MW00770737

CHAIN LYNX

THE LYNX SERIES
BOOK 3

FIONA QUINN

CHAIN

Lynx

Fiona Quinn

THE WORLD OF INIQUUS

Ubicumque, Quoties. Quidquid

Iniquus - /i'ni/kwus/ our strength is unequalled, our tactics unfair – we stretch the law to its breaking point. We do whatever is necessary to bring the enemy down.

THE LYNX SERIES

Weakest Lynx

Missing Lynx

Chain Lynx

Cuff Lynx

Gulf Lynx

Hyper Lynx

MARRIAGE LYNX

STRIKE FORCE

In Too DEEP

JACK Be Quick

InstiGATOR

UNCOMMON ENEMIES

Wasp

Relic

Deadlock

Thorn

FBI JOINT TASK FORCE

Open Secret

Cold Red

Even Odds

KATE HAMILTON MYSTERIES

Mine

Yours

Ours

CERBERUS TACTICAL K9 TEAM ALPHA

Survival Instinct

Protective Instinct

Defender's Instinct

DELTA FORCE ECHO

Danger Signs

Danger Zone

Danger Close

This list was created in 2021. For an up-to-date list, please visit FionaQuinnBooks.com
If you prefer to read the Iniquus World in chronological order you will find a full list at
the end of this book.

For my grandmother, Anna Louisa,
from whom I inherited the gift of gab, a love of books, and
my wanderlust.
Grandma, I see you every time I look in the mirror.
I love and miss you.

1

DEATH WAS LOUDER THAN I EXPECTED.

I didn't think there would be any noise at all, only a bright light to guide me.

Where were my loved ones who had passed on? Shouldn't they be here to lead me — to help me transition from the corporeal life to life everlasting? Mom and Dad should be here. My husband, Angel. My dear friend, Snow Bird...but I was alone with the sound of thundering wind and yelling.

My body jolted.

Liquid fire saturated my skin. I lay smoldering at the edge of a wide abyss. If I slid an inch to my left, I'd fall straight to the Devil's door. What did I do to find myself at Hell's Gate? My mind scrambled. I had indeed committed the worst possible of sins. I'd killed four people in my lifetime. Once in self-defense — a psychopath, Travis Wilson, had stalked me and tried to skin me alive. Surely, God would forgive me my will to live.

The other three were bank robbers. They'd taken twenty-two people hostage. A bullet tore through an elderly lady's brain. The robber was pressing his Glock to a pregnant woman's temple, making a show of his ruthlessness for the SWAT team outside. I'd been in the building, armed, on an operation for Iniquus. Protecting innocents was just an extension of my job, and killing those men were not sins in my mind. But they must have been, and this must be the road to Perdition.

Something in my soul clung to the idea of justice. Damnation was not the path I would voluntarily roam for eternity. I sensed the Devil, red-faced and gloating, reaching out his craggy hand, laughing as he tried to drag me over the edge. "No!" my mind screamed as I desperately tried to scuttle away from the chasm, the smell, the heat, and the sound. "God, help me. God, please help me."

As if on cue, peace quenched the inferno that raged through my veins. With the flames from Hell's threshold extinguished, I floated away from evil into nothingness.

Time danced inevitably forward. I felt solid again. A bright light assaulted my pupils. Not the light of Heaven's beauty, but a penlight, checking for dilation.

"She's coming around," the man in a lab coat said.

Striker's face came into view. "Lynx? Lynx, can you hear me?"

I tried to work my jaw muscles to respond. I couldn't. Something large and hard filled my mouth. The trickle of tears sliding down my cheek was the only signal I could muster. The salt stung my cuts and abrasions and burned my face.

"Lynx, if you can understand me, squeeze my hand." Striker used his commander voice, even and authoritative.

I was loopy. Heavily drugged. But that much I could do.

"Chica, you're safe. We're taking good care of you. I need you to keep fighting. Don't leave me now."

Unable to move, unable to speak, I closed my eyes and let myself drift back into the peace of the drugs flowing through my IV.

I knew that minutes and hours slid by. But it was an awareness that sat in an armchair, reading a book, muttering over the pages from time to time — not an awareness that actually held my attention or made me think.

I lay stupefied on my bed.

Slowly, I realized that Striker was rubbing a finger up and down my arm, trying to rouse me.

"Lynx? I need you to open your eyes. Look at me."

I worked hard to comply, squinting up at his face through a morphine haze. I felt the sturdiness and strength of his body beside me. I wasn't hallucinating him.

He was real.

Real?

Yes, solid. Here.

The relief I felt rushed through my body like a tidal wave, floated my emotions to the surface, and overwhelmed me. My body shivered under the light cotton blanket.

As I focused on his face, Striker gave me a slightly crooked smile with a hint of dimples. His gaze, steady and warm, held mine, though worry made tire tracks between his green eyes. I breathed in deeply to form a happy sigh until pain exploded my chest into bright colors, freezing me in place.

Striker's thumb stroked over my jawline. As I exhaled,

the pain receded into the background.

"They've taken out your breathing tube. Can you say something?" He tried to hide the hitch in his voice behind a cough.

I licked my swollen lips. They were crusty and dry under a thick layer of what tasted like Vaseline. It took me a minute and a few false tries to coordinate my tongue and teeth into intelligible words.

"Chest hurts," I croaked, toad-like.

"I'm sure it does, Chica." His grip tightened around my hand, pinching my fingers together. "We had to defibrillate you."

His vowels and consonants leaped like a gymnast doing floor exercises, swirling and spinning. It was hard to form them into understandable words. *Defibrillate.* I let the word condense into a thought. "I was dead?"

"When we pulled you from the plane wreck, you had no vitals. You must have just gone into cardiac arrest, because we were able to bring you back right away."

I tried to shift, but my body only moved centimeters. I couldn't turn my head. I was fastened by some kind of restraint. I let my gaze take in what I could. Plain, green walls. Fluorescent lighting. An IV stand. I wasn't in the desert anymore. I wasn't alone anymore.

"We flew you here to Lackland Air Force Base. You're in their hospital," Striker said.

"Texas, then. Not Honduras."

"You're on U.S. soil." His eyes hardened into his assessing look. "That was one hell of an escape plan."

I tried to screw my expression into a wry smile, but my skin wouldn't oblige. "My face...can I see a mirror?" I hadn't seen my reflection in a mirror since mid-February when Maria Rodriguez kidnapped me and hid me in a Honduran prison. It was what — sometime in late June? July?

Striker locked down his emotions. His facial muscles froze into combat stoicism. What made him brace? I lifted my hands to my face, where my fingers explored the unfamiliar terrain. Bandages and tape crisscrossed over my forehead and down my nose. Scabs, like chickenpox, dotted my cheeks. Everything felt scaly and tight.

Striker eased my hands away, moving them gently down to rest on my stomach. "Lynx, I'd rather you wait a little while before you look in the mirror. You don't look like yourself right now." His combat mask slipped a little, and I saw the shadow of sadness and concern written in his eyes. No pity, thank goodness. Pity made me weak.

"You've lost a lot of weight," he said. "You were just over eighty pounds when we brought you in yesterday. Your skin's pretty badly sunburned. Those sores you're feeling are from the toxins trying to get out of your system when you were dehydrated."

"What else?" My voice cracked. I'd love a sip of water— some ice chips. I wondered if they'd allow that. Somehow, it felt like too much effort to ask.

"Broken nose. Broken ribs and sternum. Trauma to your head and spinal column. The head trauma is worrisome because it's your second traumatic brain injury in the same year. The doctors are stabilizing you for surgery. Hopefully, that'll happen in the morning if you continue to improve."

"Because?" When I squeezed his hand for support, the tubing and tape from the IV pulled at my elbow.

"They need to rebuild your sternum and re-attach your ribs. You're strapped to a board right now." He reached out and rapped on the surface beneath me so I could hear its solidity. "But when you wake up, they're going to have you in traction for your spine and neck." His words became gruff when he drew my hand to his lips for a kiss. "Chica, it was a near thing." Emotions under his skin and behind his eyes fought for expression, but Striker's steely will held out, and he maintained his control. As always.

That didn't mean I couldn't feel his distress empathically. His energy entwined with mine until I couldn't tell us apart or tell his pain from mine—one of the many things I hated about ESP.

"I'm sorry. I'm so sorry." I couldn't handle the guilt. This whole fiasco was my own damned fault. Poor decisions. Impulsive behavior. Secrecy. I offered Striker the closest thing to a contrite smile as I could form on my inflexible face. I felt like I was treading water — my head lifting just above the black swirl of morphine. It was exhausting to struggle, so I tried to float for a minute. To rest. My words slurred together. "You know, it's going to feel so good to get home again. We can—"

"No." Striker's voice slammed into my thoughts, bringing them to a screeching halt like a brake stopping a barreling car. My eyelids stretched wide.

"You aren't going home." He softened his tone. "It isn't safe. You still have people out there trying to get you."

Monumentally confused, I played his words over again in my mind. I wanted answers, but the pain had turned into a raging monster, clawing at my chest. I gasped at the shock of it. It pulled all my attention away from here and now, and my questions of what? Why? And, who in the world? Striker pressed the call button. A nurse appeared next to me. That was all I remembered.

2

I WAS DREAMING THAT DREAM AGAIN. I HELD A BALLOON ON a long string. The sky was a brilliant, dazzling blue. I squinted up past the glistening sunrays to see my balloon, only to discover it was really a small boy, with black hair and huge eyes, floating upward. I knew I had to hold tightly to the string, or he'd float right up beyond the clouds. This time, a hand reached out to take the string away from me. I wanted to fight for the string, but I was too weak. I knew the little boy; his name was Pablo. I was supposed to protect him. I was supposed to hold on to that string.

"Pablo. Pablo," I screamed to the clouds, hoping by some miracle to call him back.

"Lynx, baby, wake up. You have to wake up now. You're dreaming." The wide expanse of Striker's muscular shoulders hovered over me. His hands grasped my upper arms, stilling my struggle against the webbing that secured me to my backboard.

"Striker, oh dear God." I panted for enough breath to continue. Sweat ran across my face, stinging the inner corners of my eyes and my open sores. "It should have been the first word out of my mouth." I frantically clawed at the sheets, trying to pull myself upright. "There's a little boy. I promised. I have to get to him. I promised."

"Lynx, lie still," Striker commanded.

"You don't understand." I slapped angrily at his hands, holding tightly to my shoulders.

"I do understand. We found your letters on the plane. You wrote to me." Striker sounded so reasonable. So in control. Antithetical to the craziness that spun my sun-bleached thoughts. "You asked me to honor your memory by saving Pablo in the village south of your prison."

"Yes, I have to get to him." My eyes felt wild in my head.

"Randy and Axel were already there at the prison, looking for you." Striker's words struck a slow, steady cadence, and I could understand them, even through my drug-hazy desperation. "They went to Franco and Elicia's cottage and brought the whole family to the States. They're in Florida." He loosened his grip on my shoulders and reached for a damp cloth on my bed table, using it to pat the perspiration from my face.

I lay still, wondering if I were hallucinating this conversation.

"Pablo had a fever when Axel and Randy brought him in," Striker said. "I received a report from Axel two hours ago. The doctors are stabilizing the boy and starting tests."

Striker's words were too miraculous to be believed. I didn't believe them. I must be imagining things again. How did they find my prison? When? My mind was set on replay, trying to comprehend these new ideas. "You found my goodbye letters in the plane?" I asked warily.

"Yesterday morning, when we brought you here, Jack was with the plane. He combed through your letters and contacted Axel. The team moved in immediately." He picked a strand of hair from my bandage and tucked it behind my ear.

I squeezed Striker's arms until my fingers felt bloodless. He felt real. But still. . . "Pablo's in the hospital in the United States?" When they sedated Mom in the hospital, she acted this way. Asking the same questions over and over again. It had taken a lot of patience to get any piece of information across to her. I felt that brain numbness. It was hard to hold onto a solid thought; everything seemed gossamer and just out of my reach.

"At a children's hospital in Florida," Striker said.

"The doctors think he'll be all right? He *didn't* die because of me?"

"He's alive today because of you."

"Oh, I need to digest that. You can't imagine." My panic calmed, giving way to cogent thought. "All those long days trapped by the storm. I knew if I died, Pablo would die, too. I promised his dad. Franco put his life on the line for me. I promised him I'd help."

"When you're up to it, I'd like you to tell me how you came to know about Pablo. Why this was so important to you."

This I could do. My thoughts and words were so much easier to form now than they were with my first few attempts at consciousness. I held Striker's gaze, wondering where to start.

"Maria Rodriguez came to the prison. She wanted to cut off my fingers and send them to you in a box," I said.

"*What*?" An emotion sizzled through Striker like an electrical current. "How could you know that?"

"I knew she was coming — I picked her up with ESP — one of my 'knowings.' So I was watching for her. I stole a key and sneaked to the office, where she was talking to the guy who ran the prison." I scratched my teeth over my top lip and wished for some water. "Maria told him the US government wasn't willing to trade me for her husband. She thought Iniquus would have broken Julio out of the federal pen by then and made their own trade for me. But since you guys hadn't, she thought she needed something to spur our team into action. She thought that a present of my fingers with an accompanying DVD of their removal would be just the incentive you guys needed."

Striker worked his jaw back and forth without a single word.

"I had been working on an escape plan…the dogs." So much to tell. All the words jumbled up together on the tip of my tongue, and I had to wait for them to line up politely to exit one at a time.

Striker sat patiently beside me, his fingers laced with mine.

I cleared my throat to start again. "When Maria headed out the door, I shadow walked my way through the prison and out the side exit, to where Franco was smoking a cigarette. Franco was one of the first guards I met there. I knew his son was deathly ill, so I used that. Used him."

I wrenched my gaze from Striker's and focused on the cratered surface of the ceiling tile, where I wasn't worried about finding censure shining back at me. Not that Striker would judge me harshly. I guessed I was feeling guilty —

manipulative and self-serving — to have put Franco's life at risk for mine.

Striker wiped the damp cloth across my mouth.

"Thank you," I said. The shame I had felt took a side-step, and I was able to focus on Striker again.

He pulled his chair closer to my head, leaning in where I could see his face clearly.

"I told Franco I was the answer to his prayers for Pablo, his God-sent miracle."

Striker squeezed my hand. "I'm glad we got to the boy in time. Axel said Pablo was in dire straits when they found him. It was a difficult rescue."

"Where are Axel and Randy now?" I was glad to shift the conversation.

"Axel's with Pablo's family, getting them straightened out. Randy's delivering Maria to the FBI."

"Oh." My emotions were bigger than that. Much bigger. But there weren't really any words to convey the enormity of it all. I wasn't sure I could fully take all this in. Pablo safe. Maria in custody. Me — alive and free. Striker here, holding my hand.

"Do I get to hear your side of the story?" I asked. "Where's everyone else?"

"They're here at Lackland. The doctors say you're too fragile for visitors. They let me in because I'm your commander, and I need to debrief you."

"They won't let my team see me?" I scowled, annoyed.

"They can come in, Lynx, but only when you're asleep. It's hard to kick Gator out when you're coming around, though." There was an odd little inflection to that last sentence. A strange little light flickered in Striker's eyes that was quickly replaced with concern when I gripped his hand with a gasp.

Striker reached out and pushed the call button again. The nurse came in, glanced at my machines, and gave me a shot that made it all go away.

3

I COULDN'T MOVE. SO DAMNED UNCOMFORTABLE. BACK aching. Head throbbing, I laid there dazed and confused and more than a little nauseated.

All I wanted was to roll over.

"Lynx, stop." Striker's voice pinned me.

I opened my lids to the institutional green walls and fluorescent lights of my hospital room. America, not Honduras. Help, not imprisonment. I pieced my reality back together.

I couldn't turn my head. Couldn't see anyone. "Striker? I want to turn over." I whimpered like a puppy.

Striker positioned himself where I could see his face. "Chica, you've had surgery. Do you remember me telling you that you were going to have surgery?"

I wanted to shake "no," but I couldn't move my head, not even a little.

"They fixed your sternum and ribs, and they put you in traction. Now you have to lie very still and quiet until the swelling goes down around your spine."

"How'd they fix my ribs?" My words had to edge past my uncooperative tongue, though my mind was being extremely supportive. I felt truly lucid for the first time in a long time. My thoughts were clear and had an edge to them instead of the fuzzy, shaded things I had conjured since the plane went down.

"You have some wires and a whole lot of screws in you. You'll probably need a doctor's note to get through airline security from here on out." His voice was teasing, but his expression was serious.

"Huh. You know, when I was growing up, Mom always said she wanted me to make a crazy quilt of experiences. It was supposed to be a comfort to me in my old age when I could wrap myself in my memories." I stopped to take a breath. Speaking in complete sentences felt as aerobic as sprinting a mile or sparring with my kung fu partner used to feel. "I don't think she literally wanted me to make a quilt of memories on my body. At this rate, I'm going to end up looking like the Bride of Frankenstein."

Striker chuckled. I guessed he found my pitiful vanity charming. "We had a plastic surgeon come in and work with your surgical team." His thumb gently stroked over my cheek. "They did everything they could to hide the incisions. Dr. Morrissey says we can have laser treatments done on your other scars. They should all but disappear. You won't look like the bride of Frankenstein. I promise."

My brows pulled together. "How could they hide scars on my sternum?"

"They did the incisions under your breasts — well, what will be your breasts."

"What do you mean, 'what will be my breasts'?" I felt a

little panicky. What happened to my breasts? I liked my breasts.

"Chica, you dropped down near eighty pounds. You don't have any fat on you. You barely have any muscle on you. You are literally a skin bag of bones, for now. After you were rehydrated, they got you up closer to ninety pounds. The doctors felt safe doing surgery with that minimum. They didn't want you to have another heart attack in the OR."

I tried to nod again, but again, it wasn't possible. "Everything went okay, though?"

"Everything went beautifully." Striker looked at me with warm eyes. "Your vitals are nice and stable. And you've been cleared to have visitors as long as you don't tax yourself. Do you feel ready? Your teammates want to come in if it's okay with you."

"Yes. Yes, please."

Striker stood and went to the door. Feet softly shuffled in. Familiar faces gathered around my bed, where I could see them from my limited vantage point. Striker, Jack, Blaze, and Gator. They looked good to me, like everything that was healthy and wholesome in this world.

"Hey, guys." I attempted a smile.

Jack reached out to put his massive hand on my knee and leaned his six-foot-five frame in to kiss my cheek. "Lynx, same old, same old. You have the adventures, and we stand around your hospital bed, watching you heal. Honestly, girl, doesn't this ever get old for you?" he asked.

"It's my hobby, Jack."

My gaze scanned across the four teammates who circled my bed. (Strike Force numbered seven in all.) They were dressed in identical gray camo fatigues, with charcoal gray compression shirts.

"Hey, you're in uniform. What's up with that?" I asked.

"We're on duty," Blaze said.

Not here to visit me. Here working. "I need an explanation." My muscles tightened as if preparing for a blow. The memory of Striker's words stood in the shadows, glaring at me — *You aren't going home. It isn't safe. You still have people out there, trying to get you.* But with Maria in custody…my gaze searched out Striker.

"You remember a guy named Jonathan Frith?" Striker asked.

I searched my memory for a minute before I reached in a back drawer and pulled out a thought. "FBI," I said.

"Yeah, that's the one. He's not with the FBI anymore. He took a more lucrative position over at Omega."

"Huh." Omega was our competitor, whose members had earned a nasty reputation for Lord of the Flies-like antics.

"Frith had a meeting with Iniquus Command. Even if he is with Omega, it seems like he still has a soul," Striker said.

I scowled, not following the relevance of this conversation. "Why was Frith talking to Iniquus if he's working for Omega?"

"Because he owes you." Striker crossed his arms over his chest. "Frith said you saved his ass once when he was on assignment. If you hadn't puzzled something out properly and gotten to him with a warning, he would be nothing but a tar smear on a country road. Instead, he got a promotion."

"Owes me?" Something was way off about this scenario. "How did Frith know I was working for Iniquus?" I asked. I had only officially worked for Iniquus for a little over three months when Maria kidnapped me. Of course, I had worked on assignments with my mentor, Spyder McGraw, for a few years, but no one had known that, not even Iniquus

Command. I had been Spyder's secret weapon, his private puzzler.

"Because the case you unraveled, which saved Frith's life, happened on what was an FBI/Iniquus contract," Striker said.

"No. That's not possible." I had to rummage around for more information before I decided. "Frith can't know me from that. That case happened when I was living in an apartment with Mom. I was working for Spyder McGraw then, and Iniquus didn't find out about me until Travis Wilson's attack. And Wilson happened almost a year after the Frith case was resolved."

Striker shrugged. "I don't know then." He perched at the corner of the bed, making it less of a strain to see him.

"Maybe he knew you from your work on the Sylanos case," Jack said. "After Sylanos died, our contract to bridge the CIA and FBI was complete, and we were taken off the assignment. Omega did follow up. Your name was sure to be in our files when we handed them over."

"Sylanos is dead? When did that happen? How did that happen?" Both hands went to my head as if I could still my swirling thoughts. A lot can happen in five months.

"We'll catch you up on all that later, Chica. Sylanos has nothing to do with Frith."

"But still, I want to know how Frith put me together with Iniquus. And second…" Whoa. Weird what my brain was doing — suddenly, it crackled with staticky sounds.

Striker reached out to hold my hand, grounding me. "And second?"

"Yeah, yeah, second, why would the FBI and CIA hire us to work the Sylanos case, and then replace us with our competition? You would think they'd stay on the same horse and not change midstream."

"They weren't changing horses midstream. It was more like they were running two horses in the same race. Omega was working on the Sylanos case at the same time we were working on the Sylanos case. As to why they kept Omega on? I'd guess it's because Omega will do things we won't touch."

"Why would someone... I'm lost. What?" Darned my head. Now I had colors kaleidoscoping behind my right eye and the tip of my nose tingled. I let go of Striker's hand so I could scratch.

Striker cocked his head and looked at me with that assessing look of his. He seemed hesitant to keep going. I wondered if I sounded as messed up as I felt. I grabbed his hand again so he wouldn't up and disappear with the team and leave me lying here wondering.

"Iniquus has to work in the gray area of the law in order to be effective," Striker said. "While we're willing to make reaches, we also have boundaries. Omega usually gets called in when they're working outside of the gray area in the black. The out-and-out bold criminal acts — in the name of American security — rendition, interrogation, assassination."

"So what did Frith tell Command?" I asked, trying to get the meat off this bone.

Striker paused, then enunciated each word with clarity. "Frith says you've become an Omega target."

My blood iced, prickling my skin with goose flesh. An Omega target. Holy shit. How was I going to go up against the power of Omega? If I thought it was bad to have Travis Wilson or Maria Rodriguez after me, they were nothing, absolutely nothing, compared to the money and might of Omega.

My team tightened their stances as if readying for a fight. And I lay tethered and incapacitated on my back with a wobbly brain.

"Iniquus will be damned if they're going to let Omega, or anyone else, hurt one of our own," Jack said.

I wanted to shake my head to clear the rubble. I swallowed hard instead. It didn't help. "But if Omega was going after me, they'd find out someone already got to me. They'd know I was kidnapped months ago."

"Right," Striker said. "Command had the meeting with Frith last Tuesday when your 911 came in. Frith said that Omega knew you were kidnapped, so your file was in a holding pattern until you resurfaced." Striker seemed to understand my distress; he had slowed his words down considerably. "I suppose they decided not to waste resources when they knew Iniquus would be beating the bushes for you while you were held captive."

"What day is today?" I asked, suddenly needing some kind of context.

"Monday, you called 911 six days ago," Jack said. "We didn't get to you until Friday."

"So Omega decided to let you guys try to recover me from Maria, then they'd move in and take me again?" I asked.

"Exactly," Jack said. "We assume that Frith didn't come to us when Omega signed the contract because Omega didn't have a spark. No spark, no fire, so no reason for Frith to put his ass out there trying to help you."

"Then something sparked," I said, tight-lipped and braced for more bad news.

"Frith said their surveillance guy picked up your 911 call same time we did," Striker said. "When we were out looking for you in the desert, it seems we weren't the only ones."

"We got to you first." Jack patted my knee, wearing a conquering hero smile. Richly deserved. He was my hero. They all were.

4

THIS NEW INFORMATION WAS ALL TOO MUCH. I CLOSED MY eyes and took a deep breath in. The oxygen from my tubing felt cold and dry in my nostrils. I didn't like how it smelled. "I don't understand any of this. Who is the client who initiated an Omega contract on me? Why is there a contract on me?"

"We don't know," Striker said.

I opened my eyes and looked down the bed at Gator. "I need to take baby steps here. Let's start at the beginning. Tell me again, where am I? How did you find me?"

Gator cleared his throat. "You're at Lackland Air Force Base in Texas, ma'am. When you called in your mayday to 911, you gave them your name and your Iniquus affiliation. The FAA contacted headquarters to update Command. They were trying to figure out where you were coming in from and what your destination had been. They needed to get a trajectory for search and rescue. As soon as we got word, they'd heard from you outside of Corpus Christi, we took off from D.C."

Striker turned my hand over and drew slow circles onto my palm. He used the gesture when he thought I needed to be calmed. "There had been a big tropical storm in the Gulf of Mexico, Lynx. Do you remember that?" he asked.

"Yes." I tried to nod, but nothing moved. "Days and days of storm. Wind and lightning, but no rain on the island where I landed. I thought it had mostly blown over. I needed water. I tried to get to the States."

"The storm stalled in the Caribbean, then moved west and stalled over Texas," Striker said. "We got into Texas airspace just as they started rerouting flights. We were told to land here at Lackland. Lucky thing, too. I have a buddy who's in command. He's been golden through this whole thing." Striker's finger tracing on my palm made me itch. I interlaced my fingers with his to make him stop.

"It's the Lackland pilots that flew your search and rescue mission," Jack said. "We took off from the base as soon as the winds died down enough to get the helicopters off the ground. We found you pretty quickly at that point because of the smoke signals you set with the tire fires."

"We weren't sitting on our hands waiting for the weather to turn, though, Lynx. We went out in jeeps for the first two days." Gator leaned over me.

I smiled at him. "I missed you all so much." Sentimental tears threatened to spill over, but I didn't want to wander down an emotional path. Right now, I wanted understanding. So I shifted my eyes to Striker. "Jeeps?"

"I broke our team up and sent them out with Lackland airmen," Striker said. "We started at the coast and worked a grid. On the 911 tapes, you said you were out of fuel and didn't have instruments or communication, so you weren't sure where you were. We figured if you were trying to fly a Cessna through that storm, you'd have put the wind to your back. You got blown a lot further inland than we expected. And you know, we got to you pretty much in the nick of time."

"Yes, thank you." I paused, looking for a stronger expression, something that conveyed the power of my gratitude. "I wish there was a better word. A bigger phrase. Thank you just doesn't accommodate all the feelings I have. I am so grateful and so blessed. Overwhelmed, in fact."

The men scuffled their feet. I thought they were probably uncomfortable that I laid my appreciation on the table like that. My team was stoic by nature. They liked black and white and symmetry, where I preferred shades and hues and dancing whirls. Somehow, we still made a great team.

I shifted the energy safely back to debriefing mode by asking, "And the uniforms?"

"You're under our protection, just like at the safe house," Jack said.

I was under Iniquus protection. My brain clouded. Protection? I searched through my haze. Ah, yes. Omega was after me. Why would Omega want me? Maybe there was something I had forgotten — something that got knocked from my memory in the crash...

"What's the date?" It was odd to flounder in a space of non-reality, with no sense of time or place.

"July the twelfth," Blaze said.

"Lynx, how is it that you had your cellphone to call 9-1-1 in the first place?" Gator asked. Like all the men on my team, Gator's build was ready for combat without an ounce of fat. He always made me think of apple pie and Saturday night football. He stood at the end of my bed, with his hands on my blanket-covered feet. The gesture was oddly grounding, and I appreciated it. My thoughts stopped swirling and resolved into linear form again.

I closed my eyes, remembering that cold February night.

"I'm guessing that you pulled off one of your magic tricks so you could keep your phone at the prison," Blaze said.

"Yes. But there were no reception bars. I knew you wouldn't find me that way."

"There weren't any pings," Jack said. "We wondered why. We figured your battery died until Randy and Axel went down to Honduras. They said your prison was in an area so remote, not only was there no cell tower, but there weren't even any landlines running in. They had to use their satellite phones for communication."

"Have you heard from Randy and Axel? How is Pablo?" I asked.

"His fever was down this morning," Striker said. "They have him scheduled for surgery in two weeks. That is, if everything continues to stay on track."

"Thank you, you have no idea what this means to me. Amazing. Just amazing that I'm here. It's so good to see your faces." I felt like Dorothy, waking up from the head injury that sent her to Oz, and here around me were my old friends. No, probably a bad analogy. My guys had heart, courage, and brains to spare—no need to go on a silly quest for proof.

"And Maria — any idea where she is right now?"

"Striker told you we have Maria Rodriguez in custody," Blaze said.

My mind stumbled around for the information. "Yes, I

think I remember him saying she had been arrested." How did that happen? And so quickly? Before the storm, she had been at the prison. "Wait. Start at the very beginning," I pleaded. Everyone looked over at Gator, our team's storyteller.

"Ma'am, I guess you're more likely to remember everything that happened until Maria kidnapped you. When they had you manacled and carried you out of the house." Gator rubbed his hand over his buzz-cut blond hair. "The ambulance arrived, and they treated me. Tammy was clutching baby Ruby with a death hold, just a shaking, and a sobbing. The paramedics had to wrestle Ruby from Tammy's grip to check on her. Ruby was fine, though. Her being in danger turned out to be a farce Maria used as a lure. The team came in right behind the ambulance."

Gator stopped to clear his throat. He moved his hands from my feet to cross them over his chest, making his biceps bulge under his compression shirt. He was leaning his hips against my footboard. I wanted him to shift back. I wanted to feel him touching me, again, reminding me this was real and not one of my prison daydreams.

"Tammy didn't have the make of her Aunt Maria's vehicle, nor nothing that would help us find you," Gator continued. "Your neighbor, Manny, saw a red van leaving, but he hadn't noticed the license plate. Even when we had him hypnotized, he wasn't able to tell it. So that got us nowhere. We put Tammy into the Iniquus Witness Protection and started looking for Maria."

Striker stood up as the door opened. Silence dropped over our group as a nurse bustled around my monitors. She checked my IV line. "This young lady needs to be kept quiet. I know you need to debrief her, but you have to be careful that she's kept calm. She's still listed as critical." The nurse's voice was no-nonsense with a hint of dictatorial.

"Yes, ma'am," Striker said.

I heard the door click.

"Chica, at first, it seemed you disappeared into thin air like one of your magic tricks." Striker put his hand on the bed and leaned in, so we were face to face. "We were pretty much slamming our heads into a wall for the first month of your captivity." Striker's lips were dry and tight, and the muscle under his right eye twitched. Except for these tells, I would think Striker was reading a grocery list; he was so damned controlled and even. "Our first clue came in when we got the video of you with the Mexican paper. But again, all this told us was that they had you, and you were alive. We didn't trust the Mexican paper because it was too obvious."

Striker sat down on my bed again and was absentmindedly drawing circles on the palm of my hand. This time, it felt good. I needed the distraction to help me deal with my pain. I didn't want to call for meds yet. I wanted my brain functioning.

"We found the file you were working on," Striker said. "I'm not sure how you figured out that Consuela Hervas was really Maria Rodriguez, or that she had married Julio Rodriguez. Your brain, Lynx, always astonishes me. We also saw that you made the connection between Julio Rodriguez and the Marcos Sylanos case. We thought that would have been a good direction to take — only, Sylanos is dead."

"How is he dead?" I asked.

"Killed accidentally when one of his security guards' guns went off. That was two weeks prior to your kidnapping. So we didn't go in that direction. We were sure this wasn't Sylanos' doing," Striker said. "Are you okay?"

I had squinched my eyes tight. I wanted to hear this. I didn't want the pain that shot across my chest to stop Striker from telling me their side of my story. I forced my eyes back open. "I'm hanging in. Keep going, Striker."

"We saw how you had found Julio down in the Florida prison. We checked the tapes and visitor records and found out that Maria went to see Julio every Sunday. We staked out the prison and watched for her. Sure enough, she showed, right on schedule. We put her under surveillance, hoping she'd lead us to you. We knew we could arrest her at any point because we had her niece Tammy's statements along with Gator's."

"You didn't arrest Maria for interrogation?" I bit my lower lip and tasted blood.

I heard the water running.

Blaze came over with a damp cloth and wiped my face. He slid an ice chip into my mouth. Sucking on the ice gave me a moment's relief from the fire burning in my throat. I listened to Striker.

"Once we got the ransom letter about doing a prisoner exchange — you for Julio — Maria couldn't go see her husband anymore. Now that Julio's name was involved, we would obviously be watching him. Axel and Randy were doing the stakeout. But by the time we got the arrest warrant in hand, she had slipped through our fingers."

"To go collect my fingers in Honduras."

There was a long silence.

"How did you arrest her?" I asked.

"Axel and Randy took her into custody in the village south of your prison. She was sedated and brought in on the same plane as Pablo and his family."

"Okay, now that Maria is in custody, Julio is still in jail, and Sylanos is dead, Command still thinks I'm in enough danger that I need a whole team for protection because Omega is out in the desert looking for me as we speak?"

Striker's eyes were as hard and sharp as broken glass. "Doesn't think. Knows."

5

"WHERE'S DEEP?" I ASKED. HE WAS MY ONLY TEAMMATE left unaccounted for.

"He's in the bunks, ma'am," Gator said. "He was out on search duty yesterday, and then he stood watch with you last night." Gator's accent was as smooth as Zydeco music and the aroma of a midnight bonfire.

"Yesterday? That makes no sense at all. You guys had already found me yesterday, hadn't you?" My energy was flagging. I needed to get some sleep; I should cut this first homecoming debrief short. But that need vied with my desperation to understand what was happening.

"We have an ongoing search going as cover for your being found." I couldn't see Jack, but his voice was some-where to my left, outside of my peripheral view. "Two days after your 911, we changed your classification from missing person to recovery." He had taken a step closer, and now I could catch a glimpse of his jet-black hair and one of his husky-blue eyes. "We hadn't given up on you, knowing your resourcefulness. We were hoping you had plenty of food and water with you, but we also needed to get Omega off the trail and keep you a little safer."

"They could still find my plane and see there's no corpse." My hands and feet went numb, and my lips started to buzz. That couldn't be good. I focused back on Gator at the end of my bed to try to still the whirlpool.

"After we found you, Deep and Jack stayed back to bury your fires," Gator said. "And to put the plane under a camo tarp."

"Now what?" I said, not really sure what information I was asking for, but wanting them to keep feeding me the news.

"Tomorrow, Lackland is going to officially call off your search. They're going to say a public prayer for your soul in the mess hall. Surely that'll get out to Omega," Striker explained.

I let my gaze drift from face to face. "I feel incredibly vulnerable in this traction device. Am I safe here? Do you think Omega can get on base?"

Striker bent in so I could see his eyes. "Listen to me, Chica. You're in a safe place."

My brow drew together. It didn't feel very safe.

"I'm friendly with Lackland's commander," Striker explained. "I ran a couple of missions with his team way back. He *hates* Omega. They put us in a lot of danger when we were in Africa together."

All right, this was personal. Now protecting me against an Omega arrest warrant made more sense. "Why, what happened?" I asked.

"An Omega unit went on a drunken civilian killing spree. It made American movement in that area treacherous. We lost all of our painstakingly built relationships, and we ended up having to abort our mission." Striker ran a light finger down the side of my face and over the hard knot of my jaw muscles. "I trust this guy unconditionally. You. Are. Safe." His voice expressed his conviction. It wasn't hard to read the seriousness in Striker's eyes.

"Okay. You trust him. But there are lots of people here who might not be on board."

"Lackland's on high alert, though they're saying that the alert was triggered by a suicide bomb threat from a militant group," he said. "Being on lockdown keeps undocumented people out of the compound. This is a secured wing of the hospital, and we have, at a minimum, two team members with you at all times." Striker looked at the machine, which was now emitting a low-level siren. "One outside of your room, one inside — but you know as well as I do, Lynx, who we're dealing with. We need you to get stable as soon as you can so we can get you moved."

My heart stuttered. I gritted my teeth against the searing pain in my chest. I heard more sirens wailing from my monitors. The nurse banged through my door. She stormed around the end of my bed to check the monitors.

"OUT NOW." I saw her arm point toward the door, and her meds floated me away.

A sixth sense tickle in my brain stirred me to consciousness. Gator must be here. My eyes blinked open. The room was dark, except for the utility light over my bed, dimly lighting the machines for the nursing staff. Gator sat on my bed, watching me.

Gator was golden tanned with sun-streaked hair, no

matter the season. He had a dusting of freckles across his nose that made him disarm, and his eyes were the kind of warm chocolate brown that made a woman think he might need a little mothering. Though at six-foot-three, with the physique of a gladiator, he was as capable as they came.

"Hey, Gator."

"Hey, Lynx. You okay?"

"I'm fine. Well, I'm going to be fine." I smiled. "Someday soon, I'll be sitting in front of a campfire, listening to you tell this tale."

"Glad you woke up." He rubbed his hands together like they were cold. "You were talking crazy things in your sleep." He pulled a foot up, balanced it on the rung of my bed, and propped his elbow on his knee.

"About Pablo?" I asked.

"Something about snake oil?" His brow raised quizzically.

"Oh, yeah? Huh. Funny that that should be on my mind."

"It means something to you?" he asked.

"It's actually letters. S-N-K-O-I-L. It was the license plate on the van that Maria and Hector used to take me to Florida."

Gator leaned in a little further, obviously excited by this piece of information. "Hector was the man's name? Do you have anything more on him? A last name? Anything you picked up on the drive that could help us find him?"

"No last name, sorry. Besides, I think he said it was his girlfriend's van. D.C. plates. You could start there." I searched my memory for anything else that might help them find Hector, but no other specific detail bubbled up. "I thought, from the conversation between the two of them, that Hector was a gun for hire and would probably trade information for his freedom. He might not know much, but then again, he might know something."

"S-N-K O-I-L," Gator repeated. "That's important." He stood from his perch, gave a knock at the door, and spoke quietly to whoever was guarding the other side.

I lay there with the demons of that horrible night stabbing me with razor-sharp memories. Gator on the ground with Hector's Taser probes sticking in his skin. The static sizzling sounds and guttural agony of Gator's torture. Baby Ruby in Maria's arms with the hunting knife poised over her heart. My fault. All of it. I felt my heartbeat ramming up behind my ribs, newly screwed into place.

The door clicked shut, and Gator sat back on my bed. I closed my eyes for the length of a breath and forced my thoughts down a calmer path.

"Can you tell me about Beetle and Bella? Who has my dogs?" I asked.

"I was taking care of them and living in your house the whole time you were gone. When the call came in, they had picked up your mayday in Texas. I took the pups across the street to Justin's and asked him to drive them up to the Millers' Kennel. I've talked to the Millers since then, and your girls are doing good."

I gave a half-smile. "Tell me about Amy. How's she doing?"

"Don't know. Amy and me aren't an item no more."

Wow. My brows went up. "Is it because of this case? Will you get back together when this is all straightened out?"

"It's a little more complicated than that." Gator eased a little closer, which brought him into sharper focus. "When you were taken, I was working around the clock to find you. We all were." Gator's eyes lost their warmth, hardening with some undefined emotion — disgust, maybe? No, that didn't seem right.

"Amy never understood what it meant when I said I was married to my job," Gator said. "She didn't understand what it meant to have a teammate in peril. I think she was jealous of you, ma'am." Gator nodded his head slightly as if re-affirming the conclusion he had already drawn. "She didn't get our relationship. I couldn't explain it in a way that helped, though I tried. She thought you were the competition."

Shit. Now on top of everything else, I was the reason Gator and Amy weren't together. "Oh," I said. In my mind, I had a lot of words — sympathetic, inspiring, hopeful, supportive — but none of those words drifted down to my tongue. So all I said was, "Oh."

"Amy wanted to get my focus off you and onto her." Gator rubbed a flat palm up and down his cheek. "I asked her if she had been kidnapped, would she like me to take my attention off finding her for any reason? She said if it were her, it would be different. And that's when I realized we were too far apart in our hearts. So I ended it."

"I don't know what to say." I fidgeted uncomfortably with my sheet.

"I guess that's cause there ain't nothing to say." Gator shrugged a shoulder. "Amy and I were in different stages of life. She wanted me to commit myself to her, get married, and have a bunch of babies. I'm not there right now. Some-day, yes, or my momma's gonna come after me with a fryin' pan. But right now? Naw."

The image of Gator's five-foot-tall, 100-pound mother, swinging a cast iron frying pan at her Goliath-of-a-son was so ridiculous that it made me giggle. Gator grinned back at me.

"Hey, you said you were living in my house, Gator. Not in the rental side of my duplex?"

"No, ma'am. There was a fire in the neighborhood. Missy's rental house had faulty wiring."

"Holy cow."

"Lucky thing Deep and me were out running the dogs, and we saw the smoke. We got everyone out. Their stuff was ruined. And the house had too much water damage to be lived in no more. So we moved the family into your rental and moved me over to your place."

"I'm so glad you did that."

Gator nodded. "Iniquus changed out the furniture I had in there for what Missy picked out at our supply warehouse. Command let her have everything she needed to set up house again. And Striker took the whole family out and bought them new clothes, books, toys for the kids, and stuff. Missy didn't have no insurance."

That was uncharacteristic of Command. I wondered why they intervened for Missy. They must have had some angle. Striker, on the other hand — of course, he did the generous, big-hearted thing. "Thank you so much."

"Weren't much." Gator patted just above my knee and left his hand resting there on my twig of a leg. "We were glad to do it."

"Is everything else okay in my neighborhood? What does everyone know about the night Maria got me?"

"It's a lucky thing you've got a detective living right there across the street. Dave had everything on lockdown right away. Had all the right people in place to start the investigation."

The longer I listened to Gator, the more his speech resembled a Shakespearean play. I was getting the gist of what he was saying, but it also sounded mildly like a foreign language. I couldn't quite wrap my thoughts around the meaning behind all his words. I screwed my attention down tight and focused in on what he was saying as best I could. The effort scrunched my face and pulled at the bandaging.

"Dave had a meeting with the other neighbors to tell them what we knew. We didn't want to scare them none, but they needed to know to come to us if they had anything at all they thought could help," Gator said.

"How did Dave explain this? Did he know the real story?" I asked.

"Dave knew what you were facing. He was in the meeting when the FBI got there." Gator paused and scratched at his chin where the beginnings of a five o'clock shadow grew. Dark circles traced under his eyes, and I wondered when he had last hit the bunks.

"About your neighbors," Gator continued. "Dave told them you had got a distress call from Tammy, babysitting across the street. That Tammy had said she needed help because baby Ruby had stopped breathing."

"And people believed this?"

"Everyone thought that made sense since you volunteered with the rescue squad."

Now that I was in traction, I realized how much I enjoyed nodding my head. I was down to words and some limited arm gestures to help me communicate, and that felt too stilted and unnatural. I tried to show Gator with my eyes that I was following the story, so he would continue.

"We had Dave stretch the truth at this bit. He said Maria Rodriguez was there trying to kidnap the children. Dave didn't say that you had been the target all along. He didn't tell them how I was on scene, too. Instead, he told how Maria was holding a knife to Ruby. Said that you talked Maria out of taking the children — convinced them to take you in their place because Iniquus would pay a lot of money to ransom you and that you were a much better 'get'. Then Dave told how you let them tie you up and put you in a van, and you were driven away. And of course, that was the last we heard of you."

"That's horrible." My hands were fisted at my forehead. "Dear god, Ruby's mom and dad must be out of their fricking minds, thinking I sacrificed my life for their kids."

Gator chewed on his inner cheek and considered me. "Everyone feels terrible," he said, his voice gruff. "Everyone was shocked."

I held his gaze. Processing. Realizing that Gator must have taken all of this on his own shoulders since he was there.

But it wasn't Gator's fault. *None* of it. Only mine.

"And they don't know I've been found?" I asked, already knowing the answer.

"Nope. Can't tell them because of Omega."

Ah. Somehow, I had managed to push the idea of Omega from my thoughts. And here it was again, front and center.

"When I took the pups over, I told Justin I was going out on assignment," Gator said. "And we put Clay in your house. Seems to make everyone feel better when there's an Iniquus man in the neighborhood."

"No doubt." I inhaled as deeply as my aching ribs would allow. "Do you know when they're going to move me?" What I really wanted to know was when *I* was going to be able to move again. Traction sucked!

"It's gonna be another few days. I don't know if you can feel it, but you're lying on a sand bed."

My brows shot up.

"The mattress is full of little beads," Gator said. "And there's a fan blowing to keep the beads moving around. That's to keep you from getting bedsores and having circulation problems, clots and stuff, from lying still for so long."

"I'm being saved by sleeping on a sand bed?" I offered up a bemused smile. "That's ironic as hell. Isn't it, Gator?"

"Pretty much, ma'am. But I think this is better." He looked up as a nurse announced herself at the door and walked in to check my IV and put meds in my line. "At first, they were gonna put you in a bed that sandwiches you between canvas." He raised his voice a little. "And they were gonna flip you, every two hours, like a pancake." He grinned over at the nurse, who snorted at the image he had painted.

She leaned over me. "We were having trouble keeping your temperature regulated. Probably because of your weight. And your blood pressure has been on the low side. Not unusual following a cardiac episode. So we brought the oscillating bed in from the burn unit."

"Thank you, ma'am," I said.

The door clicked shut as she left.

"Where will I be moved?" I asked Gator.

"We're debating that from a strategic point of view. We may take you to Striker's house. He thinks you might heal better there."

I knew that Striker had a house built on a secluded piece of land on the Chesapeake Bay, but I had never seen it before.

"It's listed in a corporate name for security sake — no

one can track the house to him, so it's a good choice," Gator explained. "Very safe location, and easily defended."

"Not the Iniquus barracks?"

"Wherever you end up, you're gonna need a nurse and a physical therapist, and depending on how you heal, maybe some other kinds of support," he said.

Fear raced across my skin. Striker hadn't given me much in the way of particulars about my injuries. He had glazed over the information when I had questioned him. Was he keeping something horrible from me? "Depending on what? Do they think that I'm going to be disabled?" Panic warbled my voice.

"Lynx, shit, I didn't mean to rile yah." He glanced toward the door. "That damned nurse is gonna come back in and yell." He focused back on me, his eyes sincere. "The honest truth is you were bad hurt. They're not sure yet what all is going wrong with you, and they don't even want to speculate. They want to go slow and see how you do, one step at a time."

My lids were wide and unblinking. "What are they concerned about, Gator?"

Gator went silent, looked back over to the door again, probably hoping someone *would* come in and yell at him to be quiet and not upset me or maybe just to field my questions.

"I'm sorry to put you in this position, Gator. But please, please tell me what their concerns are." I reached out to him.

Gator picked up my hand. "They haven't tried to get you to eat nothing yet because they're not for sure that your digestive tract is gonna be able to work." He dipped his head and was looking at me from under his lashes. "They're debating whether or not to give you a feeding tube in your stomach. Dehydration and heat led to you having a heart attack. They don't know how much damage is gonna be permanent yet. There's your head and your neck. You aren't paralyzed or nothing, but you might have some mobility trouble. Coordination trouble."

"My head?" That was my big question. What if I couldn't puzzle anymore? I'd lose my job — no more Iniquus, no more team.

"The doctors are real pleased you can talk. And that you seem to think reasonable well. You can remember things and all — recognize people. Your short-term and long-term memory's intact. You aren't forgetting vocabulary words. Those are big things, they say."

While that all sounded good, I think if the doctors truly knew what was going on in my brain, they might not be as cheerful. It was as if my thoughts were greased, and they'd slide out from underneath me when I tried to put any weight on them.

Gator waited for me to look at him again. When our eyes met, and he knew I had refocused, he continued. "When we brought you in, they prepared us for worst case. Given the extent of your injuries, and the time you spent in the heat, they said you might not be able to speak no more or recognize us."

I gripped Gator's hand tighter at the thought of not knowing him. That idea physically hurt. Gator squeezed back.

"The doctors thought you might be paralyzed from the shoulders down. So when you held Striker's hand right off, we were happy," he said.

Exhaustion blanketed me. The meds the nurse put in my

line must be having some effect. "And now?" My lids were getting too heavy for me to hold open.

"As far as going forward, it's an unknown." Gator stroked a soothing hand down my arm. "Too early to tell. You lost all your fat and muscle. So for sure, you're gonna be weak as a kitten. You have to prepare yourself that this is gonna take a long time." Then he reached for my other hand and clasped that one, too. "You're not alone in this. We're family. We've got your back. And you never got to worry about that."

"Of course not." I offered him a dopey smile. "I won't worry about it at all. I'll just take one day at a time. I'd rather be here, broken, than in that prison, whole but alone." I was slurring now, and I felt a little drool pooling at the corner of my mouth. "I guess it's all perspective, isn't it?"

He lowered his tone to just above a whisper. "Yes, ma'am."

I closed my eyes — just for a minute. Just a little rest

While Gator sat quietly on my bed, holding my hand, I nodded in and out of wakefulness. But something irritating was on my face and kept me from truly falling asleep. I itched horribly. I reached up to claw at my eyes and nose. Gator pinned my wrists to the bed, and my brain snapped. I sprung fully awake. Ready for battle. Screaming, "Maggots. Get them off me." I struggled against Gator and my traction unit, trying to thrash myself free. Gator swung his head to look behind him.

I heard, "I'm coming! You're having a reaction to your meds. I'll get you fixed up in a second." I saw blue cotton hospital scrubs and turned terrified eyes back to Gator.

"Get the damned maggots off my face. They're eating

my skin," I screamed and yanked my noodle-like arms, trying to wrest them away from Gator's grasp.

Gator leaned in close and blew lightly over my cheeks and forehead. It made the crazy sensations stop. I could feel the sedation kicking in. There was a click of the door from someone coming into my room. A smile traced over my lips. "Mmmm. I like that, Gator. Please don't stop." That's when I saw Striker's face over Gator's shoulder, and he didn't look happy.

6

MORNING CAME. I ONLY KNEW IT WAS MORNING BECAUSE they told me it was. I didn't have a window in my room. There was only one way in and one way out, and it was guarded by two of my team members at all times. Deep was in my room with me.

Deep stood smaller than most of the men on our team. At six feet of lean, hard muscles, his small stature was only by comparison to the rest of Strike Force. Deep's Italian heritage was obvious in his raven hair and tanned olive skin. His long eyelashes and up-to-no-good smile made him the object of adoration to the women who landed — by accident or calculation — in his path. Deep was telling me a story about his new nephew when Striker tapped on the door and came in.

"Striker, what've you been doing?" I asked as he moved around the bed and into my line of sight. Oil streaked across Striker's face, and it looked like he'd rolled in a dust bin.

"I was out looking for you. Deep, you're dismissed. I want you in the rack, getting some shut-eye."

"Sir." Deep reached out and rubbed my hand. "See you later." Then he left.

"And? Any success finding me?" I offered up a sarcastic smile.

Striker gave me a two-dimpled grin in return. "Nope. Nobody found you. Nobody found any signs of a plane crash." Striker stood where I could see him, but well away from me. "When I came back to base, I made a show of talking with the other men running the recovery effort." Striker pulled an olive-green bandana from his pocket and swiped his face. "We've agreed that even if you'd been supplied, there's no possible way you could have survived this long in this weather had you made landfall. And since your call came in at the far reaches of the cell tower range when you were still over the Gulf, between the wind, your electrical problems, and your lack of fuel, we have to assume you never made it to shore." Striker stuffed the bandana back into his pocket. His face was no cleaner than before he had wiped it. "Their experts concluded that since no further cell-phone pings were picked up, indicating you were flying closer to safety, you must have gone down over open water. The Coast Guard is looking for wreckage. Someone should find some soon."

"How's that?" I reached an arm out to him.

But he shook his head at me. "I'm filthy, and your immune system is down. I don't want to expose you to anything," he said. "Our team flew all the plane sections that didn't show signs of ground impact out to the Gulf two days ago. We buried the rest of the plane at the crash site. The FAA informed Mexico and Belize we're looking for Cessna pieces."

"And when they find them?" My eyebrows knitted together despite the bandaging.

"It will confirm that you crashed in the Gulf and perished."

"Striker, no. This is ridiculous. Can't we talk to Omega and straighten this out?"

"Omega is contracted. We aren't sure who hired them."

"Can we ask Frith?"

"He says he doesn't know who initiated the case. We can't negotiate with Omega. They aren't the primary, and they may not even know why you've been targeted. We have to get the contract rescinded to get you away from Omega. When you're stronger, we'll figure out how and why someone thinks you're a public enemy."

"Shit." My hands made fists against my thighs.

"You made the national news yesterday," Striker said. "They used your real name, though, India Sobado. You've caught media attention: Why would a 21-year-old girl be flying a plane through a tropical storm?"

"Good question," I said.

"Here at the base, they're lowering the flags to half-staff. They'll be saying a prayer in your name at mess tonight."

"The doctors and nurses know differently."

"In this part of the hospital, they're used to this kind of thing. The medical staff here has higher clearance rankings and understand how to keep their mouths shut. When you came in on the gurney, I was lying with you — we had a blanket up. No one saw you coming in; they saw me."

"Go back to the news. They're reporting me dead?"

"They're reporting that a mayday was received from you during the storm and that search efforts have been fruitless. They're repeating the conjecture that you went down over the Gulf. And they're asking boats to keep an eye out for parts from your plane."

"My friends and family will think I was killed in the crash." My voice was whisper-thin. I couldn't imagine the grief this was causing.

"Lynx, right now, we don't have a lot of options. I wish we could have had a victory parade, announcing you were found and safe, but Omega is too formidable to play around with. You're too fragile." Striker stood, hands on his hips, leaning his weight onto one leg.

"I wish I knew what the hell I did wrong."

"I doubt it's something you've physically done. My guess is it's something you know."

"What could I possibly know that they want to silence? It must be really bad. And here's the thing, I'm the Puzzler. The information comes to me, then I hand off the results to Command. Whatever it is I know or have done or seen, it's not just me. Others would have had access as well. Did Jonathan Frith explain?"

"He's not directly in the loop. He came across this accidentally and did a little digging on his own." I could see Striker being patient, repeating the same information that I had asked again and again, and would keep asking until I could hold it in my memory bank. I blew out another sigh. I needed to get off my damned back and on to this case. I wanted to let everyone know I was okay. My emotions thrust me forward, wanted me to leap into action. Frustration at my restraints made me claustrophobic and angry. Since there was nothing I could do about it now, I figured my best choice was to change the subject. "Is something else wrong? I'm surprised you came in looking like this."

"Nothing's wrong. Everything took a little longer than I

expected, that's all. I'm going to shower in your bathroom. It's a big day for you, and I wanted to be here for it."

"More information, please."

"They're going to try to get you to eat."

As if on cue, the nurse came in with a jar of baby food. She stood at the end of my bed and held it up for me to see — Beeches Stage One Oatmeal.

"Oh, HELL no," I yelled when I saw that. "Oatmeal, rice, and beans will never pass my lips again." These three foods were the only ones that showed up on my prison tray. Nothing else. Ever. From February until July. I sealed my mouth tightly, so she knew I was serious. The nurse turned on her heels and went right back out again.

Striker grinned broadly, dimples flashing. "Say it like you mean it, Chica. I bet you were hell on wheels when you were three-years-old."

"Yeah, I don't mean to be childish, but *no*. You know?"

"Got ya. How about some good news?"

"Finally. Yes, please."

"Pablo's family is all set up in their new life in Florida. Randy and Axel arranged visas for the family. Franco's got a job as a custodian at the Arnold Palmer Hospital in Orlando. That's where Pablo is a patient. They specialize in pediatric heart patients."

"Oh, awesome. And Elicia? Does she work there, too?"

"Elicia stays with Pablo during the day, and her mom is keeping their apartment. It's just a short walk to the hospital."

"And Pablo's surgery?"

"Still on track."

"You have to thank everyone for me. Please." Even with the beads circulating beneath me, my bottom had gone numb. I tried squeezing and releasing my fanny muscles, but there wasn't much for me to work with.

"In that same vein, Elicia and Franco want you to know they're praying for you every day and send their love."

"You let them know I was alive?" I gave up on the isometrics and tried wiggling my toes instead.

"It was a little touchy on how to handle that. Franco and Elicia don't know your real name. Apparently, there wasn't a file on you at the prison. When Randy and Axel were down in Honduras, everyone who knew of you referred to you as Santa Blanca." That got me another Striker grin. "Randy told the family you had disappeared on assignment, and no one knew where you went or if you were okay. He said that Iniquus only found out about Pablo because we received a letter asking for our help with the family. When they left, Randy and Axel asked that if anyone were to contact them about you, to please let us know immediately — we're anxious for any word of you."

"You think someone could figure out that they're here in America?"

"No. Just covering all the bases. We needed to let them know there are still some very bad men out there who want to hurt you."

Anxiety attack. I white-knuckled the bed rail.

"Chica, take a deep breath. Try to relax. You're safe. You're getting the help you need. Pablo is doing well. It's looking very good for their family. We'll win."

"How do you know that?"

Striker moved closer. "Because we're the good guys, and the good guys always win."

He was close enough now that I could smell him — dirt,

aftershave, and conviction. "Okay. We'll run with that story-line. Are Randy and Axel coming here?" I asked.

Striker shook his head. "They're going after Hector, now that we know the van's license plate."

"You're sure no one knows about Pablo's family?" I was suddenly scared for them — didn't want them sucked up in the vortex of craziness that seemed to constantly pull me toward its center.

"As far as we can tell, that contact is clean. Their surname was changed to Garcia here in the US. They've moved into the FBI protection program. FBI will call Franco and Elicia to the stand at Maria's kidnapping trial, though now I think they'll be adding murder one to her charges."

"For me?"

"The authorities think you're dead. So yes, for you."

The nurse came back in. "How about peaches?" She looked at Striker with a scowl. Probably ticked that he was contaminating my room with his search party filth. Striker sent her a wink and a grin, which had its usual disarming effect. I rolled my eyes at him.

"Okay. I can try peaches. Just no beans, no rice, and no oatmeal."

"Got it," the nurse said. "All right, my name is Barb. Here's what we're going to do. I'm going to be the momma, and you're going to be the baby." Barb had an aging pixie face and a friendly, crooked-toothed smile. "I'm going to be using this infant's spoon." She held up a red plastic spoon that would hold about a quarter teaspoon of food. "I'm just going to put a little in your mouth, so you start to salivate, and we'll watch how things go from there. Are you hungry at all?"

"No."

"Thirsty?"

"No." The thought of swallowing past the glass shards that seemed to line my throat made me reticent to down anything, even something as smooth as baby mush. Okay, I was really reticent to find out that I could never eat again. *A life without food?*

7

"**W**HO'S HERE?" I ASKED SINCE I COULDN'T TURN MY HEAD.

Striker moved into my view. "Hey, you're awake. How's your stomach?"

"I'm okay. What time is it?" I had woken up in semi-darkness.

"Seven," he said, rubbing my leg.

"A.M. or P.M.?"

That got me a smile. "P.M. It must be weird to have so little context."

I let my gaze travel over Striker. He was a handsome, handsome man. A dichotomy — hard as stone, capable, and smart, and at the same time…something in his full lips, his soft mossy eyes that made him…huh, I wanted to use the word vulnerable, but no. That was *definitely* wrong. Striker was strength personified. Chivalrous and complex were much better descriptors. I smiled weakly. "That's for sure. You look cleaner."

"It's your turn now. The nurse was waiting for you to wake up so she can give you a bath and change your catheter. Since we watch every move that the staff makes, I thought you'd prefer it if it was my turn to do the watching."

"You're watching every move because you think the staff might have an Omega operative?"

"Never know — can't make assumptions."

I blew out a huff of air and turned red.

"Are you okay?" Worry edged into Striker's gaze.

"Yeah. Are you sure you can't just trust the nurse?" I grimaced.

"Lynx, I've seen it all before. I've seen you naked, and I've seen your catheter changed — they have to do that every time you're unconscious."

"Striker, it's hard to be embarrassed when I'm unconscious." I was whining like a three-year-old again. I blamed it on my restraints and how infantile they made me feel. Completely incapable, which I hated with a capital H. "And then when I wake up, I can pretend it never happened." I twirled the sheets between my fingers.

"Okay, well, I've seen you mostly naked when you were up and prancing around." He stroked a hand over his chin. "I remember New Year's Eve very vividly when you were down to a pair of heels and a couple of pieces of string."

"And that's the only way I want you to see me naked. When we were in Miami for New Year's, you looked at me like I was a piece of art. You told me I was beautiful and soft. I'm not sexy now, Striker. I'm disgusting, about as far from desirable as a girl can get, and that whole body-fluids thing is gross."

Striker's face was serious, but his eyes sparkled with laughter. "Lynx, I never thought of you as vain before. This is a whole new side of you."

"I don't think it's vanity as much as humility. This is going to be humiliating."

"You'll make it through, Chica." He dropped a kiss onto my forehead. "You know, when you love someone, you take the good with the bad." He reached over and pressed the call button. "And when we're through this little chapter, I'm planning to take you away to somewhere very pleasant and very private and put a whole lot of energy into the good."

The tone in Striker's voice and the glimmer in his eyes gave me a rush that left me breathless. He must truly love me if he could imagine past the visual I was presenting. Striker was watching my reaction with satisfaction when the nurse came through the door.

"Whoops! This looks like a private moment. Sorry to interrupt, but we're about to get personal in other ways." The nurse moved over into my field of vision so I could get a look at who was talking to me. "Best if I start by introducing myself — I'm Penny."

"Hey, Penny." I wasn't sure if I should introduce myself back or if I was Jane Doe here, so I left it at that.

Penny wore her gray hair cut like a man's. She was short, squat, and very good at what she did. Even though Striker was watching her every move — and Penny was letting him — she still managed to drape the sheet in such a way that the most private things were kept mostly private.

Penny spent a long time trying to comb out my hair so she could wash it. "I don't know, honey, it might be that you're going to end up having to cut your hair short. You're just this side of being a Rasta, and it's still full of sand and debris."

"Crap." Tears stung my eyes — partly pain, mostly self-pity.

"I'm not giving up, though," Penny said. "I've got all night. You're my only patient, so if you can take the tugging and yanking, I'll keep working on it."

"The pain meds help. If you don't mind, I'd be grateful if you can try to save my hair. Right now, it's my only vanity." I looked over at Striker. "Don't say *anything*," I commanded.

"What? My mind was a complete blank." He grinned. I was holding both of his hands and squeezing them hard with every tug.

"Here's some good news," she said. "You've been gaining weight. You weigh 92 pounds now. How much did you weigh before your—" Penny stopped to search for a word, and then said, "—circumstance."

"A hundred and thirty."

"And you're how tall?" Penny asked.

"Five-foot six."

"Hmm, a hundred and thirty is a little underweight for five-six. But you have small bones."

I grimaced as Penny ripped a snarl free. "I was athletic."

"And you will be again, I'm sure. It's just a matter of time. You have a PT coming in to assess you tomorrow morning. Actually, you have a lot of tests tomorrow. They want to do another MRI, and a neurologist is going to be in doing a workup. They're hoping to take you off traction and leave you in a collar for a few days. That way, we can start you trying to sit up."

"That would be a relief." I sucked in some air, sending sharp pain across my chest.

"No doubt. Your skin's in much better shape. The sunburn faded, and the open sores have closed. Since you aren't scratching at yourself and picking at the scabs, it seems to me the scarring will be pretty minimal. How's your stomach feeling?"

"Okay, I think. Are they going to give me more baby food today?"

"Yup, peas later this evening."

I whimpered from behind tightly sealed lips.

"Hey, are you okay? Should I stop pulling at your hair?" Penny asked.

"It's not the hair. It's my back. Yowza. That really hurts."

I heard Penny go out and come back in. She put some medicine into my IV. Snap. I was out.

The bright oscillating mirage of a "knowing" framed my dream. I was Snow White, with black hair and ruby lips, dancing through a meadow strewn with wildflowers and singing songs with twittering-bird back up. A craggy old woman approached and complimented me on my voice. She reached into her basket to offer me a shiny red apple. She held it up, and as I reached out my hand, I saw that the side pointing away from me was dripping with…

"Pea time," I heard Penny calling to me. I didn't want to wake up for peas. I tried to cling to my dream, but it wavered out of reach.

"Come on, I need you to open your eyes whether you want to or not. We have to do this on a schedule, so we can monitor your progress."

I blinked my eyes open and made a face.

"Oh, it's not so bad." She smiled encouragingly. "If you do well with this, tomorrow we get to try green Jell-O and a soft-boiled egg," Penny said. "Same as you did with Barb, I'm going to be using the smaller spoon." She held it up for me to see. "If you start gagging, or feel like you might be getting nauseated, give me a sign. We don't want you aspirating vomit. That would give us a whole new set of problems, okay?"

"Yup."

Penny spooned mushed peas in my mouth. I let it sit so I would start to salivate, reminding my body of its duties.

"You'll be glad to know that while you were sedated, I was able to get the knots out of your hair." She slipped another spoonful of peas between my lips. They needed salt desperately — or something. Blech.

"Took a few hours, and I was a lot less delicate about it since you couldn't feel anything. Your head is probably a little sore." She gave me an apologetic smile. "Oh, the price we women pay for beauty."

Before I could answer, Penny put another micro-spoon of green in my mouth.

"I washed your hair. Didn't use the institutional stuff, either."

My stomach wasn't so happy with peas. I tried shallow breathing, hoping I could finish. I definitely didn't want a feeding tube.

Penny kept chattering and spooning. "Since I knew you were going to be getting a thorough cleanup today, I brought my shampoo with me and a deep conditioning mask. You have beautiful blonde hair."

I realized Penny was trying to distract me. "Thank you. And thank you for your kindness."

"Not at all." She winked. "We women have to stick together, help each other out. It can be tough holding on to your humanity when you're lying here like this. I was in a car accident once. I know what I'm talking about."

When Penny left, I shifted my focus over at Striker. "You look beat. What time is it?"

"Almost midnight. I should hit the rack, but I don't want to leave you."

"Afraid I'll disappear?" I rubbed at the rash around my IV tape.

He laughed softly. "Last night, I lay awake, considering microchipping you. That way, whenever I wanted to know where you were and what you were up to, I could check a computer."

"And you think I'd let you do that?" My voice sailed up a full octave.

"You'd never know. The chips are the size of rice, and I'd just shoot one under your skin with a hypodermic."

I narrowed my eyes. "You've done this before?"

"Only for my niece's dog."

I didn't doubt for a minute he'd try something like that. My voice dropped to a horrified whisper. "Did you do that to me, Striker?"

"Nope. In the end, it might give me peace of mind, or it might be a treasure map for any pirates out there."

"Looking for booty?"

"Yeah, I'm the only one who's allowed to chase after your booty." He wiggled his brows rakishly, making me giggle.

"Good one, funny man. I know that technology doesn't exist. There's no way to power something like that. The best you could do is microchip me, so if someone found me, they could contact you. Even then, they'd have to know to run a scanner over me, and who in their right mind would do that?"

"Yeah. It was all just aimless thoughts before I fell

asleep. Would you like me to tell you about some of my other thoughts?" Striker asked, bringing my hand to his lips, making me smile with his kiss.

"Maybe later." My eyelids were heavy. It seemed that I could only stay awake for little snippets of time. I was having a love-hate relationship with my pain meds.

"Okay, later. Deep is outside. Blaze is inside for the next four hours. I'm actually going to have to rotate people home to D.C. to make appearances and get them back here undercover."

"Explanation?"

"If we gave up on finding you, we wouldn't be hanging out at Lackland anymore. Jack and Gator have headed home now. They'll turn right back around after they've made some appearances and sneak back out. Then Blaze and Deep will go. I'm the last to rotate home. I'm really hoping we're going to get some excellent news from your doctors tomorrow. As soon as we safely can, we need to get you out of here."

8
_____

"WHAT DOES 'OUT OF HERE' LOOK LIKE TO YOU, STRIKER?" I blinked back the fatigue, but each blink made it that much harder to open my eyes.

"We have some options. I want to know what you want to do. Are you up to weighing some pros and cons with me?"

"Yes, thank you." I yawned deeply. Striker looked dubious, so I gave him a reassuring smile.

"We have the option of taking you out of the country. It would mean everyone would have to have a new identity. We'd have little to no support if things went bad. And Iniquus is concerned about things coming to a head off American soil. We need to protect our reputation and America's diplomatic interests."

"Agreed, I think out of the US is a no go. Even something like Hawaii is bad. It's too limiting." I reached up and scratched at my nose, where the oxygen tubes tickled my nostrils.

"We talked about somewhere else, maybe the West Coast. The thing is that our group has been working as a dedicated team since last fall when you were under our protection at the safe house. If Omega has done their home-work on any level, they'd know who your teammates are. That means in order to keep you safe, we'd have to leave Strike Force back in D.C. and assign a new team."

The idea of being alone with strangers fired adrenaline through my body and wiped away all my fatigue. It put me in survival mode. Panic must have shot into my eyes because Striker squeezed my hand. "I nixed that idea out of the box."

I breathed an audible sigh of relief. "Yes, thank you."

"The team has narrowed our choices down to D.C., either at Iniquus, or you know I have a house on the bay. At Iniquus, we could get you medical help easily. You would stay in my barracks apartment."

"You don't seem happy with that option. Why?"

"Frith thinks Omega's got eyes on the lawn. That means they think we might sequester you at Iniquus, and if you came outside, you'd be targeted."

"That's ballsy." I wiggled my nose to readjust the breathing tube. I'd be glad when that was gone.

"Yeah. I'm not going to repeat what Command said about that. At Iniquus, there's the added benefit of the shel-ters under headquarters."

"You mean in case Omega starts bombing?"

"It's a stretch of the imagination. I'm just offering the pros and cons. The big con about sequestering you in my apartment — without your being able to go outside — is your mental health. If you felt like a prisoner there, I'm afraid of how that would affect your working for Iniquus, your relationship with the team, and frankly, your relation-ship with me."

"What about the bay house? Gator says it can't be traced to you."

"I'm no-profile when I'm at my house. No one in the area knows me or has seen me. There's a lot of land around the place, and I go there for seclusion. The house has plenty of room to bunk the team. There's a gym for your rehab. And there's a lot of fresh air."

"No one knows you own the place?" Why would anyone have a house on the water, big enough to bunk a team of people and not invite guests? All right — women. Why hadn't he taken women there?

"I picked the area for safety. I thought one day I'd end up having to safeguard my sister because of her associations, and I'd need to hide her and Cammy away. Believe me when I say it's state of the art for protecting my family."

No doubt. Striker would go to any length to keep Lynda and Cammy safe.

"The added benefit of being there is that we could take you, under a false identity, to the local emergency department if you needed to be hospitalized again. And we could do that without raising alarms."

"So you'd just have the team make a show of being home and then being sent off-grid?"

"Exactly, then we can work with you to figure this mess out — who thinks you've broken what law? Why is there a bounty on your head?"

"Big ass bounty." I meant to be funny and relieve some tension, but the look in Striker's eyes made me understand there was nothing humorous about my situation. "Would we leave Randy and Axel on the outside loop to do footwork?" I asked.

"Yeah, they've been off-grid since they left for Honduras, so they're the obvious choice."

"The bay is your preference."

"I've thought it through, and I feel confident in either the Iniquus option or the bay option. I'm not confident in any of the other options."

"Agreed. And based on what you just said, I would suggest we go with the bay option, with Iniquus as back up."

"Then we have a plan. All we need now is for the medical team to sign off, and we'll get you moved."

"Gotcha. Now go to bed. That's an order." I tried to screw my face into a serious scowl to put weight behind my words, but somehow, lying there looking at Striker, all I could conjure up was a dopey grin.

"Yes, ma'am." He gave me a salute, then bent over to give me a soft kiss.

9

THE DOOR OPENED, AND THERE WAS A QUIET EXCHANGE. Blaze came into view.

"Hi, beautiful. You look nice, all washed up." He leaned over, scrutinizing my face. I was starting to feel like a circus sideshow. "Your cheeks are starting to get softer. You were pretty skeletal when we found you. Scary." He gave a mock shiver from head to foot.

"Sorry." My voice came out as a whisper.

Blaze sat gently on the bed.

"Striker won't let me see a mirror," I told him.

Blaze considered me for a minute. "Yeah, that's probably best."

"That bad?" *What the hell did I look like? Was I disfigured? Was it permanent?* My nerves buzzed, making me tingle with claustrophobia. I desperately wanted to pry myself loose from my traction unit. I tried to still my heart. No matter how much I wanted to get up and out, it wasn't going to happen. It reminded me of how I felt in prison. I still wasn't free.

He shrugged. "It was worse. You look tired."

"No, not tired. Bored. Why don't you tell me a story?"

"That's Gator's gig. I'm not a storyteller. I can tell you this, though. Axel and Randy got hold of the snake oil van. It was impounded for parking violations."

That was a big step forward. I had spent almost every lucid moment trying to wrap my brain around why Omega was after me. All I could come up with was that somehow, someone thought I was in cahoots with Maria. Part of some elaborate plan to get her husband, Julio, out of the federal pen. Julio Rodriguez was sitting on a hundred-year sentence for terrorism. My involvement in an escape plan would get any number of agencies' hackles up — CIA, FBI, ATF. And a court would seal the file associated with terrorism charges —that made sense.

I had cast a wide net, fishing for any other reason Omega could be targeting me, and I'd come up empty-handed. I was pinning my hopes for getting the Omega contract rescinded on understanding the what, how, and why of my kidnapping. Why me, for example? Why would Maria choose me as her kidnapping target? And if she were just trying to kidnap me, it didn't make any sense that she would buy a house, move into my neighborhood, and try to get to know me before the kidnapping.

I had lots of questions. Lots. But I'd start with, "What about Hector?"

"Haven't caught him yet," Blaze said. "But they're working on it. Seems he's got a very angry ex-girlfriend who's more than willing to help us find him." He smirked. "Randy and Axel are hoping they get to Hector first. The ex looks like she might do Hector some damage. They got his last name and his background — shouldn't be long until we have him in custody."

"Can you let me know before he's interrogated? I'd like to be in on that as much as possible."

"Absolutely. I'm sure that's the plan." Blaze ran a hand down his thigh and rested it on his knee. "About the van, they ran forensics to see if there was material evidence to prove it was the vehicle used to kidnap you. They found a clump of hair pulled out at the root. Axel says it's your length and color. They have your old toothbrush up at forensics for a DNA comparison. Did you do that on purpose, or did they pull your hair out?"

"My head was in a bag, so they didn't really have access to my hair. I was trying to leave evidence, and I thought if you found my hair, you could prove without a doubt it had been me. I didn't really have a lot of possibilities. I was so drugged, I thought I might have just dreamed all that and had actually left you nothing."

He smiled. "Nope, you did good."

I smiled back. "*Gracias*."

Blaze looked at me like he was trying to make up his mind about something. "I have some more info if you're okay to hear it," he said cautiously.

Uh oh. "Sure, go ahead."

"Did anyone tell you that we found your prison? Axel and Randy got to your area just before the storm hit the Caribbean."

"Yeah, I heard about that. It seems I was a day early and a dollar short with my escape. If I had waited, I might have a very different outcome right now."

"Except that Maria was there for your fingers." Blaze was stone-faced.

I quirked one side of my mouth up. "There was that."

"Sometimes, things have a weird way of working themselves out for the best," Blaze said.

"More?"

"If it weren't for your psychic ability, and your ability to puzzle through the communication problem and get us concrete details, we would never have made it down to Honduras. From what I can tell, your escape and our movement in the area were only a few hours apart.

"Randy and Axel found the airport, and sure enough, twenty kilometers south there was a prison and ten kilometers south of that was a village. The guys got a room above the cantina. They said it was like moving back in time a hundred years. There was nothing there — very secluded, no landlines, no cell tower service. Just dirt roads and poverty."

That was true. The place was less than third world; it was like landing on Mars.

"The storm got bad, and the guys were stuck. They thought that, even though they were posing as tourists exploring the Honduran coast, it would look strange to go out in the severe weather. They were trying to gather intel, though, the best they could under the circumstances. They spent a lot of time in the cantina, buying rounds, making friends, and listening for local talk."

Blaze had my full attention. I had wondered about all this.

"Gossip had it that there had been some non-Honduran Latinos there a few days before. Soldier types like Randy and Axel. They had been buying a lot of drinks and asking a lot of questions about the prison. Randy and Axel had their radar up, but they didn't know what it could mean. It was apparent, though, that some group had been asking the same kinds of questions that Axel and Randy were asking."

I was desperate to get up and pace. Taking all this in lying down was seriously overwhelming. "Omega?" I asked on an exhale.

"Frith doesn't know. He thinks it's possible. He's kept his ear to the ground since he saw your name on the file. He said he heard some noises about Central America, but the first real sign that Omega was making progress came with your 9-1-1 call. For now, we're all assuming it was Omega down there. Though how they could have found you…" He shook his head slightly. "Of course, before Frith contacted Command, we had no idea that we had competition. So, had Maria not shown up at just that time to force your escape, and had the storm not hit, then Iniquus and Omega might have dueled it out down there. I can't imagine that we'd all stay healthy."

I couldn't imagine it, either. "Someday, I'm going to tell Frith how very grateful I am for his help. He's got guts, for sure. Okay. Good then, that I left. There's one piece of guilt pie I don't have to eat."

"No. If we're looking for silver linings, that's one we can focus on."

"So if Omega catches me, then what? I get sent to an American prison? I move through the American judiciary? That might be okay. I might want to just give myself over to them so I can clear my name in the courts."

"We're still not sure of the endgame with Omega. It wouldn't go through the courts, though, that's for sure. Frith doesn't know what the order is, but he knows it isn't good. You're classified 'Eradicate.'"

Eradicate? What? I was too stunned to talk. I wanted to

launch myself up and into a fight for survival. How ridiculous was that notion, right now, tethered to this damned bed the way I was? Blaze glanced over at my monitors. No sirens. I guessed he decided I was handling this information okay because he cleared his throat.

"Frith says that could either be a kill order, or it might be an interrogate, then kill order. I, for one, am not going to let either happen."

I gripped at the safety bar like a drowning person clutching at a lifeline. Holy shit. *Eradicate*.

We were silent together. I could empathically feel his nerves bristling, and I tried to will the sensation away from him and from me. I had my own nerves to deal with.

He buffed an agitated palm up and down his thighs. "When we heard from Axel, we figured you had run away from the prison before the storm hit the Caribbean and, being in no man's land, you wouldn't have had any warning."

"I saw the storm coming up. I knew it was a bad idea to fly. I had no idea it was a tropical storm when I took off. Even if I did know, I was out of options at that point."

Blaze nodded. "From when Randy called to say a plane was missing at the Honduran airport until we got the 911, I had a terrible feeling in the pit of my stomach. I didn't want to think we'd lost you." His eyes hardened, and he made a fist over my hand, squeezing my fingers. "I'm not saying that I was hopeless. I'm saying from a pragmatic point of view, with the storm and all, your chances of survival seemed pretty slim."

Blaze seemed to be venting — like he needed to say these words out loud to relieve the pressure that had been building up. I decided not to ask any questions but just let him say everything he needed.

"When we got to you…that was horrible. The scene was surreal — it was hard to imagine that the skeleton we were saving was actually you."

Blaze stopped talking when a nurse walked in my door. In my peripheral vision, I saw flashes of blue as she passed through my room. Barb and Penny were the nurses usually assigned to me. I didn't recognize this nurse's voice as she acknowledged Blaze. She was fussing about something across the room where I couldn't see her. Blaze and I sat quietly together, waiting for privacy.

A siren went off in the hallway. It was loud enough to wake the dead. The lights over my bed flashed on and off. Trapped by my traction unit, all I could do was flail my arms. I was easy prey.

With the first sound, Blaze jumped to his feet, Glock in hand pointed at the nurse.

"Hands up!" Blaze's voice was threatening as hell.

"What are you doing? Put your weapon away, soldier."

The nurse moved close enough to me that I could see she had her hands up near her ears, and in her right hand, she held a syringe of clear liquid. She took a step closer to my bed.

"Freeze!" Blaze commanded.

There was a scuffling sound and an "oof" as a body hit the wall. More alarms sirened — this time from inside my room — my monitors were going ballistic. The nurse was yelling at Blaze to lower his goddamned weapon and let her the hell go so she could help me.

My door crashed open, and Deep called, "Let her go, Blaze. Burnt popcorn catastrophe — all's clear."

A very irate nurse stomped her way over to my monitor bank, then everything went black.

10

Slowly, I became aware. My eyes, heavily sedated, didn't want to open yet, though I kept telling them it was time. The silicone pellets in my specialized mattress gently oscillated beneath me, and its fan unit hummed. An arm cuff swelled automatically to check my blood pressure as it did every half-hour. The cold air flowing through my nasal tube tormented the cilia in my nose—a disturbing combination of scents — oxygen, rubbing alcohol, and salt.

Something was different.

The difference prickled around the outer edges of my consciousness. I ordered my eyelids to blink open.

I was no longer in an industrial green room. This room was butter yellow, with natural — not fluorescent — lighting. No traction unit tethered me in place. I could turn my head slightly, painfully, to the left, where French doors revealed a cloudless blue sky. Pine trees were to the right and choppy gray water to the left of my view.

And I was *pissed.*

The door opened on my right. Heavily booted feet saun-tered over a wooden floor.

"I had you on the monitor. I was waiting for you to wake up." Striker pointed up to a wall camera focused on my bed. "You're at my bay house in Maryland now."

"I figured that out." Sarcasm. I was a little sensitive about someone moving me around without my blessing or knowledge. With memories of my days locked in a jail cell still raw, I wanted complete control over my life and limbs. "You brought me here with no warning."

"Didn't have time." Striker used his soothing voice. I guessed he realized he'd crossed some invisible line. He could hear my internal warning alarms sounding. "The nurse at Lackland put you out when the burned-popcorn-cata-strophe all but gave you another heart attack. The doctors decided to keep you out while they ran your MRI."

"Okay." I really didn't want to hear it. "Everyone's East Coast now?"

"Yeah." He sat down gingerly on my bed, hiking one knee up and leaning forward to squint at me — his assessing look.

"That's a funny little 'yeah.' What's up?" All right, maybe I did want to hear it. "Why'd you take me out of Lackland so quickly?"

"Jack and Gator were in D.C., making sure they were seen. When they went to Headquarters, Command had another visitor. Jack and Gator got to meet Frith."

"Frith? Why? Does he have more information?" Excite-ment bubbled up. I wanted this stupidity solved and done.

"Not much new — he wanted to tell us that Omega was pulling out of Texas. But Omega thought the high alert at Lackland was suspicious."

My fingers played with the silken edging on my blanket. "Those two thoughts don't go together."

"Omega found a hole to plant an embed at the base hospital. Frith didn't believe they'd find anything, though. Wanted us to know he was sorry for our loss. Thought very highly of you. He hoped there could have been a happier outcome."

"Huh." My lips tightened, and I screwed my mouth to the side.

"Okay, what's your take on this?"

Disappointment was my take on this.

All right, think! I ordered my head. "No one at Omega knows that Frith has any connection to me, or to the case we worked on together, right? He's reporting what he's seeing going on over at Omega Headquarters. Does Omega have any clue we know they're after me?"

"Absolutely. After your 911 call, their Command realized we'd be out on the search." Striker crossed his arms over his chest and looked like a Rambo prototype, only much cuter and with rusty-brown hair. A little smile played across my lips at the thought, and Striker gave me a sideways look, then continued, "They sent word they had a warrant for your arrest. If we had any contact with you, we should pass that information on to them immediately. Failure to do so would mean we were aiding and abetting. Everyone involved would be subject to arrest and imprisonment."

"I see. So I'm fraternizing with a criminal element?"

"Afraid so, Chica." He bent to give me the kiss I'd been waiting for.

"Well, if I were Omega, I wouldn't just pull out — the embed makes sense. On the outside, I'd be gauging Iniquus' reaction. Observing movement…yeah. I think they're testing the waters, trying to make Iniquus feel safe, so if I were alive, and if I had been located, then maybe we'd get sloppy enough to make a mistake. Frith wanted us to have a heads up."

"Agreed. But we aren't going to make any mistakes, babe," he said.

"Thanks." I shifted the little bit that I could and felt the beads shifting with me. "How's Command doing with all this?"

"They're pissed as hell. Omega doesn't dictate to Iniquus, and Omega doesn't go after Iniquus operators. You've got two snarling alpha dogs ready to tear out each other's jugular." Striker's mouth was grim. "Iniquus isn't going to back down. Command thinks you must have put your thumb on the pulse of something big and ugly. There's someone or some organization out there that's got money and power."

I frowned and looked out at the gray line of the horizon. Striker waited.

"Sylanos is the only one that comes to mind," I said.

"Not when he's dead. Did you know that before you figured out the name Sylanos, the CIA had to refer to him by a code name? In their files, Sylanos was called Nemean. That should tell you how daunting they found him."

"As in Nemean lion?" I asked. "Impervious to attack. But that would mean he was a standalone, and we know that's wrong. They should have named him Hecatonchires."

"Yeah, but no one could spell that, and no one but you could pronounce it." Striker warmed me with a grin — double dimple action.

"Hydra, then. After all, that's what Spyder called Sylanos' metamorphosis. Point being, Sylanos wasn't a one-man-show. He was a monster with many heads. Even if he were dead, that doesn't mean the Hydra is, too."

"Even if?" Striker shook his head. "We had men on scene. Sylanos is dead. Before we marked Sylanos off the list, we thought maybe your case had something to do with the Colombian government. We had our contacts down there put up their antennae for you."

"Colombia? I'm lost."

"Spyder was coming in from Colombia last Christmas when he passed out at the airport. Before he collapsed, Colombia was our mission plan. Command tapped the three of us to head downrange. Our Colombian team concluded that whatever was going on was American run. Omega involvement seemed to confirm that. But then, somehow, you got shelved in Honduras, so now we're back at square one."

"Go back. Spyder was in Colombia? Who told you that?" I gripped at my blankets, wishing I could sit up to gain some physical control.

"Got it straight from the source."

"You talked to Spyder? Is he better? What was wrong with him?"

"Malaria and diverticulosis. He's a hundred percent and headed back out on assignment. He sends you his love."

What? Headed out? That made no sense what so ev— *Wait*. "Does Spyder know about me?"

"I didn't tell him anything. He thinks you're in D.C. at headquarters, safe and sound in the Puzzle Room. We only had a three-minute window. I thought it would serve you best if I pulled the most information I could from him. He's en route to Indonesia."

"Because?"

"Coup plot that could put American industry and military interests at risk, not to mention the local population's peppered with American ex-pats."

"And Spyder's supposed to stop this?" I asked.

"Yup."

"Single-handedly?"

Striker gave me a nonchalant shrug, but I could tell by his quick peeks at my monitors and the stiffness in his neck that he wasn't feeling as offhand and detached as he'd like me to believe. "I'm not sure what he's got for a team. My guess is he's already got a network in place."

Striker let me have a minute. I looked out at the bay with stormy eyes. I was angry, and I wasn't sure why I was angry. But there it was. When I looked back at Striker, the vitriol still hardened my gaze.

"Let it go, Chica. This is who he is. And he didn't know anything about you. Not the kidnapping. Not the plane wreck. Not Omega."

"*Because* no one told him. Not even you."

"Exactly." Striker gave me his commander face: hard lines, hard eyes, intelligent and unwavering. He had to have a reason. A good one. And if I asked, he'd just say, "Classified, Chica." Some parts of this job sucked.

"Okay, I'll let it go." I tapped my fingers irritably and pursed my lips until I could tuck my Spyder-thoughts into the back of my mind. Spyder was my mentor, my surrogate dad. I selfishly wanted him by my side, helping me to figure out my mess, not off combatting a distant coup. "Let's go back to the idea of Sylanos," I managed after a few minutes of turmoil.

Striker sat quietly.

"If Sylanos were already dead when I was kidnapped, it

would be hard to explain Maria's success. Sure, she wanted her husband out of jail. But could she have pulled off such a complicated scenario on her own?" I needed more wake-up time or fewer painkillers before I plunged into puzzling mode. I pushed my hair from my face and ran my tongue over fuzzy teeth. Yuck. "That doesn't feel right to me, though. Maybe she was under someone else's orders. Second in line?"

Striker shook his head. "I wouldn't think so. Sylanos's death and your kidnapping came too close together. If new leadership moved up, it would take some time to reorganize. And I can't imagine that Julio held such a high priority. He'd been in jail for months before Maria came after you. That was the only ransom demand — Julio out of jail and back with her. You were just the vehicle she was using to get there."

"And Julio was sentenced last September." I rubbed my index finger back and forth across my lower lip.

"Then Maria moved into your neighborhood in January, four months later," Striker added.

"But didn't kidnap me until February...yeah, this doesn't make much sense. Now that Maria's in custody, it's going to be good to get some answers."

"FBI's working on that." Striker stood up and went to adjust the blinds to keep the sun from hitting me in the eye.

I followed him with my gaze. "Thank you. Hey, can I read the transcripts from the Maria and Julio interrogations?"

"They aren't talking to anyone — nothing to transcribe," Striker said. "I bet they'll want to lay out their story for the DA first before he talks to Hector. And if not, then Hector might lead us to another player." Striker paused. "Hector's in custody, by the way," he said. "That's one item on my list of good news to tell you this morning."

"A whole list, huh?"

He sat back down on my bed. "You're alive. Safe. In my house, out of harm's reach. All the rest is just icing."

I looked at Striker long and hard. Any residual anger I had in my system had simmered off, and I was left with incredulity. He was right — as usual. Did I really care how I got to the bay house? Or should I focus on the fact that I was so darned freaking lucky to be back with my team? I laced my fingers possessively with Striker's and rested my other hand on his thigh. He was solid. Whole. Healthy. Here. These thoughts would probably take a while to integrate. I had to keep reminding myself.

"Axel's scheduled an interrogation in a little while. Maybe Hector can give us a better direction to take," Striker said.

"What did they charge him with?" I asked.

"Kidnapping and murder one. They don't think they can make the murder stick without a body. They're hoping to use the added charge to get him to cooperate."

"You said Axel's doing the interrogation?"

Striker looked at the wall clock. "In an hour and a half. He'll be wearing a communicator. We have two cameras in the room — one that will be a close up on Hector's face and one that will monitor his body movements. You'll see them split-screen on the computer, and you can tell Axel anything you want to be worked into the questioning."

I must have looked dubious because Striker quickly added, "Axel's good at this. Did you know he's Dr. Axel White? He has a Ph.D. in criminal psychology."

Hmm, the things you learn along the way.

"Another thing," Striker said. "I have a message for you from Command."

My face screwed into a grimace like I was waiting for something painful to happen.

"They said to stop lollygagging and get better. There's a six-month backlog sitting on your desk." Striker stopped to offer up a half-smile. "I know it's not the most sensitive of messages — I can't say that Command is overly sentimental. I think it's the best they could do to express their concern. They've had your back the whole time. This operation's extremely expensive, and there's no client. It's all coming out of the corporate pocket." Striker stopped and tilted his head. "That is to say, Lynx, they value your talent and care about you."

"Not to mention they don't like having a silver-backed ape thumping his chest outside of their gate." I instantly regretted that thought had bubbled up and popped out of my mouth.

"Omega's only recent." Striker's tone was mildly chastising.

"That did sound ungrateful. I'm sorry."

Striker nodded. "You're all right. Did anyone tell you about Missy's fire?"

"Yeah. Thank you for everything you did. And please thank Command. That seems out of character."

"They have a soft spot for you." Striker rubbed his finger over my wrist. "You do that to people — get under their skin."

"Like chiggers?"

"Yup, you're pretty irritating."

11

"Testing," I spoke toward my computer.

"Got you, Lynx. You ready for this?" Axel's voice rumbled back at me. He shifted something, and his image came into better view.

"We'll see." *No, not ready.*

A door opened, and a guard ushered in a man of medium height and slight build. He wore his orange jumpsuit with the arms rolled up to show gang tattoos. Long, black, greasy hair fell across his face and pooled on his shoulders. He slouched onto the gray metal chair, one leg extended, feet ensconced in white socks and plastic shower shoes. He tried to look cool, but I could see the tension in his shoulders. His chest rose and fell with the cadence of an anxiety rush. Handcuffed wrists brought the man's hands up to his face, pushing his hair back behind his ears. Hector.

The last time I saw this man was in a gas station's putrid bathroom somewhere along I95. He had leered at me with greedy eyes as I vulnerably sat there trying to pee. Then he thrust a bag over my head, took me to the airstrip, and dumped me like a dirty-laundry bag onto the plane that eventually flew me to Honduras. And prison.

I hated him for that. But more, I hated the memory of Hector that I tasted every day, like bile slicking the back of my tongue. It was the memory of Hector's eyes behind a black ski mask, laughing as he tortured Gator with the Taser. I spent long, imprisoned hours thinking about how satisfying it would be to watch Hector's central nervous system light on fire from my Taser attack. To hear *his* guttural agony.

Axel was calm. His voice sounded reasonable. Pragmatic. He laid out all the evidence against Hector: Tammy's testimony, the DNA found in the van, surveillance tapes from gas stations heading toward Florida, the statement from Hector's ex-girlfriend. It seemed conclusive. Hector looked sideways at Axel with a half-smile. Hector knew something that made him feel safe.

"Hector, you're going to prison for a long time. I want to make a deal with you. I need details. Names. In exchange, I'll get them to drop the murder one charge."

"Nah." Hector smirked and shifted around. He pushed his hips forward on the chair and spread his knees wide, letting his hands dangle there on the excess crotch fabric of his jumpsuit as he leaned back.

Arrogance comes from knowing you have power. Spyder told me about an assignment that had to do with a diplomat's teenaged boys. They knew they were above the law — any law. And they knew their host country would make any wrongdoing disappear in order to preserve the diplomatic friendship between our two governments, even if it was really only a veneer of friendliness. These boys would go out and rape the local girls, scoff at the newspaper accounts, and make scrapbooks of the articles. The contempt that Spyder had described on those boys' faces was what I saw now in every move Hector made. Axel wasn't going to make any headway until he found the power source and pulled the plug.

Axel nodded his chin at Hector's tattoo. "I see you're marked. El Primo. New York City. How'd you get down to D.C.? You're off your turf."

"I'm out of that life, man."

"That may be, but here in D.C., the prisons are run by Hellhound. They know you're the enemy, Hector."

Hector raised the left side of his lip in a smirk and blew out derisively.

"You won't last here. I can get you moved to New York. At least you'll have your homeboys at your back," Axel said.

"I abdicated. I'm just as marked there as here."

Axel was impassive. He had offered Hector two bones, and Hector hadn't sniffed at either one. Bones. The word tickled the tip of my tongue. I could feel a thought trying to form.

T-Bone.

T-Bone is dead.

That was my thought. A psychic "knowing." No idea what it meant. Words with import came to me like that. This one wanted to push its way out of my mouth.

"T-Bone is dead," I said into my microphone.

Axel stopped. Maybe he thought I'd have more information for him. I had nada.

"Hector, tell me about T-Bone," Axel started nonchalantly.

Hector went still. He slid his left foot behind the leg of his chair and rubbed his palms down his thigh. Bingo. Vulnerability. He's trying to hide something. I saw the moves register with Axel.

"What about T-Bone?" Hector asked.

Axel looked at Hector without a word.

Hector shifted again, pulling at his pants leg. "T-Bone don't mean nothing to me, man. I was only in his cell one night when they brought me in. After I talked to Mr. DA yesterday, I got me moved to a new cell all by myself. Luxury suite. Ain't seen T-Bone since."

"You and T-Bone hit it off, though. You had a nice long talk, didn't you?"

Hector held eye contact with Axel. Neither moved. It was one of those *mano-a-mano* moments to see who would be the first to blink.

I watched Axel's face. The scar tracing from his brow to his jaw reminded me of a pirate: willing to take risks, ruthless, a life of hardship that made him steely and unrelenting.

Hector read this too; I could see the flicker of doubt in his eyes.

Axel won.

"T-Bone don't matter none. He in for assault. He a gangbanger. No one believe nothin' he'd say. He want to tell? Go 'head. He just trying to trade me in for a free walk, man." Hector rested his eyes on his knees.

"You told T-Bone your story."

Hector looked up at Axel and back down at the floor with a scornful huff.

"And now T-Bone is dead," Axel said.

Hector all but threw his body out of his chair. He moved

back in the tiny interrogation room, away from Axel, to stand in the corner. He was cornered.

"What you mean, T-Bone dead?"

Axel said nothing.

"He was alive this morning when I got moved."

Axel gave a slight nod. Hector stalked back to his chair, sat down, and leaned forward, tightly wound, focused. "T-Bone dead?"

"This is bigger than you could ever imagine." Axel's voice was quiet. Eerily free of emotion. "*You* are smaller than you could ever imagine. You, Hector, are a bug under someone's shoe, and you are about to get squashed. I want to know why."

"I don't know why. It shouldn't-a been nothing. Maria had a drive job for me. I borrowed Loquisha's van to make the run. Maria pay me, and that be that. Now I'm charged with kidnap and murder one."

"You were just driving a van. You needed some cash. You didn't mean anyone any harm," Axel said.

"Damn straight, man." Hector took the bait.

"Things didn't go exactly as planned. Maria lied to you. This is all her fault. She should do the time, not you. I want that for you. I want Maria to do the time, and I want you to go on with your life."

Hector nodded. *Yeah, let Maria take the wrap.*

"When did you realize things weren't going right?" Axel set the hook and was now watching Hector thrash around, wearing himself out. Then Axel could reel him in.

"We got to the house and waited for the girl to be alone. I saw her out the window. She were a little bitty thing. She ain't no hassle. We had to keep her fresh, though. No guns. No knives. Maria give me a Taser to use in case she fight us.

Maria said the girl couldn't have no bruises on her for the video."

"Did Maria tell you where you were going?"

"Yeah, the drive was for Florida."

Axel's hands rested on the metal table. "So, you waited. How did you get to Lexi?"

"Maria's niece, Tammy, be calling over to the girl to get her to come help with the neighbor's baby. The boyfriend was the one that came out, though."

"Her boyfriend?" This obviously confused Axel. And me. Striker had been out of town.

"Yeah, big ass mother fucker. Soldier boy."

Ah, Gator. Yeah, I guess since he was living with me at the time, Maria probably assumed...

"He had a gun out." Hector pantomimed as much as his handcuffs would allow. "He knew something was up. And all I had was the damned Taser. Then the girl come running out the house, talking on her cellphone. Boyfriend was hiding behind the car out front, watching our house. When he saw her coming, he jumped up and ran out front, all macho shit. When he come through the door, I shot the Taser. I was afraid to let up off the trigger. Damn straight, he'd be all over me."

"The girl came in behind him," Axel said.

"She screaming to stop hurting Gator. He looked like a gator there on the floor, flopping around. Maria had a knife on the baby. The girl said she would go with us no problem, and Tammy put her in shackles and cuffs." Hector looked down at his shoes.

After a long minute, Axel said, "Go on."

"I picked up the gun the alligator dude dropped. I wanted to shoot him and Tammy. Leave no witnesses. Maria wouldn't let me, though. She said that would bring the police, and we wouldn't get away clean. We shackled them up. Gagged them."

"Then, you drove away."

Hector glanced briefly up at Axel, then cast his gaze toward the blank wall. "We heard sirens, so we got out of there."

"Down 95 to Florida."

"I put the girl in the back of a little plane, drove Maria to some apartment building, and left her off."

"In Nelson, Florida."

"Yeah." Hector worked his jaw back and forth. "That was it, man. See, I didn't kill nobodies. I didn't do no harm."

"Has anyone contacted you since then?" Still that easy monotone. Soothing. Hypnotic. *Yup, Dr. Axel was very good at this.*

"Not until I got arrested."

"And you only told this story to T-Bone."

"I shouldn't have, but when they brought me in, I was drunk and doped and feeling sorry for myself, and I guess it spilled out." Hector hung his head, hiding behind his curtain of stringy black hair.

"You gave details to the DA?" Axel asked.

Hector ran his hands down his thighs. "No."

"He knew everything already?"

"Naw, man." He shook his head again. "We didn't talk about it none."

"He said something else to you." Axel drew a circle on the table with his index finger, then gave a tap. "Something that made you feel safe."

"He said he getting me a room of my own away from the

gangs, and if'n I keep my head down, all this was about to go away."

"Did he explain how?" Axel asked.

"No." Hector leaned forward with his elbows resting on his knees, his hands linked together. He looked like he was in prayer...or pleading. "What happened to T-Bone?"

"He didn't keep his head down."

12

STRIKER CLOSED THE COMPUTER AND TOOK IT AWAY FROM MY bed. "T-Bone?"

"It just came to me." I ripped the top off two packets of Splenda and poured them into my tea mug sitting on the hospital table in front of me. I wondered, now that my traction unit was off when they were going to let me sit all the way up. Hot tea from a straw was a weird experience.

"He's not someone you met along the way. 'T-Bone's dead' just came to you. A psychic 'knowing.'"

"Yes."

Striker looked at my mug. When I followed his gaze, I saw that I had poured the Splenda onto the table, three inches to the left of the mug, and had put the paper packets into my tea.

"I think my perception is a little off," I stated the obvious.

"No guns for you until you've got your vision straightened out. That's an order."

I gave him a mock salute. I didn't actually think I had the

strength to lift a gun. And if I did, the recoil might just take my arm off. "Can Axel try to find out if T-Bone really is dead? Maybe Hector spilled a few more details when he was inebriated, and T-Bone would be willing to share."

"I'm sure Axel's already on it." There was a light tap on my door. Striker stood. "You have visitors."

He opened my door, and the Iniquus medics came in. These men had been with me both at the safe house and again at Headquarters when I was recovering from my Veil walking episodes.

"Hey, Lynx." Andy's drooping eyes had a cartoonish quality to them. He was a light man with oversized feet and hands that grew out of the cuffs of his starched white uniform. He moved over to the monitors and looked at the readouts. "This looks good. You're settling in."

Chris moved further into view. "Hey, Lynx."

"Hey, yourself."

"Thanks for the vacation. These are some pretty swanky digs," Chris said.

"Are they? I haven't looked around yet," I said.

"You will. Your physical therapist is out front waiting for you. I bet she'll want you out of this bed soon." Chris was dressed identically to Andy, but where Andy had a nimble feel about him, Chris was more of the squat, big-necked brand of husky wear.

"What's the story the PT was told?"

"Your injuries were sustained in a car accident," Striker said. "Back when you were a teen, you had a bad hospital experience, and now the smell of hospitals makes you break out in hives. You insisted on going home to recuperate, but home was problematic because of logistics. Your dad, Bill Henderson, is on some board with Jimmy Johnson, the guy who owns this place. Your family is rolling in dough. Anything you need, you just snap your fingers, and it appears like magic."

"Awesome. I need a toothbrush." I snapped my fingers.

"In a minute." Striker put his hands on my ankles. I wondered if he was trying to ground me, so I could focus. "You know nothing about Johnson; you've never met him. You're here because Jimmy's doing a favor for your dad."

"Got it," I said.

"Andy and I are private, for-hire nurses," Chris said. "We don't work for any company. We do independent, individual contracts for long-term cases. Johnson recommended us. We helped him out after his stroke last year. So again, your dad's name is Bill Henderson, and the owner's name is Jimmy Johnson."

"Bill Henderson. Jimmy Johnson. And me?"

Chris waved my medical file at me. "You're Anna Louisa Henderson. People call you Annie."

Striker crossed his arms over his chest and leaned a shoulder into the wall. "You're 27, birthday April Fool's Day — you've been ribbed about that all your life. You've lived all over the US. You call nowhere home. You're an aspiring writer working on her first book — a thriller — there's a plot against the US government from inside the Pentagon. Right now, you're in the research phase. You like to talk to my team. We're answering your questions about how the military works, and you're learning our vocabulary so you can make your dialogues believable."

"Believable dialogues are essential to a great thriller. Okay, that explains me, but how do I explain the team?"

"We're veterans home from Afghanistan. We're working on developing a reintegration program for returning vets with various disabilities," Striker said. "The program is sponsored by the Johnson Family Trust, and Jimmy's putting us up until we get the project's wheels in the air." Striker was speaking slowly and clearly, which I appreciated. It helped the details form into a clear picture in my mind. "We live in the east wing of the house, so if you're walking around with Laura — Laura McCaffrey, the physical therapist — then you'll decline to go into that area. The rest of the house and grounds are at your disposal. You ready?" Striker wiggled my toes.

"As ready as I'm going to be."

Striker moved closer and gave me a kiss. "I'm going to go. I have a case that needs some direction. I'll come back in and have dinner with you later."

"Is the case something interesting? Do you need a second set of eyes?"

"Nope. You aren't on this assignment. Your plate's full. Don't be greedy."

Striker's face was close to mine, hovering there after the kiss. I looked into his eyes, only paying half attention to his words. I loved Striker's eyes. Mossy green, flecks of gold, concern, filled with affection. I missed his eyes…mmm, and his spicy, warm cologne. Yup. Greedy summed up how I was feeling. A little smile played over my lips. He kissed me again, gave me a wink, and left through my French doors.

Chris went out through my hall door and was quickly back. "Annie, I have someone I want you to meet."

A tall woman moved toward my bed. "Hi, Annie. I'm Laura. I'll be the one who makes you cry every day." She held out her hand. I could see that she bit her nails. Her only jewelry was a sturdy watch—no mark where a wedding ring would go.

"Do I have to cry *every* day?" I asked and shook her hand.

"I won't feel like I've done my job unless I wring at least one tear out of you."

"Fair warning."

Laura was in her mid-thirties, dressed in loose scrubs, and had the feel of practicality that was painted over with ebullience. Weird word *ebullience*. I didn't get to say it often. I didn't get to think it often, but that was the word I wanted.

Even though Laura was grounded and solid, a professional from the chin down, there was this quality of bouncy cheerfulness about her face, where her freckles chortled across her nose and forehead. It was as if Mr. Potato Head had the big pink lips and the mustache on at the same time. It was an odd mishmash of energies. A good mishmash, though. Laura wouldn't be the prying gossiping sort; she was here to do her job. I liked her immediately.

"Alrighty then, let's get started. Chris, I'm going to let you take out Annie's catheter. She won't be using it anymore." She turned her attention to me. "Today, you're going to walk to the bathroom." Laura cocked her head to the side. "What's your pain level?"

"I'm ignoring my pain level. I want out of this bed."

"Give me a number anyway." She raised her eyebrows and tapped a no-nonsense young lady pen on her file.

"Four. My pain meds are still doing their thing." Okay, really more like a six or seven, but I wanted to get up.

Laura put her hand on my mattress. "You're on a Clinitron. That's going to be problematic."

"I beg your pardon?"

"Your bed. It's state of the art. The silicone beads

blowing around are absolutely fabulous to protect you from getting bedsores. But we have to follow sternal precautions with you. You can't pick up more than five pounds. You can't lift anything up over your head. And we can't let you use your hands to get momentum."

I guess I looked confused because she explained, "You have to sit up without your hands. On this kind of bed, it's going to be hard to use your stomach muscles alone..." Laura looked me over, then opened the file in her hands, glancing through the pages. "Your accident wasn't that long ago. There's nothing in here..." Laura flipped through the papers again. "There's no condition listed here to explain your weight." She looked at me to fill in the blank.

"I was way underweight when the accident happened. I'd been at a low point in my life and wasn't eating properly. I have a high metabolism, so the weight fell off."

All the merriness extinguished from Laura's eyes. "Is this an ongoing issue? Your progress depends a great deal on your motivation levels."

"The problem I was facing is resolved. My motivation levels are extremely high. I'm ready to work night and day. I need to be strong again."

"Okay, then. Let's get started."

13

"TODAY MUST BE WEDNESDAY — CHICKEN SOUP IS NANA Kate," I said when Striker set the tray on the table in my room. I'd been sitting there in a straight-backed chair since Laura had left for the day. The effort of staying upright made tiny beads of sweat tickle under my nose. An IV kept me hydrated and kept my electrolytes even.

"Yup. Good old, all-American, it-will-cure-anything-that-ails-you chicken soup." Striker set the bowl of golden broth and slippery noodles in front of me. "I bet you missed being in the kitchen," he said.

"I missed everything when I was in prison. But thinking about my Kitchen Grandmothers helped keep me sane." I twiddled my spoon in my fingers and watched the steam rise from the bowl.

"How so?" Striker handed me a napkin and sat in the chair next to me.

"Master Wang once told me about his imprisonment in the re-education center in China. He said that having a daily routine gave rhythm to his days and helped him make it through. He also said it had been important for him to have little changes."

Striker nodded, his face impassive. It was hard for me to think back to Honduras. My prison days were open, seeping wounds in my psyche. I could tell from the way Striker's muscles tensed, and his pupils contracted that we had this in common.

I forced a smile to show him I was okay. "What could be a better way to have both continuity and change than to follow my teenaged pattern for visiting the Kitchen Grand-mothers?"

Striker seemed to buy into my everything's okay charade. "I explained your Kitchen Grandmother traditions to the cook. He's going to do his best to follow along. I thought that would make you feel more at home."

I smiled at him. "Home is where the heart is, Striker. I'm fine as long as I'm with you."

"That was cheesy, but I'll take it." Striker leaned across the soup to kiss me. It was a nice kiss. A really nice kiss. But he broke it off when his phone buzzed on his belt. Striker looked down at the display. "It's Axel."

I nodded and scooted back in my chair. Striker's face was closed off — he was in soldier-mode. He pressed the end button and put his cellphone back in its case. I waited.

"Axel says that Jamal Patton, a.k.a. T-Bone, was killed by a Hellhound gang member one hour after Hector was moved from their cell."

"Does Axel know anything more?"

"Yes," Striker hesitated. "Hector's body was found in the showers forty-five minutes ago. He had a bar of soap shoved down his throat."

I blinked. *What?* "I know it would be a HUGE stretch of

the imagination. But is it possible that these were gang targets, and they have nothing at all to do with his case?"

"Hector's tattoos marked him as El Primo, but Axel said that T-Bone was a Hellhound member."

Electricity flashed over my skin, making the hairs stand up on my arms. Two murders with one degree of separation? That was outside the scope of coincidental. But why?

"Striker, can I get a timeline from the prison? Hector said he moved after he met with the DA. I wonder if he meant immediately after?"

"I'll make sure we bring all the data in-house that has anything to do with T-Bone or Hector."

I sat frozen, staring out the French doors with unseeing eyes. When I looked back, Striker was watching me patiently.

"Is Command certain Omega has a legitimate contract on me?"

"Iniquus lawyers looked into the authenticity of the warrant. They found it valid but court sealed. We don't know the charges or what agency brought them. Command contacted Omega with a request for information, including the agency that hired them. Omega sent back word that all information concerning the India Sobado case was classified."

I swiveled my spoon through my soup. "I thought I was a pawn. But I'm not."

"How so?"

"This isn't chess. It's more like Chinese checkers, isn't it?"

"Keep going."

"At first, it was Maria and me. Was she working for herself or someone else? If it was someone else, then whom?

We speculated it was Markos Sylanos, but that would be a working assumption, something that needed more evidence."

"If he weren't already dead," Striker said.

"Right." My fingers drummed the table. "After the ransom letter came through, it looked more like Maria was working for her own ends."

"But you think looks are deceiving?" Striker leaned back in his chair, stretching his long legs out in front of him, crossing them at the ankle. He shot me a steady gaze.

"There are more choices. Assume Maria wasn't on her own — did she act by consent? Or was she also an unwitting counter? Someone might have been threatening her or her husband — that could be anyone, really. Now, add Hector to the plot. He looked like a mule. Sounded like a mule. Just a guy for hire. Why would Hector be moved to his own cell?"

"To make him safer? To keep him from talking? To make him feel privileged so he would talk?" Striker had his fingers steepled under his chin. His thinking position.

"Maybe it was to get him alone for a take out? No to the last one. Hector was in the showers, a public space, when someone got to him. Whatever the reason, having a single cell had to initiate from an order from someone pretty high up, I would think. Hector had to be important to someone with clout." My gaze locked onto Striker's. "With the prisons grossly overcrowded, giving a kidnap/possible murder one case a cell his own? *All* to himself? That's weird. I don't get any of that."

Striker shook his head. He didn't get it, either.

"Maybe there's something on the first interrogation tape that Hector didn't tell Axel about," I said. "I'd like to hear the conversation between Hector and the DA."

"I'll have Axel work on that." Striker pulled out his phone, looked at the screen, and put it back away.

"The DA told him to keep his head down, and this would all go away. Weird."

Striker wrote on his notepad: timeline, DA interview tapes.

I pushed my bowl to the side. "Then we have Hector looking smug, thinking he's safe from Hellhound here in D.C.? That's pretty damned bold. So Hellhound must be involved, or at least someone with enough power to pull their strings or put out directives. That's a lot of power. I even think that's beyond what Sylanos could muster up. Nothing in the lines of the Markos Sylanos cartel that I puzzled out for Iniquus had anything to do with Hellhound."

"You haven't worked that case in two years. Things can change."

"Hmmm…no, I don't think so. If Sylanos had gang leadership or was on his way toward leadership, I would have seen some connection."

"Does it matter? Sylanos is dead. He couldn't give the order to Hellhound from the grave."

"You know his being dead makes everything just that much more complicated." I huffed out an exasperated sigh.

Striker chuckled. "Lynx, you're going to short wire your brain if you keep this up."

"I need to make a diagram so I can think. Striker, can I get a whiteboard to start drawing this stuff out?"

"Not in here. We have a puzzle room set up for you in the east wing, where Laura and the house staff are off-limits. You'll have to go over there to work. We don't want to have anything around that might pique anyone's interest."

"Understood." My brows knit together. My brain was off at a gallop again.

Striker took a bite of the sandwich that was part of his dinner. I didn't get one. I was still on mushy foods.

"Go ahead and say it out loud, Chica. You look like holding it in is taking too much effort," Striker said.

"There has to be some US government involvement. Some agency that believes I'm tied to something. They could think I was conspiring with the Sylanos cartel, but that would have been CIA. We had the case before they put Omega in control. Striker, do you think they pulled the case because of me?" Before Striker could answer, I plunged on, "I can't see that as a possibility because I was on the team feeding them the intelligence. If I were culpable of something, the CIA would have addressed it with Command immediately. So not the CIA. Who then?" I screwed my lips together tightly to help me think. "A different agency. An agency that may or may not have anything to do with Maria, Hector, T-Bone, or Hellhound. Oh my god. This is crazy. I can't sit down to think this through. I need to pace."

"Soon enough," Striker said between bites. "I'm having trouble keeping your thought lines straight. They're tumbling all over each other. Eat your soup, Chica. You need the calories."

"FBI."

"FBI?" Striker slid my bowl back in front of me.

"Frith was FBI. You said he left to go to Omega. Could he have known about me because he had heard my name in conjunction with a different case contracted with the FBI? I still don't understand how Frith knows I work for Iniquus."

"Lynx, eat. That's a command."

"I'm not in your line of command. Listen, Striker, can

someone ask Frith if he heard my name at the FBI? God, I wish I wasn't dead. I really need to talk to Frith. He's the key to this whole mess. I know it. Striker, will one of your FBI contacts talk to you off the record?"

"I'll check. Eat your soup."

I put a spoonful obediently into my mouth and tasted nothing. My hand moved from bowl to mouth in a mechanical motion. I was in my head groping around.

"You know what, Striker? It just occurred to me…" I waggled my spoon at him.

"What's that?"

"This is bigger than Maria wanting her husband out of prison. People were dying to protect some piece of information, or crime, or something. Hellhound was involved and willing to eat their young. There was money — is money, a lot of it — pumped into Omega so they can find me. I'm worth enormous amounts to someone. But it couldn't be one group, now could it?"

"How do you mean?"

"Frith says that Omega, paid for by god knows who was trying to get me away from Maria. And from what you told me about Axel and Randy in Honduras, you're speculating that it was Omega operators who were trying to find me at the prison, right?"

"Yes. We made that assumption based on the timing of the Americans' appearance in Honduras and the timing of the first Frith interview with Command. No one thought that there might be a third group looking for you."

"In any case, Maria got to me first, and then Omega got the contract. If it had been the other way around, then I'd be in an Omega cell — or dead. Here's a crazy thought."

"Another one?" Striker lifted a brow.

I made a face, childishly sticking out my tongue. "I'm serious. Maria kidnapping me, saved my life. *Wow.* That makes my head spin a little bit." I grabbed at the table.

Striker reached out to put a steadying hand under my elbow.

"Striker, I think I need to get a T-shirt made that says 'Everybody Wants Me.'"

"That doesn't seem to be too far from the truth."

14

"MORNING, BEAUTIFUL."

Striker's words popped my eyes open in surprise. I was waiting for the morning church bells to signal me that Grandma Oatmeal was delivering my morning mush. *Maryland, not Honduras*, I reminded myself.

Andy moved to Striker's side. "Time to get you up and out of bed." The men lifted me up and over to the side of the bed, where I sat and dangled my feet until my head cleared. Andy went into my bathroom to set things up.

"Did you sleep okay?" Striker asked. He pulled a chair up next to me, keeping a steadying hand on my shoulder while I acclimated.

"My drugs are amazing, but they make me feel a little bit like my head is stuffed with cotton. I'm glad you came in when you did, though. I was having a miserable dream."

"What about?"

"I saw the queen from Snow White, standing in front of her reflection. 'Mirror, mirror on the wall, who's the most clever of them all?' Then I was running through the haunted woods, and I feel like I've been running for a very long time."

"Yup. Meds will do that to you." Striker knelt beside me and rubbed life back into my toes.

Andy brought my walker to the side of the bed. I felt absolutely stupid shuffling along behind the darned thing, but I also felt grateful for the stability it gave me. The men positioned themselves on either side of me, supporting some of my weight as I pulled to a standing position and lumbered toward the bathroom.

"What's on the agenda today?" I asked as we made our way forward.

Striker flashed me a grin. "You are scheduled for healing and recuperation. Laura is going to be here in an hour to start your torture session."

"What about the case?" I raised one eyebrow.

"We'll have a meeting tonight if you're up to it."

"I'm up to it." I set my teeth for the last five feet of my hike to the bathroom.

Striker bent to kiss my cheek. "I have to go. Work hard. I'll have a special treat for you tonight."

I looked up to catch his eyes. "Hint?"

"Nope." Striker threw his head back and laughed when he saw me pout. It was a wonderful, full-throated laugh. I'd missed that.

Andy and I emerged from the bathroom. He had wrapped a towel around my wet head, and I was now dressed in black yoga pants and a T-shirt. I sat in the straight-backed chair while Andy combed the tangles out of my hair and braided the damp strands into a rope down my back, out of the way. I ran my hand over the lumps. God bless him for trying, anyway.

My gaze wandered around the room. The walls glowed with a gentle, soft buttery yellow. Artistically distressed white French farmhouse furniture stood counterpoint to my modern hospital bed — safety wings, wheels, and all. On one side was my nightstand, on the other my monitoring equipment.

Shelves to the left of the French doors displayed dozens of conch shells in various sizes, easily visible from my bed. The fabrics in the room duplicated the shells' warm shades of pinks and peaches in soft cotton. Being in here felt like inspiration for my recovery — fresh and clean and healthy— the exact opposite of my cell.

Above my bed hung a painting of a village scene with darker hues, browns, and shadows. The doors of the houses were painted verdigris, which contrasted beautifully with the fabric palate in my room and kept it from becoming cloying. The only subject in the painting was a small, lithe girl, maybe five or six-years-old. Her hair fell thick, like a black velvet curtain, to her waist. She stood with her back to the viewer, under a tree heavy with pink cherry blossoms. The canvas was both winsome and sad at the same time. I knew immediately that Striker must have painted it from the delicate brush strokes. I'd have to ask him the story behind this — it seemed like something poignant was happening.

On the right-hand side of the French doors was my table with two straight-backed chairs and a vase of wildflowers that Striker brought in when he set the table for last night's soup. This morning, he'd set out a soft-boiled egg, a peanut butter protein shake, and toast.

"Have you had breakfast already, Andy?" I asked.

"Yes, ma'am."

"Honestly, I can't stand how you stare at me while I'm eating."

"Orders, ma'am. Laura wants me to report on how well you swallow different textures. You see, you have a thick fluid, something soft here, and something chewy there. If you do well with this, you get chicken at lunch."

As if on cue, someone tapped at the door; it pushed open just enough that I could see Laura's broad smile through the door. "Was that my name I heard?"

Laura didn't let me sit for long. I walked along a corridor of plain white walls. She laced a belt around my waist and held onto it from behind me in case I lost my balance and tried to do a face plant on the floor. I felt like a dog on a lead. Up and down the corridor. Up and down. My knees wobbled, and my head spun. I was glad I could lean like an old lady on my walker, pushing it forward on its little fluorescent green tennis ball feet. I walked for forty-five minutes — well, shuffled for forty-five minutes. Then I lay on a mat on the floor where Laura stretched and massaged me, attached an e-stim unit to my skin, and let the electricity contract and relax what was left of my muscles. I wouldn't have thought it would be exhausting to lie there and let a machine do the exercising for me, but after about twenty minutes, I was panting.

I must have been a successful swallower because the lunch that Andy brought me was chicken parmesan with angel hair spaghetti, a peanut butter smoothie, and peaches. Okay, not a combination that Nona Sophia would have put together, but at least the cook gave a nod to the flavor of the day.

If I'd been sick at Nona Sophia's apartment, she would place a heating pad on my feet and an ice pack on my head. Nona thought that if you confused your body, the white cells would know to rally and fight. It was a pretty good theory; it seemed to work for headaches. But I'm not sure that it would apply to a broken sternum and a swollen vertebral column.

After lunch, I swallowed a handful of meds and took a nap. Laura sat in a cozy chair at the far side of my room, reading a book on her Kindle, waiting for me to get up so we could start all over again. She was hardcore. I appreciated that. But mostly, I appreciated my soft pillow and sleep.

15

Striker wasn't around for dinner. It was Chris, Andy, and I. Laura went home at five, thank god. Tonight we ate *ribollita*, an ancient Italian soup full of veggies and beans. Nona Sophia claimed that back in the Middle Ages, the nobility would eat their meals off plates made from large slices of dried bread called trenchers. After the meal, the peasants would gather the trenchers, full of the meal's juices and leftover tidbits, and took them home to boil them for their own dinners. That was the origins of ribollita. I always thought it sounded gross, but this ribollita tasted pretty darned good, not at all like boiled leftover trenchers.

The three of us ate in silence. I was bushed.

Andy cleared off the table, helped me into my pajamas, and hooked me up to the equipment to do a systems check. When Striker came in, he nodded at Andy, who walked out the door, closing it softly behind him.

"You look zonked," he said, sounding tired himself.

"Laura is dedicated to her job."

Striker smiled. "Good." He sat on my bed, leaned over,

and gave me a kiss. His eyes held mine. "You look better. I'm starting to recognize you again."

"I have to say, it was a good call not giving me a mirror on day one. If this is an improvement, I must have been horrific."

Striker didn't answer, but I could see emotions straining toward the surface. He dammed them back. The muscle in my thigh twitched at a steady pace. The top of my leg moved like a metronome.

"Are you doing that on purpose?" Striker asked.

"Could you do that on purpose?" I rubbed my palm up and down my leg.

"That's weird. Does it hurt?"

"It's distracting and irritating, but no, not painful."

"Does it happen all the time?"

"Different muscles at different times. The doctor said it will stop, eventually — maybe. Are you the only one here?"

"No. The team is in the west wing. We had a case come up that needs our attention. We have to pay the light bills while we try to figure you out."

"Absolutely. Do you have anything for me? Was Axel able to get more information?" I asked.

"He sent a tape of Hector's DA interview, but it's visual only. They didn't record audio. You still might get something from it since you're so good with body language, but I couldn't get anything. Axel said the timeline went like this: T-Bone was in prison for two weeks prior to Hector's arrest. His charges were assault with a deadly and resisting arrest. T-Bone had a cellmate, another Hellhound member, who was moved to solitary — consequences of a cafeteria fight over pudding."

"Ah yes, well, pudding often has that kind of deleterious

effect." I pursed my lips and shook my head in mock consternation.

"Chocolate pudding," Striker added.

"Chocolate pudding? Even worse. The staff should have known that would end badly."

Amusement brought out Striker's dimples. "Are you done?"

"Are there any more food fights in this story?"

"Nope. We're back to somber facts. Axel and Randy captured Hector on Tuesday afternoon. He was drunk when they arrested him, but not so drunk that he was incoherent. He was booked into the prison and put in a cell with T-Bone. Wednesday morning, Hector met with the DA and returned to his cell with T-Bone. My guess is that there was a time lag to do some rearranging of bunk assignments. Ninety minutes later, Hector moved to his own cell in the minimum-security wing where he would have more privileges and no gang members. An hour after that, T-Bone's neck was broken."

"Where?" I asked.

"The exercise yard. Wednesday afternoon, Axel interrogated Hector. Then Hector went to dinner, he had time in the community room, watching television, and went to the showers. A commotion called the guards' attention to one end of the showers. When they turned around, Hector was on the floor dead — no obvious reason for the death. They handcuffed him and took him to the hospital wing, where the doctors discovered a plug of soap shoved deep in his throat. A security tape showed Jesus Manchuro, a Hellhound member with a life sentence, standing over Hector. No one knows how a gangbanger with his record ended up housed in that wing of the prison — some kind of administrative glitch. I have the security tape for you, too."

"Good. Thanks," I said. *No, not good. Not good at all.*

"I have another tape. Command got an interesting visit today from our friend, Frith."

That *was* odd. "Why would Frith risk more contact now that I'm dead?"

Striker pushed a button on my bed to elevate my head and pulled the hospital table over my lap. "Exactly. Frith doesn't think you're dead." Striker reached down for his laptop, played with the keys, then turned the screen around for me to watch.

I recognized the image on the video as the conference room at Headquarters. This was the executive wing where the carpet was plush, the ceilings high and coffered, and the wood paneling richly polished. The receptionist, former Miss Arizona what's-her-name, in her uniform of tight black pencil skirt and her fifteen-hundred-dollar Christian Louboutin python-skin stilettoes, led a man to the Queen Anne table in the conference room. He was fifty-something, with a full head of gray hair and a well-fed physique.

"I'm guessing this is Frith?" I pointed at the screen.

"Yup."

"You do a background on him? Are you sure he's really Frith from the FBI?"

"You've never seen him before?" Striker raised a questioning brow.

"No. When I puzzled his case, I was under Spyder's wing, and Spyder allowed no contact between the clients and me. I only know him on paper."

"Command knew him already. I've met him before. He was our contact on three cases."

"Can you tell me what they were?" I asked, pausing the video.

"The first was a case we shared with the FBI and ATF. We were monitoring a separatist group, Patriots United, in West Virginia. The second one was the case that you puzzled over, the million-dollar drugs-for-gold bust, the one where you saved his ass. Spyder was Lead on that one. I guess he had good feelings toward us when he not only survived but received a promotion to boot. He's the one who hired Iniquus to help investigate the torture and murder of an FBI senior administrator's daughter."

"Frith hired you for the Travis Wilson case?"

"FBI was our first client on the case, then CIA. As each agency took their own hit, each one added their name to the contract. Frith was our contact at FBI."

"Wow. Small world. Now I have to thank him for his help protecting me from Omega and for his good judgment in bringing you guys onto the Wilson case. I don't think I would have survived Travis Wilson if the team hadn't found me, pulled me out of the hospital after Wilson's first attack, and put me in the safe house."

"You did a pretty good job of staying alive on your own. We weren't around when you shot him."

"Yeah. You know, sometimes I wish Wilson was in custody instead so I could ask him what was going on. I still have so many questions."

"What do you want to know?" Striker asked.

"Why did he send death threats as poems? Was that just to make us victims feel terrorized? Or was there more to it? What was his MO all about? I don't get the naked-unmo-lested-razor-sliced-vinegar scenario. It must have a backstory."

"I have a few questions of my own. Where did he get his training? His surveillance equipment? They were professional grade. And why bludgeon the others to death?"

"It would have made more sense to strangle us or slit our throats. I'm lucky that's not what he did, or I wouldn't be sitting here feeling puzzled by him. It's not easy to kill with a single blow."

"Unless you're trained how to do it," Striker said.

"There is that. And he was able to accomplish his murders six times out of seven." I tapped my pen on the tabletop in a distracted tattoo.

Striker leaned forward, planting his elbows on his thighs. "Seven's your lucky number, Chica. It must be hard not having the answers you need to get closure. But some good did come out of this. Iniquus found out that Spyder had you as his private puzzler hiding up his sleeve. We got to hire you on. That's a good thing. As far as thanking Frith goes, he did hire us in for the FBI connected murder, but he had no knowledge that Wilson was a serial killer until it hit the papers after the fact. The agencies weren't talking to each other about it. Frith wouldn't have heard your name. He only knows you from the drug bust."

I turned back to the screen and pressed play. Mr. Spencer walked into the conference room with a harried quickstep. He sat down across from Frith. "What have you got for us?"

Frith slid his coffee cup to the side. "I'm worried about Sobado."

"She's dead." Spencer's voice was flat.

"I don't think so, and more importantly, Omega doesn't think so."

"Why?" Spencer leaned in, his eyes lighting up. "Does Omega have information? If she's alive, we need to get to her quickly to protect her. Is she hurt?"

"I don't know. Omega's antennae are up. They know you're making inquiries at the prisons down in Nelson and Bellington — Maria and Julio Rodriguez. Since they're the ones who took Sobado before Omega could move, Omega thinks you're pumping them for more information, trying to find out where Sobado is shelved or could be hiding."

The muscles in Spencer's shoulders slacked as his energy level dropped. He looked resigned and maybe a little sad. "We have an ongoing interest in Maria and Julio. Maria kidnapped our operative and used her as a counter to exchange for her husband. We plan to make sure that neither one breathes a single breath of free air in this lifetime. Maria Rodriguez has been charged with murder one now that our operative is dead," Spencer added.

"You'd better be damned sure, Mr. Spencer. Omega has its nose to the ground. Until they test DNA, the team won't give up. Omega men are like Pitbulls. They have their teeth into this thing, and they won't let go until it's resolved."

Spencer stood up. "Why?"

Frith tilted his head toward Spencer. "They don't like to lose, not even by the death of the target, and they especially don't want to lose to Iniquus."

"I'd say it was Iniquus' loss." Spencer widened his stance; he leaned his weight into his knuckles on the table. He had a ferocity on his face that I had never seen there before. Aww, he did care about me.

"Maybe. Maybe not," Frith said.

Spencer went still. After a full minute, he said, "Excuse me while I make a phone call." And stalked out of the room.

Frith fidgeted around in his chair, pushing it back a little so he could cross his ankle over his knee. He drummed his fingers on the high gloss of the table, reached to pull his coffee cup back over, but pushed it back again when he heard the door open behind him.

Spencer strode into the room and back to his place at the head of the table. "I talked to the search and rescue leader. Lackland has pulled the recovery search. They don't believe the plane ever made it to US soil. They're sure it went down over the Gulf. The Coast Guard informed Mexico and Belize that we're looking for plane parts. Our search team returned to Headquarters, and their Lead reassigned them to other cases."

"So the embed is sniffing down the wrong trail. The person hospitalized at Lackland is not who they think it is?"

Spencer walked around the table to stand next to Frith, who stood up, so they were eye to eye. "I wish to god it was. Frith, Iniquus... I — I am very grateful that you tried to intervene on her behalf. She was truly an amazing woman. Surprising. Smart. Funny. We really lost something when we lost her. If you're ever in need of something, and it's in our power, please let me know personally. I'll see it gets done."

Frith shook Spencer's extended hand. "Thank you, Mr. Spencer. If she *is* dead, then I offer my condolences to you all. I wanted you to know, though, Omega is still on the hunt. There's a deep pocket behind this. No one on my side thinks she's dead."

Spencer's forehead creased. "You think I should put another team out there?"

Frith shrugged. "I don't know. I don't want her to be dead. I certainly don't want Omega to get to her. I got a peek at the file — it's an extraordinary rendition order and final tap. So if they get to her, they'll torture her for information until she expires."

"Any idea why?" Spencer asked.

"None. Getting anything at all has been tricky. There would be consequences if Omega found out I intervened. I'm only doing this because she saved my neck. I don't know that I can manage any further contact."

"Understood. That deep pocket you mentioned. Any idea who's wearing the pants? FBI?"

Frith shook his head slowly from side to side with pursed lips. "That I can't say. But no, I don't think it's the FBI. I'm not even sure it's a government contract. Maybe she's stepped on too many toes, and some ring wants her stopped before they lose any more ground. Maybe look over her caseloads and see whom she might have pissed off. Omega doesn't care who signs the contract, as long as the contract makes them fat and happy."

Spencer nodded solemnly.

Frith walked out of the office. As the heavy door closed behind him, Spencer turned and looked directly at the camera as if he were looking directly into my eyes, and mouthed, "Be safe."

I closed the computer and handed it back to Striker. "Huh."

"That's what Spencer thought."

"This gets curiouser and curiouser." I tapped my index finger to my lips.

"And that's what I thought."

"It felt a whole lot like a fishing expedition."

"I'm sure that's why Spencer played it the way he did. It pays to be cautious. How much energy do you have?"

"About a half a pound. Why?"

"I have that surprise for you, remember?" Striker stood and moved his computer to the table by my French doors. He pulled back my covers and scooped me up to a sitting position, then brought me my walker and pushed the call button on my bed. With Andy and Striker's help, I slid in a snail crawl up the hallway that I had paced earlier today. This time we rounded the corner into the main room.

It was huge — completely breathtaking. A cathedral ceiling soared two and a half stories above my head. The enormous glass panes that looked out over the bay formed the walls that surrounded me on three sides. The fourth side opened to a modern kitchen, separated from the main room by a breakfast bar, with a corridor on either side.

The furniture sat low and white. Though streamlined, it all still managed to look comfortable and inviting. The fabrics were various shades of Caribbean greens, blues, and deep purples. Striker used these same colors when he painted the massive, modern seascapes that hung on the walls in his barracks apartment back in D.C.

Andy and Striker shepherded me over to a straight-backed chair. I sat down and took it all in—the bowl of sea glass on the coffee table, the massive round column of the freestanding fireplace made of the same rocks that I had seen from my French doors. Beautiful. A lovely sense of Zen quietude permeated this house. This was a house built for serenity and healing. I completely understand why Striker wanted to bring me here to regain my strength.

"What a wonderful surprise, Striker." I smiled over to him.

He was watching me closely, gauging my reaction. He nodded with satisfaction. "Glad it's to your liking, Chica, but this isn't your surprise." Striker pushed a button on his cellphone. "She's ready."

A door opened at the end of the east wing that branched out in front of me. I heard the clickity-clack of nails on the wooden floor. A joyful cacophony of barks and whimpers went up as Beetle and Bella vaulted, in a riot of shiny black Doberman fur, into the room, dragging Gator behind them with a tight grip on both of their leads.

"Oh my god. My babies!"

Striker laughed and pulled the walker out of the way so my girls could get closer to me. It took all three men to keep Bella from climbing into my lap. I rubbed my hands over their glossy fur. Talk about medicine for the soul. This was it. This was bliss.

16

"Chica, you're having a weird dream. You need to wake up." I felt a hand on my hip.

I blinked at the early morning light coming in through my doors and turned toward his voice. "What time is it?"

"Zero five-thirty. What in the hell were you dreaming about?"

"I dreamed that you were on the other side of a lake of honey. I wanted to get to you, but it was too thick and gooey for me to swim through. The only way I could get to you was to wear Gator like a coat. I put him on, dove in, and I swam as hard as I could. I've been wearing Gator and swimming for a long time — I'm glad you woke me up."

Striker's mouth was set in a hard line. He didn't say anything. I thought that image would make him laugh. But his eyes glowed with a weird light. I would have called it jealousy, but that was beyond preposterous. Since he didn't see the humor in my sticky swim, I changed the subject. "You're in uniform."

"I have to go to the office today. You have Deep and Blaze on security. Also, Chris, Andy, and Cook are here."

"When I got here, I was surprised to see Chris and Andy were my medical support. How'd you swing that?" I asked.

"I put in a request that we get the medics who worked with you before. They're very circumspect. I've never heard a word about you, or your odd condition, around Iniquus."

"Odd condition?" I quirked a brow.

"Odd is a euphemism." Striker's hands rested casually on his hips. "When you've gone behind the Veil and sustained the injuries of the victim you're trying to help, and they find you covered with blood and slime, looking like something out of a horror movie, that's not normal. When the medics walk into a room and are given zero in the way of explanation, that's not normal. When you go to sleep for days on end, completely unaware of anything at all, and then you miraculously heal without so much as the tiniest scar, that's not normal, either. Yup. Odd is about the most benign word I could possibly use. If they wanted a good story to tell, yours would be it. In other words, I completely trust these men not only with your health but also your safety."

"Agreed."

Striker looked at his watch. "Laura will be here in a few hours. The rest of us are heading in. We won't be back until late — the commute takes a while."

"If you have anything that needs my attention, you could bring it back with you," I said.

"Nope. They've officially removed you from the payroll. Your only job right now is getting better. I do need to know where you want to go next with the investigation now that Hector got pulled off the stage."

"I guess I need to follow the chain up." I stretched and pushed the covers off me.

Striker reached out to run his hand up and down my bare leg. "Where's this chain lead?"

"To my shackles on one side." I thought maybe I should have shaved.

Striker put his arm under me and lifted me to my dangling/acclimating position. I waited for my head to stop doing cartwheels.

"Understood. And on the other?" he asked.

"Maria and Julio." I caught hold of his hand and kept my focus fixed on one spot on the bamboo floor while the room spun around me.

"Axel's on it. Since we don't have anyone on Maria or Julio's prison visitation lists, and there's no way they'd sign off on one of us, we need to go the official route. Axel tapped a friend with the ATF in Florida who's willing to help. The agent submitted forms for Maria and Julio's inter-rogations. We're waiting for the official nod to go ahead."

"That was nice of the agent. Is the ATF guy the one who will have to interrogate?" I asked as he went to retrieve my walker.

"The Agent's going to try to slip Axel in with him. If that doesn't work, then yes, he'll be the one who does the inter-view. We're going to push hard to get Axel in there. If it works out, he'll wear a wire-cam, but he won't be able to wear a communicator. You won't be in on this one. You need to think about how you want this to go and make sure you get a script together. If you're going to have any 'T-Bone is dead' moments, you need to have them now."

"I wish it worked that way."

Striker nodded. "Me, too." He had steadying hands on my hips; I liked his hands there. They felt...possessive.

"In the meantime, I've uploaded a file named 'Julio-Nelson.' In it are his records." Striker pointed to the computer on my breakfast table. "It includes everything the prison has on him — all of his reports, the video of his visits. There's a video of his interrogations, but no audio. The audio is classified."

"And Maria?"

"We're still working on that." Striker checked his watch. "I've got to go."

"Okay. Thank you."

Striker bent and gave me an absent-minded kiss that missed my lips by an inch. I grabbed his hand. "Hey, what was that? Is something wrong?"

Striker canted his head and gave me a half-smile. "Nothing's wrong — I'm distracted, that's all."

It felt like a lie. I tightened my grip on his hand, and he kissed me again. This time it was a real kiss — the toe-curling kind that made me want to pull him back into my bed with me. When he looked at me again, there was laughter in his eyes. "Better?"

"Unfair! You can't kiss a girl like that and leave!"

Striker gave a full-throated laugh as he walked out my door.

Chris came in to monitor me in the bathroom because who needed modesty? Especially doing the yoga of shaving one's legs.

When I was clean and dressed, Cook brought in my

breakfast. I was definitely over these peanut butter smoothies. I woofed everything down so I could get to work at the computer.

The first files I opened were of the interrogations with the federal attorney. With no audio, I scanned through these. In the picture was Julio in a chair as if he were a naughty boy sitting in the principal's office. He set his feet primly side-by-side. His hands rested on his knees. With eyes focused straight forward, he maintained a blank stare. Once in position, the time-lapse indicated he sat there immobile for hours. His butt must have been numb. I have never seen anyone sit that still for that long. Both my Kitchen Grandmother, Biji, and Master Wang taught me to meditate, but I don't think even they could sit that still that long. Ten. Ten times the federal attorney came in and met with him, laid papers in front of him. Talked at him. Yelled at him. Nada. He was dedicated to his strategy; I'll give him that.

The next file I opened was a commissary list of Julio's purchases: shower shoes, socks, Tabasco sauce, Charmin toilet paper. Nothing interesting there.

There was a file that contained his visitor applications and approvals. He was incarcerated in September. Maria was the only one on his list until March. That's when my team got the ransom note. After that, there was a new name: Brody Covington. I didn't know that name. It wasn't part of the Sylanos file. Interesting.

Maria had visited Julio every Sunday. That's a hell of a practice, considering that she had to get from D.C. to Florida once a week from September until February when I was kidnapped. February, she moved to Nelson, Florida. She never missed a Sunday. After she demanded Julio's release as a prisoner exchange for me and knew that Iniquus would be monitoring the jail, Brody Covington took up the practice. It was every Sunday — never any other day. That was striking.

I didn't get any further than that. Laura stuck her head in my room. "I'm here!"

Laura walked me down the hall, through the great room, to a door on the first corridor beside the kitchen. Behind the door was a gym. Mirrors lined one wall where there were free-weights. There were machines in the center. On the left, there was a matted area with boxing equipment and a heavy bag. We headed to the back, where Striker had an endless pool.

"I thought we'd put you in the water this morning to give you a little resistance."

"Is that allowed? Chris and Andy won't let me take a shower. They don't want my incision wet yet."

Laura smiled and opened her shoulder bag. She pulled out a roll of Glad Press and Seal Wrap.

"You're kidding me," I said.

"Nope, works like a charm. Can you hold your arms out to your sides?"

Laura pulled off a piece of plastic and lifted my shirt. She stopped. She was looking at my side where Wilson's knife went in under my arm and had slid down to my hip, the second time he attacked me. It took a hundred and fifty-two stitches to sew me back together. The scar had faded to a white line with little dots on either side. When it happened, the Iniquus men called this my "bragging rights," a source of pride that I had faced the enemy and survived.

Pride is not what I saw on Laura's face; what I saw there was pity.

Pity commanded me to cover up and feel weak.

I fought against those feelings.

Laura's gaze moved to my torso where a spider web of white lines crisscrossed my skin from the first attack when Wilson chloroformed me and followed his serial killer MO by slicing me with a razor and reviving me from my stupor by pouring vinegar in the open wounds. Cooking my flesh like ceviche. Leaving little for the plastic surgeon to glue back together.

Laura wove her eyebrows together and cocked her head to one side as she tried to figure out how someone could get these kinds of wounds. She looked up with a question mark. I stood there, stoically. I had nothing to say on the subject. Laura went back to work, covering the stitches under my re-emerging breasts and getting me into the water. It was a quiet workout; I wasn't in the mood for light banter. My mind was back on the Julio files.

Finally, five o'clock came, and Laura left.

I needed to nap before dinner.

Laura had squeezed every ounce of energy from every cell in my body. I wasn't sure I could lift my fork or chew, not that I wanted to. It felt as if someone took a hot knitting needle and stuck it in my right eye. Every noise felt like a physical blow to my head. When I retreated to my bed, Chris shut the screen over my French door, leaving my room bliss-fully void of light and sound. An IV drip was set up to give me respite from the nausea and the pain of my migraine. I closed my eyes and let the meds pull me under.

At seven, Chris got me up for a plate of roasted vegeta-bles, aromatic rice, and Masala Dal — foods from my

Kitchen Grandmother Biji. Today must be Tuesday. I really needed to get a calendar put up so I could get a better rhythm for passing time.

Next to my plate, there was the ubiquitous peanut butter smoothie. Sigh.

After dinner, I went back to the Julio-Nelson files. The videos of Julio's visits with Maria and Brody were bizarre. They were short. No one said anything; mouths never opened. Expressions never changed from blank. Julio sat at a visitor's window.

Maria sat down in front of him.

Julio would place a piece of torn notebook paper in front of him with a number written in pencil. Time passed. She'd get up and leave. Later, Brody took up this same ritual. The only thing that changed was the number on the piece of torn notebook paper.

I went through each of the visits and wrote down the numbers. It was a painstaking process. The camera angle was good, but the faintly penciled numbers were small and difficult to discern. Chris came in and gave me a handful of pills at one point. I was vaguely aware that I swallowed them.

———

I felt Striker come into my room. He squatted beside me, where I had my head pillowed on my arms, and reached out to turn off the computer.

"Chica, this is bad for your back. You can't do this. You need to go to bed."

"Chris doped me."

"So, he said. You wouldn't follow his instructions."

"I have to puzzle the numbers."

He chuckled softly. "Tomorrow, you can puzzle the numbers."

"Tomorrow…"

Striker gently leaned my head onto his shoulder, scooped me into his arms, and carried me to my bed.

Chris was there to pull down the covers, check my vitals, then he left.

Striker gently smoothed my hair out of my face.

"I'm dreaming about pine cones and pineapples," I mumbled.

"That's very weird," Striker said.

"You have to tell me tomorrow. *Very* important. Promise."

"Go to sleep." He didn't need to tell me twice.

17

Wednesday passed much like Tuesday — luckily for me, Wednesday is Laura's short day. I desperately wanted to work on those numbers. They must mean something. Right now, they meant nothing.

I ate dinner: meatloaf, mashed potatoes, green peas, and apple pie (with a peanut butter smoothie) in the great room with the team. They were excited about a bust they made in the wee hours of the morning. Gator was jealous that he wasn't in on the gunfight. He had pulled the short straw to babysit me and hold down the fort. I have to admit I was a little jealous too.

Not of the gunfight. I didn't do daring deeds of do or die, not when I could help it at any rate.

I did miss the tension and release of a good case.

I missed my office.

I missed driving home.

I missed home.

I missed my neighbors…

"Hey, Lynx, why the long face?" Striker asked, reaching out to rub my wrist, concern darkening his eyes.

"I was having a pity party about the things I'm missing from my old life."

"I bet I have something that will help. I'll show you after dinner."

I gave Striker a weak smile and sipped my smoothie.

As soon as I could, I slipped back to my room. The guys were in such a great mood, and I was in such a not-great mood; I didn't want to deflate their balloon.

I spent the evening watching tapes of Julio in his cell. Julio read, paced, and went to the bathroom. Day after day. Week after week. I was glad for Julio that he had reading material. It would have helped me enormously during my imprisonment to have an escape through the words on a page. Living in solitary was beyond hard. My experience down in Honduras made me wonder even more about Julio's visits.

If someone had come reliably every Sunday of my captivity, I would have used that day as motivation to get through my week. I would have had a million questions and begged for news and new thoughts. Anything, absolutely anything, to help me walk back into that cell and not die a little more each time the door clanged shut.

The very last thing I would do is sit there stoically with a number in front of me during a visit.

Not a single word.

I wouldn't have fully understood how bizarre and ludicrous these non-exchanges were had I not lived through the last six months in solitary myself.

There it was again, on the tape where the prison officials monitored Julio's activity in his cell. Sunday morning held the only deviation from the rest of the week. Instead of reading and pacing, Julio took out a marbled notebook, the kind sewn together instead of spiral binding. He pulled out the front page and wrote, moving his hand from left to right, and the second line from left to right, and then he wrote, moving his hand right to left.

I moved the video back and watched it again and again. There was more to this. First, Julio tore out the top sheet from the notebook. He took his pencil and shaded on the top of his page. Then he wrote from left to right, then left to right again. There was a slight downtick before he wrote each character from right to left. He reopened the notebook, placed the sheet he was working on over the top of the page, and hunkered over this while he wrote. He must be leaving an imprint for next week. A reminder. He closed the note-book and pushed it back out of the way. The rest of the page was confettied and flushed down the toilet. This left Julio with a seemingly blank notebook and a code in his pocket.

We ended up with a number. A number that increased from line to line and week to week. This must have been a calculation. A numeric code? That didn't feel right. This felt more like a key. A key to a lock that changed from week to week. Ugh! My brain. I needed a whiteboard. I needed to pace. I couldn't think like this.

Actually, what I needed were meds and a nap. My brain thrummed. Bright arcade lights of flashing color blurred my vision. I popped a couple of pills. Chris produced an ice pack that I draped over my neck. I momentarily rested my head on the desk. Even though my mind whirled with the light show, I was a bloodhound on the hunt. I wasn't willing to let up.

The papers that Julio displayed for his visitors were numbers. I needed to figure out the equation he was using to produce those numbers so we could get the next codes. If I could produce the next code, we might be able to trick Brody. Take him aside, show him our code. Tell him we know everything, let him go in and see Julio to get the same code from him. This would verify that we knew what was going on. We would hold Brody for questioning — he'd tell us everything. My brain stumbled forward. Yes. He'd tell us everything that could use to leverage Maria and Julio. We'd crack the case. The bad guys would get punished. Omega would go away. I would get to go home. Easy peasy.

I took out my sheet of numbers and stared at it. I willed my mind to cooperate and make sense of what I was seeing. I looked up as Striker came into my room.

"Are you pouting?" he asked.

"Mulling."

"Migraine?"

I propped my head into my hand. "Yes. Whisper, please."

He put the box he was carrying down by the door and strode over on his long legs. Striker stood six-foot-three. His build was like the SEALs he commanded— very distracting.

He pulled a chair over to sit beside me. "What are you mulling?"

"Look at this and tell me what you see." I handed him a page with the numbers from Julio and Maria's first five visits:

1-297-121-5073

1-480-752-6976
1-777-874-2049
1-258-626-9025
1-203-650-1107
1-329-512-8009

"Where did you get these?" Striker asked.

"Each time someone goes and visits poor mute Julio, he puts a piece of paper out on the table in front of him with a number on it. Each visit is a new number. They never replicate."

He ran a finger down the sheet. "Phone numbers?"

"That's what I thought, but none of the three-digit sets following the number one are actual area codes except for the 480 number — that's Phoenix and the 203 number — that's Bridgeport, Connecticut."

"He wrote them that way to look like phone numbers to cover up what they really represent?"

"Here's my thought process. Phone numbers are handy, aren't they? They're convenient for several reasons. The first one is yes — they look conventional." I pointed at the list. "Heck, some of these may actually be working phone numbers. Let's say an operative like me takes the trouble to write out each of these numbers, culls through to find out which are working phone numbers, and which are not, and then sends an agent out to check on things."

"That would suck a whole lot of resources," Striker said.

"Exactly." My ice pack had thawed. I set it aside on the table. My meds had done their job. My head had settled down to the beat of a single kettledrum.

"If they're not phone numbers, what are they?" he asked.

"Key codes. It's interesting that they are in numeric form. Most people can remember words better than numbers. As far as numbers go, there were some psychological studies done in the 1950s that came to the conclusion that human beings can hold seven digits, give or take two, in their short-term memory. Other studies indicate that human number memory is more consistent with four or fewer digits. If we take the two studies together, we find the advent of modern phone numbers. The seven-digit numbers have a division to reduce the segments to bite-sized morsels, and we get a memorable phone number sequence."

"What about the area code?" Striker asked. "That expands the sequence to ten."

"You can look at it as a sequence of ten or a sequence of three numbers- three numbers- four numbers." I shook my head. "Doesn't matter. My task here is to try to figure out how he's developing this week's code."

"They're not randomly constructed or numbers he's memorized?"

"Nope. They're calculated." I rubbed my fingers over my scalp and fluffed at my hair. "I've been at this for two days, and I haven't got a clue. Deep put them into a cryptography program, but the computer hasn't generated anything, either. I guess I can't feel too much like a failure."

"Julio could be using a cipher gadget. This might be indicators from a piece of literature or something."

"Sunday mornings, he does a calculation. Here, I'll show you." I pushed the play button on the computer, and Striker watched.

"He indents the last set of numbers into the top of his notebook and shades the reveal on the next week. Clever boy. What's the plan from here?" asked Striker.

"I think I'm going to take some more pain meds for my head and then take the problem into my dreams. Maybe my subconscious can work this out." I reached for the bottle, tipped two blue pills onto my palm, and swallowed them down.

"You tried that last night, and it wasn't very helpful." Striker handed me my glass of water.

"How do you mean?"

"Last night, when I came in, you were asleep over your notes. I had to carry you to bed. You told me you were dreaming about pineapples and pine cones, and I should tell you in the morning."

I sat perfectly still.

The color drained from my face.

My voice dropped to barely audible. "You didn't tell me that this morning, Striker."

"No. I didn't think anything of it. You're always having crazy dreams and telling me stuff when you're half asleep."

I turned from him and pulled up a Google search. I ran my finger down the list of numbers that came up on my screen. I shouted out a victory whoop and slapped my hands over my forehead. I clunked my head down on Striker's shoulder.

No yelling. Lesson learned.

When I lifted my head, Striker was quietly waiting for an explanation.

"These are Fibonacci numbers, Striker."

"The number continuum where you use the sum of two numbers to create the next number in the order 1+1=2, 1+2=3, 2+3=5, and so forth?"

"Never-ending." Excitement painted my voice.

"Never-ending," Striker said.

I turned my computer for him to see. "Look, Julio started at number 47 on that continuum. The sum at this point is 2,971,215,073. If you divide that number with dashes instead of commas, where one would normally make a division for a phone number, and then add the necessary 1 in the front to depict a long-distance call, use the first 10 digits you have, then you can see the progression for the next three codes."

"And the fourth code doesn't continue the pattern?"

"It does, but he didn't add a one in the front because this number begins with a one. And look." I scrolled back in the films to find the 4th Sunday. "That time, he underlined the one. I'd bet he did it so Maria would know that one was part of the code."

"This works all the way through?" Striker shifted his gaze back and forth between the list on the computer screen and the list in his hand.

"Looks like it." I felt like a parade — a combination of jubilation and drumming head.

Striker put the paper down. "Couple of questions. One, pineapples and pine cones?"

"Fibonacci developed his number sequence based on his observations of nature. When I was a little girl, my mom and I used to observe the Fibonacci effect in pine cones and pineapples."

"Okay, second question, how would your subconscious have figured this out in your sleep?"

"Because Julio started with number 47. If he started much later in the sequence, I would probably never have guessed."

Striker slipped down in his chair until his head rested on the back. "More information."

"When Spyder mentored me, one of the computer

training programs he had me work through taught me to see number series quickly and hold them in my memory. One of my tasks was to memorize the first fifty Fibonacci numbers."

"That's a hell of a task."

"The first thirty-five weren't as hard as the last fifteen."

"Because…"

"Number thirty-six was an eight-digit number."

Striker shook his head at me, wrapped his arm around my neck, planting a kiss on top of my head the way he used to do at the safe house. "Still my little surprise party. I never know what's going to pop out of your head or your mouth next."

"Now that I can set aside this particular puzzle, tell me what's in the box." I pointed toward the door.

"Are you up to this? Do you need to lie down?"

"I think that second round of pills did the trick."

Striker brought the box to my table. It needed two hands to carry. He opened the flaps and shut them again, laying his hand over the top.

"I'm not sure about this, timing-wise. I'm going to depend on you to know your limits here, okay?"

Curiosity wrinkled my brow. "Okay," I agreed.

Striker opened the box again. "This is from the time you were in prison. They're your letters and gifts your friends sent to you. A lot of them are from your twenty-first birthday; those came in from all over the world. Much of this is from closer to home…your neighbors."

Oh.

Tears stung the inner rim of my eyelids and held there, blurring my vision. Now, I understand Striker's hesitation. This was going to claw at my heart, and he wasn't sure I was strong enough to handle it. I wasn't sure, either. Missing everyone was a knife in my heart. I peeped in. There were letters on top that someone had slit open with a blade at the fold. I spread the envelope open and glanced at Striker.

"We looked at all your mail. We were hoping for clues, Lexi, not prying. I promise you."

"I know." I rifled through the top layer.

"We contacted each person and told them what was going on, in case they heard from you or had any information."

I reached in to take out a mauve piece of paper folded in half. I opened it, and there was a baby's handprint in black ink surrounded by a hand-drawn heart. It simply said, "Ruby." I couldn't catch my breath. The last time I saw baby Ruby, Maria's hunting knife poised over her heart. Then they thrust the bag over my head.

Striker lifted the drawing from my hand and put it back into the box. He lowered me to my chair and knelt beside me.

We were there together for a long time, with my forehead resting against Striker's.

Sometimes the enormity of my emotions engulfed me. I felt like that tiny sailboat floundering in the Gulf waves as I flew overhead on my escape — both of us desperately struggling toward safety before the full brunt of the storm hit. Tossed by reality, trying valiantly to stay afloat. That was where I was at this moment.

Striker stood up and pulled me to my feet. He undressed me, tugged his T-shirt from over his head, and put it on me. It hung almost to my knees. He put me into bed and climbed in behind me. There, spooned against his warmth and stability, with a blanket of melancholy covering us both, we fell asleep together.

18

I LOOKED UP. "YOU'RE IN UNIFORM AGAIN."

"I'm back on grid today." He glanced at his phone. "I only have a couple of minutes. Laura's going to be here, and I don't want her to see anyone other than Andy, Chris, and Cook.

"Does Cook have a name?"

"As far as I know, it's Cook or Cookie. I've never heard him called anything else. It's hard to communicate with him. Cookie's English is limited."

"What does he speak?" I asked.

"Polish. I'm surprised you didn't hear him cussing this morning. He's having a little trouble figuring out how to make your nutritional parameters work with Puerto Rican cuisine."

"Why?"

"Too spicy, from what I can gather. That's why we're having flan and fruit for breakfast," he said with a smile.

"I'm not complaining. Abuela Rosa gave me flan all the time when I wasn't feeling well."

"Listen, I'm not going to be around for the next few days. I need to head over to Somalia."

"More information, please." I let the cool sweetness of the flan slide down my throat.

"It's a private contract. A CEO and his family were captured on their yacht when they were coming around the cape in the Gulf of Aden and are being ransomed," he said.

"And you are…"

"Delivering the ransom, safeguarding the family, taking out the pirates."

"Oh, just a walk in the park then," I said, hiding my anxiety for his safety behind my napkin as I wiped my mouth.

Striker laughed.

"Good thing you're a super-hero." I reached for his hand and held it tightly. It was his job, but it still made my heart leap around in my chest. I tried to smile past my feelings so he wouldn't think I doubted his success.

"Yeah, good thing," he said with a wink.

I needed to change the subject. I felt a big, sloppy sob gathering strength. "I never hear a car leave when you guys are heading out. Are you teleporting?"

"Next best thing. Most of the time, we take the sub." He grinned at me, full dimples.

My eyelids stretched wide, and my brows were at my hairline. "You're kidding, right?"

"Not at all. See the boathouse?" Striker turned me and pointed out the window to the far right where a long, low boathouse hovered over the water. "It houses my Cigarette boat, a cabin cruiser for day sails, and a six-man submarine for getting to the office."

I shook my head, confused. "There's no dock at Iniquus. Is there?"

"No dock. There's a tunnel from the Potomac up to one of the McMansions on the edge of the Iniquus campus. We have a small fleet of subs under there."

"The bad guys can't find their way to the tunnel?"

"We protect the mouth by an electrified gate. Only a few people know about our subs."

"Why do we have them?"

"Fun." He gave me a boyish grin. Good god, but he was cute. "I don't think they've been deployed on a case yet," he said. "Iniquus took down some high-volume drug runners. Command kept their run-boats and submarines. They gave me a sub since I live on the Bay. Each of the Company Leads got one of the cigarette boats as their Christmas bonus that year."

"That's a hell of a bonus." I leaned back into him, and Striker wrapped his arms around me.

Striker snorted. "Shit, yeah."

I turned around now, so we were hugging, and I could rest my ear against his heart. "Can I see it?"

"The sub? Not today." He brushed his hand through the length of my hair. "My communicator just buzzed. Laura must be driving up the driveway. I'll take you for a ride when I get back."

There it was again, that wave of fear for his safety. Striker must have felt it in my tightening grip because he bent down to kiss me and whispered, "I promise," and kissed me again. Boy, he was good at that kissing thing. Any bad feelings melted away. The waves I was feeling now had absolutely zero to do with safety.

Laura came. Laura tortured. Laura left. I wandered over to the west wing. No one was in the puzzle room. I moved down the hall to the command center, where I found Deep sitting in front of a bank of computers.

"Hey, Deep. Are we alone in the house?"

"Cookie, Andy, and Chris are here. I think they're downstairs playing pool. Do you need anything?"

"Nope. I'm letting my thoughts marinate." I picked up a file on his desk and leafed through it. "Striker says that he commutes to the office by submarine. He took the rest of the team with him?"

"Things are busy at the office. The guys are running on all four burners."

"I wish they'd give me something to puzzle. I'd like to be working," I pouted as I dropped the file back on his desk.

"I think everyone would prefer you put your energy into healing and figuring out what's going on with your case. Iniquus doesn't like Omega's saber-rattling."

"I'm sure it pisses them off." I crossed my arms over my chest and leaned a hip into my walker. "We must be pretty safe here if they didn't leave you back up. The rest of us are useless when it comes to a fight."

"This won't happen often. We just couldn't find a way around it today. Chris and Andy might surprise you. Cookie would probably be good in a knife fight. It won't come to that, though. This place is Fort Knox. Has anyone explained Striker's compound?"

"Nope."

"Let me get Andy to watch the computer bank, and I'll show you around. I think you'll like this."

When Andy settled in, Deep and I headed back to my bedroom.

"What do you think of your room, Lynx?"

"It's beautiful. The style is different from the rest of the house. Was this Lynda's room?"

"Striker never brought his sister here. It used to have white walls and modern furniture like the rest of the house. When we were deciding where to hide you, Striker had this fixed up for you."

I ran my hand over the shelf and picked up one of the shells. I looked around with a different eye; Striker designed this with me in mind.

"It's wonderful."

"In more ways than one." Deep's chest swelled with satisfaction — maybe a little smug in there, too. "You know how you say that you like looking like a piece of fluff? That people underestimate you, discount you, and let you go places where you otherwise could never go? This room is exactly the same. It's a panic room. You are surrounded by steel with Kevlar panels on the four walls and the ceiling. Beneath our feet is a cement reinforced foundation. You have your own power battery that will run this room for seven days, your own air and water supplies — enough to support ten people for a week. Over here, you have your emergency closet." Deep sauntered toward the wall on the right-hand side of the bathroom and pulled a latch under the chair molding. It opened up to show a deep closet with emergency medical equipment, including oxygen tanks, gas masks, and iodine tablets. There was communication equipment, flak jackets, helmets, and enough firepower to take out a small village.

"Over here, you have your food." Deep opened a similar

closet on the left of my bathroom. There was a shelf of books, DVDs, and games. There was an array of foodstuffs, mostly MREs, stored above a counter outfitted with a range top and a microwave. Plates and cookware were stored below.

"Wow." My voice conveyed my surprise. Fort Knox? Deep wasn't kidding.

"That's not all. Your French doors are made of one-way bullet-resistant glass. You can shoot out, but no one can shoot in. It won't hold back everything. It would give you enough time to press the panic button if it came to that. And it would only come to that if there was a mole." He pointed to a gray pad near the head of my bed.

"What happens when I press the panic button?"

Deep grinned. "I'll show you." He depressed the communicator on his belt. "Andy, put us on test mode."

"Roger. Test mode activated." Andy's voice came out of the box attached to Deep's belt.

"Go push your button," Deep said.

I moved to my bed and touched the pad. There was a grinding sound, the floors rumbled, and steel doors slid out of pockets on either side of the French doors and across the door that accessed the hall.

"You're completely sealed in. We're safe from everything from biological warfare to atomic blast. When we aren't on test mode, pushing that button sends a satellite distress signal directly to Iniquus." Deep crossed his arms over his chest and rocked back on his heels with obvious satisfaction.

"What if there's a breach and someone puts the room on secure mode, we're besieged, and the enemy waits for us to run out of supplies?"

"You have an independent, back-up satellite communication system in the supply closet."

"How cool is that?" I examined the door, then turned back to Deep. "You said someone could only shoot at the door if there was a mole. I can see ten different ways to get to the house."

"Not undetected, you couldn't. An electronic dome protects the entire property. The cameras that feed into the command room light up by motion." Deep depressed his communicator. "All clear, Andy. You can open us back up and put us back online."

"Roger Wilco." Andy's voice crackled from Deep's belt.

The steel doors slid back into their hiding places.

"Electromagnetic locks?" I asked.

"Yup. Follow me."

We went out the sliding doors in the great room and stood on the patio. Deep gestured at the water. "We're on a peninsula—ten feet above the water, safe from any storm surge. The house is steel beams, storm glass, and concrete. No fear from hurricanes, tornadoes, fires, or earthquakes. You name it, this house can withstand it. The panic room is the icing on the cake," Deep said.

"I'll say."

"So what I wanted you to see out here is that the architect designed this house to be nature friendly. The lines of the structure are supposed to blend in with the environment. After it was built, Iniquus safety engineers came in and painted it 45% forest green, 45% light green, with black and light brown detailing."

I looked at the house. "It's painted camouflage?" It didn't look like camouflage.

"In a discreet way. No one looking at it close up would

say that's what Striker did. Laura, for example, would think it was a green-colored house with brown and black trim. From a distance, from above, from the water, the eye can easily miss it. The windows are one-way, non-reflective glass — we can see out, no one can see in."

"This gets better and better." My eyes scanned over the house, looking for weaknesses, thinking about what I would do if I wanted to breach the security. I wasn't coming up with much. I shielded my eyes against the glare. "What about water entry? Could a boat come up or a scuba team?"

"Nope. See those buoys?"

The sun glittered off the water; I had to squint to see. "Yep."

"Our safety dome and visual field go out that far. Those buoys have feelers extending down to the sand beds. If anything over 20 pounds were to pass by the buoys, either on the water or immersed, an alarm sounds in the command room."

"Why 20 pounds?"

"Pelicans."

"Ah. Say an alarm sounds by the buoy, then what?"

"We check it out on the camera feed, and we send someone down to the beach to have eyes on. Sometimes teens show up, thinking they found a good place to party, and they need dissuading. The rocks around the compound are difficult to scale by design. There are stairs down to the beach and a walkway from there to the boathouse. Once the alarm sounds, a steel gate cuts off access to those stairs and secures the boathouse. Up here, if we don't want to hunker down, there are trucks to take down the driveway or four-wheelers to take through the woods."

"Why the hell did Striker make this place? It sounds like

an evil mastermind recluse would live in a place like this." My brows were furrowed. This just seemed…over the top.

"Or someone with a lot of enemies," Deep said.

"Is that it?" I turned to look Deep in the eye.

"No. At first, Striker bought the land to build a private retreat — somewhere to do his paintings and to boat. Then he realized that Lynda mixed in with some dangerous people. He thought that at some point, he'd have to hide her and Cammy out here. He wanted it to be as safe as possible. Then I think it took on a life of its own. This is his hobby. He gets to try out all these cool systems. He does have an engineering degree. He loves gadgets."

"Striker toys?" That thought amused me.

"It's a great big adult Legos set for him."

"What a geek." I shielded my eyes from the sun. "You said Lynda's never been here. If he built it for her…"

"He built it with her safety in mind. If Lynda and Cammy hung out here, Lynda would tell people about it, and the bad guys would know where to look. She has no idea this exists."

"Understood. So who comes here?"

"The team's been here on retreats, and you."

"No one else?" I asked with my innocent voice.

Deep cocked his head to the side. "Are you fishing about his past?"

"Kind of. Yes. Did he bring other women here?" I focused on the seagulls circling above so Deep couldn't see my eyes.

Deep considered me for a minute, then said, "Striker was circumspect with women. He dated a lot, but he kept his dates out of his personal space. He went to the women. He didn't let the women come to him. As far as I know, you're the first woman to come here. Even the interior designer was a guy — a very effeminate guy, but he still had male packaging."

"Thanks for the 'he dated a lot,' that makes all of my jealous feelings melt away." Sarcasm painted my words an ugly color. I had seen one of his exes in Miami. Gorgeous. I, on the other hand, looked like this.

Deep shook his head, with his hands planted solidly on his hips. "I've been with you two since the safe house. Believe me, Lynx, you have nothing to be jealous about. Striker, on the other hand…" Deep stopped. There was a long pause.

I looked him hard in the eye. "What?"

Deep balanced his weight from one foot to the other. "I don't want to stand here gossiping."

"Spit it out, Deep." I used Striker's commander voice, hoping to pry the lid off Deep's resistance.

"Nope. That's as far as I'm going to go. We live way too far down each other's throats for me to start something."

I clucked like a chicken and flapped my arms like wings, using my body language to call him a coward.

Deep looked at me with exasperation in his eyes. "You know what, Lynx? You're some kind of crazy smart. Your background makes you take all that smart and live sort of extemporaneously — most of us have a script that we follow — more or less. Having you as a teammate gives us the edge, and I think you're great. But you'd be hell-on-wheels to date."

I was taken aback. Hurt even. "You wouldn't date me?"

"Not for a million dollars. I'm not a glutton for punishment."

"Wow, Deep. You think I'm punishing Striker?" My

voice squeaked out.

"I think this whole conversation is making me uncomfortable."

Now I was pissed. "You kicked the door open, have the courage to walk through."

"Okay, here it is: I think you're unique. And what others would normally see and feel may not be your reality at all."

My hands clenched around my walker. "I don't know what to do with that. I need more information."

"This is Striker's problem, and you don't need any more information. I've said enough." He was heated and yelling at me, his Italian heritage on full display.

"Deep," I hollered back.

"Seriously. *Basta*. Enough!"

I stormed back to my room. Well, I stormed in the slide clunk, slide clunk, slide clunk kind of way that my walker would allow.

Too bad that Laura wasn't here now. I had some spit and vinegar to bolster my workout.

Cookie saw me moving past the kitchen with a thundercloud brewing around my head and went to hide in the pantry. Good thing. I didn't want to torment poor Cookie with my extemporaneously punitive self!

I moved on down the hall to my room, lay on the floor with Beetle and Bella, and waited for calm to return. It took a while. Hmph. I must believe that Deep was telling the truth if it felt this bad. I didn't mean to punish Striker. This was unfair. What if circumstances were reversed? What if something happened in Somalia and I needed to go find him? What if he were hurt? Would I act any differently than Striker was acting toward me? Would I be less loyal? Less concerned?

That wasn't what Deep was talking about. It wasn't mission-related; it was relationship related. Deep thought I was hurting Striker because I wasn't seeing what a normal person would see. *He thinks I'm abnormal.* Well, doesn't that make me feel like a Martian? I *was* normal — in an unschooled, out of the box kind of way. It was true that I was socialized differently than most kids, but I never felt awkward about how I related to people. Up until now. Now I felt...guilty, lonely, and worried sick for Striker.

Okay, this misery was mostly about that. Love makes us vulnerable. So says Spyder. So says Master Wang. When my husband, Angel, was in Afghanistan, I thought I learned that lesson first hand. Then it hit me like a locomotive when an IED exploded his convoy.

After his death, I had decisions to make. Could I allow myself to be that vulnerable again? Could I be that vulnerable with Striker? When I was in prison, I thought yes. When I hunkered down on the Isle de la Juventude trying to outlast the storm, I thought yes. When I crashed into the desert, living to tell Striker that I loved him sustained me. Pushed me. Compelled me.

I wrote to him — he said he found my goodbye letters on the plane, so he has read how much I loved him. But I haven't said it to him. Not once. Not ever. And now he was in Somalia. Somalia of all places. *Goddammit.* If Striker needed me, I couldn't help him. Being powerless made me feel...exposed — ANGRY. Being unable to function made me angry.

There was a knock on my door. It slowly pushed open, and Deep stuck his head in. He saw me lying on the floor, flanked by Beetle and Bella.

"You okay?" he asked tentatively.

"I'm having a hissy fit, followed by a pity party."

"I can see that. Am I invited?" he asked.

"You can come in, but the party's over."

Deep walked into my room and sat cross-legged nearby. His back rested against my bed. Deep was a pretty brave guy.

"I shouldn't have opened my big mouth. I'm Italian." His hangdog expression made me smile.

"Are you really making your heritage the scapegoat here?" I asked.

"It usually works."

I chuckled. "You're okay, Deep."

"Nonetheless, I apologize. Striker loves you. You love Striker. Someday you'll get married and have beautiful *bambini* who will patrol the school playground at recess and kick all the bullies' asses."

"I was homeschooled, Deep. My kids won't go to school."

"Cool. Then we can deploy them like little mini spies. And I get to be their godfather."

I sighed. "Striker and I don't have that kind of relationship. Striker's not the settling down kind. You're right, though. I love him. And I'm worried about him. Who's on his team?"

"Striker took Jack and Gator with him."

"That's good. Those three together will have the pirates walking the plank in no time flat. How'd you and Blaze get to stay stateside in Hotel California?"

"Blaze is working a case that needs his attention, and I'm assigned to you for computer and technical support while you puzzle out your house of cards. If we need backing, we can get Randy in after today."

"And Axel?"

"He's up at Headquarters. He has to fly down to Florida Saturday to meet with the ATF guy. Sunday, he's going over to Nelson to get eyes on Brody — see if he can't follow that trail. Brody might lead us somewhere interesting." Deep looked across the room. "I see that Striker brought you the box. Have you gone through it?"

"I'm working up to it. It's painful. Makes me miss home."

Deep gave me a funny kind of look. I couldn't interpret what it meant — hurt, maybe?

"Don't get me wrong," I said. "It's wonderful to be here. Wonderful to see you all. Everything is a thousand percent better."

"But you're still a prisoner of circumstances," Deep concluded.

I shrugged. "I'm looking forward to being able to go home. I feel cowardly hiding here while my loved ones think I'm dead. While Sarah and Bob think I died to save their children." I reached out my hands, and Deep gently pulled me to sitting.

"So you haven't looked through?" he asked.

"I stopped at Ruby's handprint."

Deep nodded. "When you feel up to it, you'll find a birthday gift from Biji in the bottom."

"Biji? She went back to Punjab to live with her sister. Is she still there?"

"Yes. She said in her letter — you do know we read everything, don't you?"

"Yup. It's fine."

"She said that she contacted everyone from your apartment and your friends — Master Wang, the librarian, people who knew your parents, and she asked them for pictures that have you or your parents in them. She put them in an album in chronological order. It ends with the newspaper article from the night of the fire. It was a hell of an inferno."

"It was. One minute there was an apartment building. The next minute, there was an ash pile. Everyone lost everything. I was lucky. I was able to get two boxes out with me — my laptop and my folks' journals."

"In the album, I got to see pictures of baby Lynx. Why in the hell were you always wearing Playtex gloves as a kid? Did you have a skin condition? Were you OCD?"

That got me to laugh. "I was playing Nancy Drew, and I didn't want to damage any of the evidence by getting my fingerprints on stuff."

"What a weirdo. You would've been beaten to a pulp in my neighborhood, walking around looking like that."

Before I could zing him with a good comeback, his cellphone buzzed. He listened for a minute. "Do you have an ETA? — Roger that. See you, man."

Deep put his phone back on his hip. "Randy's coming in. He just got into Reagan. He has to get through customs, then he'll head over to Iniquus. Striker left the sub there."

"That sounds like something from a James Bond movie. My life is so strange." There was a knock at the door. I lifted my voice. "Come in."

"I know. I saw the pictures, Playtex glove girl," Deep said.

Chris poked his head in. "Hey, time to get cleaned up, pills, and bed."

I looked over at Deep.

"No telling how long he'll be held up at the airport," Deep said. "You'll see Randy in the morning. Maybe he has something new for you."

19

RANDY SAT AT THE TABLE ACROSS FROM DEEP WITH A coffee mug in front of him, reading the paper. I clomped down the hall with Beetle and Bella beside me, their nails clickety-clacking on the wooden floor, calling attention to our approach. Randy stood to greet me. I saw the surprise that crossed his face was quickly and intentionally replaced with a warm smile.

This was the first time he'd seen me since I was taken hostage.

"Randy!" I shouted as I ran forward at the speed of a snail.

"Hey, Lynx. Long time no see."

Randy leaned over to give me a kiss on the cheek. "I take it that your being here isn't a social call. Where did you come in from?" I asked Randy.

"Honduras."

My eyebrows went up. "At the prison?"

"The capital, Tegucigalpa. I went to visit Julio's family. Since he's not talking, Axel and I figured we might be able to get something to put some pressure on him. We thought with enough background, we could convince Julio he was putting his family in danger," he said.

"Did Axel get authorization to interrogate Julio?" Deep asked.

"Still in the works. He's down there with his ATF buddy waiting for the okay. They think it might be tomorrow morning."

"And you're here." I put my hand on the table so I could move my walker out of the way.

Randy pulled out my chair and helped me to sit down. "Striker said you're scripting the interview. I thought you should get the background."

It was Sunday. No Laura. And Cookie got to make whatever he wanted since that was my free day with no Kitchen Grandmothers. This morning, Cookie chose scrambled eggs, fruit salad, bran muffins, and (sigh) a peanut butter smoothie.

"Thank you. Was the family willing to talk?" I asked, taking a bite of my eggs.

"They've been worried about Julio. They haven't heard anything from him since last September. By that, I mean they haven't had any money come in since last September. Julio had been sending them checks, very sizable checks, up until that point. They would like to have their income restored."

"I'll bet. So what's his story?" I chugged the peanut butter smoothie to get it finished.

"Julio came from a poor background. His dad had been a day laborer. When he was growing up, his family lived in a cement house with a latrine and access to a community water pump. There were three kids: an older sister, Flora, Julio, and a younger brother Henrique. The other two kids were average, where Julio stood out. The sister grew up, got married young, and lived the same life as her mom. The brother went to prison for a while on theft charges. After his release, he moved with his parents and does nothing but hang around, play cards, and drink."

"You'd think the dad wouldn't put up with that." I took a bite of I don't know what. I was too focused on Randy to care.

"He's okay with it. See, Julio bought his family a house in a middle-class neighborhood and furnished it. His dad retired, and they've been living off Julio's monthly support checks. No real reason for the brother to go dig ditches."

"Ah." Well then, they'd definitely want to get those checks back in their mailbox.

"His story goes like this: when Julio was a little boy, he was very bright. He taught himself to read from his sister's schoolbooks when he was three years old — very studious — and learned everything he could from every resource he could. Everyone thought that he was headed for something big. American missionaries spent a summer working with the Rodriguezs' church when Julio was a teenager. One of the missionaries arranged for Julio to go back to the States with him to finish his high school education and go to college on a Catholic scholarship. Julio jumped at the chance."

"Wow. There was a piece of good luck." I smiled.

"He didn't squander that luck. He worked hard in school. The Rodríguezes showed me their album with the letters from Julio and his report cards. He deserved the scholarships he received. He went to grad school, got a Master's in software design, and headed to Google for his first job."

"It sounds like a Cinderella story. That's when he bought

the house for his parents?" I pushed my plate away from me. My stomach still wouldn't hold much, and right now, it was full of smoothie.

"On his first vacation, he went down to visit and surprised them with the money for the house. Julio spent his trip helping his parents find the place they wanted. That's also the visit when he met Maria Castillo. Consuela Hervas being her alias."

"*Dun. Dah. Dun.* And so the story turns." I grimaced.

"You've got that right." Randy put his arm on the table and leaned in. "Julio and Maria fell in love. Julio's family didn't like her. She wasn't Catholic. She was a loose kind of girl, and they thought she only wanted to marry Julio because of his job in the US. They warned him against her but didn't press too hard. They thought the relationship would end when Julio went back up to the States. They showed me pictures of young Maria. She was very beautiful. Have you seen Julio?"

"Early Julio? No. He was in a picture I saw with Beth Sylanos, but he was turned to the side and in a shadow," I said. "I have seen footage of him at the prison."

"In the pictures, the Hernandez family showed me, Julio seemed scrawny and awkward. Not exactly what you'd call a babe magnet. When you see a picture of the two of them side by side, there's a disconnect. It doesn't look like they belong together at all."

I leaned my head back, gathering my hair into a ponytail to get it out of my face. "Maria must have loving feelings for Julio, or why would she go to the trouble of kidnapping me to get him out of prison?"

"The whole thing has me baffled," Randy said.

"Did Julio go back to Honduras to see Maria?" Deep asked.

"After Julio went back to the US, Maria went up to California within the month to visit him. They got married while she was there."

Deep snorted. "Much to the joy of Julio's momma."

Randy shook his head. "Momma didn't know. The family wasn't told until almost a year later when Julio and Maria took their belated honeymoon. They stopped in to see the folks for a few days, on their way to the beach in Costa Rica. By this point, Julio had sent them enough money that the dad had stopped working and got medical attention for his knees. They had a secondhand car. They had plenty of clothes and food for the first time in their lives. Henrique was released from jail and back living with them. Things were looking good."

I angled my chair to get better eye-to-eye with Randy. "Are they doing okay now that they don't have money coming in?" I asked.

"The house and car are paid in full. The family lived frugally, so most of Julio's money went into the bank. I got the impression that they were so used to being impoverished that having this relative wealth made them feel uncomfortable…fearful. From the stories they told, I think they knew Julio was doing something wrong, and the money was somehow tainted. His parents didn't like that much, but never asked questions, either."

"They had no idea what he was up to?" Darn it.

"None," Randy said. "But what they did remember was that on their honeymoon trip, Maria and Julio planned to meet with friends in Costa Rica, Amando and Beth Sylanos."

"That's when they took the picture. Wow."

174 | FIONA QUINN

"Wow is right. Something big happened on that trip. When Julio went back up to the States, he quit his Google job and took a job somewhere else. The family didn't know where. They thought his job had to do with writing software applications for a shipping company."

"And so Julio starts his life of crime. That must be when he signed on with Amando's cousin, Markos Sylanos." Deep's voice was excited.

"I think so," Randy said. "The Rodriguez family checks almost doubled after that."

"How long ago did the checks double?" I asked.

"Nine years," Randy said.

"Julio visited with them? Brought them up to see him in the States?" I drummed my fingers on the table.

"Nope. They never saw him after the honeymoon trip. You want to know something even more curious?" Randy leaned in and dropped his voice.

I held my breath.

"The checks came from a CPA in Sacramento. The Rodriguez family didn't know where Julio was living. The letters that they addressed to the house Julio lived in before his honeymoon came back stamped 'undeliverable.'"

Oh, interesting. "He thought they might be in danger? That someone might use his family as leverage?" I asked.

"It wasn't easy to find them. Someone would have to be motivated and have the right resources. We traced the family through Henrique and the courts."

"Julio's family is a soft spot." I nodded as my thoughts came together. "Julio might like to know how they're doing. We might even be able to convince him that his family is suffering now that the checks aren't coming in, losing the house, illness…we could intervene in exchange for information. Offer to give his family money and protection." The men nodded as I thought out loud.

"I'm not sure, though," I said. "I have to think this through. Julio might have been fulfilling his filial obligations, and that's all. He could have stayed on the straight and narrow path with a beautiful wife, an excellent job, a loving, proud family. He traded in his relationship with his family for his work with Sylanos. If only I knew what drove him to make that choice."

20

"Lynx, you're a girl." Blaze set his elbows on the table at our Sunday night family-style dinner and looked over at me.

"Blaze, your powers of observation amaze me," I said, taking a sip of water.

"What I mean is you might be able to interpret Faith for me."

"Like a foreign language?" I quirked a brow.

"It's foreign to me. I don't know what her problem's all about." Blaze shifted some food around on his plate.

"I don't know, Blaze. When I was a teenager, my mom was terminally ill, and I was working with Spyder. Those two things took up all my time. I didn't socialize the way most girls did. My experience with dating relationships is definitely limited. I can give it a shot, though." I doubted I'd be helpful, but curiosity tickled me.

"Things have changed with Faith and me. She seems angry *all* the time. We were doing fine until Gator and Amy broke up, and then boom. I can do no right."

"You and Gator used to go on double dates from time to time. Did the girls get close?"

"Faith got along okay with Amy, but they didn't have a lot in common. Faith sort of put up with Amy — she thought Amy was self-centered and princess-y."

"Yeah. You know, I could never figure out the whole Gator-Amy dynamic," I said.

Deep snorted. "You saw her, right?"

"She was beautiful, and she had enormous boobs. I get that. But this is swamp Gator and the Barbie doll. What in the world did they talk about?"

"Uh, Lynx, do you really think their relationship was about deep conversations?" Blaze asked, and the men laughed as if that were the best joke ever told.

I waited for them to get it back together. "Amy wanted to marry Gator."

"Amy's a shallow piece of work who liked how she looked walking around with her G.I. Joe." Blaze's disdain was more than apparent.

"Barbie and G.I. Joe? That's a whole lot of plastic and make-believe," I said.

"Exactly. Gator had it in the right perspective. He wasn't in the relationship for the long term. He wanted a little affection and a lot of—" Deep caught himself before he finished.

"Physical satisfaction?" I asked.

Deep choked on his drink. "That would be a way to put it."

I turned back to Blaze. "Faith got angry with you after Gator broke up with Amy. She knew that Gator was dating Amy for the thrill ride, and she knew that Amy wanted Gator to marry her, even if it were for superficial reasons. So let me ask you this: why are you dating Faith?"

"I really like her. We have fun together. Had. We *had* fun together."

"Is she *the* one?"

"I'm not in the market for *the* one."

"And you told her that?"

"Yup." Blaze had his fork in one hand and his knife in the other, holding them like reins on a horse. Braced.

My gaze fell off to the side while I thought this through. "Gator told Amy that he wasn't going to marry her because he was married to his job."

I was thinking aloud, but Blaze answered, "That's my understanding."

"I would guess this girl sees herself going the way of Amy. Used and discarded. I would say she's sending you the signal, 'shit or get off the pot.'"

"Damn, Lynx, your language." Deep's face was comically shocked.

I gave him a wink. "I've been hanging around you guys *way* too much. You're rubbing off."

"Shit or get off the pot?" Blaze asked. Lost.

"Yeah. Look, she's what, twenty-five-years old?" I squirmed in my seat to relieve my back.

"Twenty-six. She had a birthday while you were gone."

"I'm not saying that her biological clock is ticking, and I'm not saying she's even looking for a ring. I think she might be looking for the grand gesture that tells her you see her and your relationship as having more value than what Gator had with Amy. She wants to know the direction you're headed together so she can make some decisions." I paused. "Do you see a possible future with her?" I asked.

Blaze shrugged. "She's a cool girl. Smart, pretty, kind. I

could see her being a great wife and mom. I don't see me being a husband and a dad right now."

"But later, can you see the possibility of you two together or no?"

"Later? Yes."

"Then you need to tell her that, and you need to make a grand gesture that makes her know she's on your priority list."

"I don't know what that means," Blaze said.

"You guys take your girls to chick flicks from time to time, right?" I swear to god, if these guys could take out a pad and paper, they'd be taking notes. They all looked at me as if I was about to disclose the holy grail of womanhood. If they only realized how pathetic it was, they were turning to me on this subject. "Look, they make those movies to appeal to women, and it's a simple formula. The guy sees a girl and wants her to be his. The girl cooperates or doesn't, but something always gets in the way. There are hurt feelings and a lot of misery. How does the guy win the girl in the end and make everything all right? He makes some grand gesture — he does the thing that is counter-intuitive to his spirit but speaks to hers. He has to overcome himself to get to her. The girl in the movies wants the guy to swim through fire to be with her," I stalled and pointed an emphatic finger at Blaze, suddenly feeling like I should protect Faith, "but if you make the grand gesture, you have to make sure you mean it."

Blaze nodded gravely.

Deep cut a bite of chicken. "So Lynx, what was Striker's grand gesture?"

"Striker's grand gesture?" I scanned the men's faces. "Since I've known you guys, I've been a woman on the precipice. I've needed a whole team of men making the grand gesture in my direction." Deep, Randy, and Blaze nodded.

"And I know, without a doubt in my mind, that you would dive in front of the bullet to save me. And that, according to the movies, is exactly what every girl wants to know. When push comes to shove, is she safe with you?"

"From bullets?" Chris asked.

"From a broken heart," I said.

"Shit." Blaze looked down at his plate. "A grand gesture."

The table went quiet as we ate. I had obviously given the guys something to chew on beyond their dinners. I was in Lala Land myself, studying a piece of yam dangling from my fork when Blaze caught my attention.

"What are you stewing over, Lynx?"

"Oh, I was thinking about yams." I popped the bite into my mouth.

"Yams don't take a whole lot of thought," he said, looking down at his plate, carving a bite of steak.

"Well, I was really thinking about a story that I used to read when I was a little girl. It's an Anansi tale that Mrs. Shelack used to tell during story hour in the library." I let a little smile slide over my mouth. "I always think of Spyder McGraw as Anansi. He's such a trickster. It's a good thing for everyone. He puts his mind to work for the good of humanity. He would be a formidable villain if he ever decided to turn his brain to self-serving exploits."

"Amen to that," Deep said. "How does the story go?"

"So the name of this story is called *Anansi is Dead.* I was trying to remember — it goes something like this:

In Africa, the monsoon had not come. Several moons had passed since the rains were expected. The plants had with-

182 | FIONA QUINN

ered and died. There was almost no food left. The animals were hungry. Anansi was hungry. He decided to fill his belly by playing a trick on his family. He told them he had gone to see the sorcerer. The sorcerer had seen a clear vision and told Anansi he was about to die. The sorcerer instructed Anansi on what should follow in the way of burial. If the family followed the instructions, they would be spared from the famine. Anansi said that when he died, they should bury him in the sweet potato patch.

'Yes. Yes. Anansi,' they promised, 'we will do as you ask.'

'And when I die, and you bury me in the sweet potato patch, you must bury me with a pot and some matches.'

'Yes, oh yes, Anansi, we will do as you ask.' Then Anansi died. The family was in mourning. He was a trickster, but he was still family. Everyone gathered and spoke kind words about him and buried him in the garden near their last surviving sweet potato plant.

Each night Anansi crawled out of his burial hole and ate some roasted sweet potato. Soon the family started to notice that their plant was not producing as much food as they expected. They devised a plan. They decided to make a man out of tree sap and put it in the garden.

Later that night, Anansi crawled out of his hole and saw the man in the light of the crescent moon. Anansi was afraid that the man would take all the sweet potatoes, so he went to attack the man. Anansi got all eight of his legs stuck in the tree sap.

The next morning Anansi's family came out to see if their trap caught the sweet potato thief, and they found Anansi alive, but not so well, stuck in their trap."

"That's it?" Deep put his fork down on his empty plate.

"Yup."

"Is there a reason you're thinking about this story?" he asked.

"It's one of the ways my brain gives me information. You know, like my subconscious is working through a problem in the present tense, and I'm given a bridge to the answer that I picked up in the past tense. Most people do this. Sometimes they're unaware that they should be listening. A lot of times, it's a song that gets stuck in your head. For example, what do you think about when you think about Ghianna? Do you have a song?"

"Probably the one I think about when she's not with me is Epic's *Lier's Eye*," he said. "But I sing it 'Ghianna' instead of 'Donna.'"

"Isn't that the one about…" Chris stopped and shoved a huge bite of food in his mouth, making a show of chewing it. The other men let their focus land distractedly around the room, giving Deep a little privacy as blood rose to his face.

"Deep, it's not a foolproof system. You know — don't take it too literally. Your subconscious might not be warning you that Ghianna's fooling around so much as it could be telling you that you would care if she were — that it would devastate you. Maybe you have more invested in the relationship than what you're thinking on the surface." Deep didn't seem to buy my interpretation. I floundered around for something he could accept. "It could even be as simple as you like the tune and Ghianna rhymes with Donna." Shoot. That wasn't how I expected the conversation to go. Why couldn't he have said something fun and happy?

Deep still looked unconvinced.

I reached out to put my hand on Deep's arm to make him listen to what I was saying, not just hear placating words coming out of my mouth. "So don't go running off accusing her of something that's probably not happening."

"If that song played in your head when you thought of Striker, what would you do?" Deep asked.

"To be honest? I'd try to figure it out. You can't pick the most obvious solution. Sometimes the subconscious is subtle, especially when you're not used to listening and deciphering." I squeezed my hand where it rested on his arm. "Promise me you're not going to go off the deep end, excuse the pun. Don't take this conversation too literally."

Deep wiped the hard line of his mouth with his fingers. He was pissed.

Blaze came to the rescue, changing the subject back to where I had started. "And your 'Anansi is stuck in the gumman' bridge leads you where exactly?"

"To Marcos Sylanos," I said.

"You still think Sylanos is alive?" Blaze leaned forward, his gaze intent.

"I *know* he's alive. I can feel him alive. I can feel him laughing at us as he hides in his dark hole, coming out while no one's looking and taking what he wants." My eyes had hardened. No fluff-mode here. I was ready for battle. "I want to get him. I want to trap him and expose him just like Anansi."

"How does this lead back to Omega and you?" Blaze piled more food onto his plate.

"I'm not sure it does. But the same players keep showing up." I shook my head. "I can't figure out who is competing on what team is all. Or if they aren't all on the same team, for that matter. Omega should have given up on me by now, don't you think? Maybe I can go back to Washington to work on this."

Blaze and Deep shot a glance at each other.

"Okay, I take it Omega hasn't given up. How do you know that?"

My two teammates seemed to have a full conversation with their eyes in a language that I didn't understand and couldn't interpret until the final raised eyebrow that asked, "should we say?"

"Spill. What are you guys hiding?" I ordered. They weren't in my line command, but my job title did give me a certain amount of authority. Wait, I didn't have a job. Command took me off the payroll.

"Omega put tails on us. All of us," Blaze said hesitantly. "We can't seem to shake them. We can't leave Iniquus without someone showing up in our rearview mirror."

"But if you're undercover, Omega chasing you would increase your visibility and put you guys in danger." I scanned the faces of my teammates.

"We need to be out working to prove we're out working," Deep said. "We've had to take on a lot of out of state and overseas assignments to get us away from Omega operators. Jack was outed the other day. He lost the tango. It killed the case. Nearly killed Jack."

"He didn't say," I muttered, trying to assimilate this piece of news. I looked at my lap while I processed. Cases were being blown, which would hurt Iniquus' reputation. And worse, I was putting my guys in the direct path of danger. I thought I was the only one at risk, and now come to find out, my team was in jeopardy because of me. Here I was safely tucked away from harm, and my team was out being stalked by assassins. They wouldn't be safe until I solved the case, or I was captured and dead. Rendition with final tap, that's what Frith told Spencer.

A shiver raked my body.

Randy looked up from his phone. He had been sitting at the end of the table, watching all of this play out. "Text from Axel — ATF got clearance, and the interrogation is set for Monday afternoon."

21

RANDY, DEEP, BLAZE, AND I WERE IN THE PROVISIONAL Puzzle Room in the east wing of Casa Striker.

I had sent Laura home early, telling her I had a raging migraine.

We had a visual from Axel's cam glasses — not the best in terms of clarity. Axel was suffering from allergies. His sneezing gave the whole interview a rollercoaster feel, or maybe that was just my stomach doing loopty-loops.

I needed this to go well. I wanted answers. The audio was staticky. That was the problem when depending on the spyware for real-time information. The sound recordings that Axel would send over later would be cleaner.

Julio was ushered into the room. He sat down just as he had seated himself for all ten of the federal attorney's interviews. He positioned himself for the impassive long haul. There were no introductions. On the computer screen, I saw Axel's hand push a piece of paper forward. It was exactly like the papers that Julio had created, displayed, confettied, and flushed each Sunday. This one had the next code.

Julio looked down at the paper. He looked at his knees. His lips moved ever so slightly as he calculated in that genius head of his. He looked up, and a bead of sweat slid down the left side of his face.

"Brody is in custody. He's very cooperative," Axel said.

Julio looked blankly at Axel, and his shoulders gave a slight shrug. He didn't seem to know the name Brody.

"Brody Covington is the legal name of the man who visited you each week to get the codes, and now he's working with us."

"Oh. He's on my visitor list as B. Henry Covington. Covington doesn't know how to produce the codes." Julio's voice had a fey quality like he wasn't living in his body but floated outside his corporeal self.

"Fibonacci," Axel said.

Julio blinked rapidly. He ran his handcuffed palms up and down his pants legs. His right foot started to tap, tap, tap on the floor. Axel let him sit in distress. Neither Axel nor the ATF agent, Ken Dalton, moved or spoke.

"I'm dead then," Julio said very softly.

"Not necessarily. Today's Monday. We have until next Sunday to take over for Brody. We understand your codes. We need to know how you're applying them and what they're protecting."

"Me," Julio whispered. "They're protecting me."

"Not anymore they aren't, unless you get real cooperative, real fast," Dalton said.

Julio nodded. "May I have some water, please?"

Dalton picked up the pitcher sitting beside him on the gunmetal gray table and poured the water into a plastic cup, holding it out. Julio sipped, put the cup back on the table, and focused on his feet. "The number codes connect to a computer housed at my CPA's office in Sacramento. It's actually their computer. They have no idea I placed a program on their hard drive. The Fibonacci code is entered each Sunday before eight P.M., and nothing happens."

"What happens this coming Sunday at 8:01 if no code is inputted?" Dalton asked.

"If I was not dead already? They'd kill me, and Maria would be killed as well."

"You know that Maria is in prison for kidnapping and murder?" Axel asked.

Julio nodded. "When Covington started coming, I knew something bad had happened. I didn't know what for a long time, until I saw her in the newspaper."

"Did you help her plan the kidnapping?" Axel used the same soft monotone that he used with Hector. It had a hypnotic quality to it that made me want to share my inner-most secrets. I'd have to watch my tongue around Axel.

"I have not spoken to my wife since I was arrested. Everything I know about India Sobado comes from the paper. I can tell you that Maria was never going after those children the way they reported. Maria loves babies, always wanted her own. Eight. She wanted to have eight children. It was the Sobado woman Maria was after. I'm sure of it."

"Why would Maria want to kidnap Miss Sobado?" Dalton asked. He rested with his thigh on the table, and his arms crossed over his chest. He tilted his head back, and the whole set up gave him an arrogant, almost pugnacious, air. I thought that stance probably didn't play well with Julio. Dalton should soften up.

"Maria is not a very educated woman." Julio's eyes took on the distant look of introspection. "I think in her mind, she believes America works the same as in Honduras, that she could trade Sobado for me. Sobado must have some connection to wealth or political power. I would imagine Maria was trying to set up a trade." Julio sighed deeply and gave a sad shake of his head. His gaze moved back to his shoes. Guilt? Embarrassment? No. Shame, I think.

"I read in the papers that Sobado died in a plane crash over the Gulf," Julio said. "I have to assume that my wife hid Sobado with her family in Honduras, that Sobado was able to escape, and was trying to fly home when the storm hit."

"India Sobado was on the East Coast of Honduras," Axel replied. He sat on a metal folding chair in front of Julio with his knees apart and his hands resting naturally on his thighs. In my opinion, this was the best approach for Julio — to be on the same level. Open. Non-threatening.

"Yes, so it was with her uncle, then. He runs a prison. That would be the perfect place to hide the girl," Julio said.

"What's the uncle's name?" asked Dalton.

"Alejandro Castillo," Julio reached for the cup with shackled wrists and took another sip.

"Why would Maria take such a risk?" Axel asked, his voice colored with compassion as he leaned slightly forward.

"I would like to say it's because she loves me." Julio gave a little laugh. "I imagine the real reason she did this was she is afraid of poverty. She didn't want to go back to her life in Honduras." There was a long silence. Then Julio continued to muse. "She has no way to earn a living. She would be a maid or a street vendor, living hand to mouth. She is here illegally. We both are. I let my work visa run out after I left Google."

"Maria didn't want to live with your parents in Tegucigalpa?" asked Axel casually.

Julio flinched. He stared hard at the wall behind Axel's left shoulder. "You are very thorough."

Neither Dalton nor Axel responded.

"My parents would not have helped her. You probably already know I've not personally had contact with them in over a decade." Julio sighed loudly. During this interrogation, Julio's gaze seemed to land around the room like a bird hopping from branch to branch, but he never looked directly at Axel or Dalton. "Sacrifices had to be made so that I could provide for my parents and provide for Maria and myself. I'm sure that my family believes it is Maria who has kept me away. They are not softhearted, forgiving people, my family."

"What if Maria was successful in effecting a prisoner exchange?" Axel asked.

"Maria did not understand that the people she was saving me from, and the people who she thought would save us, are one and the same."

"She wanted to get you out so you could continue to work for Sylanos?" Axel adjusted his glasses, making the image waver.

"Yes, I believe that's what she was doing."

"But you think you are in prison because of Sylanos," Axel said.

"I know I am."

"I'm listening." Axel sneezed, then blew his nose.

Julio twitched around in his chair. His head nodded slightly back and forth rhythmically as the mechanisms in his brain whirred. Finally, he pulled his lips in and shook his head no. He wasn't going to cooperate. Our having the codes wasn't enough. He still thought his best chance at survival lay in silence.

"Here is the fault with your codes," Axel said. "It was very risky to set up this way, human error being what it is. People aren't dependable, like computers. Maria could have gotten sick, or incapacitated, even dead. Then what? What if she found someone else to take care of her? Another man? A man named Hector?"

Julio's eyes were black onyx, hard and opaque. "I trusted Maria over the short run. My imprisonment shouldn't have gone on this long. I thought it would only be three weeks, four at the most."

"Before what?" asked Dalton.

"Before I was released."

"You were tried for terrorism," Dalton said.

Julio nodded.

"Very quickly, too," Dalton pressed on. There was something threatening in his tone, though his voice quality didn't demonstrably change. "Usually, it takes a year or so to mount a case. This one came to trial in two weeks. That's highly unusual."

"My crimes have nothing to do with terrorism. They needed me on ice, and they have power in all the right places. They can make almost anything happen."

"This is Sylanos?" asked Dalton.

Julio nodded. "Sylanos, yes. And those who benefit from Sylanos."

"If they needed you on ice, why didn't they take you out?" I couldn't actually see Dalton as he spoke. Axel remained focused on Julio.

"They'd like to. They're trying to figure out what to do with me. I don't fit neatly into the plan."

"How so?" asked Axel.

"I was tired of crouching under the radar in fear. I had lived very frugally here in America. Sylanos laughed at me, my little apartment, my modest lifestyle. I sent money to my parents, as you know. Not a huge amount for living in the US but very nice — a very nice lifestyle — for living in Honduras. I put money in an offshore account. I was going to get enough together, so Maria and I never had to worry, and then I was going to leave."

"You have enough together now. You were making noises like you might be leaving the organization," Axel said.

"I can't walk away. They have people everywhere. I have watched the cartel deal with their retirees before. I needed to leave with their permission."

"And that explains Maria."

Julio lifted an eyebrow.

"Maria knows that you stashed the money. She doesn't know how to get to it."

Julio licked his teeth behind closed lips.

"We know that you were involved in the first leg of the Sylanos shipping triangle. We know you were involved in bootlegging software and entertainment — movies, music, games. They have no one else who could do this?" Axel asked.

"I have a master's degree in software design. It would take someone with my level of education to carry on."

"A big asset," Axel said. "I imagine it would be hard to recruit someone like you."

"Exactly," Julio said.

"You were friends with Marcos' cousin, Amondos."

Julio nodded gravely. "Dead. Him and his wife, Beth."

Axel shook his head, making the computer picture nauseating to watch. "Beth is alive. She's an informant for the CIA."

The shock on Julio's face was almost comically drawn.

"It's Sylanos who is dead." Axel delivered this piece of news like he was ramming a knife between Julio's ribs.

Julio sat like a frozen rabbit, waiting for the fox to move on by. Then he threw his head back. Julio's laugh burst from his lungs. It was too big for his small frame and bent him in half, almost dumping him from his chair. Tears slid out the corners of his eyes as he righted himself. Julio used the sleeve of his orange jumpsuit to wipe his face dry.

"Good one. If Sylanos were dead, I'd be dead."

Axel slid the newspaper clips over to Julio. Julio was reticent to pick them up. He looked at the articles laying on the table for a long time. "These are in Spanish," he said finally.

"This was reported in South and Central American papers. It's not newsworthy in the US. No one knows Sylanos's power up here," Axel replied.

After several minutes, Julio reached out his hands and pulled the papers into his lap. He read each one and then read them again.

Without looking up, Julio said, "The truth is, I didn't ask Sylanos to release me from the organization. I knew that was the kiss of death. I went to the Attorney General."

"Here in Florida?" Dalton asked.

Julio nodded. "I thought that if I testified against the organization, that the people who could hurt me would be imprisoned. I thought that the American government would help me with a new identity. Maria and I could go live somewhere obscure, Indonesia or New Zealand. We have plenty of money to live a simple life somewhere. We are only 35. We still have time to start a family." Julio's voice trailed off; his unfocused gaze slid to the right. After a few moments, he roused himself. "Little did I know that the fucking AG, Jim Noble, is in bed with Sylanos. He arrested me on the spot. I had no contingency plan for this. I was completely surprised. I thought he was going to take me out right there and then, or order the gang CQ2 to do it."

"You thought that Noble would pull in a gang chip?" Dalton asked.

"Absolutely. He's used them before. CQ2 is all over the prisons. Even in solitary, even in Max, they can get to me. All Noble needs to do is raise an eyebrow, and I'm gone."

"Then there's a reason you're not gone," Dalton said. "There's a reason why you haven't opened your mouth from the time you were arrested until today."

"I documented everything to do with Sylanos from the beginning of my tenure with him. I updated my computer files daily. The data contains everyone's name, how they fit in, when they did something, how they did something. I had it all. A decade's worth of data."

"They trusted you with this information?" Dalton asked.

"They trusted me with their computers. I wrote the software for the organization. It all backed up into my Sacramento files and floated in cyberspace. I have everything…" Julio was thoughtful. "I must have something that I don't know about. Something that implicates Jim Noble himself."

"Or someone he's protecting," Axel said.

"Yes." Julio nodded his agreement.

"You told Noble you had documentation of Sylanos' organization."

"Yes. They needed to know it was more than my memory

— more than my word against theirs. After all, in their eyes, I'm merely an undocumented worker."

"You must have told Noble that the computer was programmed to release the information," Axel mused. "That you had no control. It was automatic. That way, they couldn't torture you for the information."

"Right. If I gave them the wrong information under duress, they'd be exposed. I said if anything happened to Maria, that too, would create an automatic release of information. She may think of me as a paycheck, but I really do love her. I guess sometimes you take what you can get," he said wearily.

"This makes no sense," Dalton said. "If the AG has you on ice while they try to figure out how to protect themselves from you, why didn't they figure out the code? Arrest Maria? Arrest Brody? They could do what we're doing."

"Maybe they tried. Maybe you're better than they are. I thought I was very clever about my system. There are other players, too. There's more to this."

"Who? What?" asked Dalton

"That I can't tell you. I collected the data. I didn't read the data. I only know about the software pirating. If I had read the data and understood the connections, I would never have gone to the AG, now would I?"

"You knew he was connected with CQ2?"

"Yes. We used Blackhearts for some projects, mostly weapons mules up 95. The two gangs have overlapping territory that causes a lot of collateral damage. I overheard some phone conversations that maybe I shouldn't have heard. In one of them, Sylanos said that if CQ2 stopped another shipment, he was going to put Noble's head on the chopping block. That's why I thought he and Sylanos were competitors, and going to Noble would be the best way out."

"Let's go back. I still want to know why you haven't said a word to anyone in almost a year," Dalton said.

"Noble told me he had decided we should negotiate."

"There are no tapes of you talking to the AG, only the Fed."

"No, these were private conversations," Julio said.

"Go on." Axel rested his elbows on his knees, mirroring Julio's body stance, giving Julio the psychological sense that this was intimate, and Axel was conspiring with him. Julio nodded in agreement. Good. He was reading this the way Axel wanted him to.

"He said that someone had called the newspapers and news outlets reporting that I was a terrorist. The unknown caller said my plot had come close to taking out key players in the government, but the Feds were trying to keep this under wraps ahead of the election cycle. A media circus surrounded me."

"Could Maria have done that to protect you?" Dalton asked.

"Maria's not that smart. This was someone very clever. The more I thought about this, the more I saw the genius of it. Not only did the media save me at the moment, but it's also ongoing. I get five, ten, fifteen requests every day from authors who want to write my story. People are watching me. People with skills and resources. People with possibly big paychecks on the line. If I were to suddenly disappear, there would be lots of questions."

"Ah. That better explains your good health. You've got media working in your favor, but you're still playing your code card?"

"If the writers are asking questions after I disappear, it doesn't do me a whole lot of good, now does it? I have to stay here and stay quiet. The deal is that I keep my head down, and as soon as things have cooled off a little, I'd be free and have my new identification papers. Noble was afraid that if someone got the information out, from a reporter, for example, that I would leak some of my data. Noble said that I should shut my mouth — literally not open my mouth once, from that moment on. If I said anything, I would be drawing the whole thing out longer than anyone wanted."

"How could they release you if you've been to trial and convicted?"

"I signed papers as to my guilt. There was only a sentencing trial. As I said, they have players in all the right places. Evidence and a good cover story could show up any day."

"You believe that?"

"It's the fantasy I'm telling myself until I die. Now that this interrogation has taken place, you have Brody, and you figured out the codes, it should be any time now."

22

"THAT WAS DAMNED DEPRESSING." I RUBBED MY LOWER back and leaned into the chair for support.

"There were a lot of holes in that story," Randy said.

"It was the Swiss cheese of all stories." Blaze reached out to turn off the display that had gone to static.

"I don't think he had any more to give us. I think he dumped it all on the table, hoping for a miracle," I said.

"He seemed surprised we didn't care about his work with Sylanos." Deep turned to check a monitor that lit up. A turkey buzzard flew low to the ground across the screen. Deep pushed a button to signal a false alarm. "Darned raptors. I think there's something dead in the woods. I need to find it and move it out of the controlled zone."

"I wish I could interview Brody before we talk to Maria," I said.

Randy flicked his pencil in the air in a high rotating arch; it landed neatly in his hand. He used it as a pointer to waggle at me. "Axel sees Maria in the morning. We'll have to run the script you already wrote."

200 | FIONA QUINN

I nodded. "The AG's gonna have a heads-up we chatted with Julio. He'll have the tapes and know everything we do."

"Nope. Axel scrambled everything not on his frequency; all they'll get is static," Blaze said with a grin.

"But it's six hours of static. You think that bodes well for the guy?" I asked.

"Honestly, it's his past actions that might save him here. You saw the first ten interrogations. He sat on the chair for hours on end without a peep. Not even a bathroom break. Why would number eleven be any different? In the end, we have little to no control over this situation. We don't know if the AG is at the top of the pyramid, wringing every drop of power from his tenure," Deep said.

"Or if Julio was out-and-out lying, or something in between. When is Noble up for election?" Blaze leaned over Deep's chair and launched a search engine.

"I don't think Julio was lying," I said, looking over Deep's shoulder. "He was confused. He drew some faulty conclusions. Hmm, no, I think he was as honest as he could be."

Blaze pointed at the screen. "Noble's running for the US House of Representatives in the November election."

"With CQ2 in his pocket? How is it no one's picked up on that?" Deep asked.

"This might be one of Julio's false assumptions. He came to his conclusion based on phone conversations he overheard. So many questions…" I stretched and rubbed my back. It was well past my bedtime — and well past my meds time. I was trying to ease off the pain pills. I'd weaned myself down to only a couple of nighttime Tylenol, but at that moment, I'd have been very appreciative of some stronger relief. Six hours in a metal chair staring at a monitor was five hours too long when you weren't getting your questions answered clearly.

"Randy, do you know who the CPA is in Sacramento?" I asked.

"I have copies of their bank transactions," he said.

"Do you feel like a trip to the West Coast?" I reached for my walker. "I think we need their computer to go to our forensics lab. It might hold the key to the universe. My universe, at any rate."

Randy pulled out his iPhone and checked the screen. "I can go Tuesday night. Is that soon enough?"

I was in the water, walk-jogging in the pool current while Laura leaned over the side, dangling her hand in the water, and saying encouraging things. "You can do it!" "What an improvement!" "Look at you go!" I felt like a kid at a Little League game cheered along as I ran to the next base.

The next base today was weightlifting. I'd taken a special trip to the imaging center on Friday. I was just shy of the requisite healing time before I lifted anything over my head, but the doctor gave me permission to proceed.

I sat in a chair and lifted two-pound weights, both arms moving up at the same time, and sweated from the exertion. This was ridiculous. Even in prison, I worked out harder than this.

I grunted my agitation.

"Don't get discouraged, Annie. You're moving ahead at a good pace. You have to build back your stamina and strength. It's a time game."

"I'm frustrated," I snapped, as my arms wavered like

202 | FIONA QUINN

overcooked spaghetti noodles over my head, struggling to hold up mini dumbbells.

"Yeah? Well, let's look at the positives. Today, you're lifting. A few more days and the doctor says you'll be safe enough to move around without the walker, then we can go outside and work on your balance. It's a beautiful property."

I gave Laura a half-smile. My mind wasn't really on my therapy. I was thinking about Maria. Axel and Dalton should be with her right now. Since they didn't have a two-way communicator, it didn't matter whether I watched in real-time, or waited and watched the feed later. I had already given up a half-days work over Julio for no particular reason beyond impatience. Strength had to be my priority. I needed to be ready if Omega found me.

My monitor showed Maria's swollen face. Red stippled around her eyes from a crying jag that had gone on almost an hour, according to the timestamp at the bottom of the screen. I scrolled through her sob session. It was a pitiful scene, but I couldn't work up a sense of compassion. To be truthful, I was happy she was bathing in her pain. I wanted her to suffer. A tiny metallic voice tapped on the edge of my consciousness, reminding me that Maria had very likely saved my life by kidnapping me before Omega goons grabbed me. I tried to ignore that voice and revel in my satisfaction.

Axel, on the other hand, had had enough. "Are you done?" He reached up and adjusted his glasses, making the image jiggle.

Maria shifted around in the hard metal chair, folded her

arms tightly over her bosom, and glared across the table at the men.

"We've been chatting with Julio. He's had some interesting things to say."

Maria arched her eyebrow at him. She obviously thought he was trying to trick her.

"Julio is having some problems in prison. Looks like CQ2 targeted him. Rumor is, he won't make it to testify at your trial," Axel said.

"Oh, he'll make it to my trial, all right." Venom dripped from her words.

"You sound very confident," Axel said.

"I am. He's not going to die. The politicos won't let that happen."

"Who do you mean when you say, 'the politicos'?" Axel asked. That tone. I needed to learn how to modulate my voice into that tone. It was genius.

Maria said nothing. She pursed her lips together and twisted them from side to side, a you'll-get-nothing-out-of-me response.

"Are you referring to Sylanos and his friends?" Axel asked.

Still nothing. I guess she thought since the sympathy card hadn't worked, maybe she'd try stonewalling.

Axel opened his laptop and played a small section of yesterday's film — where Julio explained that Maria was trying to get him out of prison to access his money. He didn't believe she cared anything about him at all.

"He's not in your corner, Maria. You're on your own." Axel's soothing voice made him the support she could lean on. Encouraged her to lean on. "Your husband won't stand with you. Sylanos' organization won't stand with you. You are an illegal who took an American citizen captive, hid her in a foreign prison, and tried to negotiate a trade for an affirmed terrorist."

"Julio is *not* a terrorist!"

"Maria." Patience. Kindness. Like petting a kitten. "Julio signed court papers admitting to his guilt. He's serving a life sentence in maximum security. You tried to negotiate the release of an affirmed terrorist who tried to harm the American government by using a young American girl as your pawn. In trying to escape and get back home, this young girl died. What do you think is going to happen to you?"

All the bluster rushed from Maria's lungs. She looked like a wounded child. Vulnerable. Axel had kicked a goal shot.

He tilted his head sympathetically to the side. "Maria, you can turn state's evidence, like your friend Beth Sylanos. You don't have to rot in prison, waiting on death row for your execution."

Maria moved her hands to her lap. She turned inward, eyes scanning the floor in front of her, then her lips tightened down again, curling inward. Just like Julio, she'd decided not to cooperate.

"Hector's dead," Axel said it like he was saying, "We need milk." A normal, everyday kind of statement.

Maria leaned forward and puked. Axel's wire-cam focused on the puddle of half-digested food, corn, and some beef chunks. Dalton walked over to the door and rapped at the window to get the guard's attention. After sticking his head out the door for a brief conversation, Dalton sat back down. "He's getting a mop."

"How did Hector die?" Maria wiped a sleeve across her mouth.

"Gang hit within twenty-four hours of his arrest," Axel said.

Dalton reached over, poured a cup of water, and held it out to Maria. She shook her head, so Dalton took a sip and put it back on the metal table. How they were sitting there with undisturbed faces, and the smell from the puddle of puke at their feet was beyond me. My stomach rolled and bucked at the image alone.

We waited. For the mop? For her to digest the information? I didn't know. It was a long wait. Fifteen minutes went by, then twenty. A guard came in and swiped a mop through the pool of puke, sprayed some disinfectant, then wheeled the bucket back out, shutting the door behind him. I'm sure the room was much more pleasant now.

Still, there was silence.

It was around the forty-minute mark when Maria met Axel's eyes again. She had made her decision. "Julio has been hiding our money. We have lots of money. Julio sent some to his family. He sent most to his bank account. We had little to live on. It was a better life than I lived in Honduras, but I wanted to buy pretty clothes, have my own maid to clean the toilets. I wanted to eat restaurant food. I don't see why I couldn't have had a little money to do that," she complained. "But no, Julio has to hide it away. He wouldn't tell me where. I said to him, 'What if you die? Then the money is gone, and I'll be a widow living on the streets.' He should tell me where he hid the money."

"Julio said he was ready to leave the organization — to take you and the money and go live in Indonesia. Was he worried that Sylanos wouldn't let him leave?" Axel asked.

"It didn't matter what Sylanos wanted. He had to release Julio," Maria said defiantly.

"Julio might be dangerous to let walk around, knowing everything he knows about Sylanos and the operations," Axel said.

"Very dangerous. That's why Julio documented everything over the years. That was his safety net."

"Why do you think that Julio signed the documents that said he was planning a terrorist attack?" Axel asked.

"He's doing what he was told to do. Julio went to jail because he told the wrong guy the wrong thing. Once Julio was part of the system, they had a hard time making it go away because it got media attention. Someone planted the story that Julio was a terrorist. Too many eyes involved. They told Julio he had to sit in jail and that when things cooled off, they would get him out." Maria stared at the wet spot on the floor.

Axel waited for her to shift her gaze back to him. "And when you say 'they,' you're talking about…?"

"I'm not sure." Maria hunched her shoulders. "The politicos."

Axel had moved to the corner of the room while the mop guy did his thing, but now he came back over to perch on the table in front of Maria. "We know about the codes that Julio gave you each week. We know that Brody Covington took your place after you sent the ransom note. We know how to calculate next week's code."

Maria looked silently at Axel, then slowly nodded her head.

"How do we find Brody?" Axel asked.

"I don't know," she whispered.

"Maria, you have to cooperate here, or we can't help you." Suddenly, Axel transformed into Papa Bear. His voice growled in warning. You don't mess with Papa Bear. Maria's body jerked when she heard the tone; she knew there was danger there.

"I will tell you what I know. I can't tell you what I don't know. I don't know how you can reach Brody. He's underground."

"What's his involvement?" Dalton asked from behind Axel somewhere.

"Brody gets five hundred dollars a week to show up, memorize the code, and type it in on the computer."

"How do you know he will follow through?" Dalton asked.

"If anything were to happen to Julio or me, then he doesn't have a paycheck anymore, see? He's doing it for the easy money."

"Who's paying him?" Dalton asked.

"I am. It's set up with an accountant."

"That's a whole lot of money, Maria. You were living a frugal life. How are you getting the money to pay Brody?" Axel stood up and leaned into the wall. The angle of his glasses made Maria catty-corner on my screen. I tilted my head so she'd be upright, and I wouldn't get seasick.

"The Man gave me a lot of money. I thought it would be enough to last until I could exchange Lexi for Julio. When Julio was free, then we could get to our money."

"How long do you think that will hold out?" Axel sat back down, and I was able to hold my head up again. I rubbed my neck.

"I only have a few weeks of money left. After that, Brody won't put the codes in," Maria said.

"What happens when Brody doesn't put the codes in?" Axel asked.

"The computer will release the documentation that Julio

has collected for the last decade and send it to the government agencies. Then Julio and I will be killed." Maria's cadence was like a dirge.

"Like I said, we know how to create the code. I can put the code in for you. Protect you. How do I do that?" Axel was back to his hypnotic tone.

Maria leaned forward and gestured toward the pen Dalton was tapping on his knee. Maria wrote a web address on a piece of paper that lay on the table. "On Sunday afternoon, and *only* on Sunday afternoon, you can pull this up. Otherwise, it will give you an error code. When it comes up, there will be a box and no instructions. Type the code into the box and press enter. You will see a smiling face if you did it right. If it is wrong, you have two more tries. That's so if I type wrong, I have a chance to make it better."

"And if four codes go in incorrectly?" Dalton asked.

"The computer sends the documentation to everyone from the President of the United States, to the presidents of Colombia and Honduras, Iniquus, the media, everyone Julio could think of."

"How do you think they could kill you in prison?" Axel asked.

"These prisons in Florida are filled with CQ2. They will have no problem killing us."

"Is this someone with Sylanos who will give the kill order? We need to know who's in charge so we can stop them."

Maria nodded, all seriousness. She was at the edge of her chair, her feet planted wide for stability. Her gaze lasered in on Axel. He was the man with the life vest. Axel might be able to save her. "I think it is a man with the politicos. A group named Omega."

Omega? *Omega*. Holy cow. I felt the blood drain from my face. I was completely lost now about what was happening. I sat forward in my chair, leaning hungrily toward the screen. I held my breath and waited for what would come next.

"Maria, go back. You said 'a man with the politicos' and you have also said 'The Man' who gave you money — are they one and the same?"

She looked up at the ceiling, processing. Maria bobbled her head. "Yes. Yes, they must be…"

"Maria, you will start at the beginning and explain your connection to The Man and Omega." Dalton was using a captain-in-command voice. Quiet authority. No other choice but to comply.

Maria nodded. "Julio was arrested. He was on the news all the time. I had to move from our apartment and change my name to Consuela Hervas to hide from the reporters. I was afraid that the border police would come and make me go back to Honduras. I thought that I had hidden pretty well. One night, when I was asleep in my apartment, a man broke in. He came to my bed. I woke up with his hand over my mouth."

"Did you ever see him?" Axel was on his feet again.

"No. The lights were off, and he was behind me."

"Accent?" Axel asked.

"Anglo."

"How big?"

"Average height, heavyset — you know middle-aged kind of heavy."

"Anything else you can tell me about him?" Axel moved in front of Maria and crouched down eye-to-eye with her. His voice was flat and barely audible. I could see Maria's pores, her sweat, her twitching right eyelid. Maria was used to being hit. Axel could see what I saw. With his psych background, he would interpret her body language the way I was interpreting it. He must have wanted to pressure her with a physical threat.

I would have done this differently, but I looked a lot different than Axel. Before all of this, I looked like a young happy-go-lucky piece of girly fluff. It was my planned and practiced disguise. Now? Well, it was going to take a while to put my disguise back in place.

And Axel's strategy seemed to be working.

Maria was revealing her secrets.

23

MARIA SWALLOWED VISIBLY.

"What did he want?" Axel asked.

"He had a job for me to do. He knew that I had money problems, that Julio had been stingy with the money. He said if I cooperated, he would make sure I had everything I needed and help me get to Julio's offshore accounts."

"And if you didn't work for him?" Axel asked.

"He never said. I never asked. I needed the money. I was okay working with him. He left two thousand dollars on my bed when he left."

"Why you?" Dalton said.

"Because I had a connection with Lexi Rueben."

Rueben, my maiden name.

"Okay, let's focus there. Tell us about your connection," Dalton said.

"My best friend, Beth Sylanos, used to live in Washington D.C. under the name Jenny Agnew. I wasn't supposed to know that because she was a federal informant and is in their protection program. But Beth contacted me and kept in touch with me. Lexi used to babysit Beth's kids while she worked at the hospital laundry. The Man knew all about Beth. He knew everything about everything. He needed me to make friends with Lexi."

"Why?" Dalton asked.

"He never said," Maria replied.

"Did Lexi know Jenny Agnew went by another name?" Axel asked.

"I don't have a clue what Lexi knew or didn't know. I would seriously doubt she thought anything about Beth at all. Lexi was a girl when she babysat — a young teen."

"The Man thought that you had a foot in the door even though you knew a woman named Beth, and Lexi knew her as Jenny Agnew?" Dalton sounded confused. He should stop talking. Maria needed someone with authority to confront her one on one. Sharing a leadership role with Axel weakened Axel's position and helped Maria gain power. She needed to be powerless.

"The place Beth was living was like this little apartment village. All the families shared with each other and helped each other. It was a very important place for Beth. The neighbors there were like family. Beth thought of Lexi like a niece."

A niece? Huh. Mrs. Agnew must treat her family like shit. She was mean, surly, and sometimes even vicious.

"There was a fire at the complex," Maria continued. "The whole building burned down. Everyone lost everything."

"Where did Beth move after the fire?"

"Beth had to move before the fire happened. She thought that someone had found out about her, so she ran away. I haven't heard from her for years. Not since she lived in the

D.C. apartment building. The Man said that Lexi got married, moved to a house after the fire, and that she would be missing her life at the apartments now that everyone was living in different places. Lexi's parents were dead. Her husband died in Afghanistan, and she was alone. He said that my having a connection to Beth, well Jenny Agnew, would feel comforting, and since I knew about Spyder McGraw, we could talk about him."

"Do you know Spyder McGraw?" Now that Maria was doing well, Axel leaned on the edge of the desk in front of Maria instead of crouching. —Good thing. He had been making me cross-eyed.

"No, I know enough about him from Beth to fake it, though. And The Man left me pictures of him."

"How did you buy your house on Silver Lake?" Axel asked.

"The Man arranged for it. He put money into an account, and I bought it under the Consuela Hervas name."

"You moved into the house at the end of December. You reached out to Lexi. Did you become her friend?" Dalton's disembodied voice came from behind Axel's head.

"I've never met a more unfriendly person in my life. The Man was getting mad at me. Threatened me. I was trying. I made friends with the people in the neighborhood. I invited my niece Tammy to come over. Tammy and Lexi are nearer to the same age. I thought that would help. It didn't. I lied to The Man, though, and made it seem as if we were getting closer."

"Tell me again, why did the man want you to befriend Lexi? What did he want?" Axel asked.

"He told me nothing. He was always asking about

Spyder. Had I seen him? Did I know where he had gone? Did I know when he would be back from his assignment?"

"What did you say?" Axel asked.

"I lied. I said he would be gone for a long time. He wasn't planning on coming back. I didn't know what else to say. He had me bug Lexi, and then bug her house to listen to her private life."

"What did you find out?" Axel focused on the door. A guard was looking in the window. He nodded at Axel and moved on.

"She washed the first bugs that I planted on her and her boyfriend, Gator. Then one night, I went with another neighbor, Manny and his boys, over to Lexi's for dinner. I wasn't invited. I just went. I had to get inside to put the bugs in her house. I don't think anyone saw me plant them, but Gator discovered them and destroyed them."

"How did Gator know to look for bugs?" Dalton asked.

"I have no idea." Maria shoved her hair back from her forehead. It was damp with sweat and stuck up from her head, making her look crazed.

"You moved away suddenly," Axel said.

"I guessed Gator figured out I was the one who planted the bugs in Lexi's house. He must have planted bugs in mine to understand why I wanted to listen to her. But they were found."

"How did you get the equipment and training to find bugs?" Dalton asked.

"The Man found them when I was out shopping. I came home, tried to turn on the lights, and everything was out." Maria reached under her cuffs and rubbed at her wrists, where red marks had formed. "I could see that the neighbors all had their porch lights on. I thought maybe that a breaker tripped. I went to go fix it, and there was The Man sitting at my kitchen table."

"You said you didn't know what he looked like," Axel reminded her.

"I don't. It was dark. I only saw that someone was there. I recognized his voice, though. He said someone had discovered me somehow. I believed he would go ahead and kill me. I told him that Gator was a paranoid soldier type…he must have that PTSD. I said how it doesn't matter if my house was bugged. No one could have gotten any information from me. Gator had bugs in my landline, my computer, and my walls. It didn't matter, though. I was smart. I was careful. I contacted no one but Tammy. The only thing Gator would have heard was me watching TV."

"Then what happened?" This time it was Dalton pushing the story along.

"The Man wanted to know what information I had. Wanted to know if Lexi and me were friends now. I said how I was getting to know Lexi, that I had had dinner at her house the other day. He knew about the dinner and said that that was good. After he left, I got to thinking. If he knew about the dinner, then he'd know that the bugs got messed up. The game was over. I was afraid if I stuck around, The Man would kill me. I packed up and moved down to Nelson, Florida."

"If The Man was set on killing you, you don't think he would find you in Nelson?" Axel asked patiently.

"Why would he look for me in Nelson?" Maria sounded genuinely confused.

"That's where Julio is imprisoned," Axel said.

"The Man knew me as Consuela Hervas or Maria Rodriguez. When I moved to Florida, I called myself my maiden name Maria Castillo. He wouldn't know to find me under that name. He'd look under Hervas. I was safe using Castillo."

"If he knew everything about you," Axel said, "surely he knew that you flew to Florida every Sunday to see Julio. The Man could watch the prison on visitor days and see if you showed up — or he could have just paid a PI to do it for him. They'd simply follow you home."

Maria's eyes stretched wide. "Oh, I didn't think of that. I guess The Man didn't think of it either, because I'm still breathing." Maria stilled; her focus moved to her knotted fingers. "Not for long, though," she muttered. Maria raised her eyes to meet Axel's gaze. "If you decide not to put the codes into the computer, Brody will only come a few more times. I hope Sylanos will hurry up and get Julio and me out."

"How will Sylanos do that?" Axel asked.

"Sylanos will talk to the bigwig politicos. They make sure that everyone looks the other way when Sylanos wants something done."

"Because?" asked Dalton.

"Sylanos funds them. Funds their yachts, funds their European vacations, funds their political campaigns. So as soon as Sylanos says they should let us go — when the media forgets about Julio — then they will set us free."

"Why didn't Julio play his Sylanos card to stay out of jail?" Axel swung his head around to watch Dalton tap a tired-of-being here pencil on the table, making pinging noises. Was this a technique of some kind? Like Chinese water torture? I sure wished he'd stop already.

"Like I said, Julio went to jail because the wrong guy got involved. Once Julio was part of the system, they had a hard time making it go away because it got media attention. Too many eyes involved. They told him he had to sit in jail, and when things cooled off, then they would get him out."

"That's your whole plan? Wait for Sylanos?" Dalton's tone was derisive.

"Shut up, Dalton," I yelled at the screen.

Maria glared at him.

"When you say politicos, do you know whom you're talking about?" Axel was back to his hypnotic voice, trying to soothe Maria into complacency, like an Indian snake charmer with his flute.

"Different people. No, I don't know each one. I just know from what Julio said. And I know the name Omega."

"Omega. Anything more?"

Maria shrugged and played with folds of her tan prison uniform. "Julio told me that there were actually two groups working to take Sylanos down. There was Omega, and there was Iniquus. Spyder McGraw works for Iniquus, and Lexi's boyfriend, Gator, works for Iniquus. But Omega was never a threat to Sylanos."

"Come again?" Dalton said.

"The politicos got their money from Sylanos to begin with. So, do you see? If Omega took down Sylanos, Sylanos could no longer give money to the politicos. If the politicos had no money, they would not have funding to win their elections. Once they are elected, the politicos order the agencies to hire Omega to do their agency support work. Omega has fat government paychecks because of this chain that starts with Sylanos. Julio says that Omega knows not to bite the hand that feeds them. In this case, it's Sylanos feeding the politicos who in turn feed Omega with contracts. Julio says that's why Sylanos is safe. Omega will make sure of it, and the politicos know this and depend on it."

"Omega was not a threat to Julio. Omega was protecting Julio?" Dalton asked. Axel turned the camera toward Dalton. This piece of information seemed to sharpen Dalton's focus — at the very least, it stopped his pen from pinging and seeding a new migraine behind my right eye.

"This is right. Julio didn't worry about Omega at all. Iniquus was the threat. Iniquus could not be bought with money. And Sylanos had no mole, though he tried to plant Julio."

"What does that mean, Maria?" Axel asked gently.

"Julio tried to get a job up at Iniquus, so he could plant software onto the computer systems. He was not hired. He didn't pass the security clearance. He tried to plant spyware and send viruses, but they were not successful with that, either. Julio said he would like to meet the head of Iniquus IT."

"Was Julio mining for something specific?" Dalton asked.

"Yes. Sylanos wants to take down Spyder McGraw."

A guard unlocked the door, and Dalton asked the direction of the john. Speaking of bathrooms, I needed a break, too. I paused the video. "Intermission," I said, using my walker for balance as I pushed to my feet.

As I waited for my teammates to get back, I scanned my notes from Maria's interrogation. Randy was in the air, headed for California. He had a federal search warrant in his hand. I couldn't wait to go through the data on the computer he would bring back with him — maybe as early as tomorrow.

"Okay. I'm here." Deep stalked through the door, the last one in. He held a peanut butter smoothie out to me. I stared at it with my hands in my lap.

"Come on, Lynx, it'll make a man of you." He wiggled the glass at me.

"Just what every girl wants." I sighed dramatically and reached out.

Deep tapped the computer button as he sat down, and the screen filled with Maria again.

Axel was alone in the room with her. "You said The Man was interested in Spyder. Was he interested in Iniquus, or just Spyder?"

"I don't know." She lifted her shoulders and let them drop despondently.

"But you think The Man was associated with Omega?"

"He had lots of money, and he wasn't concerned about spending it, so it must have come from somewhere where money wasn't an issue. That's not how the agencies work. This must have been a private organization. I figured he was an operative with Omega, and they needed to find out what Spyder knew about Sylanos in order to safeguard their piggy bank, and they needed to find Spyder so they could tap him."

"By tap, you mean…?"

"Kill him." Maria shifted around in her seat.

"And Lexi figured into this how?"

"As bait, as close as I can figure it. The Man was frustrated one day, yelling at me over the phone, and he said something like, 'What's it going to take to get him back? Her funeral? I can arrange that.' He was not a nice man. I was deeply afraid of him." Maria sat silently for a long time. She rubbed her hands through her hair, down her pants, over her stomach. "After he came to my house that time, I figured I should do like Beth did — pack and run — but I only had the money The Man had given me. It wasn't going to last very long. I needed to get Julio out of prison."

As Maria was speaking, Dalton was let back in the door, and he must have heard that last little bit because he said, "So you could get to his stash?"

Maria was quiet for a long minute. "Well, anyway, that's when I thought that Lexi would be a good trade for Julio, and I made my plan. I had to go quick before The Man got to her first. I hired Hector. We took her to Florida. I knew a burro who would fly her to Honduras for not much money."

"The Man got to her first? Or Omega?" Axel asked.

Maria looked like she was really trying. Her eyebrows came together, making deep wrinkles across her brow. Her lips pursed and skewed to the side. "I don't know. Maybe The Man was Omega. Maybe not."

"You kidnapped Lexi and sent her to Tito Alejandro." Axel's voice shifted. The quiet in Axel's voice sounded deadly.

Maria shot a startled glance at Axel. I didn't know if it was from his using the right name for her uncle or that she was reading Axel's mood, too. I bet it was palpable. I wouldn't want to be sitting in a locked room with him at that moment.

Maria's hands came protectively to her throat.

24

I WOKE UP TO STORMY SKIES. I DIDN'T EXPECT LAURA TODAY — some kind of a family obligation. She e-mailed me a list of things she wanted me to accomplish: the treadmill at a slight incline, holding on to the sidebars, weightlifting, stretching. She was ambitious for me.

Chris attached the e-stims to my back. As I lay there with muscles contracting, I could hear the rain pattering on the roof. It was a sleepy kind of day. I had decided to let the case filter through my subconscious. I needed to figure out the next steps.

"You get a break after this cycle." Chris handed me the machine so I could adjust the amount of zap I could stand.

"I wonder what Cookie's making for lunch. I heard him singing in the kitchen this morning. He's in a good mood."

"For once." Chris snorted. "I bet I can guess the menu — peanut butter smoothies."

I wrinkled my nose. "It's a napping kind of day. I think I might crawl into bed after lunch and look in my box."

"What kind of box?" he asked.

"My mail that came in while I was away. They put it all in a box and brought it to me."

He grimaced. "The only mail I get is bills."

"I hope there isn't anything like that in there. I'll go home to a financial mess."

I curled like a slug on my bed. Outside, Thor was in battle mode. He threw bolts of lightning and stomped angry feet, making us mortals feel the full wrath of the god. A lesser house would shake with the concussions in the air. Striker's fortress stood solid.

I rolled over as streaks of lightning reflected in the water. The rain had stopped. This reminded me of the storm over the Isle de la Juventude when I landed on my flight to freedom to refuel. I had used a drug runner's landing strip, far from any population, cut out of a pine forest on the top of a mountain. By the time I landed, the storm raged in full fury. I hunkered down in the back of the plane with the meager supplies that Franco gathered for me and waited. It was a lonely kind of waiting. I had been waiting for weeks and months in prison. You would think that I'd be used to it. It was torturous to be so close to freedom. So close! If the storm hadn't stopped me…

What if the storm hadn't stopped me? I would have flown home to the US. I would have been none-the-wiser about Omega's contract. Frith wouldn't have given Iniquus the heads up. I would be right back in prison, only worse. Rendition with final tap? *Shit.*

While I cursed the storm at the time, and I even cursed

fate for obstructing me, I guessed I should feel gratitude that nature conspired to keep me safe.

Huh. Wasn't *that* a selfish as hell way to reflect on that storm? All those people who suffered. All those people who died. And it actually flashed through my brain that Mother Nature organized herself to save me. How narcissistic was that?

I carefully gathered up the box and placed it on my bed. I concluded that the bravery I needed to confront the contents of that box wasn't so much about me and my brokenhearted homesickness. It was more about my pangs of remorse for causing pain to the people I cared about.

If someone I knew were kidnapped, I'd probably feel horror and anxiety, sadness, powerlessness. It would add layers of emotions, much more jumbled, if someone decided to go with a kidnapper to protect me or mine. Gratitude. Guilt. I'm sure that Sarah woke up every day burdened by this. That was who Sarah was — tenderhearted and kind.

I pulled out Ruby's handprint and pushed the knife memories aside. Ruby was a bliss baby. The Zen-dumpling of all babies. When I missed my husband Angel — engulfed by my loneliness and fears for him — Ruby would sit in my lap, and her calm would wash those awful emotions away.

Given a chance, I would absolutely have put my safety on the line for my Ruby. But it didn't really play out that way. The truth was that I endangered Ruby. Her heart was under the knife so Maria could capture me. If I had not been there, Ruby would never have been threatened. I wasn't a hero here — I was the villain.

I laid the mauve paper to the side, heartsick. Next in the pile were two construction paper art projects that had a lot to do with dried beans. These were from Fletcher and Colin, the Murphy twins. I have known them since they were newborns. I even cooked for their christening. I couldn't quite make out the designs the boys were going for. The glue wasn't doing an exceptional job of holding the weight of the elbow macaroni, and now I had a meal's worth of dried foods on my bed.

There were some letters asking me to continue donating to my charities, The Wounded Warrior Project, SPCA, Smile Train, and JDRF. Striker had noted on each piece the amounts of the donations he had made in my name. Very generous donations. God, I loved him.

Please be safe. Please rescue that family and come home to me.

And that led me to a letter written by my seven-year-old neighbor, Jilly-bean. I started donating to the Juvenile Diabetes Research Foundation after her diagnosis. The whole neighborhood had rallied around her. We walked together at the annual fundraiser, wearing our matching purple t-shirts, with a picture of Jilly messing around with my guitar. I loved that. I loved that whole day. The sense of community and caring. Jilly loved it, too. She was the princess, a small recompense for everything this terrible disease did to her little seven-year-old body.

Jilly wrote to me that she had a new British lab puppy from my friend Cathy at the Millers' Kennel, where Beetle and Bella had got their start. Cathy had trained two dogs to do diabetes alert: one for Jilly, and one for her friend's grandson, Patrick. Jilly said that she had named her puppy Hope. That was a wonderful name for a diabetic alert dog. It was nice that Jilly would feel safer with the dog working for her — that now Jilly-bean had help.

As I read down, Jilly explained that she had named her

puppy Hope because she was thinking of me and was hoping every day that I was okay and that I could come home soon.

That last part started a boo-hoo festival to beat all boo-hoo festivals. I admit I was more than a little out of control. This was like weepy PMS to the tenth power. It felt horrible.

Chris and Deep burst into my room. I waggled the sheet of blue paper with the sparkly fairy at the top toward Deep so he'd know I wasn't injured or in physical pain. He took it from my hand and read it over.

"Yeah," he said. "When we heard that, we all got choked up. Gator needed to go for a run. He was gone near half the day before he came back."

Chris handed me a box of tissues and a glass of water. He stood at the end of my bed, shifting from one foot to the other, not nearly as comfortable around my tears as Deep was.

I blew one last time into my tissue. My emotions back under control. Deep reached over, put the artwork and letters back in the box, closed it up, and moved it to the table. "That's enough for today. It's dinner time."

"What, already?" I glanced at the clock. Sure enough, six on the dot.

Cookie had made a pot roast with roasted root vegetables, sourdough bread, a big green salad, and a bowl of grapes. It was exactly the right thing to eat on a stormy night when the wind wolf howled and bent the pine trees. Nana Kate would have approved.

Since we were running on the solar battery back-up, we didn't have to worry about the electricity going out. At home, I liked it when the lights went out. I liked the sudden jolt from modernity. I would light jar candles and fill the room with the fragrance of sage and lemongrass while I read from a paperback and listened to the storm brew.

I shoveled up a bite of roast and wondered where Striker was with a big sigh.

"I know what you're thinking," Deep said.

I looked over at him and realized my fork was dangling in my fingers. "What's that?" I put the bite into my mouth.

"Striker," he smirked.

"Mmm. It would have been nice if you'd turned psychic a few months ago. Helpful even," I said.

"Doesn't take a psychic to read your mind when you think about Striker." Chris clapped a hand over his mouth, and his eyes got huge with a, "Did I really just talk to my superior that way?" kind of look. Andy laughed behind the screen he made with his napkin.

"You're okay, Chris. I'm not offended or surprised." I looked over at Deep. "Have you heard anything?"

"I was on my way to your room to tell you when I heard the emotional explosion."

"My doctor said it might take a while to regulate my moods after the head trauma."

"Understood. Striker and the team are stateside. Gator said to turn on the national news at 6:30. The family's going to make a statement about their rescue and return — thank all the heroes over at Iniquus." Deep winked.

"Ten minutes." Chris went to turn on the TV. Andy moved my plate to the other side of the table and carried my chair there for me, so I could watch and eat at the same time.

The news reporter's face filled the screen:

"Today came the end of a black-hearted love story, which seems inexplicable. Julio Rodriguez was housed here in the maximum-security facility within Nelson Federal Prison in

Nelson, Florida." The news reporter gestured with an open palm, à la Vanna White, at the low industrial-looking building behind her and walked to the left, so the signage came into view. "Held on terrorism charges — sentenced to life in prison."

The report cut to video of Julio walking shackled into his trial, protesters outside the courthouse, and his lawyer expressing his frustration and inability to mount a proper defense since Julio was unwilling to communicate. The image cut back to the reporter now standing at a three-quarter angle beside a lovely tree, with the leaves framing her brunette hair.

"For six months, Julio's wife, Maria Rodriguez, came to visit him every Sunday, and still Julio never said a word. It turns out that birds of a feather do indeed flock together, and Maria was soon to become a jailbird herself. Maria was being held at Bellington Correctional Facility for Women in Bellington, Florida, not thirty minutes up I75, awaiting her trial on kidnapping and murder charges. Last night, within the same hour, the couple committed suicide, each by hanging themselves in their cell on ripped sheets. The couple had had no communication since last March. Was this a suicide pack? Had they decided prior to their arrests the date and time that they would die? Or was this a miracle as the hearts of two people, deeply in love, spoke through time and space? I guess we will never know the answers to the hows or whys of this great, criminal love story, so reminiscent of Bonnie and Clyde. It was Bonnie who wrote before her death: 'Someday they will go down together: And they will bury them side by side. /To a few it means grief, /To the law it's relief, /But it's death to Bonnie and Clyde.'"

"Oh my god!" I gasped, not only at the news of Maria

and Julio's deaths but the idea that a great love story played out in this reporter's mind.

Randy hunched his shoulders, snickering.

Deep waved at us to be quiet. "Shhh, I want to hear this train wreck."

"Today, it was death to Maria and Julio. This is Michelle Thompson in Nelson, Florida."

"Excellent report, Michelle. Thank you. When we come back, we'll have more breaking news. Stay tuned." A Tide commercial filled the screen. Deep muted the TV.

"When did you guys find out that Julio and Maria were dead?"

"I had no idea. Axel..." Deep's cellphone vibrated. It was Striker. Deep put him on speaker.

"Are you watching the news?" Striker's voice rose from the phone.

"Yeah, man," Deep answered. "Gator told us the family was doing a victory lap on national news. We just turned it on to see what they had to say, and instead, we hear that Julio and Maria are the new Bonnie and Clyde."

Striker snorted. "That woman is nuts. Lynx, they took your queen and rook."

"Yeah, I get that," I said.

"What's Axel saying about Brody?" Striker asked.

"Axel got caught behind a five-car pileup Sunday and missed Brody at the prison. His ATF buddy was incommunicado, so Axel had no backup. We missed the opportunity," Deep said.

My eyes widened. This was the first I heard about this. "A *huge* miss. No more Julio? No more reason for a Brody visit," I said.

"I'll leave Gator down here to find him." Striker didn't

seem to be phased by this piece of bad luck. "Gator has some pals from his Marine days in that area. He'll track Brody down." Confident. I wasn't so sure, but I crossed my fingers under the table to add a little good luck juju to the situation.

"Striker, Gator may be looking for a needle in the wrong haystack. Remember that Maria flew down to Florida every week. Brody could live anywhere."

"Deep, go back and check commercial flights into Orlando, just in case," Striker said. "Brody wasn't being paid by an organization. This was from Maria's pockets. I don't think we need to worry about private planes and municipal airports. Check motel logs. We know he's not staying at Maria's apartment. We had that staked out after Maria's arrest. She was evicted as soon as she missed her first month's payment," Striker said.

"Yes, sir," Deep replied in soldier-mode.

"Why wasn't Brody picked up before all this?" I directed my voice toward where Deep's phone lay on the table.

"Glitch. We had no way of knowing that someone was going in to visit Julio. When we did our research, only Maria showed up on his approved visitation list," Striker admitted.

Hell of a glitch. But to be honest, I would probably have missed it too, since the target was Maria, not Julio. "I think we need to get to Brody before someone else gets to Brody," I said.

"Agreed. We're on it," Striker said.

We? Wait. I wanted Striker to come home. I needed to tell him…

25

THE CLOCK FACE GLOWED TWO AM WHEN BEETLE AND Bella welcomed Striker home, whimpering and clattering around his heels. As I slowly shuffled down the hall, I saw Striker on the ground, wrestling with the dogs. The girls licked at his face as they jumped back and forth over him, trying to find a new spot to kiss.

Now or never, I told myself. I slid-clunked my way into the room. Striker had plenty of time to untangle himself, wipe his face off with his shirt sleeve, and start toward me. But before he could say anything, I yelled, "I LOVE YOU."

Striker stopped mid-stride, threw his head back, and gave a full-throated laugh. He pitched himself forward with his hands on his knees and gasped for air.

My mouth formed a hard, tight line. My eyes narrowed. I waited for the hilarity to calm down. I *hated* it when people laughed at me. "My saying I love you is *not* funny."

"It is if you're standing in my shoes." He put his hands around the front bar of my walker and leaned in to give me a kiss. I moved back so he'd miss and raised my eyebrows in a question mark.

"I've seen that face about a thousand times — a soldier headed into a life or death battle. Were you in your room, psyching yourself up?"

I turned, looked toward my door, and turned back at Striker with chagrin. I worked my mouth open and shut a few times until words formed. "That didn't work out quite the way I had imagined it."

Striker folded me into a hug, my walker compressed between us. "Understood." He kissed the top of my head. "Why don't you try again?"

I nodded into his chest, took a deep breath, and tilted my head back so I could see his eyes. "I love you."

Striker wasn't out and out laughing at me; he was sort of quietly in his mind laughing. I could tell from the merriness that danced flecks of gold over the moss green of his eyes and the tears that clung to his eyelashes.

"My, my, my Miss Lexi, then I guess we'd better get married and make some babies so Deep can be a godfather."

"I guess we probably should." I smacked at him. "Deep's had a conversation with you."

Striker trapped my hand and held it to his heart. "The one that went. 'Lynx is upset about the women you dated because I riled her up by accident, so be ready for trouble when you get home?' Yup."

"I'm sorry I didn't say it before."

"You did." Striker smiled. "Just not in plain words."

I took a deep satisfying breath. "I'm glad you're home."

"Glad to be home. Look at you. You're almost back to your regular weight."

I tugged my t-shirt down and turned slightly to the side. "I have boobies."

"I noticed." Striker grinned with full dimple action.

Heat rose in my cheeks, and I didn't quite know where to look, suddenly embarrassed and self-conscious. I knew my body didn't look anything like it did when we were in Miami when he wanted to make love to me. Now I was… "I swear to God, Striker, if I drink one more darned peanut butter smoothie."

It was a graceless change of direction — too sharp of a turn, and that got Striker laughing again. I amused him. He found me entertaining. I sighed.

"Are you here for a while?" I thumped my way into the living room and eased onto the sofa. Striker sat beside me.

"That depends on how things shake out."

"With Gator?" I asked.

"With you. What are you thinking about all of this?"

"Snow White, oddly enough."

Striker's lips wriggled. "Of course. Anything more?"

"I don't know more. Snow White is the story that keeps bubbling up."

Striker looked at the ceiling, thinking. "You must be Snow White." Striker focused on me; his eyes were merry.

"I guess," I said.

Striker was having trouble keeping a straight face. Laughter danced behind his twitching lips. Yes. Sometimes my way of thinking sounded ridiculous, even to my own ears. And this was definitely one of those times.

"And in this scenario, our team plays what role?" he asked.

"Well, that would make you all the…" Heat rushed to my face.

"Seven dwarves?" Striker asked.

"I guess." I couldn't help but grin at him. "It is apt, though, when you think of it. You found me in the wilderness in distress. You saved me from the witch by hiding me away in your house in the woods. Each day, I see you go whistling off to work." I laughed. It was pretty comical, thinking of these all-American heroes playing the role of Sneezy, Dopey, and Doc in my drama.

Striker reached out and twirled a stray piece of my hair around his finger and gave me a mock-serious look. "So who's the Prince Charming in this story? The one that gets to kiss Snow White awake?"

"Snow White doesn't need a Prince Charming in this story. She figures out there's a poison apple and decides not to take a bite. Prince Charming has to wait for a different story."

Striker actually looked disappointed. He traced his finger over my jawline and down my nose. Looking at me with an artist's eye and pleasure.

"Of course, with the way my life's been going for the last two years, it probably won't take long until one is needed. Why? Did you want to audition for the role?" I asked sweetly, batting my lashes. I loved playing with Striker.

Striker threw back his head and laughed. The good kind of laughing that really meant he loved me.

"Absolutely," he said, and then he showed me how Prince Charming really could bring his princess to life with the mere touch of his lips. I was sorry when he pulled back. The game was over. He was somber again.

"Chica, I never want to kiss you back from death again. Twice I've had to do mouth-to-mouth on you. That's *enough*.

Do you hear me? You stay whole and healthy from this point on. That's an order."

"Yes, sir." I gave him a salute.

"If you don't understand your Snow White metaphor, I guess we have to stick to facts. Fact is, your pieces are falling off the board. Where do you want to go from here?"

"T-Bone, Hector, Maria, and Julio — all dead. I'm almost afraid to play anymore. I don't want to be responsible for more deaths — imprisonment absolutely — death? Not so much."

"You can't take responsibility for any of their deaths." Striker had his hand on my thigh, just where I like it.

"I kind of believed that myself, until I died."

Striker's brows drew together. "More?"

"When I was dead, and you were defibrillating me, some part of me was aware, and that awareness was heading straight to hell. It didn't seem to matter that the people that I've killed were killed for a good reason. I killed them and that damned my soul."

"I think that you were in hell at the plane crash, and what part of you that was aware perceived that. It was hell for me, that's for damned sure." Striker's gaze locked with mine. "If you're going to hell, Chica, I'll be heading there right beside you. I hope that isn't true. I have to believe that intention makes a difference." There was sincerity in the gruffness of Striker's voice.

I felt his love empathically. It was so big that it was almost heavy. Striker full-on is intense. I mentally took a side step. "At any rate, they may be taking my chess pieces, but I'm still going after their king."

Striker tilted his head. "Who's the king?"

"Sylanos," I whispered.

"He's dead, Lynx."

I shook my head. "He doesn't *feel* dead to me."

Striker leaned forward. "Is this your intuition speaking?"

"It's my reasoning. Look at the crimes. If the king went down, there should have been a lapse until his number two stepped in and established his command. That's not what happened. According to the data I've been trolling, things have actually picked up."

"And you're taking this in what direction?"

"Mmm… I could follow the politicos," I said.

"Are they listed in the phone book under that name?"

"No. Sadly, they aren't. Did you see the tapes of Julio and Maria?"

"I did, and I talked to Axel."

"He's very good at the interrogation gig. How did he get to be Dr. Axel White? I assumed he was on our team for demolition."

Striker pulled a throw pillow over and tucked it behind his head as he lounged across the sofa. "That's a hobby. Axel was a pyromaniac as a kid. He spent some time in juvie for blowing shit up. The psychiatrist there gave him some assessments and found out that his IQ was Mensa quality. Somebody made a phone call to someone else. The Marines liked the combination that Axel presented, so they recruited him. The judge agreed to let Axel out of detention if he joined up."

"And he got to blow stuff up for pay." I smiled, remembering Axel's glee when we blew up a briefcase bomb on the Iniquus lawn last fall.

"Blow stuff up and get an education, paid in full."

"When Axel was on my team at the safe house, you

didn't know you'd be blowing anything up. Was he there for me?"

"He was tasked with profiling Wilson. And yes, he kept an eye on your mental health at the same time — checked how you were handling everything."

"Ah." Well, that made sense. "Did he get Wilson right?"

"Axel said the stalker was a fifty-five to a sixty-year-old white male. Hetero — no long-term attachment. Advanced college degree. Organized thinking. Military background. Probably involved with crime prevention in some way."

"Like a CSI or something?"

Striker shrugged.

That was on the opposite end of the spectrum from Wilson. "Hmm," I responded.

"Yeah. That's what Axel thought, too," Striker said.

Beetle snored at our feet. I reached out a foot and rubbed her soft fur.

"With the amazing Dr. Axel plucking at Maria and Julio's brains, did you pick up on something specific?" Striker asked.

"I wondered about the AG, Jim Noble. Maria said Sylanos was funding politicos campaign funds. Noble is up for election in November, and he was playing an odd role in the Julio story."

"We need to keep our eye on the Lexi Sobado ball," Striker said. "What would Noble's election, and its funding, have anything to do with you?"

"It doesn't, I guess. It was just odd." I leaned closer so I could look Striker in the eye.

"Here it comes," he said.

"What's that?"

"Some great synaptic leap." Striker grinned.

I gave him a bemused smile in return. "No." I leaned back to cradle my head against the sofa pillow. "More like a coincidence that caught my eye. Did you get my text with the picture of the lapel pin?"

"Yup." Striker's lids drooped.

"Did you recognize it?"

He yawned loudly. "It's an Assembly pin."

"The federal agent who went to see Julio wore that pin, so did Noble, so did the DA who talked to Hector and told him he would keep Hector safe and make everything go away."

"It sounds like a conspiracy theory." Striker peeked out from barely open lids to look at me and shut them again. "Maybe Annie Henderson could use that as a plotline in her novel."

"You don't find that a little too coincidental?"

Striker rolled over and stood. He reached for my hands and pulled me up beside him. "I think that when you do a little research tomorrow, after Laura leaves, that you'll see it's as significant as all those men wearing gray suits with white shirts." He pulled my walker over and started me down the hall toward my room.

"What are we doing?"

"I'm going to put you to bed so I can cuddle with you. When my being there cramps your back, or I mutter obscenities in my sleep, you're going to elbow me in the ribs. Then I'm going to wander back to my room and sleep for about twenty-four hours straight."

26

"STRIKER, HOW LONG IS GATOR GOING TO BE IN FLORIDA?" I lay on the sofa in the great room with an ice pack on my head, a heating pad on my feet, and an IV cocktail of pain inhibitors and anti-nausea medicines stuck in my vein. Luckily, it was doing the trick; my migraine was easing.

"I nccd to pull him back up in the next day or two." Striker was reading briefs in the chair next to me, being very quiet when he turned the pages.

"I was thinking. I'd like Gator to go check on Pablo's family since he's right there. I'd like to talk to Pablo's parents on the phone."

Striker's phone buzzed on his hip. "I can arrange that." He swiped the screen. "Hey, man, what's the word?" He walked toward the east wing.

"Thank you," I whispered after him, then I closed my eyes and fell asleep.

Striker woke me and hauled me to my feet. "Babe, that nightmare was intense. Let's walk you around. You can't *do* that." I wondered what "that" was.

I didn't remember having a nightmare.

Striker was using his commander's voice, so I followed his directive and thumped down the hall with his hand gently on my back.

"Who called earlier?" I asked.

"Randy." Striker pushed my IV pole along beside us.

"Oh, good. Is he heading back now?"

"Heading back? Yes. Good? No," Striker said.

"Shit. What happened?" I turned to lean my back against the wall so I could see Striker's face.

"No computer. Four days ago, the CPA's office caught fire and burned down to the ground. Nothing left but the toilets."

"What? Four days ago, it was Monday. That's when Axel was interviewing Julio. I thought from what Maria and Julio were saying, no one knew about the location of the CPA."

"The fire wasn't intentional. There was a grease fire at the diner three doors down, coupled with morning rush hour pile up on the highway that jammed rescue. The fire trucks didn't get there until the block was wiped out."

"Morning rush-hour in California. The fire happened before Axel and Dalton even arrived at the prison for the interrogation. This is nerve-wracking." I paused while the new fiasco sunk in. "But surely, the CPA had offsite backup — Carbonite or something. Maybe that —"

Striker shook his head. "This guy wasn't as much detail-oriented as he was an alcoholic. He didn't have a lot of clients left. The guy didn't bother with back up."

I worked hard to stopper the geyser of emotions crashing

to the surface. The effort left me panting and was mostly ineffectual. The doctors said erratic, overwhelming reactions would affect me temporarily. Of course, the doctors had no clue that a torture and kill order hung over my head. These feelings were probably more rational than not. I spoke through a tight jaw. "That seems odd to me."

"Odd or not, I am absolutely sure there was no backup. Randy was thorough."

"Which means?"

"Randy was thorough," Striker said with a hard glint in his eye. "That's all you want to know."

Gator was in place when Franco got home from work. He was on a wire-cam. We watched on the computer as Gator presented pictures of Axel, Randy, and his Iniquus ID. He showed them a picture of me before my prison stay and called me Santa Blanca.

Iniquus files listed Gator as bilingual.

If someone were to ask him, Gator would say he spoke three languages: American, back bayou, and Spanish. I would say that Gator seasoned his Spanish so heavily with Creole spices that it was almost unintelligible.

Gator dialed my safe phone and put a very confused Elicia on the line.

"*Hola Elicia ¿Cómo estás?*" I asked.

Elicia spoke no English. I learned my Spanish from Abuela Rosa. I flavored my own accent with the aromas of Puerto Rico and spoke very differently from Elicia. Even some of the Honduran vocabulary she used was different. We struggled along together. Gator had her on speakerphone.

"Elicia, Pablo is doing well?"

"Beautifully. Thank you so much. You are an angel—a saint. We pray for you every day. My mother says a rosary for you."

"Thank you. Your prayers have served me well. For the moment, I'm safe, too. Some bad men are looking for me. They are the same people who put me in prison. Elicia, I need your help to try to figure out who they are."

"Oh, no. I can't help you with that. I have no idea why you were there."

"There was a man who acted like he was in charge when I arrived. He was tall with a thick gray mustache. Do you know who he is?"

"Sr. Alejandro Castillo. He is the man who runs the prison. He lives in the big house outside of the gates."

"Yes, I saw it. Was he a good boss? What kind of person was he?"

"He did not speak with me. He was a very rich and important man in our village. Now that I am here in Florida, I see that life outside of our village is different. The houses are huge here in America. Everyone has electricity, clean water, toilets, and food. In our village, Sr. Castillo had all these things all the time. He and his second were the only ones."

"Did you ever meet his niece, Maria Consuela Castillo?"

"No, I don't know this name. Mommy? Mommy, do you know a girl named Maria Consuela Castillo? Yes, Mommy knows her. I'll have my mother speak to you."

"Hello?"

"How do you do, ma'am?"

"Bless you, child. I bless you. Thank you for our new life. Thank you for Pablo's health." The voice that warbled over the phone was soft and warm, like the pink blanket, my mom would wrap around me when I had nightmares as a little girl.

"I'm very happy we could help you, Abuela. I'm trying to find out why I was put in prison near your village. I was wondering about a woman named Maria Consuela Castillo. You knew her?"

"Yes, little Maria. I knew her when she was young. She came to our village from the capital to live with Sr. Castillo after his mother got sick. Maria took care of Senora Castillo."

"How old was Maria then?"

"Let me think. Young. Maybe ten or eleven years old. She was taken out of school. We did not have a school for her. She read books all the time. She was a good girl."

"Is there anything else you remember about Maria? Was Senor Castillo good to her?"

"I don't think he paid any attention to Maria."

"What clsc do you remember, Abuela?"

"Well, Sr. Castillo had a second-in-command at the prison. His house is the smaller one next to Sr. Castillo's. This man, Sr. Tabora, had a daughter named Elizabet. She was a few years older than Maria, but they were best friends and always together until Elizabet left our village."

"Do you know where she went? Why did she leave?" I asked.

"Her father was a harsh man. Cruel. It was his job at the prison to get information from the prisoners. He beat them, sometimes to death. I do not blame Elizabet for wanting to leave. I think maybe, though, that when she left, she found herself in the exact same place she was trying to run from."

"I don't think I understand."

"She married Sr. Sylanos. He was a very hard man, too. They all were — vicious, evil people."

"Is this Amando Sylanos?" I asked.

"Si, si. Sr. Amando Sylanos."

"Did Amando live in your village?"

"No, he brought the prisoners in on the plane. He would stay with Sr. Castillo while he questioned them in prison."

"Did he work for the government? The army?"

"I believe that he worked for his cousin. But this is a very long time ago. When Elicia was a toddler."

"What was the cousin's name?"

Abuela Garcia paused for a moment. "That I do not know."

"Did Elizabet come back to the village after she was married, or would Amando come alone with his prisoners?"

"Sr. Sylanos had a different job. He moved to America. He took Elizabet there to live. Elizabet looked American like her mother and spoke English like her mother. But Elizabet's mother died, and that's when Elizabet took up with Sr. Sylanos. We never saw or heard from her after that. Maria was very lonely. She ran away when her grandmother died. We don't hear about her, either."

Not surprising. "Is there another man who brings the prisoners now?"

"Oh, yes. When we left, yes. He was a terrible person. He beat the prisoners unmercifully. They would scream and scream. Elicia, she hated to work there, but there was no other work near our village. We needed the money to pay for Pablo's doctor."

"What's the man's name who is bringing the prisoners?"

"His name was Sr. Vega."

Vega. I didn't know that name. "And when you left, he was still bringing in new prisoners?"

"He is the one who brought all of the prisoners in on the plane."

"Do you know anything else about him?" I asked, hopefully.

"We all stayed far away from him. He was a devil."

"Do you know Sr. Vega's first name?"

"James," Abuela said with an American pronunciation.

"Was he Latino?"

"No. He was from the US."

"Thank you, Abuela. This has been helpful."

I sat with my phone in my hand. Huh. Beth was Maria's childhood friend. Maria's uncle ran the prison. Maria tucked me away in that prison, either for herself or for someone else. It seemed to me that someone needed to talk to Tio Alejandro.

Striker watched me. When I looked up, I caught his steady gaze.

"I'll get Deep to help me research that prison," I said. "My guess is that no one knows it exists. Striker, all those people, they were in such bad condition. They might have been normal people just like me."

"You consider yourself normal?" he asked.

I squinted my eyes at him by way of reply. "Be serious." This was definitely not the time to play. "If they were kidnapped like me, we *have* to help them."

Striker nodded grimly. "I'm on it. Looks like Axel's heading back to Honduras," he said. "I can't spare Randy right now. I need his skills on a project we're attached to."

He paused. "This isn't reconnaissance. This is a full-blown mission. I'm not going to pull anyone from your detail other than Axel. We'll need him down there for interrogations. I'll get another team from Iniquus. Command's going to have to work the diplomatic end."

I sat there, thinking about all those people down in the Honduran prison suffering in the sweltering heat with no relief. I felt overwhelming sadness welling up inside me. Emotions so big that I didn't know how I could hold them inside of my skin. Before we left Texas, the doctor had suggested meds to try to "flatten my affect a bit." I knew I had to keep handling this on my own. I relied on my feelings and instincts for survival, and hearing about the vicious men attached to the Honduran prison threw me headlong into survival mode.

27

RANDY AND STRIKER HEADED DOWNRANGE THE NEXT DAY, somewhere in the Middle East. Classified. Don't ask. No, they didn't know when they'd be home, and even if they did, that'd be classified, too. I missed them — well, Striker, mostly. I worried.

Last night, I dreamed about IEDs again, like I did when Angel was over there, right before one killed him.

Chris made me take medicine at night now.

He said I kept screaming.

This morning, I was in my usual yoga pants and a tank top, waiting for Laura to arrive at nine. I sipped my breakfast smoothie outside on the patio, where a fluffy white cloud masked the brightness of the morning sun. A nice breeze cooled the air and brought the smell of salt up from the water.

Beetle and Bella splashed around on the beach. Gator threw sticks for them to chase out into the waves, their barks joyously punctuating the air. It was the kind of day that made a great backdrop for fun summer adventures and good times with friends. Yet, I couldn't quiet my humming nerves and tight stomach muscles as I thought about the guys down-range. I would make a terrible SEAL. The men on my team had the clichéd nerves of steel; they thought this was fun and games. The whole team was envious that Command tagged Striker and Randy for duty. I sighed and projected good juju toward my guys out in the god-knows-where desert.

For me, today was more of the same with Laura in the gym. I kept my balance, standing like a flamingo on the BOSU ball. Well, I tried my best, at any rate. I moved against the current in the lap pool. I stretched and lifted.

After Laura put me on the treadmill, walking on an incline for an hour, I had a stitch in my side and a sweat-soaked shirt.

"Your weight isn't moving up anymore." Laura tapped her pen on her graph paper.

I looked down at my shirt. "I think I'm filling out."

"What size bra were you before you lost all the weight?"

"32 DD."

Laura tilted her head to size up my chest. "You have a ways to go. Are you drinking the peanut butter shakes with your meals, like I asked?"

"They were good the first few hundred times. Six times a day is five times too many."

"I have a few more recipes you could try. The peanut butter is the most caloric, though."

I stuck out my tongue. She reached over and turned down the pace from snail speed to sloth speed so I could cool down. "I used to be worried about you staying out in this deserted place all by yourself when your nurses were off-duty, but apparently, you have housemates."

"Yes." Uh oh.

"I saw two of them jogging up the drive yesterday as I was leaving. Very cute. Big!"

"Big, yes. Cute? Laura, I thought you had a new beau."

"I do. It doesn't change my eyesight. Are they military?"

"They were. They're a group of ex-Marines who are developing some kind of project to reintegrate vets when they get back stateside." I climbed down from the machine and stretched.

"That's nice for you," she said.

"How so?" I sent a curious glance her way.

Laura grinned broadly. "I wouldn't mind being in a house of ex-military guys, especially when they look like that."

"Yeah? I don't see them very much. They stay in the east wing, doing their thing. I try to take advantage of the times they hang out in the great room in the evening. It's helping my book. The military has its own vocabulary and cadence to their speech. I try to pick up phrases to color my writing – give my conversations a touch of realism. They'll answer my questions about weapons and tactics. I try not to pester, though."

She pushed the stop button on the treadmill and handed me a towel.

"Mostly, I talk to you, Chris, and Andy." I patted the towel over my face and neck. "Other than that, it's almost like living alone, which is great for me." I stretched my back. "If I don't hole myself away when I'm writing, every-thing and anything becomes a distraction. If you ever go to a writer's house, look in their closets — they're always clean."

"Why's that?" she asked, adjusting my stance and making the stretch I was doing a thousand percent more painful. *Oof.*

"Procrastination," I grunted.

Laura nodded and patted the leather-covered massage table draped in a crisp white sheet. "Up you go."

I lay on my stomach with the e-stim pads polka-dotted across my back. The tens unit zapped me while Laura knitted booties for her soon-to-be-born niece.

"How's your book coming, Annie?" she asked.

"Fits and starts. I try to write two thousand words a day, even if it's crap."

"What do you write?"

"Thrillers. This one's about a power grab plot from within the Pentagon. The military thinks that the three branches of government are too slow of a system. The brass wants all the power for themselves."

"A military coup?"

"Sort of. The military is going to disrupt the government enough that it's not functional, and they have to step in." I was making this up on the spot and hoped it came off as credible.

"How could they do that?"

"They explode the Capitol Building while the President is giving his State of the Union address. Everyone dies." I thought I was probably telling the plot of a Tom Clancy novel.

"Supreme Court, Senate, House members, what a mess. But I thought the military showed up for that." Laura picked a knot from her mint-green yarn.

"Some of those military leaders aren't part of the coup plot and need to be disposed of anyway. The others don't show."

"Wouldn't that look weird? Maybe not at the time, but later, when they were figuring it all out."

"Yeah. I'm still trying to find my way out of that box. Anyway, when the President is giving his speech, they always send a cabinet member into hiding. I'm sending the Secretary of Defense, but she's actually in on the gig."

"She? That makes a good twist."

"Wish I knew where I was going with this. I had it all worked out in my head. Then my head got bashed in."

"Are you having memory issues?" Laura stopped her needles and looked up. I saw concern in her brown eyes.

"More like creativity issues. I remember the gist of the story. Right now, all my characters are cardboard cutouts. I can't seem to breathe any life into them."

"I bet that feels frustrating."

"Like I said, I write my two thousand words a day. Then the next day, I delete most of the previous day's work, and I plug on. You know what, Laura? I'm not feeling very well. I think I need to stop for today."

Laura turned off the e-stim. "What's going on?"

"I feel a migraine coming on. I'm starting to see auras."

"Tell Andy to hook you up to the IV now before it gets a good hold and get some sleep. I'll pack myself up and let myself out. I'll see you tomorrow."

"Thanks."

I slid off the table and delicately made my way back to the west wing. Andy caught my eye when I passed by the kitchen and followed me to my room. On silent feet and without a word, he set up the IV. With the infusion set taped to my arm and the meds flowing down the tubing, Andy shut the blackout screen on the French door and went out.

. . .

Hours later, I walked out into the great room. Chris and Andy were there, playing video games on their computers with earbud cords dangling down. Gator sat at the table doing paperwork, and Cookie moved around in the kitchen as quietly as possible. Everyone looked up when I shuffled in.

"I'm better. Thanks for the silence. I really appreciate it."

"What's your pain level?" Andy asked, walking toward me.

"Two? Pretty much no pain. A little double vision and a sticky tongue, probably the aftermath of your joy juice."

I reached past Cookie to get a glass from the kitchen cupboard and moved to set it on the counter. The glass crashed to the floor, splintering into a million pieces against the granite tiles. I had missed the surface by a good six inches. I stood there barefooted amongst the shards for a second, processing my mistake, then everything went black.

28

IT WAS A WEIRD, WEIRD, WEIRD EXPERIENCE TO BE IN ONE place and in one position, and then fast forward in time and become aware again in a completely different place and position. The last thing I remembered was the kitchen at the bay house. I was definitely in a hospital bed now.

I didn't feel bad. I felt like I was waking up from a good night's sleep after taking a Sominex — a little woozy, but otherwise normal. I pressed the call button and waited for a nurse and an explanation. The door opened, and a man came in dressed in mint-green scrubs. He was short, light on the balls of his feet, with a devilish goatee and a big grin—lots of teeth.

"Surprise!" he said with jazz hands. His voice was sing-songy. "I'm Caleb. I'm your nurse on duty. You're probably wondering where you are and what happened."

I nodded my head.

"This is Siena Hospital. The ambulance brought you in yesterday afternoon after you passed out in your kitchen.

Your boyfriend will be back in a minute. He's in the cafeteria getting some breakfast."

"Breakfast?"

Caleb looked at his watch. "It's six A.M."

I wondered who my boyfriend was. Striker should be out of the country. Unless I've completely scrambled my brains and I remembered incorrectly, which was a very distinct possibility.

"Do you know why I blacked out?" I asked.

"I'll let the doctor discuss it with you. Dr. Kloss has your case and is making rounds. He should be in soon."

"What kind of doctor is Kloss?"

"Neurologist." Caleb sort of half-smiled, half-grimaced. I wondered what that meant.

Gator walked in the door with a baseball cap pulled low, an oversized t-shirt that hid his muscles, and thick overnight stubble. I almost didn't recognize him.

"Hi, honey," I said.

"Babe." Gator took my outstretched hand and gave me a big smacking kiss on my lips. "You okay?"

"I'm about to find out. Did the doctor say anything to you?"

"I'm not family until you agree to marry me." He squeezed my hand affectionately. "I guess I'll find out when you do. They've run a lot of tests, though. Laura came by last night to talk to them about your medical history, her work with you, and all."

The door opened again. A bald and diminutive Dr. Kloss walked in with his arm stiffly extended in front of him. He shook my hand in an unnatural and practiced way that told me he didn't like to deal with the whole bedside manner mess; he'd rather stick to the science. I didn't expect warm and fuzzy from him.

He adjusted his glasses and spoke to my file rather than me. "How does your head feel this morning, Ms. Henderson?"

Ah, yes. I was Annie Henderson. "Like I'm a goldfish in a small bowl."

"No pain?"

"None," I said as Gator moved to slouch into a chair in the corner of the room. I wondered what I was supposed to be calling him.

"Good, good." Dr. Kloss let his focus move to my knees. "So we ran some tests. We did an EEG and an MRI on you when you came in. I was concerned about swelling. Your test results indicate that you have a lot of fluid built up around your brain. That is probably what has been affecting your visual perception and causing your migraines. We have some forms for you to sign." Kloss looked at Caleb, who handed me a clipboard and pen. "I want to do a spinal tap to run some tests, and as a side effect, it should relieve the pressure. After that, we'll see how you're doing. If you still have a buildup of fluids, I will want to put in a shunt. The fluid I pull out is sent to the laboratory to check to make sure it is clear."

Caleb pointed at a line. "Can you see well enough to read this?"

I nodded, scanned down the page, and signed where Caleb had indicated.

"Good," Dr. Kloss said. I found his robotic speech irritating. "I will be back after my rounds. We can do the procedure right here in your room." With that, Kloss turned and left. Caleb gave me an apologetic smile and followed him out.

"Spinal tap. That sounds like fun." Gator moved to the edge of my bed.

"Better than a final tap." I attempted a smile. "This is the joy ride that never stops. Hey, what's your name?"

"Joe King."

I stared at him wide-eyed. "You're joking."

"Yeah, I'm Joe Mama."

"Gator!" I swatted at him.

"Okay, for real, I'm Joe Campbell. See?" Gator reached in his pocket and showed me his Virginia state driver's license.

"Huh. Thorough. Do I have one of those?"

Gator picked up a pocketbook I had never seen before. He pulled out a wallet and showed me that indeed I had a whole little life in there — credit cards, insurance cards, driver's license, and a picture of me with Gator. "Where did you get this picture, Gator?"

"We have a stack of them that Deep Photoshopped, in case one of us had to take you in. It would verify that we had an attachment to you."

Caleb came in with my breakfast tray. I wasn't hungry. I pushed the scrambled eggs around on my plate. "I'm so sorry that I put the bay house on the map."

"How do you mean?" Gator watched me play with my food.

"You had to call 9-1-1 and have an ambulance sent out," I said.

"No, we used the one in the garage. Chris and Andy pulled on their EMT jumpsuits, and I followed in the pickup truck."

"Are you kidding me? Striker has a freaking rescue squad in his garage?"

"Iniquus has three of them. They make a great cover. Real handy for going into situations and extracting our mark, especially if we have to drug them first." He took a swig from his Styrofoam coffee cup. "Iniquus lent one to Striker in case something like this happened. We could move you and keep your location undercover. We rented an apartment in the next city over, so you have a local address and phone number." Gator pulled out a driver's license and handed it to me. I looked over the information, committed it to memory, and handed it back to him. "Thorough," I said again.

"We try." He turned to put the purse on the counter, then sat back on my bed.

"Nice kiss, by the way."

"Line of duty, ma'am." He winked and gave my leg a pat. "Maybe you should be eating some of that, not just pushing it around on your plate."

"Hey, Joe?" I was interrupted by Caleb coming in with an instrument cart. The sight of the syringes spread across the table made me feel green.

"Whoa," Gator said. "What are you going to do with those gonzo needles?"

Caleb picked up the syringe with a gloved hand. "Dr. Kloss is going to insert this into your lumbar spine, Ms. Henderson, and suction off the fluid. We expect to get several vials, but we only have to place the needle once. You're going to lie on your side in the fetal position and be very still while we do the procedure." Caleb looked over at Gator. "You won't be allowed in here while the doctor is working, Mr. Campbell."

I believed that I detected relief on Gator's face.

Kloss came in, did his thing, and I was going to try to forget the whole experience. After the spinal tap, Kloss let me rest, but he told me I still had an arteriogram yet to go.

"Joe" was back by my side. He had gone down to the hospital gift shop while I was playing pincushion. He came in with an armful of flowers, balloons, some chocolate — always a good thing — my favorite novel, *Pride and Prejudice,* and a bobblehead alligator wearing sunglasses and a smile.

We waited for the test results.

After dinner, Gator got a text from Striker and set up the computer so we could all chat over Skype. Randy and Striker looked like they'd come in from a sandstorm. There were sweat streaks on their faces that made mud rivulets down their cheeks.

"Hey, guys. Been playing in the sandbox?" I asked.

"Something like that." Striker took a cloth and rubbed it over his face.

I cocked my head to the side. "Successful?"

"Mostly. The client still has boots on the ground. Our part is over," Striker said. "I hear you got bored at the bay house, decided to go into town, and do some shopping."

"They have a lovely antiques mall here," I replied.

"Cute. What's really going on? What are the doctors saying?" he asked.

"I'm fine. They think they figured out my migraines and fixed it."

The nurse peeked around the door. "Good news. That was a negative on your arteriogram."

"Great. Thanks." I gave him a wave and the door shut.

"What test was that?" asked Striker.

"It was the craziest thing. Chris told the doctor that when I set my glass on the counter, I missed by about six inches. I looked down to the left at where the glass crashed and passed out. So there's this weird medical problem that trauma patients can develop, something to do with the artery running up the back of the head. It's called vertebra-basilar insufficiency. Have you ever heard of such a thing?"

"Can't say that I have. It didn't come up in SEAL medic training."

"Yeah, well, it seems there are some people who aren't allowed to look down at their left armpit because it makes them blackout."

"Every time?" asked Randy.

"Yup. If the test had come back positive, I would never see my left armpit again except in a reflective surface."

"Glad that's not an issue, Chica. It is kind of funny if you think about it — you're in a fight with a bad guy; he throws a right upper-hook. You look down for the block, and he TKO-ed you without landing a single blow."

"Less bruising that way." I smiled. "Yeah, I was afraid I was going to be the Harriet Tubman of the spy world."

Striker laughed. "That would have made life interesting."

"Is that a client? I don't know that name," Randy said.

"No — sorry, Randy. Tubman was a slave here in America back in the 1700s. She's one of my all-time heroes. When she was a little girl, her owner hit her in the head with a heavy weight. After that, she would fall into a deep sleep just whenever, and no one could wake her up. When she grew up, she escaped from her owner, ran away to the north, and later she made a bunch of trips back down to the south and brought other slaves up to freedom, too. Can you imagine how courageous that woman had to be? I mean, Tubman could have had a bloodhound on her heels, chasing her down, and she'd take an unexpected nap. She was awesome. But I'm not her kind of brave. If I really had that arterial thing going on, it would change a lot of things."

"You couldn't do fieldwork, that's for sure. You'd put the team at risk." Randy reached up and scrubbed a hand over his head, sending sand flying.

"You're right. Command would put me in the Puzzle Room, and I wouldn't get to go out and play anymore."

Randy's hands landed on his hips. "Glad to hear you're okay."

"Thanks, Randy. Me too. And so?"

"So we're headed home. What is that thing?" Striker squinted at the screen.

I had been absentmindedly flicking the alligator, making his head bobble around. It was close to the computer. I pulled it back so Striker could see. "My boyfriend, Joe, brought it to me with these beautiful flowers and the balloons." I gestured with my hand. "He was down in the gift shop, enjoying himself, while I had an elephant's hypodermic stuck in my spine. Least he could do, don't you think?"

"The very least." Striker's voice sounded as dry as the dirt on his uniform. The look he shot me was the same one my dad used when he caught me in a lie of omission — a *huge* sin in our household. I ducked my head and coughed to hide the heat rising to my face and the guilty tears that stung my eyes. My reaction was surely the result of childhood habit; I was just too tired and too provoked to push it to the side. "When can you come home?" I asked when I looked back up.

"There's a carrier heading stateside in an hour. Randy and I are going to catch a shower and hitch a ride. We'll be on the bay tomorrow."

"I hope I beat you back to the house," I said. "I have to wait to hear what the doctor thinks went wrong with my head."

29

AFTER KLOSS RELEASED ME FROM OBSERVATION, MY TEAM waited until dark. Spotting a tail was easiest when they had to use headlights, especially on lonely country roads. We drove over a lot of those roads. Deep and Chris were in the follow-car with extra firepower in case we picked up a shadow.

The house was empty when we got back. Striker still wasn't in the next morning when I got up. I was anxious for him to be home. I decided to put my mind to work on the case, instead of all the things that could have gone wrong between the desert and here.

I liked a good puzzle. I enjoyed it when someone handed me a pile of disparate components and said, "We need the full picture." It was a creative process. It was an intuitive process. Right now, wading through this pile of junk was a pain-in-the-keister process.

The Assembly. The Assembly, on the surface, was a prayer group. A bunch of guys with connections to Capitol Hill who decided that every year everyone with power, in the political sense of the word, should get together with the people with power, in the I-have-a-direct-line-to-God sense of the word, over breakfast. It turned out that it wasn't that simple, and it wasn't that innocent.

The Assembly men — and as far as I could tell, they were all men — thought of themselves in the vein of medieval royalty. Not quite human — closer to divine. They were the chosen ones. The ones that God said could and should rule the Earth. The mundane among us should have rules, regulations, and laws, but the Assembly members were above that. They were above regulation. They believed this. They preached this. Quietly.

Now, I had to admit that I liked having my own set of rules. At Iniquus, they didn't want to make rules an issue for me because they thought it might wither my creative thinking vine. Command let me color outside of the lines when it came to the rule manual. I didn't take advantage of it — well, not too much advantage, not so much that anyone had felt the need to take away my crayons. I stayed in the guest room in Striker's apartment when they barred other women from entering the men's barracks. I wore whatever I pleased while everyone else had a uniform—pretty benign stuff. The Assembly, on the other hand—wowy-kazowy! They did as they pleased. And they got away with it, too.

Members of the Assembly included House representatives, judges, senators, presidents — past and present. Power. It was all about control and manipulation.

One set of rules for us commoners, one set of rules for the Assembly.

Lately, a Nevada state senator and a South Carolina governor, both Assembly members, had their affairs revealed in a media storm. Neither man thought they had done much wrong. The Assembly believes that fidelity is for mortal men (and all women), not for the chosen ones. Now, these guys didn't come right out and say it, but one could easily read between the lines.

A reporter, Bill Kennedy, had somehow copped an invitation to live in one of their Assembly houses. In these houses, the newest generation of the Assembly was trained and brainwashed. His entre was bizarre because the Assembly gains its supremacy through secrecy. They are the undercurrent, the political and financial riptide of our nation. Kennedy spent two years walking in the very expensive, highly polished shoes of a member. He researched, compiled, and wrote his findings.

Almost every library in the US has Kennedy's book on a shelf, and yet most Americans were blind to the Assembly's existence. Though right there on Wikipedia, of all places, it had a comprehensive article that said Assembly members took a required vow of secrecy. Their leaders explained the organization's desire for secrecy was based on biblical reproaches against public displays of good works, and also if they acted publicly, they would not be able to tackle delicate diplomatic missions if they drew public notice.

In major national papers, they reported the long arm of the Assembly, even to countries in Africa like Uganda, where Assembly members had been instrumental in developing laws that would put homosexuals to death. That kind of delicate diplomatic mission didn't sound very Christian to me.

The secrecy component explained why I had never heard of them. Striker had, though. I asked him earlier if he was a member. Turns out Iniquus bans membership to this group.

Command thought the Assembly was antithetical to American ideals and counter to our mission.

My mission this week — along with trying to figure out what the Assembly was all about — had been to see if I could figure out which of the people in my own little saga happened to play on Team Assembly. Kennedy had set up a website where he posted all his documentation, everything he had gathered over the years of research that he synthesized into his book. That's where I spent my time.

I found my federal attorney and DA. I found Noble. Today, four long days into this expedition, I stumbled on a little treasure trove. Jonathan Frith was a member, and so was Judge Wallace. Wallace had signed the warrant that allowed Omega to go after me.

Night fell, and I was giving up on the idea that Striker would get in tonight. This late, if he were here in the States, he would probably go ahead and stay in the city. I watched Gator, who stood in the great room, bouncing tennis balls. Working the girls into a frenzy. "Here you go," he'd say as he rolled two balls down the hall. I pushed myself up against the wall to get out of their way as they galloped past.

"Gator, cut it out. You're going to ruin the floors." I sounded like my mother.

"Nah. Striker knew the girls were gonna be in here. He had everything sealed."

"Have you heard anything from him?" I asked.

Beetle and Bella ran back toward Gator, each with a ball in her mouth. "Striker? Nope." He rolled them again as I thumped my way toward the sofa. The florescent-green tennis balls ricocheted back into the great room. Beetle and Bella did sliding stops and hurtled back toward us.

They each dove for the balls.

The balls on the tips of my walker's legs!

With a lunging tug, Beetle and Bella pulled my walker out from under me. I was falling backward when Gator scooped me up.

He was laughing full out with me in his arms when Striker walked in.

"What's going on?" Striker was *not* laughing.

"I'm done using my walker." I pointed to where Beetle and Bella tugged the balls from the feet. They were wedged on pretty well — it was turning into the ultimate tug-of-war chew toy.

"I'm not even going to ask." Striker's eyes were hard, hands on hips, feet wide. Immovable. "What's the word, Gator? Did your Florida pals find our man?"

"Not even a hair on his chinny chin chin." Gator set me gently on the sofa. "Brody's a ghost, man. My guys have their ears to the ground. I'll get a call if anyone spots him. We have his license plate, and there's a BOLO issued. Hopefully, he's driving around, and some traffic cop will catch sight."

"Better than nothing." Striker picked up his briefcase and tossed it onto the table. "You hear about the Peterson case?"

"Yes, sir. When do we head out?" Gator asked, back in soldier-mode.

"Command is working out logistics. Soon." Striker looked down at my walker, then back at me. "You're okay?"

"Good thing Gator got trained in scoop-and-save at the safe house. Felt like old times," I said.

"I heard you're still working on your conspiracy theory," Striker said.

"I wish Brody would show up, willing to talk. I don't know where else to go but to conspiracy theories. Sylanos, Omega. Sylanos, Omega. Sylanos…why does the Assembly keep popping up?"

"That's a very good question. I sent you some computer files that Command thought might be helpful."

Striker looked tired. I felt a twinge of guilt, though I wasn't sure why. I went over to give him a welcome-home-I-missed-you-loads kind of kiss.

"Thanks for the files." I smiled up at him. "Are you hungry?"

Striker's eyes dilated to black. He held me tight against him. "Starved."

I gave Striker a smile, and Gator made a show of leaving the room.

I snuggled my head against Striker's chest. "You look like you could use some sleep."

"That's for sure." Striker tilted my head up. "Are you trying to send me to bed so you can start looking through the files?" I could tell by the warmth of his eyes that he had taken off his Commander's hat and was wearing something more domestic and comfortable.

I smiled and shrugged. "Judge Wallace is on the Assembly list." I reached out and popped a strawberry in my mouth from the bowl that Cookie had set on the table.

"Everyone's on the Assembly list." Striker bent to kiss me, then sat down on the floor with Beetle and Bella, his long legs stretched out, leaning against the chair. I sat in the chair across from him.

"Not everyone — you're not. I'm not. It's invitation only.

The list is long, but it's prestigious. Not everyone gets to sit at the Assembly table."

"I hear you." The bland look on Striker's face told me that he wasn't convinced that this was meaningful. I sighed. He could be right, but I didn't have any other direction to go. "I did a search on Wallace. He retired two weeks ago. There was a big hoo-hah in the paper about him and his sendoff party at the Smithsonian. Lots of politicos were there," I said.

"Not surprising." Beetle curled her body and put her head on Striker's leg to get her ears scratched.

"If he was the judge who signed my arrest warrant, and now he's retired, someone else is in charge of my file. Maybe even — and I know this is a long shot — someone who isn't in the Assembly."

Striker nodded his head speculatively. "The Assembly idea is an interesting twist. If you're right, that would be the Mount Everest of takedowns. Even you couldn't win that one. Iniquus would be powerless to help."

I stilled as a frisson of cold nerves swept over me. "Wow. That's quite the statement."

Striker rubbed a finger over his bottom lip. "What does your gut tell you?"

"That I've just spent four days down a rabbit hole."

"Funny thing about rabbits: they breed like crazy, and then each one takes off in a different direction."

"I hear you, and I understand. I need to pick one rabbit and chase it down. Otherwise, I'll be running all over the place like a crazy person. Which, by the way, is exactly how this mess makes me feel."

Striker looked at me thoughtfully and pursed his lips. "Let's focus on Wallace for the time being. I'll call Spencer, see if we can't get the new judge to open your file, and let us take a peek."

I held up crossed fingers.

"I have some news. The Honduran project got a green light. Axel's wheels are up."

I grabbed for Striker's wrists in my excitement. "You're kidding me."

"Nope. Maybe Sr. Alejandro Castillo holds the key to your lock."

30

STRIKER WAS BACK AT HEADQUARTERS, REVIEWING logistics with Command and the Honduran consulate. After that, they were going with Iniquus' legal counsel to a "big meeting." They had an appointment with the judge to see why I was a public enemy. I would make a very bad criminal. I felt hugely guilty even though I didn't think I actually did anything wrong.

I walked down to the edge of the bay and sat on the beautiful little beach that Striker had created. The sand was silky white and still hot from a day of ninety-degree heat. It felt good to feel the warmth radiating up underneath me as the cool twilight breeze winged over the water and blew my hair around my face.

I reached back to pull the strands into a ponytail bun and watched my girls playing in the water, barking at the passing fish and birds. They were happy here. I was happy here. Striker made an oasis—a little safety zone in a turbulent world where evil could never find me.

My strength was returning little by little, though the

doctors only signed off on baby weights. My coordination was slower. I wouldn't dare walk out on the mats to spar with someone. But I felt like I was finally making progress. There was a sense of freedom that came from physical power, from feeling capable. Weak as a kitten did not fit well with my personality. Neither did being sequestered. As safe as I was here, I was ready to get this resolved. I wanted to hear a judge's gavel bang, putting the bad guys away for good.

At least today, some good was coming from my prison stay. Axel's squad had moved into place. I had been anxious all day. Agitated. Another tropical storm hit the Honduran coast. We had no satellite feed. Deep monitored the airwaves from the command room in the west wing. Every once in a while, he picked up a sporadic sentence or two. The general vibe was the mission followed along the planned trajectory. I wondered about the inmates, about the guard dogs, and worried.

Command, Striker, and Iniquus lawyers were probably still meeting. My freedom depended on the outcome. I worried about that, too. Judge Talbot opened and reviewed the sealed file from Judge Wallace's court. Judge Talbot needed more information.

Iniquus lawyers, as my posthumous representatives, along with Striker and Spencer, were meeting with FBI lawyers to figure out the charges and the supporting evidence for the warrant. It turned out that Judge Talbot had a niece working for Iniquus as a copy girl. Lucky me. At least with her poking at her uncle, I got some attention. It also didn't hurt that the Iniquus reputation was pristine. It was hard for Talbot to believe that Iniquus would have a rogue agent, and our commanders wouldn't be the first in line to slap on the cuffs to protect their image.

"Lynx." I turned around to see Deep standing on the stairs. He walked over to where I was sitting and held out his hand. "Come on. You've got to go get yourself fixed up."

I looked up at him with expectation.

"Striker called in. They dropped your charges. The whole team is on the sub, heading in for a celebration dinner. Cookie isn't quite sure what's going on, but he understands the word 'party.'"

I reached up to give Deep a hug. "Wow. Oh, wow. I can go home."

Deep put his hands on my shoulders and took a step back. "Don't get your hopes up too high," he said. "Striker says it's still complicated. He'll catch us up to speed tonight."

Crap. I knew it was too good to be true.

I waited on the stairs as the men walked up from the boathouse. I didn't see the sub come in. I didn't even see the water ripple. I only knew they had arrived because I had been standing in the command room, waiting for the warning alarm that picked up something weighing more than twenty pounds passing by the buoy sensors.

When the men walked up the path, they saw me with my hands on my hips, my feet set wide. I was sure that the look on my face read very plainly that I wasn't in a partying mood. "Don't get your hopes up," Deep had said. "It's complicated," Deep had said. Enough was enough already. Honestly!

Striker had a full dimpled grin on his face when he

caught the first glimpse of me and raised his hand in a salute. As he came a little closer and could read my body language, the grin dropped from his face.

That hurt.

I was hurting him, and he didn't deserve it — didn't deserve me. Like toxic waste, my moods clouded the air. Who could live, let alone thrive, under such poisonous conditions? I've been nothing but trouble since the day he took on the Wilson case. At some point, I'd have to pull up my big girl panties and set things right. What that meant frightened me because I knew — and, if I were honest, had known for a long time — the best thing for Striker was that I let him get on with his life, without me.

"Deep told you that we had a win and a caveat," he said as he got closer.

"Deep said not to get my hopes up for a trip home." Tears filled my voice. Life without Striker? I was bereft at the mere thought.

"Come inside, and I'll catch you up." Striker put his hand on my lower back and shepherded me inside, reaching down to ruffle Beetle and Bella's ears on his way to the puzzle room. There, he shut the door. "I understand you're upset. Let me lay everything out, and then we'll see what you want to do about it."

"I'm listening," I said, still choking on the thought of life without Striker.

"Judge Talbot reviewed the sealed files. They didn't follow the normal protocol for obtaining an arrest warrant. This should have gone through a grand jury. It turns out the FBI insisted the warrant be issued. They used an aspect of the Patriot Act to keep it quiet, demanding the case be sealed."

"And Frith didn't know that? Did the FBI give a reason?" I asked.

"Not in the file. The judge contacted the FBI and explained he was taking over most of the cases that Wallace had on his docket. He wanted immediate response about the India R. Sobado case."

"What did I do?"

"Nothing. Not a damned thing. The only file that the FBI has that includes your name is the Wilson case. In that case, it is very clear that you were Travis Wilson's victim, and you killed him in self-defense. The FBI had no reason to issue an arrest warrant, with or without the seal." Striker crossed his arms over his chest, mimicking my stance. His hip leaned into the side of the table.

His gesture was more out of habit; mine was a sign of self-protection. *I'm toxic, Striker, one problem after another. One worry after another. Are you tired of me yet?* Deep said it to me that day when he was showing me around, "You'd be hell-on-wheels to date. I wouldn't date you for a million dollars. I'm not a glutton for punishment." My loving Striker punished him. Oh, God, that thought was so painful I could hardly breathe. Tears shimmered my vision.

"How did a warrant get issued then?" I rasped.

"Chica." His eyes warmed with concern. "You look miserable. Are you in pain?"

All I wanted to do at that moment was crawl into the corner and sob. When you love someone, they're supposed to feel joy, not constant anxiety. "My brain's misfiring. I swear, I'm fine. Do you know anything about the warrant and how it was issued?"

"They can't tell, and Wallace says he has no recollection of that case ever coming before him."

"Wallace is an Assembly member," I said.

"Lynx, powerful people populate the Assembly."

I paused as the phrase ran through my head. "I bet you can't say that three times real fast." I smiled at him and tried to climb down from the emotional cliff I was standing on. I didn't want Striker to feel punished by my bad mood. He was working hard and had been working hard for a long time —all for me.

"Talbot dropped the charges and cleared your name," Striker said. "The FBI followed the trail and found they had signed a high-priority contract with Omega concerning India Sobado. It was a very expensive contract, attached to other work Omega was doing in Afghanistan. The Afghanistan contract is upward of a billion dollars, so this didn't catch the attention of the bean counters. It passed right through the internal audit."

"How did the contract read? Who signed it?" *Relax. Breathe. Listen*, I reminded myself.

"It was exactly what Frith said: extraordinary rendition, final tap. Who signed it? Jenkins."

"Deputy Director Jenkins? He's an Assembly man."

"Lynx." I'd pushed that button one too many times, and Striker was clearly exasperated with me ringing that bell.

"I know. 'Powerful people populate the Assembly.' Go on. Why did he sign it?"

"He says he didn't. It's his signature, according to our forensic computer analysis, but he says it's not possible that it's his signature. When that contract was signed, he was in the Bahamas, celebrating his twenty-fifth anniversary with his wife."

"Forged?"

Striker shrugged. "Can't say. It's under investigation."

"There's no warrant, and Omega's contract is baseless. What's the problem? Why can't I go home?"

"The FBI wants to know what's going on. They contacted Omega and changed the contract. The new orders read that Omega must treat you like a fragile egg and bring you to their headquarters immediately, instead of following through with a rendition order. Under no circumstances was there to be a tap — not a hair on your head should be hurt. They need you whole, and they need you healthy. They're leaving the bounty money in place."

"What bounty?"

Striker's gaze locked on mine. "Two million dollars."

"Two million *what*? That would put me on par with upper echelon Al-Qaeda leaders."

Striker nodded slowly. "Exactly why it bypassed the comptroller for their Afghanistan focus."

"Why don't they rescind the contract and let me be done with it?"

"They are asking you to sit tight and give them a little bit of time to figure this out. They've already lost a lot of money on this. Crimes are obviously being committed. There is a major breach in the judiciary and the agency. Of course, Omega hasn't done anything wrong. They're just complying with their contracted orders. The FBI wants answers. Command had them sign a contract with us, so that Iniquus expenses for your search and rescue were paid in full, that you have proper safeguards in place, and that Iniquus works on the case with FBI cooperatively, which means anything they see, we see. Anything they hear…"

"We hear. Got it." I scratched my fingers through my hair, trying to wake up my brain so I could take this all in. "What if I say no?"

"Then, you go home. Omega picks you up, takes you to Jenkins. Jenkins has to pay the two mill, and we never know why you were a target. The bad guy is still out there, and still after you." Striker reached for my hand. "Chica, there's a reason someone went to these extraordinary lengths. I can't imagine that failure at reaching their goal is an option for them."

I cocked my head to the side. "There's more."

Striker grinned. "Hard to hide anything from you. There is more. Up until this point, the FBI has prevented us from accessing anything related to Frith. My sources couldn't get their hands on either the Wilson or the Patriots United files. Command insisted that total access to everything to do with Frith, and those cases, in particular, be made available to us."

"The FBI agreed to that?" My brows shot up to my hairline. That would break all kinds of protocol.

"Spencer threatened them with a huge lawsuit, where we would ask in courts for everything we were now asking for privately. If that were the case, Command said that you wouldn't cooperate with this new ploy. And you'd want a sizable payout for your suffering. And then their agency could deal with the media frenzy."

"Ah. And so…" I looked over at Striker. His eyes had warmed. His commander stance was falling away. The way he looked at me made me smile despite myself. Striker pulled me into his arms. It was a little sanctuary of calm and safe. I was *so* going to miss this feeling. I gasped and buried my head.

"And so, Chica, we are asking you, pretty please, with sugar and cream on it, to lay low and let the systems run." Striker kissed the top of my head and let me go. "And in the meantime, that briefcase…" Striker nodded toward the bag resting on the table, "...has Frith's employment records. The rest is being encrypted and sent over to Command, who will forward it on to the puzzle room computer."

I went over to the bag, pulled out the files and a large evidence bag. I held it up and sent a questioning look over to Striker.

"Frith left on a sour note. Security escorted him from the building. They removed the food but packaged the rest of his desk drawer contents. You can see there isn't anything of interest there."

I jiggled the contents in the plastic bag to see what it held. "He didn't want this back?"

"It's noted that he did request the items and was denied."

"Denied?" I let the word sit on my tongue. I bet they didn't know.

"I think he really pissed off his commander," Striker smirked.

"I bet he was furious."

"The commander? Yeah."

"No, Frith," I said.

"Because he didn't get back his black plastic comb, Bic pens, and pocket knife?"

I looked back at the contents of the bag and slowly shook my head. "Striker, that isn't a pocket knife. That's a Mesinox flash drive."

"What?" Striker moved over to look into the bag I held out to him.

"There are no blades in this thingy. It's made to look like a multi-tool army knife, but it's really a flash drive." I took the bag back and held it up to the light to see better. "It looks like the company's high-end drive." I set the bag down on the table. "Mesinox has some amazing features. They can automatically encrypt, and they have fingerprint recognized access. More importantly, if it isn't given the right fingerprint, this flash drive can pull enough energy from the port it's plugged into to self-destruct. What do you think Frith's got on there?"

"I don't know. I'm sure the lab can pull a fingerprint off something else in the bag. Maybe the coffee mug. Either way, they can put it in the FireWire bridge in postmortem and pull everything off without it being damaged, even if it's self-destructible. It may take a while. I'll have Command bump this to the front of the queue."

Now that most of my bristles had softened, Striker's lips were soft on mine. Possessive. I laid my head on his chest and breathed in the scent of his aftershave, spicy and warm. I loved him so much. I needed to get this case solved so that Striker wouldn't be forced into this position. Right now, he had no choice but to deal with me since Command made the assignments. I'm sure with a little space and time, Striker would realize I'm not a healthy person to be around. I was a catastrophe. My heart squeezed painfully. I didn't want to walk away even though I knew I needed to, for Striker's sake.

31

AFTER DINNER, THE MEN RETIRED TO THE WEST WING. THEY were still on the clock and working their caseloads. I stood alone under the overhang and watched the glow of the last light shining through the gray clouds as rain danced in the distance — no rainbow, though. The bay swayed with white-capped waves. It was mesmerizing.

I startled when Striker moved up behind me.

"Sorry, I didn't mean to make you jump. You were in Lala Land. Is your head okay?" He wrapped warm arms around me. I leaned back to pillow my head on his chest.

"I was thinking about my dream last night."

"Rats?" Striker asked.

"How'd you guess?" I asked, twisting so I could see his face.

"You have that one a lot."

"Yeah, for a couple of years now."

Striker spun me around, so we were eye-to-eye. "That's curious. Any idea what it's about?"

"I did. I started having the dream after I puzzled the Sylanos case."

"A lot was happening then: Spyder went off the grid, your mom passed away, there was the fire at your apartment, you got married, Travis Wilson was stalking you…"

"Nope. I had the dream before the apartment and Wilson. It started right when Spyder left. I had been working on the Sylanos case. I figured out he was the kingpin of the crime ring I was puzzling. I handed the file over to Spyder, and that night I got the goodbye call from him. He was going off-grid. I was to follow the plan for shutting down his personal life. We knew he'd be gone for a long time."

"You don't think it has to do with Spyder?" he asked.

"That my subconscious considers Spyder a rat for leaving me? Are you kidding?"

"Sorry." He dropped an apology kiss on the top of my head.

"You should be. But the answer is no. I have always equated this dream to Sylanos, which makes no sense since he's dead."

"Maybe someone else that you pinpointed got away?"

"Like Maria or Julio? Dead and dead." I turned to face Striker. "I puzzled the case. I gave the information to Spyder. I thought he gave it to Iniquus, but when I was in the safe house, you asked me if I had helped Spyder on the case. You thought the case was unresolved. You brought me the file, I reconstructed the puzzle, and I showed you what I had discovered. What did you do with that information?"

"I took it to Command."

"Did they act on it? Were there any arrests?" I asked.

"I don't have that information. We took the case back to our client. It was very complicated, as you know. Sylanos had done a very good job, skirting just on the inside of the law. The client wanted to be the one with boots on the ground. They were sending in their own operators. We were involved as support and intelligence. We did the things that would have had the agents bound up in red tape."

"Were we around when Sylanos was shot?" I asked.

"Yes." Striker took my hand and started up toward the house.

"Tell me what happened to him." I patted my leg to call the dogs.

"Sylanos was at a party down in the islands, and some of the guests got out of hand. A fistfight turned into a brawl. Sylanos' bodyguards pulled out their guns — one of them was shooting into the air to get everyone's attention. Someone bashed into the guard, and the gun went wide. He shot Sylanos by accident."

I turned in front of Striker, stopping him just as we got to the door. "Sylanos died on the spot?"

"His guards gathered him up and dumped him in his helicopter to get him to the hospital. He died en route. They took his body back to his complex in Colombia, and they held the funeral there."

"Were there any operators involved at this point? Did anyone see the body?"

"We have photographs. No. No one was eyes on. The last physical contact was at the party. With Sylanos dead, we were released from the contract."

"Wait. It was the client at the party? Iniquus operators weren't at the party?" I asked.

"Correct."

"So this story comes from…?"

"Our client," came his tight-lipped response.

"CIA?"

"Classified."

"Do you refute that?" Normally, it's almost impossible to pick up a "tell" on Striker. But I guessed he wanted me to know because he gave me a lopsided grin. "I can neither confirm nor deny that information."

All right, then CIA officers were with Sylanos at his supposed death.

As the wind whipped up, we moved inside, where we sat together on the couch. The air conditioning felt good after the heat outside. My mind worked to line up the details. Striker sat quietly, giving me the space I needed to put a hypothesis in place.

Finally, I pursed my lips and shook my head. "I'm not buying it. This is what I think happened. The CIA got hungry. They didn't only want Sylanos. They wanted other tentacles from the monster. That's what Spyder was after. That's why you and I got called up on the assignment last Christmas."

I needed to pace. I stood up and walked the short distance from one end of the couch to the other, then back again. Back and forth, back and forth. "It was a behemoth, and Sylanos was only one arm. A massive arm, for sure. I think that besides calling Iniquus in, the CIA put in a shadow detail, and they watched to see where Sylanos would lead them." I paused to look Striker in the eye. "Personally, I think it was a bad decision. Greedy. Sometimes you have to take what you can get. And he's a pretty big get."

I paced again. "I think Sylanos is alive. The party was a whole big set-up, necessitated when somebody at the CIA accidentally showed their hand. Sylanos staged his death, and now he's free to act with impunity."

Striker had scrunched down on the sofa with his head resting on the back cushion, his arms folded nonchalantly across his chest, and his legs spread wide in front of him. "I can't go back to Command with 'Lynx has been dreaming about rats, so Sylanos must be alive.'"

I narrowed my eyes at him. "Of course, you can't." Then I stopped to consider the next step. "I'm sure that someone will make a mistake at some point. It's not easy to pretend you're dead for very long."

Striker angled his head. "I have a feeling that sentence is leading us to a new topic."

I smiled. "Very smart boy. Striker, when Frith approached Iniquus, what name did he call me?

"I don't know. Why?"

"Can you find out?" I asked.

Striker pulled out his phone and punched a number on quick dial. He asked whoever it was on the other line to send over the recording of the first Frith interview. I went back to the window to brood while Striker fetched his computer.

We waited. I tapped an impatient toe. I would lay money on the answer to my question, but I still needed proof. When the file popped into Striker's e-mail, I sat down thigh to thigh with him to watch. I only needed to see the first thirty seconds.

"Striker, he calls me Lexi Sobado."

"This means something to you?"

"Yes. When I solved the puzzle that saved him, I was working for Spyder. I was Alex, no last name. No one knew about me. You didn't even know about me."

"True."

"When I signed on at Iniquus, I used my formal name with my maiden name in the middle. My contracted name is

India Rueben Sobado. That's the name on all my IDs. In the field, my call name is Lynx. All of my bills and public records are India A. Rueben or India R. Sobado as well."

"Yes…"

"I was only Lexi Sobado to my friends. Never professionally. Never publicly. How did he know to call me Lexi?"

I felt the electricity run through Striker. "Shit."

"How he knew me, how he thought I had saved his life, so he owed me. That's confused me since you mentioned it in Texas. I think I need to know more about Frith. He's not feeling very much like a friend to me." I shut the computer lid. "And I need to get back to headquarters. I'll bet he laid that line about Omega surveillance to keep me away, and he wants me kept away for a reason. Did Iniquus find out how Omega could have real-time surveillance on the Iniquus compound?"

"No. And believe me, they used a fine-toothed comb trying to figure it out." He stood up and helped me to my feet, starting me toward the couch.

I stopped and caught his arm. "I want to move to the barracks ASAP."

"This house is safe, Chica. I can keep you safe here. You're making remarkable progress with Laura's help. I'm afraid of undoing that."

"I think Frith wants me to stay away from headquarters. I believe it's because Omega has zero chance of getting to me there. And that as long as I'm not sequestered on Iniquus grounds, I'm vulnerable."

"Let me get this straight. You think Frith played at being your friend so he could gather intel about you from Iniquus? And keep you vulnerable? Why would he even give us a heads up, in that case?"

I shook my head. "I have no idea. Striker, I want to go back to headquarters. I have a lot of puzzling to do. I want to know what Frith's angle is. I'm dead certain he isn't the good guy he makes himself out to be. I don't feel safe here anymore. I have the heebie-jeebies."

"From Omega?" he asked quietly.

"When I think of Omega, I feel greasy sick to my stomach. The heebie-jeebies belong to Frith." As soon as that thought washed through my mind, a wave of nausea hit me, and I leaned forward to vomit. It landed in a puddle between Striker's feet. I stooped with my hands on my knees, trying to regain my equilibrium. Striker pressed his hands to my shoulders to steady me.

I looked down at the mess. "Oh, god. I think that was the last peanut butter smoothie I'll ever be able to drink." I wiped my mouth with the back of my hand and slowly stood up.

"Yeah. Me too," Striker said.

32

Andy won the clean-up-the-puke prize. I had to go back to my room to wash myself off and brush my teeth. I was lying with a cold rag over my forehead, reading a file, when a knock sounded at my door and Striker stuck his head in. "Command wants to talk to you."

"When?"

"Now. Spencer's on Skype."

"Okay, but afterward, I need to show you some puzzle pieces I've put together."

"Roger. Come on." Striker put his hand on the small of my back and marshaled me down the hall. He had a computer set up on the eating table. On the screen, I saw Mr. Spencer swirling a whiskey glass and staring off in the distance.

"Good evening, sir." I pulled his attention to the camera with my voice.

Mr. Spencer looked tired to me — like he'd had a long day that wasn't over yet. He sat quietly for a moment, peering into the screen, then tipped his bourbon down his

290 | FIONA QUINN

throat. "I was prepared for worse," he said. "I saw pictures of you when your team pulled you from that wreck of a plane down in East-by-god-Texas. Death warmed over. You almost look like you again."

"Thank you, sir." I sat stiffly at the end of the table in the great room, feeling small for the moment under the cathedral ceilings and Spencer's gaze.

"Striker and I have been chatting about you. Congratulations, by the way, on getting your face taken off the post office walls. You're no longer a wanted woman. By the law, that is. Someone wants you, though. Bad."

"Yes, sir. Thank you for everything you've done."

Spencer waved his empty glass in the air. "You're an asset, Lynx. We protect our assets. And now we've got someone footing the bills past and present, so we're in it to win it, as my friend Hillary likes to say." Spencer pulled a glass stopper from the cut crystal decanter to the right of him and poured another thumb of amber liquid into his glass. "Well, little lady, Striker told me what all you're working on. Lots of choices and no clear route. Striker says you've been picking up Assembly lines. That name's casting through your various scenarios. The Assembly's not a big fish. It's a Moby Dick. If the Assembly is involved, this mess is going to take a long time to unknot."

I rubbed my palms together under the table. Mr. Spencer didn't usually make me feel nervous. Maybe I was afraid he was going to tell me to leave it alone. That was fine if the Assembly connection turned out to be coincidental. And so far, I hadn't found them with their hands in a criminal cookie jar. Their members seemed to stand in the general area of the cookie jar, jiggling the change in their pockets, whistling a distracted tune while others reached in and took what they wanted. Especially when it came to policy-making and signing government contracts. Extremely lucrative government contracts. On the other hand, leaving the Assembly alone was not so fine if they were the ones writing the script, for all the bad that had been happening to me and mine. "I understand, sir."

"I'm not sure you do. I need you to be discreet as you move forward and not step on any toes. Don't get me wrong. If there are laws being broken, if America's getting smacked around, it's our duty to stop it. And stop it, we will." Mr. Spencer pointed at me with his bourbon in hand. "But Lynx, from what we know of you, you will not go gentle into that good night but will rage, rage against what has come against you."

"Dylan Thomas. Very nice, sir."

He nodded with pursed lips and slid his tongue over his teeth, making a sucking sound. "Yes, well, now you've got the Assembly sitting at the table. You've got Omega sitting across from them."

"Perhaps companionably beside them, sir," I said.

Spencer acknowledged that with a slight lift of his drink. "There's a question mark at the end of the Frith sentence. And another one about Sylanos's health and well-being, which is a shame. I liked the idea of Marcos Sylanos moldering in a grave somewhere. That case has been a thorn in my backside for over a decade now. We would have taken Sylanos into custody when you first solved the puzzle back when we had you tucked away in the safe house, but our client's orders were to watch him and see where he led us."

I leaned forward. "Do you know why, sir?"

"They were trying to implicate some heavy hitter at the Pentagon. My opinion is they should have skimmed the cream off the top and watched the operation to see what happened with management gone. The cartel would have gotten sloppy and been easy pickings. This… it's more complicated than it seemed. And to be honest, it always seemed like the damned Minotaur's labyrinth to me. Soft treads, Lynx."

"Yes, sir."

He raised his glass to me. "And someday, I want you to tell me exactly how you managed to single-handedly escape from a Honduran fucking prison in a hurricane, steal a plane, and make it to Texas. You're an amazing woman. You never cease to fascinate us." He took a sip. "Yup. An awesome asset. We'll do what we can to support you."

"Thank you, sir. Good night."

My screen went black.

"That was merry," I said.

"He's worried. I agree with Spencer. I don't think you fully appreciate the power of the Assembly. I know you've got the idea on paper, but it feels different when you have to dance with them."

"Speaking of which, there was that thing I wanted to show you." I got up and headed back to the Puzzle Room. Striker followed along behind. After digging around in a drawer, I handed two photos to Striker. "That's James Vega."

"Remind me who he is?"

We moved over to sit at the table. "He's the man Abuela Garcia told me inherited the Honduran prison delivery-and-torture job from Amando Sylanos when Amando took another job in the States."

Striker nodded and looked at the photo again. "He doesn't look Latino."

"His family has been in America for generations. He lives in Miami. Guess what?"

"He's an Assembly man." Striker's voice was dry and tight.

"Bingo. Guess what else?"

Striker looked at the next picture of two men in suits at a political dinner. "He knows Attorney General Noble," he said under his breath. "This was a while ago. Vega looks considerably younger."

"This picture was taken at a thousand-dollar a plate fundraising dinner for the 2000 Florida US Senate race. Dithers was on the ballot." I pointed at the photo.

"Did Vega play a political role?"

"He was the attorney general for Florida at the time. Jim Noble was the assistant attorney general. They each gave a speech that night."

Striker gave a low whistle.

"Not only that. Look here." I moved my finger down the photograph to the right corner. There was an empty table. I picked up my magnifying glass and handed it to Striker. All the tables in the picture were so crowded that people could barely get their knees under the cloth, and here was an empty table without so much as a fork out of place. In front of the plates were nametags. I pointed to the tags.

Striker read aloud. "Julio Rodriguez and the next one you can see probably says Maria Rodriguez."

"If these are all Sylanos's people, that's a twelve-thou-sand-dollar donation."

Striker looked at me. "There's more?"

"Yes. On his federal taxes, Vega lists Omega as his employer." I stopped to smile. "Hey, that rhymes."

Striker looked at me like I'd lost my mind. "Clarification. Vega was a politician turned torturer for Omega. He took his victims to Honduras, where he housed them in Alejandro's prison, which we believe belongs to Sylanos."

"Looks that way. Though maybe not in that order. Fact: Vega was attorney general for Florida in 2000. Fact: Abuela Garcia and Elicia both confirmed that this man brought prisoners down to Honduras on a private plane, and he's the one who beat those prisoners. Abuela Garcia said that Vega started the job when Beth married Amando. Beth married Amando eighteen years ago. Vega's two jobs overlapped."

"No shit?" Striker's hands were on his hips, his legs wide apart. Soldier boy. "And he was on the Assembly roll all that time?"

"From the time he won the election for Attorney General. More facts: Vega started listing Omega as his employer only three years ago. Before that time, Vega was a freelance political analyst, making seven figures on paper. Fact: Elicia said that the most recent time she saw Vega had been about a week before the storm before the unidentified men showed up asking questions about the prison and an American woman."

"That means those unidentified men, whom we assumed were looking for you, were someone other than Assembly, Sylanos Cartel, or Omega, or they would have had access to the prison, and would have known that you were there already."

"It's possible they were looking for someone else."

Striker scratched a thumbnail between his eyes. "That doesn't feel right."

"I agree. Think back to when our team searched for my prison. Is there any possibility at all that someone could have picked this up on surveillance prior to Randy and Axel's first trip down to Honduras? Maybe someone sniffed a cell conversation?"

Striker was silent, his fingers laced and resting on his head. Thinking mode. Engaged. He shook his head. "I'm sorry, Chica, I don't remember. It could be that I took a cell call off-campus. Why? What are your thoughts?"

"That someone else was looking for me, picked up on something along the way, and hired some goons to go check it out."

"Which means Axel's on a wild goose chase."

"No. It would mean that Axel is a hero. He's saving hundreds of lives. We won't know until he gets back and can be debriefed whether he helped my situation or not."

33

THE NEXT DAY, DEEP PEEKED INTO MY ROOM, WHERE I LAY on the floor with my sock-covered feet up on the wall, thinking.

"Hey, Lynx? Can you come to the situation room for a minute?"

"What's up?" I slowly swung myself to a sitting position and adjusted my shirt into place.

"Rumblings down in Florida." Deep's eyes glittered with excitement.

"More info?" I asked, reaching for his outstretched hand, letting him pull me to my feet.

"Gator went down to try to lay his hands-on Brody Covington."

"Oh, wow." Deep and I moved as quickly as I could manage back toward the Puzzle Room. I was excited about the possibility of having some more answers.

"B. Henry Covington was picked up last night," Deep said.

I followed Deep into the room and over to the desk. "What have you got?"

"Tape from the arrest. Gator's on the line to talk to you."

"Where is he?" I asked.

"Orlando. He got the phone call around zero three hundred."

I looked at the wall clock as I pulled my chair under me and sat down. It was ten-thirty Sunday morning. On the computer screen, there was a static page from a video. Gator was eating a sandwich in the box in the upper right corner.

"Hey, Gator. Do they have our man?"

"No." Gator spoke past the bite he was chewing.

"No?" Disappointment pulled at the corners of my mouth. "Wrong guy?"

He swallowed and swiped the back of his hand over his lips. "Watch the tape, ma'am. See what you think. They had the guy's ID — my buddy said it looked almost right, hair was different, weight was different. The police haven't booked him, so they don't have height or prints."

I pressed play. The footage was from a police car camera. The timestamp at the bottom said 01:45 this morning. A man was hobbling down an empty city street, repeatedly looking over his shoulder. The police cruiser followed slowly behind him for several blocks. Then the guy stooped to pick up a rock and hurled it toward the patrol car.

With the car's headlights on him, I could see blood dripping from the guy's nose. One eye was swollen shut, his clothes were ripped and dirty, and one arm dangled lifelessly at his side.

The officers got out of the car and moved toward him. The man picked up another rock and threw it. There was little power behind the throw, and the rock landed a few feet in front of him.

"Stay away. Stay away from me," the guy screamed.

"Sir, you're hurt. We're police officers. We want to help."

"Police? No. No. Don't hurt me anymore."

The officers were in view of the camera now. Both of them held up their hands to show they were unarmed. They were circling slowly toward the injured man.

"Sir, we're the good guys. This is Officer Mulhainey. I'm Officer Orloff. We only want to help you. Get you medical attention." The voice coming from the policeman on the left had a placating quality. It didn't work.

"Good? No one is good. No one is safe." The guy didn't sound doped or drunk. He sounded terrified. "I did nothing illegal. You guys already beat me up once tonight. I don't want to die. Don't come any closer to me. HELP! HELP!" The guy's screams were high-pitched. This was not the ranting of someone mentally impaired. This was panic — deep down, gut-wrenching fear. I sat further forward in my chair completely, taken in by the scene.

"Sir, something very bad has happened to you. What happened? Who hurt you?" Mullhainey asked.

"The police did this to me. I was watching TV, having a beer, getting ready to go to bed. BOOM. They broke down my door. They grabbed me." The man was working his way slowly backward with every step the officers made. They were moving farther and farther from their car. The policemen must have realized this. They stopped moving.

"I said, 'Show me your warrant. Why are you here?'" he whimpered, his jaw quavering. "They beat me. 'What's the code? What's the code?' I don't know the code. I don't have the code. Julio's dead. There are no more codes."

He said Julio. This must be Brody.

"These were men in police uniforms?" Orloff asked.

"State. I didn't break the law. They aren't supposed to break my nose!" Brody held something up in his hand. I paused the tape.

"What has he got there, Gator?" I asked.

"I can't see what you're seeing," Gator said.

"He's showing Orloff and Mullhainey something shiny."

Gator leaned in toward the screen. "He pulled off one of the assailants' badges."

"Good for him. Are they tracking it down?" I asked.

"They have the name. Officer Saunders. He was on duty last night. They cain't make radio contact with him or his partner. They got an all-points out for them."

"Two thugs could have hurt the officers and taken their clothes," I said. "But that's a pretty far stretch. They'd have to have the right size team. Takedown two state cops? Brazen, dangerous, and stupid. Nope, I'm betting on rogue officers."

"That's the chatter, ma'am," Gator said.

I pressed play on the video, and Orloff was animated again.

"No, sir. They aren't supposed to hurt you," Orloff said. "We're not going to hurt you. We're going to get you some help."

The man's legs went out from under him. He crumpled to his knees with the one good arm knuckle-down on the road for support. The badge scuttled out in front of him. His injured arm now hung at an improbable angle, a bone tenting his skin in the wrong place. My stomach did a flip. *Gah.*

"You need medical help. Your arm is broken." Orloff took a step forward.

"Please. Please don't hurt me." The guy pulled his shoulder toward his face like a shield. "I don't want to die. I don't want to go to jail. All I did was pick up the code and put it into the computer. I did nothing else. If you put me in jail, CQ2 will kill me, too."

"Why would they kill you?" Orloff asked.

"Why did they kill Maria? Why did they kill Julio? Same night. Same time. Two different prisons. They wanted to show how organized they are, how exact they are."

"Who is 'they'?" This time it was Mullhainey.

"Not only that but the guy from the van. Hector." The injured man panted and swayed from his barely upright position. I thought he was going to pass out from the shock and pain of his injuries. Now he was rambling somewhat incoherently. I strained to make out his words.

"Soap down his throat. Who does that? He wasn't even on CQ2 territory. He was up north. Everyone who touches… shit. Why did I do this? The money wasn't even that good. Noble has no power up north. Who got to Hector? Nowhere to hide. Big. This is big. If you arrest me, they'll kill me, too. I probably won't make it 'til morning."

"Sir, you need medical attention. We want to take you to the hospital. We have an ambulance en route. We're going to get you help," Mullhainey said.

"No. No hospital. They'll get me. You don't understand. They're everywhere. They run everything. There is nowhere I can go that is safe for me. They didn't kill me yet because they think I have the codes. If I had all the codes, why would I go see Julio? They have to think I'm something I'm not. Otherwise, they wouldn't have killed Julio. They must be convinced that it was me, not him. But it was him. I swear it was him. I don't have the codes. I was too low on the totem pole. Julio never even talked to me. Not before prison and not even after, when I went in to memorize the numbers. I did reproduction. I don't do software. I never even met Julio before he was in prison. I swear. I know nothing more than the phone number I get each week."

I could see Orloff shaking his head. None of this meant anything to him. It all sounded like the ravings of a man struck in the head with a nightstick too many times. Hell, I had a clue what all this meant, and it still sounded like gibberish to me.

"You said that it was police officers who beat you?" Orloff asked again.

"Two of them in my apartment." Brody coughed, and blood splattered his shirt.

"How did you get away from them and onto the street?" Orloff asked.

"I shot them. They beat me back toward my bedroom. I had a gun hidden there." The guy was panting his words out like a steam engine trying to gain velocity. "I shot them. They're dead. Everyone who touches this is dead. Dead. Dead. Dead."

Then Brody arched back and took a long gasp of air into his lungs. "They know I know. They know I've seen him alive. When I saw him standing there, I freaked the hell out. I left Miami and hid here — I thought I'd be safe."

Orloff took a step closer and crouched down like Brody. "Who? Who's alive?"

34

"SYLANOS." BRODY'S SHOUTS ECHOED OFF THE APARTMENT buildings. Lights snapped on in the windows. The man gave a soft laugh. "And now that I've told you, you're dead, too." Then he did a face plant.

An ambulance pulled in at the crossroad. Orloff and Mullhainey crouch-walked cautiously over and patted down the injured man. They gave an all-clear sign to the rescue crew, who packaged him up, cuffed him to the gurney, and rolled him away.

"Gator, that's our man. Where's Brody now?" I buzzed with excitement. Alive. He saw Sylanos alive.

"Gone," Gator said.

"Gone?" My eyebrows shot straight up.

"Rescue took him to the hospital. Emergency got him stabilized and put a cast on his arm. When the nurse went in for the routine vitals check, he was gone. The handcuff was still dangling from the bed rail. Opened with a key."

"They got to him." I put my hands on my head and let my breath leave my lungs in a whoosh.

"Looks like it. Sorry," Gator said.

"How'd you get this tape?"

"Marine friend of mine turned cop. He works for Orlando PD. He heard the chatter and went to investigate. He's the one who got hold of the tape for me. Good thing he got it when he did. It went blank right afterward."

"No kidding. Wow." Someone else must have been listening to the chatter, too. "Brody said Sylanos is alive. He's seen him. And he said that Jim Noble ordered CQ2 to kill Maria and Julio. Orloff and Mullhainey are in danger."

"I took care of it," Gator said. "I sent a copy of the film to everyone's inbox. If you work for the city of Orlando, your copy already popped up in your e-mail."

"You're a pretty smart guy, Gator Aid Rochambeau. Was anyone able to trace back to Brody's apartment?"

"Which apartment?" Gator asked.

"More than one?" Deep asked.

"Yeah, he had an apartment in Miami. We went in, but it was abandoned, so I headed to Orlando."

"Can I have the address?"

"I'll text it to you. So Brody has a walk-up here in Orlando. Looks like there were three of them living together. The other two were out partying and missed the show. Came home to yellow police tape." Gator took another bite from his sandwich. I waited for him to swallow.

"What kind of police tape? Who's claiming jurisdiction?"

"Orlando City. One of Brody's neighbors called 9-1-1. Shots fired. Police showed up. Blood smears dragged from the apartment, down the stairs, and over the sidewalk. Spatter patterns and bullet holes on the bedroom walls. Definitely two people hit. Dead? We're not sure. Disappeared? Yup. And only one witness willing to say they saw or heard anything, and they did that on the 1-800 witness tip lines."

"And said what?" I was holding either side of the computer screen in a death grip. I wished I could use it as a portal and be on scene in Orlando.

"Four men hauled two police officers to a van. State uniforms on the downed officers."

"What about the original caller. Did he see anything?"

"The caller decided by that point that what he had heard was a car backfiring and not really gunfire, like he had first supposed."

"I see." I lowered myself back down in my chair.

"Where do we go from here, ma'am?" Gator asked.

"We're not quite back to square one. We are back on the Brody hunt, though. What's on your docket? Can you stay down in Orlando, in case something pops up in the next day or so?"

"I was scheduled to relieve Deep tomorrow. I have meetings at the end of the week in Washington. Iniquus needs the Apache back then."

I was plaiting my hair into a braid, holding a rubber band between my teeth. "Oh. I want to learn to fly an Apache!"

"I'm sure Command can arrange for that when you're back from the dead. We don't need Omega rocket launchers aimed at you, too. Expensive all around."

My lips made a hard line. "Roger that." Though Omega was supposed to treat me like a fragile egg now, they weren't really known for using a delicate hand. They were more your smash-up derby kind of guys. "Gentle" to them probably meant I could still breathe without a ventilator.

Deep leaned over my shoulder so the computer camera

would pick up his face. "I don't need a break, man. You stay there until Headquarters needs you."

"Wilco. I'm back on the scent." Gator popped the last bite of his sub in his mouth and reached out to cut our connection.

That was a lot to take in—a lot to process. I swiveled my seat around to face Deep, sitting rigidly against the hard back. Deep stayed quiet while I thought. I leaned forward. "Review."

"He doesn't have the codes," Deep said.

"He saw Sylanos and said, 'now that I told you, you're dead, too.' I would suppose that to mean that Brody saw Sylanos since Sylanos' 'death' because why else would it matter? I wish I knew for sure that sentence was accurate. But because it's supporting something I want to believe, I need to be careful about assumptions and wait for proof."

"Let's draw out possible scenarios." Deep pushed up and went to the whiteboard.

"The one that seems the most likely from what I heard," I said, "is that Brody worked for the Sylanos cartel. Brody said he was a reproduction guy — he didn't do software."

"That means he was part of the pirating side of the Sylanos shipping triangle," Deep said.

"That would make sense. Julio didn't know Brody's name. Julio knew him as B. Henry Covington from his visitation roster. Julio wouldn't have known who Brody was at the work site if Brody was a worker bee. Maria could have met Brody in the warehouse when she went there to see Julio."

Deep drew a box, labeled it warehouse, and put Julio, Brody, and Maria's names up there.

"Let's assume that Brody worked for Sylanos, and that Maria hired him to go get the codes from Julio," I said.

Deep drew a prison, put Julio in the box, and Brody on the outside.

"Okay," I said. It was good to see this going up on the board. It felt more cohesive to me and less like a flock of thought birds roosting in my head. "Julio's safety depended on the codes going into the computer each Sunday afternoon. And Julio was the hen sitting on the golden egg. Maria didn't know where all their money was hidden. She needed to keep him alive. After Maria sent my prison video and the ransom note, she could no longer pick up the codes. Brody goes each week, and each week he gets his five-hundred-dollar payment."

"Nice little paycheck for an hour's work." Deep drew a dollar sign over Brody.

"No kidding. Okay, next we know that Brody was aware of Julio's death. That was part of the news cycle, so that's not surprising."

Deep picked up a red marker and put an X over Julio's name. "And Brody knew about Maria," he said, and X'd through Maria's name.

"Brody keeps going to his normal work — say, Monday through Friday — because, while five-hundred dollars is nice, it doesn't pay the bills. It's plausible that he didn't know that Sylanos was pirating. Well, just for fun, let's make him innocent in this scenario. Brody goes to seemingly legitimate work on the weekdays, and on weekends, he goes up to Nelson to play his Maria/Julio role. He might think it's slightly weird, but hey, it's five-hundred bucks. No harm, right? He'd do the job."

"Wouldn't people know?" Deep asked.

"Maria might have told him that if he said anything, then the gig was over. I don't know. He must have realized this part was nefarious. I'm sure he wouldn't be telling everyone. Maybe he just told the wrong someone."

"The connection was made. They knew where to find him." Deep reached up to circle Brody's name and draw a big fat question mark over it.

"The attack came on Saturday night." I tapped my pen against my jaw. "It makes sense, and yet it doesn't make sense. Someone knew there were codes. The men wearing the uniforms — and let's assume they really were officers for the moment — asked for the codes. They might even know they needed them by Sunday. They hurt Brody. It was torture-hurting him, though. They weren't trying to kill him. Yet."

"How do you figure?" Deep asked.

"If they wanted him dead, it would go something like this: officers break down a door on a suspect. They have their service weapons drawn. They shoot the guy because he was armed and threatening. Done," I said. I laced my fingers behind my back and started pacing. I was a kinesthetic thinker, and movement helped me sift through the debris.

"They needed the codes to keep the information from leaking." Deep followed me with his gaze. "Do you think they would have shot him after he gave them up?"

"I guess that depended on what he gave up when. He didn't have anything real to give them. If he convinced them of that, he'd be dead. I guess he could have made up a string of random numbers and bought himself a few hours. Of course, Brody probably had no idea that the codes were meaningless since the CPA's office burned down. He might not even know what would happen if the codes didn't go in," I said.

I paced some more, then stood looking at the board. "So torture — injuries to the eye. Broken nose. When that didn't work, a step up in pain, strikes to the leg — bad enough that it made him stagger. Broken arm. These weren't professional techniques. Too much noise. Too much show. The more I think about it, the more I'm convinced the two guys in uniform really were police and not criminally professional."

Deep drew two stick figures lying on the ground with tongues hanging out, blood puddles under them, and X's for eyes.

"We don't know they're dead," I said.

"Why officers?" Deep erased the X's and drew googly eyes instead.

"Whoever ordered them in would know that an officer in his uniform can do what a citizen cannot. It would make breaking down the door okay. Cops are already there, no reason to call 911. A scuffle and yelling? Expected. They could even drag Brody out and away, and it would be all in the line of duty."

"Brody won. He shot them." Deep added some spurting blood coming out of the stick figures' chest wounds.

"Score one for the little man. Then he runs. He thinks Jim Noble called the hit on Maria and Julio via CQ2. How could he know? Why would he have any contact with Jim Noble or know about his gang ties? That's really baffling." I pulled out a chair and sat down, only to pop right back up again for more pacing.

"Brody probably thought Noble ordered the beating, which makes sense," Deep said. "Noble would know the state officers, and if he was, in fact, criminally minded, he would have a few bad eggs in his pocket." Deep drew lines connecting Noble, Brody, Maria, and Julio. And wrote CQ2 on the lines between Noble, Maria, and Julio. The whiteboard was starting to look as jumbled and unintelligible as the whole crime sequence.

"Now what?" he asked.

"Hector. Brody knew Hector's name. How weird is that? And he knew that Hector was dead. His death didn't make media. Hector was from D.C. Before that, he was El Primo in New York. Write these questions down for me, Deep. One: how did Maria meet Hector to hire him? Two: how did Brody know him by name? Three: why was Brody keeping tabs on Hector?"

Deep scribbled the words onto the corner of the board. "All good questions," he said.

35

TOMORROW, I'D BE MOVING. I WAS GLAD TO BE HEADED back to Headquarters, though I knew I'd be under lock and key. I loved Striker's bay house, but I was beginning to feel like a butterfly who had done her metamorphosis and was ready to chew her way free of the cocoon so she could fly. I was waiting for Laura and had been wasting time this morning, looking through the old pictures that Biji had sent to me for my birthday gift, laughing at myself in my yellow Playtex gloves. Deep was right; I was a weird kid.

I sat on the floor in my room with the album open in my lap and shock on my face. I had made my way to the very last page…a newspaper clipping from the night of the fire.

Emotions. So many emotions from that night. Confusing. Conflicting.

The photographer snapped the picture in front of the Safeway across the street from my apartment building. I was in the left-hand corner of the picture, dressed in my flannel pj's, with the two boxes I'd saved from my apartment sitting next to my frozen bare feet. My eyes locked onto Angel's. It was the very second that we fell in love. He had his hands under my elbows, holding me steady as I swayed from the jolt of this new feeling. Angel. That was truly a lifetime ago. I was innocent then.

In the center of the picture, flames climbed the walls of the three-story building. Fire fell from the sky along the street, where the hook and ladder trucks and EMTs had parked. I lost my way of life that night. Almost everything I owned. My tightly knit community…

I recognized one of my fellow rescue volunteers checking on old Mr. Grady. He had a heart attack that night.

But the image that caused my shock was a car on the right-hand side of the photo, obscured by the distance. My mind could be playing tricks… I squinted over the page. I could swear that that was Tom Matsy climbing into the front seat of a sedan and that the man holding open the door was… God yes, I swear it was Travis Wilson. The guy who had stalked and attacked me. He was there at the fire…with Matsy. My brain stuttered.

I picked up the album and went to the west wing to search for Deep. I found him in the puzzle room. "Are you busy?" I asked, with as much nonchalance as I could muster.

Deep scrubbed a hand over his head and stretched. "I'd appreciate a reason to set this aside. I'm going cross-eyed."

I moved forward and put the album in Deep's lap. "Am I going crazy, or do you see what I see?"

Deep looked down at the photo. "That's Angel with you?" He pointed.

"Yes." I was barely breathing.

"This is your apartment building on fire?" He looked up

at me, and I nodded my head. I was in a holding pattern — no words formulated on my tongue.

"What is it you want me to see, Lynx?"

I pointed at the cars parked on the right. Deep leaned down over the photo. "Holy cazoli." He reached over to the lighted magnifying glass and swung it around on its metal arm. Deep gazed through the lens. "I'll be damned, it's Travis Wilson."

"That's what I thought."

"Who's that with him?"

"Tom Matsy. The fire originated in Mr. Matsy's apartment. We were told that he was drunk, fell asleep with a lit cigarette, and caught his bed on fire."

Deep's brow creased. "A cigarette wouldn't start a fire like that one. It would melt the mattress and make a lot of smoke."

"Right. There was also a bottle of Jack Daniels involved," I whispered.

"Still."

"Exactly. Still…" I cleared my throat. "I have a few questions."

Deep grinned. "I bet you do. Where should we start?" he asked, rubbing his hands together.

"Can you get a better image of the license plate? We could trace that. Let's put a line out on Matsy. I want to know why he's with Wilson."

Deep took the newspaper clip from its protective sleeve and put it on the scanner plate.

"All of us neighbors were sort of cast to the wind after the fire. I don't remember hearing about where Mr. Matsy went. I guess I figured he was keeping his head down in shame and not talking to folks."

314 | FIONA QUINN

I sat back while Deep punched the keys on his computer. A close-up of that portion of the photo came onto the screen, the extra pixels filled in by the computer program.

"Son of a gun." I leaned in.

"What are you seeing, Lynx?"

"That's Frith." I pointed at the man standing with his hand on his open car door, climbing in. I followed Frith's line of sight. He was focused on Matsy and Wilson.

Deep moved his cursor around the screen and punched a few keys, and Frith, bundled in his winter wear, came into better view. Frith's car had government plates. Deep played with the picture again.

"Here we go. Wilson's plate is X94 NB87. Hang on." Deep pulled up one of our search programs. "Yup. This car is registered with Potomac Auto Rental. Their address is north of here. Let's see who's in place." Deep tapped the keyboard again, then pulled out his cell. "It's Deep. Are you having doughnuts, man?"

Jack's voice came over the speaker. "I wish. I had to run over here to check on a possible witness. I came up empty-handed. You need something?"

"I need you to follow up on a car rental. I'm sending you a file with the particulars."

"Wilco. I'm heading out now," Jack said.

Deep put an explanation and all the known data — date, plate, etc. into a file and sent it over to Jack, and then started a search on Matsy. An alarm sounded two short blasts. Deep looked over at a monitor. "Laura's here for your torture session."

"Poop. I'd rather do this." I scowled.

Deep quirked his lips. "I bet you'd rather eat raw snake."

"I hear it puts hair on your chest — makes a man out of you."

"You'd have to ask Gator about that. I cook my snake," Deep said.

"Nancy-boy."

Deep raised his eyebrows. "You want to go there?"

"Not at all. I just don't want to go there." I pointed to the door. Deep laughed as I hefted myself out of my seat and went out to the great room to wait for Laura. Thank goodness she'd be gone by lunch.

"Lynx, today I'm your best friend." Deep smiled at me as I reemerged from the gym soaked in sweat.

"Yeah? What have you got?"

"I have news about your neighbor, Tom Matsy. The night of the fire, he got dead."

"Shit. You're kidding me." I swabbed at my face with a hand towel. "This is getting ridiculous."

"I've got more. Matsy drove his rental car to a motel in South Jersey. Wilson and Matsy went in to register. Wilson walked Matsy to his room and left him at the door. Wilson got in a different car and drove away."

"Wilson didn't kill him?" I asked.

"Nope."

"Who was the room registered to?"

"Matsy. And to answer your next question, we knew that Wilson didn't kill Matsy because Matsy left his room to buy cigarettes at the vending machine near the stairwell at the other end of the outdoor walkway. It's on security camera."

"That was fast. How'd you get hold of it?" I went around to sit on a chair.

Deep leaned back with his hands laced behind his head. "Jack was already north of the city for the car rental. Turns out they had to tow Matsy's car back from a motel up the road. Jack paid the motel a visit. The motel manager was very cooperative."

I smirked. "Jack greased his palm, huh?"

"The guy's probably enjoying a bottle of good scotch and a fat-bottomed girl as we speak."

"Can I see the video?" I asked, chomping at the bit.

"Jack's getting a copy. The motel's system was VHS. He'll have a file made by dinner tonight. I watched it on the cam-wire when Jack did."

"You saw Matsy walk back into his room?"

"More than that. I saw Frith heading into Matsy's room, and then Matsy heading back with his cigs."

"Frith?" God, what was the connection? How did these two players get their paths to cross?

"Frith was bundled up in a hat and scarf, but I recognized his get-up from the fire picture. He was wearing gloves and carrying a black bag."

"Holy cow. He killed Matsy?" My eyebrows stretched up as if they wanted to jump right off my head.

"Matsy's autopsy report reads opiate overdose, accidental."

"You've been busy."

Deep gave me a satisfied grin.

"But why, Deep? That is all so weird." I let my brain churn for a moment. "Let's follow the obvious line." I leaned back in my chair and stared at the ceiling. "Frith was FBI at the time of the fire. He was working on some cases with

Iniquus and the ATF. Do you think his target was Wilson or Matsy?"

Deep offered up a shrug.

"Wilson could have been at the fire because he had targeted me already and was there on surveillance. But why would Wilson hook up with Matsy? Why would Frith go into Matsy's motel room? I'm guessing Frith followed them, went into the open motel room to do a quick shake, and see if there was anything interesting there."

"Like what?"

"The fire originated in Matsy's apartment. Fire first, then an explosion. Perhaps Frith thought — and maybe rightly so — that Matsy and Wilson were cooking a bomb, and it got away from them. Did Frith think that Matsy or Wilson was involved in a criminal plot? Huh. Matsy really didn't seem the type. I didn't know him very well, though. He had only lived in the apartments for a couple of months."

"That would make sense. Frith slipped in to look around, taking advantage of the open door. Matsy went in, did some recreational drugs, had a bad trip with no support, so he died."

"What's the timeline on the tape of Frith leaving?"

"Frith goes in, Matsy smokes a cig, Matsy goes in, light from the TV can be seen, thirty-minute lapse, Frith sneaks out, walks head down to his car, and is gone."

"What car?" I asked.

"Agency car."

"Same as at the fire?" I reached for a pencil, drew some bubbles on a sheet of paper, and layered in thought prompts.

"Yup," Deep confirmed.

I stared at the paper, trying to reason out what could explain this chain. "So Matsy gets in before Frith can get out. He hides behind the curtains, lets Matsy settle, waits for him to go to the bathroom or whatever, and sneaks out."

"That seems reasonable." Deep reached for my paper and read it over.

I gave him a minute. "Do we have a time of death?"

"No. And here's a weird little detail: the manager said that Matsy booked the room for the week, and he specifically said he didn't want maid service."

"No maids, so no one to find the body? Innocent track: Matsy didn't want to be disturbed, maybe he was afraid of publicity from the fire. Not so innocent track: Wilson helped with those no-maid arrangements, gave Matsy some bad dope, knowing Matsy would die so Wilson couldn't be named in interrogation. Wilson wanted to make sure that he was long gone, and the body was in bad shape when it was found."

Deep snorted. "Bad shape, that's an understatement."

"How so?" I asked.

"It didn't take the week to find the body. The heat was on full blast, and the body could be smelled in the lobby."

"Oh, gross."

Deep snorted. "I'm glad it wasn't my job to pour him into a bag. What's next?" He laid my paper back in front of me.

"I want to see the files from Frith's work on the FBI side and see what Iniquus has from our side. I wonder if Tom Matsy's name is going to show up in either. Hell of a coincidence that Wilson would know Matsy *and* be after me."

"Could Travis Wilson have put you on his radar screen at the fire?"

"I imagine he was busy with Matsy, and I wasn't a random tag. Wilson was after me because I'm like a daughter to Spyder. I was the sacrificial virgin for our agency. The other women that Wilson stalked were either the wife or daughter of an agency head. Each agency on Wilson's list lost one woman, which gives me another interesting ping."

"What's that?"

"Frith is the agent who was handling the murder of the girl who died for the FBI. He was the one that hired Iniquus and got you all involved. Could he have picked up on Wilson at that point and been tracking him for the murders instead of for his anti-government doings? Hmm. Hmm. Hmm."

"I have one for you."

"Shoot," I said.

"What if Wilson knew Matsy from the group Frith was watching? What was it called?"

"Patriots United."

Deep shook his head. "That's a stupid name. Okay, what if Wilson and Matsy knew each other from Patriots United? Wilson was doing his bit for God and country by trying to demoralize the various agencies by making their loved ones the target of his insanity. Wilson was over at Matsy's and happened to see and recognized Spyder. He figured out which apartment he came from, figured out who lived there, figured out from watching you two together that Spyder loved you, and boom, he's got you in his sights."

Shivers went up and down my spine. It took me a minute to process. "Deep, that timeline works. I got my first letter at the Red Cross housing the day I married Angel. That was three weeks after the fire. The fire was at the end of January. Spyder went off-grid in September; Matsy had moved in by then. I remember him at our apartment at the Labor Day picnic at the pool. Yes. It was sometime in late July or early August that he moved in. Spyder and I were working nonstop on the Sylanos case at that point. Matsy and Wilson would have had lots of opportunities to spot us. Deep?"

"Yeah, Lynx?"

"You're my new best friend."

"Don't I know it?"

And that's when all hell broke loose.

36

THE SPEAKERS' HIGH-PITCHED WAIL HERALDED AN INTRUSION into our infrared protected bubble. I scanned the monitor, expecting to find more turkey buzzards swooping in to eat whatever had died in the woods at the entrance of the peninsula. Instead, the cameras focused on two Little Bird helo's, rising ominously over the rock cliff that protected the bayside of our compound. Surely, if our team was coming in, they would have given Deep a heads-up. I tapped the computer button, and the cameras locked on the moving target, zooming the picture in tight. Gunners, in black BDUs, perched on the runners with their M-4s nestled into the flesh of their cheeks, their eyes scanning through the telescopic lenses.

Deep jumped to his feet, his chair toppling behind him. Over the intercom system, he broadcast the attack. A Blackhawk UH60 rose into sight.

I tried to deflect Deep's hand as it slammed the panic button. "Andy and Beetle are outside," I yelled.

Deep easily averted my move, and the mechanics of

Striker's house ground the bulletproof shutters and locks into place. I watched on the monitor as Andy, dressed in full security gear, took a knee on the back walkway. Beetle dashed from the tree line to flank him, salivating as her teeth chomped at the air. Andy pointed his rifle skyward. Two blasts sounded nanoseconds apart. Andy lay prone and unmoving on the slate. Beetle followed her training and covered his body with hers. A man swung lifelessly from his harness as one of the Little Birds bugged out.

Deep yelled past the helo uproar into his comms, "Man down. Op for fast rope insertion, targeting roof." He grabbed his Glock from the desk in front of him. I turned my attention to his monitor. Men, with three-hole balaclavas hiding their faces, slid from the massive Blackhawk onto the roof's landing pad. The sound from the engine and rotors was deafening, but Striker's house stood solid against the wind and vibrations.

At the door, Deep turned and pointed a directive finger at me. "Get to the safe room and shut her down. Use the sat phone to get Iniquus here, stat."

That's when the explosion ripped the roof hatch open, and I flew from my body.

When I've walked behind the Veil in the past, it was a cognitive decision on my part to separate body and consciousness, sending myself out at a distance to seek information. This time, I hadn't had time to think, to plan. The tether securing my awareness to flesh and bone had become weak to ineffectual during my time in prison. Astral projection had been a daily habit during the time Maria sequestered me in the eight-by-eight hellhole. I needed my body to function — to follow Deep's directives and contact

Iniquus — but instead, my corporeal self collapsed in a heap on the floor, and my awareness broke free to fasten to Blaze.

The explosion had knocked Blaze on his ass.

Now, he scrambled to his feet in the dorm room.

Barefooted and dressed in black boxers and grey T-shirt, a bandolier draped over his shoulder. He peeked past the door frame, squinting through the smoke and particulates that filled the air at the hole made by the blast. Coughing hard to rid his lungs of the debris, he pulled the neck of his T-shirt up to cover his mouth and nose. His rifle snugged firmly against his shoulder. As the first bad guy dropped into the house, Blaze squeezed the trigger for a triple tap. Two to center mass. One to the head. Then he dove to the right to reach the staircase. Hunkered against the wall, he covered his ears and squeezed his eyes tightly shut as a flashbang dropped into the hallway. Blaze bounded down the stairs, turning and pushing Deep, who barreled toward the enemy.

They leaped down the stairs in two jumps. Blaze threw himself into the right-hand corridor, the one that led to the offices where I had left my body. Deep covered left — where I should be right now — whole and protected in the safe room. Blaze pressed his back against the wall and sucked air into his lungs, steadying his nerves. I registered the cold and the solidity behind us, but Blaze's attention was sharply focused on absorbing information, scanning the corridor, and forming a plan.

Cookie stuck his nose around the corner, and Blaze waved him back. I could hear Bella growling viciously from the gym, scraping at the door. I must have shut the door on her when she fell asleep, keeping me company during my workout. Shit. I had to get to her and get her back to the safe room. I willed myself back to my body but stayed solidly attached to Blaze.

Deep took a knee, his 9mm at the ready. Blaze's rifle rested at a forty-five-degree angle aimed at the floor. There was time for one more breath before a four-tango stack stormed down the stairs, moving into Blaze's line of vision. Deep aimed a head shot, then swung into a doorway out of the way of a follow-up shot from the enemy, as the first in line went down.

My guys were grossly outnumbered, out supplied, and out dressed. I hoped Cookie and Chris got to the closets in my room and strapped on combat gear and did what I was supposed to be doing, getting Iniquus in the loop and deployed. I needed to get back in my body and get help. I wouldn't be much in the way of hand-to-hand, but surely, I could do something. Again, I tried to will myself away from Blaze and back toward my physical form. But my spirit clung to Blaze like a nearly drowned swimmer who had reached a buoy.

The tangos vaulted over their teammate's body. Two turned in Deep's direction. The massive one sprang at Blaze.

With the reflexes trained into a SEAL, Blaze parried the barrel of his weapon to the side with his left hand. Pressing his rifle flat against the bad guy's body, Blaze squeezed the trigger in three staccato bursts while pushing his elbows outward. As the giant fell away, Blaze reached his rifle around, shooting past him with another three-shot burst as a second tango rounded the corner. Fire and ice exploded my awareness as a bullet seared Blaze's shoulder. Blackness enveloped him, and he dropped.

"Lexi," Deep yelled. And with a pull to my abdomen, I merged with Deep. He focused down the hall on my open bedroom door. "Fuck," he spat as he swung his head back toward the command center where one of my lifeless hands was visible, stretching away from where I fell.

Bullets strafed the great room as two tangos aimed at Chris and Cookie.

Deep sprinted toward my form. A flashbang exploded, dropping him to the ground. He was so close. If I was just in my body, I could reach out my fingers and touch him. Help him. I had to help him.

Ears echoing, vision mottled, disoriented, Deep lifted himself from the floor. When he got his feet under him, he ran through the cloud of smoke that filled the hallway toward the enemy. A tango knocked him out cold with a crashing punch to the jaw.

As Deep went down, there was nowhere for my awareness to go but back to my body. And now that I was home with my own blood and sinew, my training kicked in. I was on my feet, shaking my head to clear away the pain from the punch Deep had taken. I grabbed the pocket knife I spied on the desk, flicked it open, and lunged for the door.

"Stop," a man's voice boomed. He aimed his 9mm between my eyes. "India Sobado, you are under arrest by order of the United States government. Drop your weapon. Hands in the air where I can see them." His finger lay flat against the trigger guard. He stepped forward, closing the distance between us. The threat of the barrel loomed a foot in front of me. I guess no one apprised him of my skills.

Letting the knife drop beside me, I raised open palms in the air, but not in surrender; they were ready for an opportunity.

He was going down.

From the direction of the kitchen, a gurgling scream

overrode the yells and commotion. It was enough of a distraction. My left hand parried the gun offline as my right grabbed the top ridges, knocking the slide, jamming it back, and making it ineffectual. My left palm jammed the cartilage in his nose back toward his brain stem. As blood gushed from his nostrils, I twisted the barrel to turn toward the tango. In this position, I easily pulled the gun from his hand. I thrust my rigid knuckle into the pressure point just south of his ear that I knew would put him out for at least twenty minutes and watched him crash to the ground.

Not knowing how many bullets he had fired, I dropped the magazine and unsnapped the pockets on his tactical belt, grabbing up his spares. One I smacked into place on the bottom of the Glock's grip; the second I slid into my pocket.

Striker's SEAL mantra played in my brain. *Slow is smooth, and smooth is fast.*

I emerged from the command center and made my way down the hall toward the great room.

Chris was down the hallway, dragging Blaze toward the safe room. Cookie, with carving knives in each hand, had squared off with a man who was bigger by about a foot and probably thirty pounds of muscle. The tango fought Cookie barehanded with his rifle near his feet next to another guy's body. The width of the pool of blood under the fallen man's head told me he was past help. And the knife shoved behind his collar bone told me that kill was by Cookie's hand. In a split second, I took in the slash marks that marred the tango's arms as he tried to retreat. Every time he reached for his sidearm, Cookie's knife sliced at lightning speed.

Deep rolled on the floor with another man. The tango had Deep in an arm lock and pummeled him with a fury of punches. My gaze scanned for other threats as I moved to a better angle, lifted the Glock, and took Cookie's guy down with a shot to the leg. As he hit the ground, a black-clad figure emerged from the basement stairs, his gun aimed at my center mass, his finger on the trigger. I could easily read the hatred in his eyes. My hands shook too much for me to take him, and standing here in the middle of the great room, there was nowhere to dive for cover.

The tango on top of Deep yelled out, "You're not supposed to hurt her. She's precious cargo."

The gunman's eye twitched right toward the voice, and that's when I regained control of my nerves, raised my weapon, and put my sights on the mark. Before I could squeeze the trigger, I saw Bella's black silky body pinch through the hole she had gnawed in the gym door. It took Bella a nano-second to home in on the tango, bunch her muscles and leap onto his back, taking him down with the weight of her forward momentum. His high-pitched screams filled the room as Bella sank her teeth into his shoulder. I left Bella to her prize as I trained my gun on Deep's attacker and paced forward. The tango released his hold, and Deep kicked the guy off him, rolled him onto his stomach, and used the tango's own zip ties from his utility belt to secure the guy's hands and feet.

I called Bella to me, so Deep could make his rounds, zip-tying the men on the ground.

Moans echoed off the cathedral ceiling. The enemy lay dead or injured in heaps on the wooden floor. Smoke from the explosives hazed the atmosphere, painting it in an eerie, otherworldly color.

Bella, Cookie, and I retreated to my bedroom. Soon Deep followed, darting to my bed and slapped the emergency button. We were on shutdown. Chris treated an unconscious Blaze for his gunshot wound. Deep was on the sat phone to Iniquus. After a short time, the helo's that brought the tangos in bugged out, and silence fell over the house for just a moment before the whoop-whoop-whoop of the Iniquus cavalry flew into range, riding to our rescue.

37

Тhe submarine was a strange experience. The interior was comfortable. The chairs anyway. Me? Not so much. It was a bit like being a message in a bottle thrown out in the water with crossed fingers. Once you're in the sub, you're in. This was a little too much like my cell in Honduras with the heavy clanging metal door. Only there was no open window assuring me of air — also no oatmeal, so some good with the bad.

I stared at my lap, bathed in horror over what had just happened. Blaze. Fuck. And not only was Striker's house put on the map, his retreat was all but destroyed in the attack. I had no way to make this up to him. Being around me was just bad juju. No one deserved the crap that followed along with loving me. Especially Striker. When this was over, at least I could do something about that. He could put me in his rearview mirror.

We were underwater for what felt like forever.

I spent the time reliving every second of the assault, over

and over again. When the "go-ahead" came to us over the loudspeaker, and the bulletproof shutters reseated themselves, the first thing I did was run outside to check on Andy. The rifle shot he took to the chest had winded him, but the ceramic plates that Striker required outdoor security to wear had saved his life.

My attention shifted to my dogs, whining at my feet. Striker said Beetle and Bella did better on their first ride when Gator brought them in from the Millers' Kennel. That was probably because I wasn't there sending out anxiety waves. I have grown to hate enclosed spaces from which I couldn't escape. Couple that with battle-frayed nerves and the stench of adrenaline on my skin, and no wonder the dogs were anxious.

I scratched behind Bella's ears and pulled her lips back to see if she had hurt herself on the door splinters. Beetle squirmed forward to get her share of attention. My girls seemed unfazed by the battle we had just lived through.

By the time Tidal Force leaped from our own Blackhawk, Omega had exfilled with their casualties. From the security tapes, eight had had boots on the ground. Obviously, there were more tangos in their copters. Even before we left the scene, Command had let Omega know what it thought of their little maneuver. Omega denied a hand in the battle but said they had a warrant for my arrest, and Iniquus had been warned about aiding and abetting. Iniquus responded that I had not been in the house; I was at the bottom of the Gulf, and Omega could pay for repairs, then they'd talk about what it would take to get the video feed returned to Omega headquarters instead of the FBI where their contract could see what Omega thought of the phrase "treat her like a precious egg." That was the latest update. And then there was Blaze. He was medevacked out, and I didn't know yet how he was doing.

Soon enough, we were under the Iniquus McMansion on the edge of the Potomac. Home again, home again, jiggery-jig. I was glad to be here even though we had come in under cover of darkness and horrible circumstances. Jack took Beetle and Bella for a moonlight potty run. Striker and I made our way up the path to the men's barracks. Dressed in black, no one would see me and know I was here.

The Iniquus campus sat on the south side of the Potomac, with easy access to the highway. Iniquus employees had housing on the campus so that when things got tight, Command could keep everyone going around the clock, though most people had a secondary residence. Only Iniquus employees could enter Iniquus housing. The women were quartered in a few of the McMansions arranged to look like a small elite community. These mansions also contained our warehouses, and apparently, our submarine station.

On the west edge of the woods, an eleven-story apartment building housed the Iniquus men with a "no women allowed" policy. Striker walked me as far as his door, then had to go down the hall to check in with David, a fellow Lead Commander.

I pushed open the tall, carved wood door to Striker's place and took a deep breath in. Even more than the bay house, this apartment smelled and felt like Striker to me. The designer used natural materials, durable, strong, and reliable to construct the interior. The ceiling in the front room was two stories high. The outer wall was made of glass, with a panoramic view of Washington that transformed into a bejeweled, black velvet ball gown of a view at night.

I went to use the bathroom and saw that my bags sat in the hall between the two bedroom doors. Would I sleep in my own room or with Striker? I couldn't tell if Striker was trying to make a decision, if he wanted me to make the decision, or if this happened to be where Jack put them. I was going to leave it alone for now.

I wandered back toward the great room and looked in the fridge. I wanted to cook but wasn't sure there would be any food since we'd been away. Luckily, the food fairy had come. I made burritos and put them in the oven. Striker came in; his face had the pinched look of fatigue and a busy mind. I brought him a beer and sat down beside him to stare out at the view, still a little shell shocked and not at all sure what to say. What could I possibly say, "Sorry they blew up your house"?

"Gator's here," Striker said.

I glanced over and saw Striker's eyes were dark and hard.

"How do you know?" I asked.

"You always get that little smile on your face right before he walks through the door."

"He tickles," I whispered.

"Yeah. I'm going to leave that one alone." Striker's jaw was set.

"What the hell does that mean?" My effort to control my emotions was flagging.

"You tell me what the hell that means." Striker's voice had a snarl at the edges. Was this because of Gator? His house? Had I finally found the not so sweet spot that said Striker had reached his limits with me?

The doorbell rang. I shot Striker a contrite look and went over to open it to Gator and Deep. They were both dressed up in suits like it was Sunday morning. I stood for a minute, staring at the bruises that bloomed over Deep's face. I knew he wouldn't want me to baby him; I should treat him like a warrior who had faced the enemy with valor. But god, my heart squeezed down so tightly that it took me a minute before I could step back and let them in.

"Hey guys, come on in. Dinner's about to come out of the oven." I tried hard to relax my face and dial down the sobs that wanted to surface.

"We cain't stay. Just wanted to let y'all know that Blaze's out of surgery. Good thing they were using round nose bullets. If they had been using hollow points, he could have said goodbye to that shoulder. Doctors are thinking full recovery after some rest and PT. But Blaze said he ain't gonna let Laura come anywhere near him. He's not a glutton for punishment like Lynx is." Gator rocked back with a grin. "It sure do smell good, though. Wouldn't mind if you were to wrap some up for tomorrow."

"Shouldn't you guys be resting? What are you doing dressed in suits?" I asked.

"No rest required — just another day at the office. Besides, we got dates." Gator pulled at the neck of his starched shirt and looked like he was doing penance. "The girls have some big shindig with work."

"And Deep's going like that?"

"Shoot yeah," Deep's attempted grin went lopsided by the swelling at his jaw. "Girls find out that I beat up a guy who was attacking a lady, and they'll get all hero-worship-y and want to tend to my wounds. And I've got wounds all over." He winked.

"Hero-worship-y. I didn't know that was a word." I moved in to straighten Deep's collar. "Do I know them?"

"You know Ghianna," Deep said. "She asked me to bring someone for her friend Becky."

"And if this Becky looks anything like the Becky I grew up with, then Deep is going to owe me big time."

"Ghianna's smart and cute, Gator, birds of a feather and all that. I'm sure you'll have a great time. You look fabulous, Deep," I lied. "Those poor girls' hearts don't have a chance."

Deep looked over at Striker; I saw him register the hard line of Striker's mouth. "Hey man, looks like we're interrupting something. So we'll head on. G'night." Deep whispered out of the side of his mouth, "Good luck." And they took off.

I wandered back into the living area, glad to have a little of Deep's good juju. I've seen that hard-ass look on Striker's face only once, and what happened after wasn't pretty, and luckily, was directed nowhere near me. Striker never loses control, but the situation that had upset him got controlled, that's for damned sure.

I sat down, facing him, and waited. Nothing. No words. No reaction. Striker stood there like a concrete barricade. His walls were up. He had closed himself off. He was having a private argument in his own head, and I didn't like that I was excluded. I didn't like that any conclusions he came to on his own would be his alone. Keeping me at arms' length seemed selfish. This should include me. All right, the truth was, I wanted to be in control. Though it was a little bit unethical, I searched around him with my sixth sense, and the hostile vibrations he sent off had to do with Gator. Not Blaze. Not his house. Not the battle. Only Gator.

I cleared my throat. "When I was younger, I adored reading English legends." Striker lifted an eyebrow ever so slightly. At least I knew he was listening. "I guess, with my mom's terminal illness, I was scared most of the time." I twisted my fingers into a knot on my lap. "The idea of a knight in shining armor facing down my dragons for me was very appealing. *Ivanhoe, La Morte D'Arthur, Tristan and Isolde, Robin of Sherwood.* I read them over and over again. I dreamed of meeting men with that kind of valor, that kind of code — men with chivalry."

Striker's eyes turned curious, though still distant.

I was slouched back on the sofa, trying to look casually conversational. "The men in my life, though, were ordinary men. You know, ordinary strength, ordinary problems." I pushed my hair back from my face, wondering where I was headed with this line of thought, and decided to just keep talking. "They dreamed mundane dreams, and they went through their days doing routine things." I cleared my throat, hoping that would stop the wobble in my voice. "I resolved myself to the idea that men made of legendary stuff were of the very distant past."

"Not your dad," Striker said and shifted against the wall. Atlas holding the world on his shoulders. It seemed unnecessarily burdensome to me. I was willing to take my share of the weight.

"No, not my dad." I looked out the window toward the Washington lights, but not really registering them. "I was too young to understand how incredible he was. He was familiar, though." I focused back on Striker. "I didn't have the proper perspective until after he died. He didn't wear armor that sparkled in the sunshine." I let a long breath whisper between my lips. "What I wanted at the time was fairy tale magic. When I needed him to slay the dragon, he couldn't. My mom was going to die, and he was a mere mortal."

Striker crossed his arms over his chest. I fidgeted with the hem of my shirt.

"When I was thirteen, Spyder became a big part of my life. I got to experience extraordinary for the first time. He was so exotic with his accent and his strength. As my mentor, he taught me so much. He showed me amazing things. Introduced me to Iniquus." My mouth had gone dry, and my lips were sticking to my teeth. It made the smile that I was offering Striker feel awkward and untrue. "Who knew there was such a place? That men like you existed?" Striker's gaze was too intense. I couldn't bear up under it. I was suddenly exhausted. Beyond exhausted, actually. Wrung dry of all energy. I looked down at the floor.

"Spyder filled my head with modern legends, like the ones that you and the teams were writing every day. Like today at your house — good conquering evil." I lifted my eyes to Striker's. "I'm so so sorry about your house, Striker."

He waved his hand back and forth as if to bat that idea out of the way. I guessed he wanted me to finish my thoughts.

"Back when I was known as Alex, and I was playing the role of a young guy under Spyder's wing, meeting you was like meeting Arthur himself. You were so handsome. Strong. Smart. Brave. I was in awe of you. I was completely starstruck — out of my mind, uncontrollably in love with you."

"You *were* in awe of me? What, no more?"

I looked up at him for a beat, then back at my hands. "You know what I mean."

"Not really. I don't know why you're telling me this. I've never known you to need a knight in shining armor to ride to your rescue. To support you as teammates, yes, but you've done a damned good job of saving yourself. You're hardly a damsel in distress."

I leaned forward. "If there is any myth that goes with the Middle Ages, it's the damsel in distress. Do you know what happened when those errant knights went out on their quests? They left the castle. They took every worthwhile man with them and left the battlements. Who got ditched? Old men, children, and women. Who ran the castle and protected it from the enemy? Women. Who was it that…"

"Lexi?" Striker's voice had softened, and so mine did, too.

"Yes?"

"I think you might be straying from your point."

"Sorry." I cleared my throat. "I guess my point is that when I was younger, my world seemed black and white. There were knights, and there were dragons. There was right, and there was wrong. There was no gray area. As I'm getting older, with more experiences and relationships, I understand that life is more nuanced than that. There is a whole lot of gray, isn't there?"

"Sometimes. Sometimes not." Striker moved over to sit in front of me.

"In the case of you and me? It's gray. When Spyder left, and I stopped puzzling, I chalked up my feelings for you as a teenaged fantasy and moved on. I married Angel. I loved him. Hugely. Deeply. He was gone to Afghanistan, but nothing changed for me. He was my heart. Then there was Wilson, and I got sequestered in a safe house. Who did the Fates put squarely in front of me? You. It turns out every

338 | FIONA QUINN

feeling I had for you as a teen was right there on the surface again."

Striker was watching me closely.

"I had to grapple with all of my inappropriate feelings for you. It was confusing," I whispered. "I struggled with all of that before Angel's death and afterward. Emotions are hard. They're complicated." I paused. Even though I knew I was going to have to end this conversation by telling Striker that as soon as I safely could, I would be leaving and would never see him again, I owed him this explanation. He needed to know I was going because I loved him enough to want what was best for him. I'd survive the loss...somehow. I sucked in a shaky breath.

"They can be, Lexi. My feelings for you aren't complicated. I'm in love with you. That's about as simple and straightforward as it can get."

"Not true, and you know it. Before Maria got hold of me, you didn't know what to do with me or how you were going to fit me into your life."

Striker gave me the slightest of nods.

"You said that you found my letters on the plane?"

Striker's eyes went dark. "I did," he said gruffly.

I reached out for his hand. "Striker, you know that I love all of the men on our team. They are the knights in shining armor that I longed for in my youth."

"Some more than others."

"Gator? No doubt, I have a special affection for Gator."

Striker worked his jaw. His eyes hardened again.

"Striker, I have a unique connection to him. You know that. Surely you understand that my feelings for him are not anything like the feelings I have for you." No, I could see that he didn't understand that at all. I released his hand.

"Before I was kidnapped, you told me that you were in love with me. At that point, I was too vulnerable to say the words back to you, though I felt them. I have always *felt* them. I have been in love with you since I met you years ago. I was afraid, plain and simple. Not knowing how I fit into your world scared me. In prison, well…" I stopped to breathe deeply and steady myself before I started again. "Having the answer as to my place in your world couldn't have mattered less. I was ashamed of my cowardice. I should have told you how I felt."

My hands pressed together against my lips as if I were in prayer. I trembled from head to foot. Anxiety. Funny how many life-or-death moments I've faced, and yet this is the one that made me feel the most like I could fall into oblivion. How was I going to live without him?

Striker quietly leaned forward and folded my hands in his.

I raised my face so I could look into his eyes. "When I was trapped on the plane, I thought I had no more time, and I would have no more chances to say everything I wanted to say, I wrote them. If I were going to say anything and let it be my truth, I would have said it when I thought I was going to die, and there would be no consequences. My truth is that I am *in love* with you, Striker Rheas. Only you."

Striker reached over and scooped me into his lap. He held my head against his chest. "I love you too, Chica." We sat there wrapped together. After a long time, Striker whispered into my hair. "When you first told me you loved me out loud, I meant it when I said we should get married."

I stared at his mouth as he said it. I felt my heart stop completely, then gallop forward.

Striker wanted to marry me.

Despite everything.

Was I willing to do that to him? Tie him to me and my crazy life? I opened my mouth to ask for more time, but what came out was, "I meant it when I said I guessed we probably should."

38

STRIKER TIGHTENED HIS GRIP AROUND MY BACK, AND WITH one arm under my legs, he stood up and carried me to his bedroom. Setting me on my feet, he brushed the hair from my face. His slow possessive kisses left me breathless. Gentle fingers drew my shirt up over my head. His warm hands stroked down my sides. He reached around to unclasp my bra. Like a dance, he held and moved me as the rest of our clothes fell to the ground. In his arms, I felt unscathed and unscarred. I was graceful, beautiful, and whole.

He lifted me onto his bed where the sheets were cold and made me shiver. Striker leaned over me. His fingers swept over my skin. My mind flashed to when I first saw him naked. It was at the safe house. His Bowflex model's body had sent me to crazy places in my mind. And his hands were holy shit, sending me to even crazier places now.

After some time, I thought, *I should be participating in this more than just lying here mewling*. What though? My hands rested on Striker's shoulders as he made his oh-so-slow way over my body. He had well-practiced moves.

Masterful.

And I had…read about this in a novel, somewhere…My dildo lessons with Chablis. Shit.

The image from one of my cases last year popped up, unbidden. The couple had been at it on the guy's desk, and then she… Yes. Striker would expect that.

Probably all the women he'd been with did that for him.

All of them — how many were there? I could do it, too. I *could.* I was just a little intimidated.

I groped around awkwardly, trying to…

Striker caught my wrist in his hand. "No."

He took both of my arms, pushed them over my head, and placed a pillow on top, holding them in place with its slight weight. "I've been waiting for you far too long, Chica," he said. "If you do that, I'm going to be done before either one of us wants me to be."

"Oh." Shit. I did something wrong.

He chuckled. "You're just going to have to lay there and take it until I'm done playing."

"Oh," I said again. "Okay." I looked down at his smiling face. Dimpled grin. Eyes dark and glittering. So damned cute. I, on the other hand, was white-skinned and goose fleshed, splayed out like an untrussed chicken. I have never had such conflicting emotions. In books, the beautifully choreographed sex scenes were always so simple — the couple had such single-minded intent. It was all about plea-sure. I wasn't prepared for my ego to jump out and yell crap at me right then.

"Lay there and take it," he'd commanded. I'd try that. It was *sort of* like meditation. I'd focus on the wonderful sensations, the ripples and tides rolling through my body, and not think about the mortifying-as-hell place he was flicking his tongue.

Jeezus.

He made my stomach jerk in little staccato spasms. My toes curled tight. I didn't think I could take one more second of this heat, of the tension. Filled to overflowing with emotions and sensations, I gripped at the pillow and tried to find relief, making mooshed-up crazy faces and porno-noises.

He reached into the side table and pulled out a condom packet.

I wondered momentarily when he'd put it in there.

I closed my eyes while he adjusted, opening them again when he moved between my legs, with his weight pressed into his elbows. "Ready, beautiful?" he asked softly.

I nodded against the pillow, and he slid slowly into me, his eyes watching my face.

I knew that it would be painful my first time, but with the shock of him in me, I pushed my head back into the pillow and froze.

"Only for a minute, Chica." He bent and whispered against my cheek. "It will only hurt for this one little minute." He stayed very still, waiting for me to breathe again.

His mouth found mine. His kisses were primal. He kissed away my thoughts. He kissed away my damned interfering ego. He kissed away my bones until I was supple and malleable. My hips moved under him.

Oh. This felt natural. This felt right.

He followed my rhythm and then changed it. Striker never took his eyes off mine. He watched me as I went deep inside myself and gathered the energy into a rush that left me slick and limp in his arms.

We made love all night and slept through the alarm clock in the morning.

Striker paused his fork over his breakfast and watched me as I sat down at the table after my shower. He looked like a man with a question that he wasn't willing to ask.

"Potato chips," I said, pulling my chair under my knees.

"Excuse me?" Perplexed eyes looked at me.

"You're wondering what I think about sex, and I think 'potato chips.'"

Striker looked uneasy. I guessed he wanted a different kind of answer. "Chica, you don't like potato chips," he said quietly.

"How did you come to that conclusion?" I spooned a beautiful strawberry into my mouth.

"I have never seen you eat one. Not ever. Even when we're at a party, and there's a big bowl in front of you."

"And you deduced from there that I don't like them. I offer you another conclusion. I love them. I love them so much that one bite of potato chip makes me lose complete control of myself. I not only devour every last chip in the bowl, but I have been known to lift the bowl up and lick the salt that's on the bottom. I am such a glutton for chips that I will eat every tidbit from the bag and then lick my fingers to get the very last crumbs. In the end, just one taste, and I turn into a licentious, abandoned, potato chip whore."

While I was talking, I watched Striker's eyes dilate to

black. He was up out of his chair, pulling me into him and kiss-dancing me back to the bedroom…

39

"YOU'RE BURIED THERE." STRIKER PAUSED WITH HIS KEYS IN his hands. I hadn't looked up when he came in. Beetle and Bella didn't offer warning barks, just wagged their stubby tails excitedly, so I knew who was coming through the door...and I had this one last thought that I wanted to gel... nope, it escaped me. I looked up and smiled.

"What is all that?" Striker asked, coming over.

"Autopsy reports: Hector, Wilson, Matsy, Maria, and Julio." I pointed at the pile to my left. "This next set is fire reports from my apartment building. And that over there is the data that Frith archived on the Patriots United and on Bayleigh Joseph."

"Bayleigh was Tad Joseph's daughter, FBI, the first to fall under Wilson's attack."

"Yes." I shifted the floor pillow that I was sitting on to a more comfortable position.

"What are you finding out that's interesting?" Striker came and sat on the floor near me. He crossed his legs and put his elbows on his knees.

"From the autopsy reports, nothing new. From the fire reports? It's interesting. The story that I heard was that Mr. Matsy went to bed with a cigarette and a bottle of Jack Daniels. From what I can tell, the cigarette might melt the mattress and make lots of smoke, but it would be a slow process — all night. The Jack could have sped things along, but not make an inferno that took out the whole building."

"Hold that thought," Striker said. He sauntered into the kitchen and came back, twisting the cap off a beer.

"When the alarm sounded, I ran out of my apartment, and there was smoke billowing everywhere," I continued.

Striker nodded and took up his place on the ground, using a chair to support his back.

"At one point, I crawled through the hallway, pushing my boxes out in front of me. I never saw an actual fire. It wasn't hot. The smoke was the problem. I went over to the Safeway parking lot with most everyone else. The fire trucks roared up the road, then BOOM. Flames engulfed everything."

"How does the fire report account for that?"

"It suggests that a spark contacted a gas leak from the stove. That the fire smoldered in Mr. Matsy's room, made its way to the kitchen, and blew everything up like a bomb."

"You sound skeptical." Striker stretched his long legs out in front of him, stacking his ankles.

"There was a lot of smoke. Mr. Matsy would have asphyxiated in his apartment. It seems to me… I don't know. The timeframe that they're suggesting is too fast."

"More?" Striker reached out to pick up the fire file. He leafed through the photos.

"Mr. Matsy had to know his mattress was on fire. And he

must have left his apartment fairly quickly after things started to smolder. He would have had time to pull the fire alarms and get help long before a spark could have reached his kitchen. The kitchens in the single-bedroom apartments were at the far diagonal on the floor plan."

"You said he was drunk. Would that change your thought process?"

"I didn't *say* he was drunk. I said he went to bed with a cigarette and a bottle of Jack Daniels. I saw him at Safeway, and he looked a little out of it. I thought it looked more like he was in shock. We all were. But he wasn't stumbling or puking or anything. "Here's another thing: the alarm that was set off was outside of 1A."

Striker shook his head to show he didn't understand the relevance.

"Mr. Matsy lived in 1E. 1A is a first-floor apartment on the front left of the building. 1E is on the back right. There's no visual. Someone outside of 1A couldn't have seen smoke from that part of the building at night."

"Okay. Mr. Matsy is running out, he pulls the alarm as he passes, and keeps running to the parking lot across the street," Striker offered.

"Nope. There was a sidewalk coming out of Matsy's apartment that went right to the crosswalk. Going to 1A would make him circle out of the way," I said.

"What are you suggesting here?"

"I'm suggesting that there is a missing piece to this puzzle. The explosion wouldn't have followed the smoking mattress in the correct timeframe. Mr. Matsy wouldn't have set off the alarm from 1A. And 1A couldn't see that there was a problem. It doesn't add up."

"You're awfully good at this." Striker grinned. "Too bad you don't work on crime puzzles for a living." He leaned in to plant a little kiss at my hairline. "Does the fire inspector think it was a felony?"

"They have it labeled as questionable. The poor owners. I wonder how a 'questionable' fire report figures to their insurance payout."

"Where are you going with this?"

"Nowhere. I don't see how it has any bearing on anything." I sighed and leaned back, hugging my knees to my chest.

"Is this what you were thinking about when I walked in? You were off in your head. I tried to be quiet and not interrupt you."

"No. It's okay. I was thinking about trickster tales."

"Come again?"

"Moral tales where the main character tries to trick everyone with their cunning."

"Got that, but why did you think about tricksters?"

I took a big breath in and blew it noisily back out. "I'm specifically thinking of a First Nations story — Crowe, I think — called The Coyote and the Geese."

Striker laid down on the floor beside me with his arms crossed behind his head and closed his eyes. "Okay, Chica, I'm ready. Let's hear it."

I leaned my head back to rest on his shoulder and started in with my sing-songy storytelling voice.

Coyote was coming home. It had been a long tiring day, and he had been unsuccessful at everything he had put his hand to. He had gotten as far as his uncle's place and decided to sit for a spell at the pond. Get him a drink of cool water. Coyote set his bag down next to an old tree stump and started over toward the pond.

Now, it just so happened that a flock of geese had seen that very pond from the air and had the very same thought as Old Man Coyote. That water sure did look cool and refreshing. They had been flying all day long, and they were looking for somewhere to rest. They watched Old Man Coyote putting the sack down, and they waddled over to him.

"Hey there! That sack sure do look heavy. What you got in thar?" one of the geese asked.

"This'un here? Why it's full ah songs," said Coyote.

"How'd you get all of them songs?" wondered the Geese.

"Why I have me some strong magic. These songs come to me in my visions."

"Let's have a dance!" cried the geese.

"These songs are much too strong. These are powerful songs."

Well, the geese begged Old Man Coyote to let the songs out so they could dance. Finally, after much back and forth, Coyote said, "Okay, if I do let the songs out, you have to follow my instructions. You have to dance like I tell you to." And the geese agreed. They all went down by the water's edge, and they used their webbed feet to pat down the grasses and make a real nice dancing ring.

"Now you got to close your eyes tight. These here songs are powerful songs, and if'n you open your eyes, even just the tiniest peek, why you'll be hurt!"

The geese closed their eyes. Old Man Coyote took out his

music sticks and starts tappity-tap tapping them together and singing. The geese all started dancing away, flapping their wings and hopping from foot to foot.

"Keep your eyes closed now," said Coyote, and he took one of his sticks and hit one of the geese in the head, killing her.

"Hey, now looky here," Coyote said over the dead goose, "this one opened her eyes, and now she's dead. You have to keep your eyes shut!"

The geese shut their eyes and started dancing again. Coyote grabbed another goose that started squawking for help. "That's right, my friend, you keep singing! Sing right out as loud as you can. It adds to the power of the medicine song."

The geese continue to dance, and Coyote goes after a third goose. This time one of the geese peeks and sees what Old Man Coyote is doing. He yelled, "Run away, run away, if I want to live for another day, then I run!" And he ran.

Old Man Coyote picked up the four geese that he had managed to kill and stuffed them in his sack, and he wandered on home thinking what a productive day he had had."

Silence followed my story. I was breathing heavily like I had been sprinting. I focused on the nightscape as my thoughts roiled and bubbled. The lights of the cars on the highway across the Potomac made a ribbon of glowing red.

"The geese are Hector, T-Bone, Julio, and Maria, and the one who got his eyes open was Brody," Striker said.

"Bingo." I played with the end of my ponytail, twirling it in my fingers.

Striker pushed me up to sitting as he came upright. "When did you start thinking about Old Man Coyote?"

"Today, why?"

"No. Exactly what time did you start thinking about Old Man Coyote?"

"Um. It was on the treadmill. Fourteen thirty, maybe Fifteen hundred hours."

"Have you switched channels on your psychic network?" Striker asked.

"How do you mean?"

"I was going to tell you that we have a line on Brody. Axel figured out where he was about sixteen hundred our time. You had him by an hour. It seems to me you're picking up your information differently."

"My psychic antenna is definitely bent. I'm not picking up much of anything. Though ever since the crash, my brain has been dancing with bizarre dreams and children's stories. With only the occasional 'T-Bone is dead.' But as far as the Old Man Coyote tale goes, I've always had stories as analogies as part of my ESP repertoire. Where's Brody?"

"Your Honduran prison."

I sat straight up, my arms stiff at my sides. "How did he get there?" I whispered. "Vega?"

"That's what we're trying to figure out. It would help if we knew who Old Man Coyote was."

"Ah, well, I've been trying to figure that out all day."

"Who's on the table?" Striker swiveled around and looked at me intently.

"The obvious players: the Sylanos Cartel, Omega, and a wild card. Maybe the wild card's name is Vega. I think I'm missing someone."

"You've been working on the Frith files. Do you think Frith is caught up in this?"

"There's no evidence trail. Mostly I was trying to use the files to figure out how he knew I saved his life in the gold-for-dope debacle. I was looking for the way that my name comes up in his files. Do you know whose name came up?" I asked.

"Who?"

"Travis Wilson."

"At the fire? We know that."

"Wilson's name came up before the fire. He was a member of Patriots United."

Striker moved toward my file stacks. I reached out to get him the right one and opened to the page with the Post-it Note.

"Right. Go on," he said, scanning down.

"Frith had Wilson flagged as dangerous/to be watched. This seems to parallel the explanation Deep, and I considered for why Frith was in the photo of Wilson at my fire and why Frith tailed Wilson to the New Jersey motel. There's even a record in there of him signing out an agency car that night. Which, by the way, is a little peculiar. Normally, agents don't take cars with government plates out on a tail."

"Which leads to..." Striker tried to lead the conversation in a straight line.

"Me being confused." I put my hands on either side of my head and scratched at my scalp as if by digging a furrow, I could sprout a thought. "I wish I knew why Frith left the FBI. And why they wouldn't give him back the stuff from his drawer."

"I had the same questions," Striker said. "I talked to a contact up there, and they did some snooping for me. Rumor has it that Frith was double-dipping — working for Omega at the same time as he was working for the FBI. It's nothing that they could prove. There may have been an overlap, but then again, maybe not."

"Here's a string of ifs: what if Frith worked for Omega and the FBI at the same time? What if Omega wanted his help on the Sylanos file — protecting Sylanos from the FBI, CIA, and Iniquus? Maybe Omega put Frith on their team and tasked him to check on the FBI front. What if Frith saw my name as the puzzler and did a little digging, and he did a background check on me?"

Striker's face got that hard-edged combat quality that he gets when he thinks I might be in danger. "It's not hard to find out that your name changed when you married or where you had lived," Striker said. "But, Chica, that's a lot of 'what ifs.' And still leaves a lot of important questions unanswered."

"What do you think is the priority question?" I asked, hoping he could help me sieve out the gems and let the debris fall to the side.

"How would he have figured out that you, as an Iniquus agent, are the same person who saved him from the drug deal gone bad?" Striker said.

"Okay. Let's start there since I think I have that answer. Spyder was downrange when I figured everything out about that case. I called my information directly into our FBI contact. In Frith's file, there is a communication log with a transcript of that conversation, my cell number, and my AT&T contracted name, India A. Rueben. Ha! And here I thought I was calling in anonymously. I guess they auto-track incoming calls. Beginner's mistake coming back to bite me in the butt."

"Why would he go to the trouble to follow that trail?"

"Curiosity? That's my theory. I'd want to know who saved my life." I shrugged. "Let's leave this alone for now. I don't have anything concrete to tell you. Let's talk about Axel, instead. He called you and told you he thought he found Brody? How's the operation? Is there a timeline?"

"Axel's in the air. He's due in tonight. I told him we'd debrief him in the morning."

I shot Striker a dumbfounded look. "Morning?"

"I know you're anxious, Chica. A few hours won't matter right now. He's been going full throttle since he left. He needs a good night's sleep. He'll be clearer if we wait until tomorrow."

"What about the dogs?" I asked.

Striker threw his head back and laughed.

I sent him a questioning look, wondering why in the hell my asking about the dogs would be such a source for hilarity.

"I win the pool." He grinned.

"What are you talking about?" I was annoyed. I didn't like to be the subject of the team's speculation pools and games. It made me feel like a sideshow since they usually had something to do with me.

"The team threw money in the pot on what your first question would be. I said the dogs, hands down."

"They let me escape. I owe them my life."

"I hear you, Chica. That's why I put money behind it."

"What did everyone else say?"

"Ah, let's see. Deep thought you'd ask how many people they pulled out. Gator thought you'd ask what's going to happen to the people who ran the prison, would they lose their jobs, how would they eat? Randy thought for sure you'd ask if anyone was arrested, and could you interrogate them. Jack thought you wouldn't ask anything; that you'd say that reminded you of a story you heard when you were little. And Blaze is still in the hospital and didn't get to play."

"How much was the pool?" I asked.

"Twenty a piece."

"Oh yeah? Got any special plans for your eighty bucks?" I slithered onto his lap and smiled at him.

Striker put his hands on my hips, settling me against him, and returned my smile. "I'm taking you out to dinner when you're not a wanted woman."

"There's going to be a time when you don't want me?" I batted my lashes.

"I can't imagine that. Let me rephrase — I'll take you out for dinner when you're not a hitman's mark." Striker hugged me to him as he stood up. He lowered me gently until my feet touched the floor and reached for my hand. "It's late. Come to bed, Chica."

"I will in a minute. I want to read this one thing more. I don't think I'm going to be able to sleep a wink, anyway."

"Come to bed, and I'll distract you from your mind jumble." His voice was warm, with a touch of spice.

"Oh yeah?" I looked up. Striker had that look in his eye, the one that gave me a rush and left me breathless. As he watched my reaction, his eyes dilated to black.

"I'm up for a little distraction." I smiled at him.

"Little distraction?" Striker pulled me to him and nuzzled at my neck, tickling me with soft lips.

"I'm up for a sizable distraction." I giggled and squirmed.

Striker's hands were under my camisole, over my

breasts, giving me goosebumps. "Sizeable distraction?" He pulled my hips tight against him.

"Huge. I'm up for a *huge* distraction."

Striker scooped me up and kissed me all the way to the bedroom.

40

I WAS UP BEFORE STRIKER'S ALARM CLOCK SOUNDED. TRUE to his words, Striker had worked every drop of anxiety and distraction from my body. I was able to sleep with a smile on my face. But now, Beetle and Bella tapped impatient feet on the bedroom floor, wanting their run. I'd just stood up when a knock sounded at the front door.

Jack leaned against the jamb in jogging shorts and sneakers, and nothing else. The bronzed Adonis getting ready for his morning workout.

"Hey Lynx, I came for the pups."

"Oh, great, thanks." I turned and tapped my thigh to call the girls out of Striker's room, where I had left them in a sit-stay.

"I saw Axel heading over to Headquarters. He said he has a quick meeting with Command, and then he's coming back here. I've given everyone the heads-up. They should be gathering up soon. Thought you should know." He reached out to tweak the label on Striker's T-shirt, which I had pulled on inside out and backward. "So you could get some clothes on."

I blushed hotly. *Shit, Jack knows what I've been doing with Striker.* That felt way too personal. I thanked his back as Beetle and Bella followed him to the elevator.

Striker went to take a shower. I pulled on some yoga pants, put my hair back in a ponytail, and went to the kitchen to make everyone breakfast.

Gator knocked at the door. "Did someone already take the dogs?"

"Jack. You just missed him. Come in and talk to me. I'm getting some breakfast together." I moved back to the fridge and scanned for ideas. "What do you want?" I asked, looking over my shoulder at him.

"Some of your blueberry muffins," Gator said with a grin.

"That was on the tip of your tongue."

"Always. So tell me, when you heard Axel was in, what was your first question?"

"Striker won. I asked about the dogs." I piled breakfast ingredients on the counter and set the oven temperature to pre-heat.

"Okay. I got me another question for you."

"Shoot," I said, reaching for a wooden spoon.

"All them dogs down at the jail. They ain't lapdogs by any means."

"No. They're the real deal. The jail staff kept them mean and hungry."

"But you got out past them," he said.

"I did." I poured a cup of sugar over the butter in my bowl and started to cream it together.

Gator rubbed his jawline with his thumb. "I can see how

you could use your sleight of hand skills, and maybe under the right circumstances, your shadow walking skills when you escaped. But I can't figure how you got past them dogs."

I cracked an egg into my batter and paused with the shells in my hand. "You have a bet laid on this, don't you, Gator?" I turned to throw the shells into the trash.

Gator paused. "Yes, ma'am," he admitted.

The hangdog look he gave me was endearing. But again? Really? I didn't like to have bets laid on me. True, it was better than having bets laid against me…still. "And the guys sent you in to figure out how I did it. You're on a wire right now, aren't you?"

"Uh. Yes, ma'am." Gator dipped his head, looking like a five-year-old caught with a face covered in chocolate smears and cookie crumbs.

"Nice." I sighed. "All right, it's pretty simple. I trained the dogs to follow my command and to ignore the command of their handlers."

"You did what?"

I tapped my index finger to my temple. "I trained them using my mind."

"Not even you can do that, Lynx." Gator stuck his thumbs into his belt loops and shook a disbelieving head.

"No? Look at yourself. What are you doing?" I rested my elbows on the counter with my hands interlaced under my chin, ready to have some fun of my own.

Gator looked down and saw that he was balanced on one foot, the other foot perched uncharacteristically against his knee in tree pose. He stomped his foot down and looked at me with narrowed eyes.

"Don't worry, Gator." I stood up, laughing, and moved back to my batter. "I can't move you like a marionette. We have a connection, as you well know. I used that link to send a picture to you with my mind — stand on one foot— and some part of you heard me, trusted me, and acted on my suggestion. It's something like that with dogs." I pulled out my mixer and beat the batter.

Gator didn't look convinced.

"Training dogs with the mind is not an impossible concept," I said, turning off the motor, then swatting away Gator's finger when he reached out to swipe it through my bowl. "You've seen wolves on TV when they're hunting caribou?"

He nodded as he put the paper liners into the muffin tins.

"Then you've seen that they can be well outside of their pack mates' visual field, and yet every one of them is coordinated. Dogs pick up information in the ether just like you and I can." I tapped the blueberries in and swirled them with my spoon. It was heavy. I had made a quadruple batch. My team ate big.

"Did you speak to the alpha in Spanish?" Gator asked, watching me fill the first dozen cups.

"No words. I used pictures. Feelings. It was a learning process for me, as well as for him."

"And you can do that to people as well?"

"Only special people that I love and who love me back." I smiled and slid the tin into the oven. "Thirty minutes until muffins."

I let Gator finish up while I started in on a breakfast casserole.

The men trickled in, ready to eat. Blaze set the table while the dishes finished up in the oven.

Now that Striker was up and dressed, I took my turn in the bathroom.

When Axel walked in, all the men rose to their feet and gave him a well-deserved hero's welcome with whoops and back slaps. Axel's dark skin took on a slight pink flush as he nodded his acknowledgment to the team. Humbled amidst the celebration.

Four hundred and twenty-seven. That was the number of people they found in the prison. They looked like Dachau survivors. The rescue team listed most of the prisoners in critical condition, but at least now they had a chance.

Gator set the food on the table while I poured orange juice. I went over, jug in hand, and gave Axel a kiss on the cheek. "Good to see you home safe. Thank you for everything."

"What was her first question, Striker?" Jack asked.

"About the dogs." Striker grinned and did an end-zone victory dance. Boys.

"Axel? I'm sorry, but could you start with the dogs?" I asked.

Axel took a seat at the table and put his napkin on his lap. "Sure. Alejandro Castillo ordered that the dogs be locked in their kennels. We loaded them on a transport and brought them to Maryland to the Millers'. That happened on day one. The Millers are doing vet checks and assessments on all of them. Once they're done, Command will make the final call. They think it might be good for us to have them join our stable of working dogs."

"Good. That's good. The Millers don't speak Spanish, though, and the dogs do."

"They hired a guy. It's covered," Deep said.

I nodded. If the Millers were involved, those dogs were golden.

Leaning both elbows on the table, I cradled my chin on my palms and waited for Striker to start the debriefing with an overview. As he moved to stand at the head of the table, the team focused on him.

"Axel has returned from a Honduran rescue mission developed as a joint venture with the State Department. They have a humanitarian fund that we tapped for funding. We also got them involved for diplomatic reasons, and they were a big asset to have onboard. Much of Iniquus' success in rescuing the hostages is due to State's behind-the-scenes work with the Honduran government." Striker stood with his knuckles on the table, looking like Captain America. "We were working in conjunction with the Honduran Army. They let us go in and interrogate Castillo on his own turf. After that, the army arrested Castillo and took him to the capital. And, of course, Iniquus handled the dogs." Striker gave me a wink. "A South American humanitarian group, similar to Doctors without Borders, set up a field hospital in the prison. The storm hampered operations considerably, but the medical team did the best they could under trying circumstances. They were documenting everyone and their country of origin. So far, no Honduran nationals were in the prison—a lot of Iraqi and Afghani men. The preponderance was Colombian citizens. There was a handful of Americans. The identification effort is still in progress since some of the prisoners are incoherent."

"Was there any documentation indicating who incarcerated these people?" I broke protocol by asking out of turn.

"Nothing," Axel said.

"But you think you found Brody?" My jaw tightened.

"I believe so," Axel replied. "The guy I found was badly beaten. His jaw was broken, and he was in and out of consciousness. Honduras let me bring him back to the States. He's hospitalized. His prognosis is listed as guarded."

"Did Castillo say who brought him in?" Striker asked.

"James Vega. It's the right timeframe for this to be Brody Covington based on Castillo's statements. Once he was arrested, Castillo turned the Honduran version of State's evidence, so he was still cooperating. Why don't I show you the initial interview?" With Striker's nod of assent, Deep hooked up Axel's laptop to the widescreen TV.

In the video, Axel was wearing his cam-wire. His arm came up and knocked at the door. The sky was periwinkle, and the time stamp in the lower left read 05:03.

A man with a gray mustache came to the door with a pot of shaving cream in one hand and a shaving brush in the other. Foam covered his face. He wore military-style pants and a wife-beater T-shirt with a towel slung over his shoulder, which he used to remove the shaving cream when he saw Axel standing there. To me, Castillo looked only slightly taken aback by Axel's presence — inquisitive, but not afraid.

"May I help you?" Castillo asked in Spanish.

"Axel White." Axel displayed his credentials. "Iniquus operative, representing the Honduran and United States governments. May I come in?"

Castillo pushed the door wide and stepped aside, scanning behind Axel's shoulder. I assumed he saw other boots on the ground. His face slackened with resignation.

They sat in a comfortably sized room on black leather furniture. Glazed terracotta tiles shone under their feet. "I'm looking for my colleague, India Alexis Sobado."

Castillo nodded. "She was here. They took her away."

"Who took her?" Axel had a very good accent. This was the first time I'd heard him speak Spanish. Impressive.

"That I do not know." Castillo shrugged and settled back into the cushions.

"Can you tell me what you do know? When was she here?"

"The last time my staff saw her was the day the tropical storm hit in July. They called her Santa Blanca." Castillo offered up a rueful smile. "The woman who serves the morning oatmeal started calling her that. She said a saint had come down to bless our village, that she could feel God's great love when she opened the chute on Sobado's door to slide in the breakfast tray." Castillo crossed an ankle over his knee. A man comfortable in his own home. "This created quite a problem for me. The villagers came up and wanted to touch her so they too could receive a blessing." He pursed his lips, making his heavy mustache fan. "I ended up buying some plastic crosses and handing them out, saying they held Santa Blanca's special prayers. That seemed to keep everyone happy."

"Go on," Axel commanded.

"One morning, Sobado didn't reach for her oatmeal. The storm was raging. The other server thought Sobado was moved to a different floor since she had no windowpane in her cell. Sobado's exercise guard didn't go to let her out because of the weather. I only discovered that she was missing from her cell when I went up to the village to survey the damage and drink. The cantina owner asked about her. There were rumors that Santa Blanca flew straight up to heaven in the storm. I checked Sobado's cell, and sure enough — gone. We couldn't account for her. We let the dogs search, but there was too much time and too much wind. Sobado must have been taken from the jail."

"And how do you think that happened?"

Castillo shrugged and offered open hands. "I don't know. This has never happened here before. It was odd, though. There were two men, Latinos with heavy foreign accents. They were at the cantina, asking many questions and going for hikes. I think they probably took her from the jail. I don't know how. But, yes, I think these men got to her."

"Who brought her in, to begin with?"

Castillo shifted uncomfortably and adjusted his pants leg. "A drug runner. My guards met the plane."

"This was the plane that was stolen from the airport?"

"No, a different burro," Castillo said.

"Who did they work for?"

Castillo shook his head.

Axel pushed his briefcase out in front of him and unlatched the clasps; it fell open to show that it was full of Euros. "Your time here is over. We are taking over the prison. This is to help you settle elsewhere. There are a passport and plane ticket to Barcelona. It is important that you cooperate. The other side of the coin is not as shiny."

Castillo nodded and pulled the case over next to him. "The first burro, I don't know. We are not on his usual route. The second one, the one with the stolen plane, refuels here. He works for Sylanos."

"And you work for him as well. This is his prison," Axel said.

Castillo nodded. "His cartel owns and runs this prison. I have not learned the name of the new director."

"You heard that Sylanos is dead?"

"*Si.*"

"Have you heard from your niece Maria since she sent you Sobado?" Axel asked.

Castillo startled, then shook his head. "No. She asked me to hold the girl in solitary, and make sure that she was secure and unharmed."

Liar. And if he lied about Maria going down to collect my fingers, well, that made everything he said suspect.

"We made a video of Sobado and sent it via satellite so Maria could get her husband out of jail. Since we made the video, I have heard nothing."

"Tell me about Omega." Axel used his hypnotizing voice — slow, with few modulations. No peaks or valleys.

Castillo got up and poured a glass of tequila at the bar; he signaled an offer to Axel, who shook his head. "It's early to drink. But I think this is a special occasion," he said, then wandered back to his seat. "Omega came into our lives a few years ago. They were brought in by a Sylanos man."

"Vega."

"You know much. Yes. Vega has worked here at the prison for a long, long time. He enjoys this job. It's like a sport to him. Sylanos kept this prison to pressure other families to cooperate with his demands. A very successful business plan. He was able to get the families to do almost anything he wanted them to do when they saw their loved ones being beaten, wearing rags, skin and bones. This prison operation is one of the keys to his achievements. But Sylanos? He's dead now, so no matter, right?"

"Omega?"

"Ah, yes. Omega needed a place to do their special interrogations and bury bodies. We have a hole twelve kilometers north of the airport. Omega brings bodies in, wrapped. We drive the corpses up and throw them in our hole. If the bodies come in alive? They go into the cell and get interrogated by Vega. If it were me? I'd rather skip the interrogation and go right in the dump." Castillo took a big swig and gestured with his glass. "Sylanos was very grateful to Vega for his expertise. Treated him like family."

"Vega brought down Omega prisoners as well as Sylanos prisoners?"

"Exactly."

"Did Sylanos' people or Omega know about Sobado?" Axel asked.

"No, I kept her quiet. Maria said the girl couldn't be hurt. She had to be in good shape for the tape and the exchange. If Vega knew about her, beautiful girl like that? Well, when she first got here, she was beautiful. I saw her in the yard when she had air time, and she became quite horrific. Probably dead now," he mused, rubbing his thumb and forefingers through his mustache. "I don't know how long she could survive, looking like that. Dim around the eyes, then they die, and we put them in the hole."

"Again, I'm asking you, neither Omega nor Sylanos knew about Sobado?"

"Correct."

Huh. Okay, that meant there *was* another player, one that I hadn't accounted for. Yet.

"But there were men who were asking questions," Axel said.

"Two sets. Latinos, then Americans. I'm guessing that you are one of the Americans. They told me about your scar." Castillo ran a thumb down his face to mimic the line that ran from brow to jaw on Axel's.

Axel nodded, swinging the picture on the screen up and

down. "I was in the second group. I need to know who was in the first group."

"I don't know. We didn't see them after they left, and then you and your companion moved in."

"And you weren't curious?" Axel asked.

"They were here a very short time, and no, sometimes it's better to focus somewhere else."

"Why did you keep Sobado for Maria?"

Castillo shifted his shoulders and screwed his lips into an unpleasant shape. "I'm old. I do not want to work here forever. When I give up my job, I give up my house. Life in the village is not lovely. Maria told me that Julio had a fortune hidden away. She said that if I helped her conceal Sobado, then she would be able to get Julio out of the American prison. I would move with them to Indonesia as a rich man." Castillo gave a soft chuckle. "I have magazines from Vega about the young girls over there. They do things for a man that a Catholic Honduran girl would never consider. I would like that. To have little oriental girls take care of the General." Castillo gestured toward his crotch.

Blech. I shifted uncomfortably in my chair.

"Were records kept?" Axel seemed unfazed by the visual Castillo had offered.

"I do not. That doesn't mean there aren't files somewhere — there must be. I have tallies on a chalkboard, so I know how many I am to feed, and I can tell the cooks what portions to prepare. Other than that? My job was to make sure no one ever got out and brought attention to our little prison. And I failed at my duties. Sobado is gone. You are here. And I am done. Who's outside?" Castillo glanced toward the window.

"Iniquus operators and the Honduran Army," Axel replied evenly.

Castillo got up to pour himself another drink.

"No one has ever been released from here?" Axel asked.

"The only release is death. Sweet, sweet death. I am happy for the men and women when they die." He took a swig. "The families may be told that they will get their loved ones home, but they never do, no matter what. Even after they die, Sylanos still exploited the family by not telling them." Big grin, full of tobacco-stained teeth. "Brilliant mind that man had. Absolute genius."

The men had left a while ago. They had done KP while I took a nap. Now I was up and banging around the kitchen, making a lot of noise. The stories about the prison churned through my mind, becoming a storm as big as the one that forced my plane to the ground.

I slammed a plate onto the counter with way too much emphasis.

Laser-eyed and steel-jawed, I looked over at Striker, who sat calmly on the bar stool watching me like a TV show. He held my gaze, and I reviewed the scene.

"I'm angry," I whispered.

"I can see that, Chica." Placid. How could he be so damned imperturbable?

"I'm angry that I'm angry." My voice ratcheted up a notch. "I don't want to feel like this anymore."

Striker nodded, a safe response to offer a Tasmanian devil.

372 | FIONA QUINN

"It's like someone is holding a remote control and channel surfing through emotions that I have no reason to feel with the volume up way too loud. Uncomfortably, miserably loud. And I can't turn the damn thing off." I grabbed up a dish towel to stuff over my face. "I hate this. Look at me. I'm out of control."

Striker came over and gathered me in his arms. "Shhh," he whispered against my hair.

When I moved my head, I rubbed snot and tears into his shirt.

"You've been through hell and back. This is understandable."

"It's *not* understandable. I need serious psychiatric help." I pushed my tear-dampened hair back from my eyes.

"You need freedom. You've been a caged bird for way too long." He pulled me by the hand to the sofa, where I curled, cat-like, against him, and he petted me—long, soothing strokes. "I have good news, though. Forensics has pulled all the information off Frith's flash drive. It's being translated by cryptography now. They should have something soon — maybe as soon as tomorrow."

41

I SAT DOWN AT THE BREAKFAST BAR WITH MY LAPTOP. I HAD been anticipating this moment for weeks.

"Okay, Jonathan Frith, what are those innermost secrets that you think need encryption and possible destruction?" I opened the file, more than slightly afraid that all I was going to find out was that he had a nasty porn fetish for being tickled with duck feathers while wearing Latex and women's underwear.

No...not a porn fetish. I couldn't believe what I was seeing. My mind literally went numb. I had to wait and look again. Comprehending was a process, but when I finally got it through my thick skull, I was off my stool with my fists to my head.

Striker moved over and grabbed me by the elbows, ready to jump into action.

"It's not my head, Striker. It's freaking Frith. I can't believe it. I am such a moron. I have major freaking brain damage. How is it that I could be standing there, chopping up a fruit salad, when it's been the poison apple all along?"

"I'm completely lost. Start at the beginning. When did you make a fruit salad?"

"I have been trying to put it all together, the Omega apples and Assembly oranges, Sylanos — he's bananas — and the rest. Some of it does mix together. It's all rotten fruit, to be sure. But the *apple!* The apple is what I should have had my eye on the whole time. Snow White and the Seven Dwarfs. Don't you remember me telling you that that was the story being pushed forward as a psychic knowing? I should have seen it. All this wasted *freaking* time."

"Snow White, that's you." He was using a calm, controlled voice — maybe he thought that would rub off on me somehow.

"Yes." I danced around, shaking my hands. My body buzzed like I had stuck a wet finger in a socket.

"And the poison apple is how the wicked stepmother is trying to kill you."

"Yes."

"And now you're reviewing the secret Frith files. Frith is the wicked stepmother?" Striker asked.

"Yes. This whole time he dressed like a beautiful queen — well, you know what I mean — he was dressed as a friend when he was really an old witch who wanted me dead."

"Lexi, what was on the flash drive?" Striker's tone turned glacial. His face a stone mask.

I turned my laptop toward him. "This first file is called 'Daddy's Little Whore.' In it is a series of poems in their original form, and here are the changes."

Striker moved to the counter and tipped the screen so he could read. "I recognize these. They're from the Bayleigh

Joseph case. The letters Frith brought to us when he contracted Iniquus to find her killer."

"Travis Wilson. Yes. How about this file?" I tapped the buttons to bring up a different file.

Striker scanned through the poems. "If I'm not mistaken, that's Mary Snyder, the targeted victim with the CIA."

"Why does Frith have that? The point of the different agencies all signing on with Iniquus was to keep these cases individual to the agencies and under the control of you and your team alone, so there would be no leaks. Either someone leaked…"

"Not from our team. There wasn't." Striker was emphatic.

"Agreed. The time stamp on the computer shows that these poems were placed onto the flash drive prior to their receipt."

Striker stood absolutely still. When he finally spoke, his voice was flint edged and dangerous. "The only way to get them prior to their receipt was if he knew what was going on before it actually happened."

I opened a new file. "Cry-baby Calls Daddy Home."

Striker's eyes slid over the words on the screen:

Dearest India Alexis,

O my Luve's like the melodie
    That's sweetly play'd in tune!
    As fair thou art, my bonnie lass,
    So deep in love, am I:
    And I will love thee still, my dear,

376 | FIONA QUINN

Till a' your bones are white and dry:
Till a' your veins gang dry, my dear,
And your skin melt with the sun;
I will luve thee until your heart is still my dear
When the sands of your life shall no more run...

This poem was mine. The poem that slid under my motel door the day I was getting married to Angel. And, of course, my dad was already dead. My second dad, Spyder, was off-grid. Frith wanted him called home.

To look at Striker as an outsider, you would think he was merely contemplating. I knew better. If Frith had been in the room, if Striker knew where he could be found, Frith would no longer walk the Earth.

I have seen Striker's many moods. I have seen him in life-or-death fights. I had seen him when he thought that the drug lord might have beaten his sister to death. I have never seen this; the heat from his anger burned all the oxygen from the room. I froze in place. I knew that Striker had supreme control over himself. I wanted him to have a moment to remember that.

Striker looked at me hard. "Frith met Wilson and decided to use him. That makes so much sense. No wonder Wilson was able to plant high-priced surveillance in your house and get into your garage. Wilson knew where you went and when you went there. And you had no clues to puzzle. None. Wilson had a puppet master. Axel was absolutely right about the killer's profile."

"They exploded my apartment building." Unshed tears burned my eyes and blurred my vision. I was freezing cold and trembling at the enormity of what I had caused to happen. "All of my friends lost everything they owned because of me. Here all this time, I thought it was a drunken accident by Mr. Matsy. Mr. Matsy's dead. It wasn't an accident at all. Frith and Wilson worked together."

Guilt choked me; it was hard to breathe around it. It was solid in my chest and almost unbearably painful. "I'm poison. Everyone I love is getting hurt by the bad guys in order to get at me." All the loss. All the suffering had my name graffitied across it.

"Chica, you are *not* responsible for anyone else's actions. You had no control."

I might have found some solace in Striker's words had I not died. As my team worked to pull me back from the Devil's grip, that's when I understood that, in the end, I would be held accountable whether I believed I was doing the right thing or not. Even being a catalyst has repercussions. My heart weighed more than a feather from Ma'at; that was for damned sure.

Striker got on the phone with Command. He paced away from me. I worked to hold back the sobs filling my chest — they felt self-pitying, and there was no room for that. Not when I was the cause of all this pain.

As Striker moved back into the room, he snugged his phone onto his belt. He sat down, pulled me onto his lap, and kissed my hair. "Hopefully, this will be over soon. Command arranged for an arrest warrant for Frith. We're going after him," Striker said.

"On what charges?"

"Murder. The Matsy death. Command was already getting that together with the FBI after I took them the information you had been piecing together. The FBI investigation into the Frith-Wilson connection showed that Frith didn't have a directive to follow Wilson the night that your apartment building burned down. Frith wasn't assigned to the Patriots United case at that time. The police had never seen the video that Jack picked up from the motel. They never asked for it, chalked the incident up to what it looked like on paper — a drug overdose, pure and simple. Good thing that manager put the tapes in his vault just in case. Smart man. Still, our case is circumstantial. The lawyers think it's enough, though, so we're going for it. That'll get Frith off the streets and behind bars while the FBI aligns the Wilson murders with him."

"When will they arrest him?"

He shook his head. "I don't know, Chica. I'm sorry, but it looks like Frith went underground."

"How far underground?" I wasn't blinking.

"He sold his house and car. He closed his bank accounts and emptied his safe deposit boxes. Gone."

"So Iniquus and the FBI were already in action? Already trying to pick him up? This is icing?"

Striker nodded.

"Could Frith be holed up on the Omega campus?" I asked with the smallest glimmer of hope.

Striker shook his head. "Not that we can tell."

"You have it under surveillance?"

"Yeah. After Frith said Omega had eyes on our lawn, Command decided to reciprocate. We have cameras with face identification software tracking their comings and goings."

"No Frith."

"He never went on campus."

"Maybe he was disguised?"

"Nope. Our cameras flagged everyone not identified by

the computer program. We tasked one of the support staff with making a positive ID. I've gone over the files. They're clean. Frith didn't work or live at Omega Headquarters."

"Poop."

Striker gave me an "I love you" smile, the kind that is a little bit on his lips, mostly in the eyes. He planted a kiss on my forehead. "Tidal Force is working around the clock. We're slowly moving the parameters wider. We'll get him," he said.

I rolled over and untangled from the cocoon I made for myself with last night's tossing and turning. I could hear Striker in the shower.

The sun glittered on the Potomac outside the window. It was a beautiful end-of-summer day—the kind where fat, puffy sheep clouds wandered around the sky. I stretched and gasped. The pain that shot down my spine was so intense that sweat beaded under my nose, and my feet went numb. I slithered out of bed onto the floor and lay there, staring at the ceiling with my knees bent up, my breath coming in shallow gasps. That's how Striker found me when he came into the room, wrapped in a towel, looking totally edible with his wet hair and smelling of aftershave.

"What are you doing down there, Chica?" He towered above me.

"This is as far as I could get this morning."

"Do you need help?" He reached out a hand.

I shook my head. "I'm going to lay here for a minute and see if I can't get my back to cooperate. I need to call Laura's office and see if she can't work on me today."

380 | FIONA QUINN

"Today's really not good." He squatted down beside me.
"I can see you're in pain, but Strike Force is out in the field
today with Tidal Force. We have a bead on Frith, and I need
everyone involved. No one's around to take you."

"I can go by myself," I said. I needed help. I couldn't just
lay here for days until I fit neatly into someone's schedule.

"Not a good idea," Striker's tone changed. A little more
commander slid into place.

"Why not a good idea? Besides our team, Cookie, Chris,
and Andy, no one knows about me. I'll take a company car
with tinted windows and drive around for a while, then circle
over to Laura's office. I think she said she was going to be in
the Arlington office this week. I hope so, anyway."

"The cars are followed in Control."

"That's easy enough to disable." I tried rotating my
knees to the left. Bad idea. "*Agh!*" I righted myself and
panted with my hands shoved under my back.

Striker had his hands on his hips. A man ready for an
argument. I could see him weighing options. "I'm not going
to get a say in this one, am I?" he asked.

I looked up the length of Striker, his calves, his thighs,
the muscles that rippled across his abdomen, and his goody
trail that slid behind the low-slung towel. If I was feeling
better — it wouldn't take much — a little tug would have
that towel on the ground. Darned this pain. "I appreciate and
understand your reasoning, Striker, honestly. But I need to
go out for my sanity's sake, and my back's sake."

"No heebie-jeebies? No feelings that the bad guy is
hanging over your shoulder?"

"To be honest, I've not been able to shake the heebie-
jeebies feeling since the attack on the bay house."

"You'll take every precaution? You'll have your gun?"

That was his Commander checking on the troops before battle voice. Honestly. I was just going to see my PT; I wasn't going hand-to-hand with Gaddafi-esque dictator and his battalion of Amazons.

"The doctor said no guns until my brain settles down, and my fingers stop twitching despite what happened at your house." Shame for destroying Striker's beautiful house settled heavily on my shoulders. How would I ever make that up to him? "If it makes you feel better, I could take some pepper spray."

"No, it doesn't make me feel better, but I'll take what I can get." Striker looked uncomfortably resigned. "If you go," he pointed an emphatic finger at me, "you need to wear a communicator, and you stay in touch with Deep the whole time. He's going to be point man for logistics today."

"I can do that."

Fortunately for me, Laura was in Arlington. Unfortunately, she had a full schedule. I must have sounded desperate on the phone because the receptionist said that she would squeeze me in during the last appointment slot.

I iced, stretched, took pain meds, and kvetched. It was not a good day. I accomplished nothing beyond my little pity party.

By the time I got in the SUV and barreled onto the highway heading south, I was only mildly improved. It was weird to be behind the wheel again. It was a good weird, a normalizing weird. I hadn't driven a car since last January. Here I was, acting like an average person taking care of business. I was independent of my security detail — well, mostly independent.

I depressed the button on my communicator. "Lynx. Check."

"Deep. Reception clear." His voice rose from between my breasts where I had taped the wires.

"I'm on I95. This should be boring, so don't expect to hear anything from me."

"Good enough. I'd appreciate a check-in when you're done with your appointment and heading home. I'm following coordinates from your phone. I have you up on my screen," he said.

"Roger that. Out."

When I got to the physical therapy office and signed in, I found out that the man before me was a no-show, so the assistant was able to get me right back on to a table. I lay on my stomach with my arms crossed under my head. Laura came into view. She stood there in her blue scrubs. Her jaw opened and shut, opened and shut like a marionette. She seemed beyond surprised to see me. She was awkward and processing. I wasn't quite sure what was going on. The assistant handed Laura my file.

"I'm a last-minute add-on. I hope this doesn't mess up your plans for getting out of here early."

"No. You're fine. I didn't see you on the schedule this morning." Laura lifted her hand to bite at her thumbnail.

"I woke up in pain, and I wheedled my way onto your roster after you got started with the day. I bribed your receptionist with homemade brownies." I smiled.

The assistant attached e-stim pads to my back and handed me the control.

"I need to make a quick phone call, Annie. We'll let the machine do its thing, then I'll come back to do an evaluation."

"Thanks." *Huh. What was that all about?*

Laura wasn't gone long. She felt different to me. There was a shift in her energy. I couldn't quite put my finger on the change. There was a distance there — repulsion. I didn't think I smelled bad. I did take a long bath this morning. When Laura came back, she was brisk and professional. No warmth.

Laura kept me on the e-stim for a second round. My teeth were buzzing from all that electricity. The receptionist and the assistant left at five, turning off the lights in the waiting room and locking the front door. I had a major case of the heebie-jeebies.

"Laura, look at the time. I need to leave. I'm meeting my publisher for dinner in the city."

"Can you wait another few minutes for me to stretch you?" she asked, her eyes tight with anxiety, her hands trembling.

The feeling of danger grew into something palpable. "Nope. Thank you for working me in. Thanks for the e-stim. It helped. I've got to go now." I was off the table and moving toward the back door that led to the parking lot.

"Wait a second for me to grab my purse, and I'll go out with you."

As Laura turned out the lights and followed me out the door, I depressed my communicator and whispered into my shirt, "Heads up, Deep. Something bizarre is going on." I got a double buzz back, acknowledging me. I moved quickly toward my car.

Laura called, "Annie, wait!"

I turned to see Laura standing by the door with a gun in her hand, pointing it at me. This was so antithetical to the way I thought about Laura, that it took me a full breath before my brain would register the image. I was too far away to get the gun away from her and too close for safety. "Laura, what are you doing with a gun?" I asked evenly, channeling my inner Striker.

"I can't let you leave. You have to stay here." Her voice was high pitched and manic.

"Why?" I offered her a sympathetic smile. "Laura, put the gun away and tell me what's happening."

"You're a terrorist. You're plotting against the president." Her hand was shaking so hard that the gun was visibly wavering, and I was afraid she'd accidentally put too much pressure on the trigger. My hands went up protectively in front of me as if to ward off any wayward bullets.

"You weren't writing a book. You were making actual plans. I need to keep you here until he comes to arrest you," Laura said.

I heard very quietly, "Jack and Randy, sixteen minutes out," rise from my T-shirt.

"Laura, I'm a writer. I write about terrorists who plot against the president. It's fictional. No one wants to arrest me. Laura, accidents happen. Lower your gun barrel."

I had my hands open so she could feel she was in control. "I'm not going to move. We're going to talk this through." I was using my EMT voice, the one of clear, reasonable authority. "Point your gun at the ground." I saw Laura process for a moment, and the barrel moved down a few inches.

"What are you going to do with the gun, Laura? You're not the kind of woman who could shoot someone. I'm your patient. Your job is to make me healthy again. You don't hurt people. You help people. You can't shoot someone. It's not who you are."

"I could shoot someone to save the president." Laura's tone — solid and plaintive at once — told me she was trying to convince herself as much as me.

"Laura, please tell me what you're talking about," I said. I needed her to talk. I needed to know where all of this was coming from. Laura had never shown signs of being unstable. She must be acting on someone's directive.

"I saw your picture on the news Saturday night when Wyatt and I were having dinner at my house."

"My picture was on the news?" Now I was really confused.

"Your name isn't Annie Henderson. It's India Sobado."

Uh oh. "And you came to this conclusion because you saw a photo on the news of some girl who looks like me? Why was this girl on the news?"

"*You.* You were on the news because Belize found a plane tail washed up on their shoreline. They said it was from a plane that disappeared over the Gulf during the tropical storm and that India Sobado was the pilot who called in a mayday before they lost contact. I recognized you right away. It sent chills up my spine." Laura's face was ashen. Her cheek on the left side ticked spasmodically, making her wink and pulling up the corner of her mouth in a lopsided and incongruous grin. "You said that your injuries were from a car crash, but they weren't." Laura shook her head back and forth and raised the sight on her gun to level. She double fisted the Glock with seriously shaking hands. This wasn't a suburban housewife's gun. Someone had given her this gun —a man.

"You were injured when your plane crashed. I asked Wyatt why he thought you would lie about something like that. Why would you want people to think you were dead? And Wyatt said that there was a warrant for your arrest."

"Who's Wyatt?" I asked.

"My boyfriend."

"And why would Wyatt think there was a warrant out for my arrest?"

"Oh, he told me everything. He was with Homeland Security. He told me how they started investigating you two years ago as a terror suspect. You want to take the government down. You're planning to kill the president." Her shrill voice echoed from under the metal overhang about two octaves too high. "He said how he had seen you on tape cheering when the towers came down on 9-11."

Wyatt. Wyatt? The only Wyatts I could think of were Wyatt Earp and a city somewhere in southwestern Missouri. Made up name? "Laura, think. I was sixteen years old when the towers were hit. I had just gotten my learner's permit. I went to school on a bus, acted in the school play. I worked in an ice cream shop when I was sixteen."

"Not as a child, as an adult in your meetings," Laura said. She was completely convinced. Her voice was full of conviction.

"My meetings?"

"Your anti-government planning meetings with the anarchists. Wyatt said they have your plans to murder the president. It's Wyatt's job to stop you."

"You said Wyatt *was* with Homeland Security. If he isn't with them anymore, then how would he have authority to stop this India Sobado person?"

Laura stopped and looked at her feet while she thought

that one through. I took a careful step toward her. When she looked up again, her gun was aimed an inch lower.

Doubt.

"This is weird, Laura. Don't you think it's odd that I'm your patient, and you are dating a man who is trying to arrest someone named India from Belize, and we are one and the same? The likelihood of that happening has to be about one in a bajillion. Things like that don't happen in real life. I couldn't even use this scene in my novel. It's too unbelievable. My readers would put the book down and say the plot was too cockamamie to keep reading." I took a breath. "You don't really believe this, do you, Laura?" I saw her waver. I saw her questioning herself. I took a step closer.

"Tell me again, Laura. You were watching the TV, and there was a news report. They said that a plane tail was found in Belize, and that India had died?"

"Yes."

"If the authorities think that India died, why would you think that I am India?"

"Wyatt said you didn't die. You were rescued by your group."

"This is the anarchist group?" I asked evenly.

"Yes." Laura held the gun in one hand while she reached to push a ginger-colored curl back behind her ear. She was breathing too fast. Anxiety. Good. I pushed harder. I wanted her gun in my hand before whoever it was that was coming actually arrived. Laura couldn't shoot me on purpose, but I felt sure that, whoever this Wyatt guy was, he could and would.

"It seems that if someone were rescuing India that that would cost a lot of money. Laura, you've seen anarchist groups on the news before. Did they look like they had any money?

"Well, no," she said. The gun got heavier with time and confusion; her conviction was wearing thin. The sight lowered to my hips. Still lethal.

"And the news said that the plane went down over water over the Gulf of Mexico. Do my injuries look like injuries that could have been sustained in a water crash?"

Laura was thinking hard. I took another step toward her. This was a little bit like playing Mother-May-I, with deadly consequences if I took a wrong step.

"Some of them, yes. The sternal problem. The spine and head wounds…"

Nope — don't want her making any affirmations. Cut off that line of thought, now. "Laura, let's be rational about this. How could I have survived a crash in the Gulf?" A mini-step closer. A few more, and I might be able to get the gun.

Laura took one hand off the grip to wipe the sweat off on her scrubs. Her hand left a wet mark on the cloth. "Maybe if you had a floatation device?"

"Come on, Laura. What if I did have a floatation device? What if I had a rescue raft with fresh water and supplies? It was a tropical storm. Fifteen-foot waves. Waves as high as a two-story building. As high as this building." I gestured up with my arms, and she turned to look. I took another step. "Do you think that in my physical condition, hurt as I was in the *car* accident, skin and bones, weak as a baby, is it possible that I could have survived until some anarchist group organized itself to come and find me?"

She shook her head. Good. Some of this was getting through to her.

"And once they found me, they had enough money and

enough wherewithal to bring me to Maryland, of all places, and hide me in Jimmy's house? Jimmy, who is president of the local NRA? God-and-country, ex-marine Jimmy? Under the same roof with the war heroes who were planning to help other soldiers as they transitioned home? Is any of that probable or even possible, Laura?"

"No, but Wyatt said…"

I stretched my arms out and waved my hands to distract her as I took a final giant step forward. "*Who is Wyatt*?"

42

"**I**'M WYATT." JONATHAN FRITH SWUNG AROUND THE SIDE of the clinic.

"Oh, thank God." Laura dropped the gun to her side. Her shoulders sagged. She had valiantly tried to do her duty as a good American to save the president, and her duty was over.

"Hello, Frith," I said loudly for Deep's benefit.

"Sobado. You're very good. Clever as they come. You almost talked poor Laura out of her gun."

"You've been feeding poor Laura a bunch of hooey."

"I told her what needed to be told," Frith said.

"You didn't tell her about all of the women you've killed."

"I've never actually killed a woman. Why get their Jezebel blood on my hands?"

"It really does seem too much of a coincidence that you and Laura are friends." Stall. Stall. How many minutes had passed? How far were my teammates?

"Coincidence? No. One of your problems, Lexi, is that

you think you have all the brains. You think you are smarter than anyone else is. In the end, it's your conceit, your arrogance, and vanity that creates your Achilles' heel. You never saw me coming. You never saw me pull the strings on my puppet."

"You're calling Laura your puppet?" I gestured over to where she stood, wide-eyed, and still as a statue.

Wilson. I needed Deep to record Frith explaining his role with Wilson, so no matter my outcome, they could still indict Frith.

Frith was a narcissist. Of course, he'd be here to gloat and make the last move himself. It wouldn't be enough for him to pull the trigger. He'd have to rub my nose in it like a puppy who had pooped on the carpet. He'd want to extend my punishment by hitting me with his brilliance.

I was going to use that—all of it. If I were going to die, first I'd get a full confession.

A narcissist of his caliber? It shouldn't be hard.

It would just take some the right choices of words.

"Laura is one of my *many* puppets." Frith smiled coldly.

"How did you find her?" *Come on, Jack. Get here.* Frith was looking very relaxed. I wouldn't be talking him out of anything. But when he ran out of words, he'd take action.

"It wasn't all that hard. Iniquus would have wanted their baby girl close. They would have wanted the best for you. I Googled. Laura's reputed to be one of the best physical therapists within a two-hour drive of D.C. Hats off to you, Laura." Frith's eyes slid momentarily in her direction. She responded with a high-pitched giggle. Verge of hysteria. Why didn't she back into the building and call someone with real arrest authority? *Go, Laura.* I egged her on with my mind.

"Dedicated, too. She was in the chat rooms and doing research on how she could best support your recovery. Omega has some impressive computer programs. I tapped in my search parameters, and away it went, coughing up possibilities. Who was looking up emaciation and head trauma at the same time? Oh, it was Laura. No. Not hard at all to find and follow her. It was entertaining. I got to screw your therapist. I was banging her from behind, thinking about my gun going *bang* and killing you. My imagination splattered your brains and blood all over the walls and sheets. *Very* sexy. I came like a wild man."

The sun popped out from behind a cloud and glinted in Frith's eye. He moved into the shadow of the building. "I found your little get-away. Sad that Omega handed me their idiot team to capture you. Just couldn't convince them that in your condition, you'd be a problem. Tidied some jackasses from their duty roster. I'm sure they want to thank you personally for clearing away the debris. Ah, but still, it would have been a thing of beauty to see your blood coloring the bay water, darkening that glittering white sand. Not dead, mind you — you still have a purpose to serve. But a heartbeat away would have been nice. I could almost write a poem about it."

Disgust replaced my blood and thrummed through my veins.

Deep's whisper wafted up from my T-shirt, "Three minutes out, stall, keep him talking." I narrowed my eyes and recited:

"*Now, at your last gasp of love's last breath,*
   When your pulse failing, passion speechless lies,

When faith is kneeling by your bed of death…"

"You memorized my little rhyme." Frith offered up a sardonic smile. He was enjoying this *way* too much.

"It's etched on my brain. Like your scars are etched on my body."

"I didn't do that. Wilson did."

"And Wilson was you. You trained him. You gave him the women's names. You wrote the poems. You set the kill dates."

"I particularly enjoyed working on that last poem, Lexi, knowing what would follow. Oh, I wish I had been there." He chuckled. "Wilson said you screamed like a banshee. Did you enjoy it? Did you like the pain, Lexi?" Frith licked his lips. "I bet it made you hot. Did it turn you on? Make you wish that Wilson would fuck you? All taped up. The little victim. Isn't that every whore's fantasy?" Frith stretched his mouth into a sneer. His face transformed into something hideous and satanic. I could almost smell the sulfur.

"I won that one, Frith. I'm alive, and Wilson is dead."

"No. I won that one, Lexi. Wilson was killed. He needed to be. I couldn't leave him walking around. He knew too much. My hands look clean. Not a drop of blood is visible on them."

"I can prove otherwise. I have evidence of you at my apartment fire. Was it you who struck the match? Or Wilson?"

"That was actually a lot of fun and so easily done. We went into your neighbor Tommy's apartment. He was a dependable drunk, wasn't he?" Frith leaned nonchalantly against the brick wall, acting as if this were a friendly conversation between colleagues at the end of the day. He even had the audacity to cross his ankles. "I turned the gas on the stove up to high and laid a flammable debris trail back to the bedroom. Poured a bottle of Jack Daniels on the bed next to a box of cigarettes. Wilson and I slapped Tommy to consciousness and got him to our car. I went to the other side of the building, pulled the fire alarms to get everyone out, and then BOOM. It was marvelous."

"Why did you care if the people got out?"

"I didn't care about the people. I cared about you. I had to keep you alive for Travis. It wouldn't be any fun unless you suffered. And, you have been suffering since the fire burned your apartment to ashes. I've enjoyed watching your misery."

"You are not without a drop of blood on your hands. You killed Tom Matsy. You and Wilson duped Matsy into the back of his car, you put him up in a cheap motel, and you gave him the drug overdose. You staged the scene. I saw you going into Matsy's room on the motel security tape with my own eyes. I saw your car license plate at the fire and the motel. Even if I couldn't prove anything else, you'd still spend the rest of your life in prison for his murder. Ex-FBI don't fare well in our penal system."

"FBI?" Laura asked. "I thought you were Homeland Security."

Frith ignored her. "You're a clever girl to figure that out, though, it won't matter in the end. I have a nice little nest egg sitting offshore. A pretty little pleasure palace on a beach far, far away. And a new identity. I have one more little errand to do: I need you dead, and then I'm out of here and onto my life of luxury."

I thought probably at that point I should have been

afraid. I wasn't. I was many things, nauseated, revolted, infuriated, but no, not afraid. I had a feeling that when this was over, I'd turn into a pool of jelly. Thank god for Master Wang's training in mental sparring.

"Congratulations." My voice was dry and sarcastic.

Frith gave a slight bow. "Thank you."

"My team will never let up. There will be plenty of money to go after you, too. With you manipulating Wilson, you've racked up seven murders: Matsy, plus six from the different agencies, and two attempts on me."

"Yes, attempted murders, up until now, that is," Frith said.

"There were others. Since I'm going to die anyway, at least satisfy my curiosity. Why does the Assembly want me out of the picture?"

"You think the Assembly cares about you? Tsk, tsk, tsk. There's that vanity again. You really are tremendously egotistical. Omega, on the other hand, would like you badly. They are none too pleased that their men died when you did not. And, the operation cost is dripping red on their ledgers until they hand you in. I don't plan on letting them get to you, though. There is a sizable bounty on your head. You lost me my windfall once, and now I get to earn it back in spades. You are going to be quite the cash cow once you're lying in the morgue. I know they said, 'treat with kidgloves,' but beggars can't be choosers, and accidents happen. So, I will bypass the Omega assholes and claim the money for myself. Then I will drink a toast to your memory with my evening margaritas on the beach at my new home. Maybe even invent a new drink, a shot — that would be ironic, the Bloody Lynx." He looked pleased with himself.

My mind scanned for anything that made sense from this

new puzzle piece. "What do you mean that I lost your windfall?"

"You are so stupid, Lexi. You puzzled out the drug case and called in the information to save my life."

"You aren't showing a lot of gratitude."

"Gratitude? You ruined everything. I was set to pick up a stockpile of gold. Untraceable! A million dollars' worth! The explosion that you pre-empted wasn't going to kill me. It was going to be my cover. Everyone would think I was dead. No one would be looking for me. I'd leave just enough gold behind so that they would find the traces and think it had melted away. I would leave safe and rich. See how lovely? See what an idiot you are? Save my life? You moron, you ruined my life!"

"So you decided to take your revenge on me. That explains me. What about the other women? You had some of them killed before I ruined your plans."

"There were plenty of people before you came into the picture that needed to be taught a lesson about arrogance. Practicing on the first six gave Wilson time to perfect his skills."

I had tried counting down the seconds in my head until help arrived. I had passed the mark when I should hear tire squeals fifty-Mississippi's ago. My internal clock and reality did not jive, but surely any second now... "You went to the meeting, you listened to Wilson talk, and you realized that you could use him as a tool. So you created a modus, developed Wilson, and then you set him loose."

"I couldn't set that idiot loose. He would have botched everything. I had to control his every move. It wasn't as easy as I made it look. It was satisfying, though."

"I happened to be last."

"You know, Lexi, you are not the dog that I was chasing. You were merely the tick on the dog that I am taking pleasure in crushing between my fingernails."

"Spyder McGraw." Anger bubbled to the surface of my skin. I wasn't sure I could mask it and maintain my look of indifference. I didn't want my emotions to bring Frith more pleasure and goad him along.

"I thought that you were more important to Spyder. I misunderstood your relationship. Watching the two of you together, it was like father and daughter — well, father and son when you were playing your ridiculous charade as Alex-from-the-hood. He couldn't care less about you."

Uh-oh. Frith had reached in and tweaked a nerve. He was going for psychological warfare.

"One would think that your father-figure would come home and be supportive when your mommy died. Or that he would come to help out when his daughter's apartment blew up or when a stalker was on her trail. But no."

"He didn't come because he didn't know."

"He didn't know because you didn't get word to him. You could have gone to Iniquus. But in your heart, Lexi, you knew he wouldn't come because he doesn't love you. Spyder-daddy played you. He only cared to use you and your brain to line his own pockets and inflate his own reputation. Why else would he keep you secret after you were eighteen? You could have been the Iniquus Puzzler out in the open and gotten your share of the pie. Spyder McGraw is a selfish, self-serving manipulator. I should know. He's my mirror image."

"Spyder McGraw is an honorable, wonderful man. He would never use me the way you used Wilson."

"No? Why are you yelling, Lexi? Feeling defensive? Did I pour vinegar on your wound? Where was Spyder when you were kidnapped? Where was Spyder when you were in a plane crash, and all of Iniquus was on the search?"

"He was ill. He knew nothing about me."

"No? He doesn't watch the news? He was well enough to head off-grid. But *not* well enough to care about you. Ah, she wavers. I see you're trying to justify him in that little pea brain of yours. There's no rationalization. He is me, and you are his Wilson."

All I could do was shake my head to reject what he was saying. He was good. This did hurt.

"You set the fire to get Spyder home." I tried to turn the rhetoric.

"No. I set the fire to get you out of the nest. Too many mama birds for Wilson to be successful. I needed to cull you from the herd, if you will."

"I survived." My voice was flat. I had grabbed the reins on my emotions again.

"Not because of your actions, but because of my orders. Travis wasn't supposed to kill you. He was merely to follow the MO of the other women and hit you in the head, not hard enough to kill you, just hard enough to put you out. Your being the lone survivor of the serial killer, who was slaying the agency daughters and wives, would have Iniquus on you like maggots on shit. I thought surely at that point Spyder-daddy would crawl from his hole and come to the rescue. But no, he still wouldn't come home. I wished to god that I had any other bait. You were obviously meaningless to him."

Inspiration flashed like lightning. "You're *The Man*."

Frith looked at me, blankly.

"You were trying to gather intel about Spyder through Maria Rodriguez."

"What a waste of time she was." Frith stood with his hip pressed forward, like he was swilling a drink at a cocktail party and telling a story about just how blasé life could be.

I decided to throw out the theory that seemed to arrive in my frontal lobe fully formed and ready for this moment. "And, since she was such a waste of time, you went with bigger guns. You hired Omega. You used your affiliation with the Assembly to get Judge Wallace to sign an arrest warrant for me on behalf of the FBI. You had the FBI sign the Omega contract as an agent before you left and joined Omega. Then you waited with the contract in your back pocket until you needed them to rally."

"See how I'm the most clever of all? The Chess Master." He grinned.

"Not really. Uneducated Maria outsmarted you. She got to me first. You had to find me. It took you months, but you did. You hired the Latino men to check out the prison in Honduras. How did you know to look there?" That was a part of this equation that was a variable.

"Because Maria was uneducated, her world was very small. Mine is very big. I have friends in interesting places."

"Like the Assembly?"

"In this case, yes. I was planting evidence for them down in Miami. They needed an enemy removed from an election cycle and living in a jail cell. I met a man named Vega. He and I have a lot in common, it turns out. He, for example, enjoys the sound a human makes when they are in so much pain, they think that they will die. It is a very specific cry. It's wonderful to hear. He gets to hear it all the time in his job. I would like a job like that. They wouldn't even need to pay me."

"At the Honduran jail," I specified.

"Yes, he told me about his jail. He told me about the man who ran things down there, Castillo, and how he used to have his little niece Maria living there with him. After Vega tortured his enemies, he was horny as hell, and little Maria was young and soft, ripe for the picking like a sweet mango. Vega had a great time with her. Loved to tie her up and listen to her beg."

"That's sickening." My stomach churned. I had to swallow hard so I wouldn't throw up.

"Vega said that Maria ran away from him, but he saw her from time to time in Miami. She had married Julio Rodriguez — one of Sylanos' special few — so Vega couldn't touch her anymore. Wasn't that serendipitous, Lexi? Don't you think the Fates wanted me to find you? All I had to do was figure out where the prison was, somewhere on the east coast of Honduras. Then I could go pay the uncle a few bucks and get you out."

"Why didn't you ask Vega to do it for you?"

"Because you used to be beautiful. I couldn't imagine that Vega could pass you up. He would have fucked you into oblivion, and I wanted you all to myself. Of course, if I knew you had become this," Frith gestured the length of my body with his gun and sneered, "I would have let him, have you. You're disgusting. I'm going to have to skip the part of my plan where you got to play the role of little Maria. I don't think I could get it up for you. I'll go right for the gore."

I could feel Frith salivating at the thought. I needed to move his attention away from his fantasies and delusion. "Well, surprise. I escaped the prison."

402 | FIONA QUINN

"And almost made it home. Congratulations. It was more than I thought you had in you. Of course, as in everything you do, Lexi, you failed. And I picked you up on the 911 call."

"Then you handed the contract to Omega, who saw the money dangling out there and went after it full force. You pretended to be my friend with Iniquus to get information. Only it hasn't worked out."

"Yes, Omega is largely ineffectual as I knew they would be. As I needed them to be. I had to intervene a couple of times to keep you alive. Convincing them to use round-nosed bullets at the bay house and not shoot you in the head...but that wasn't too difficult."

My attention slid left to Laura. Until this point, I had forgotten that she was in the picture. Tunnel vision. She had sunk to her knees, hands balled to her gut. By now, she should have slipped away. What the hell was wrong with this woman? Wasn't she listening? Our lives were on the line here.

Frith never wavered from his masturbatory explanation of his brilliance. "I merely wanted the contract in place so that I could go after the target on your back with impunity. I could serve you up cold and pocket the ransom. And look how well it's all worked out? You're here. There are no witnesses. I will hand you over with a hole in your head. Spyder will come to the funeral, and he can join you at the Pearly Gates. The cherry on top. Revenge complete. And you provided me with an alternate income."

"All you have to do is kill me and hand my body over to the FBI." *Jack? Randy?*

"Well, you and Laura. Then it's off to the warm sands, blue sea, and riches."

He was winding down — I had to keep him talking. Think. Think. "Some things I don't get. Why did you call a kill order for T-Bone and Hector? It seems that leaving Maria and Julio alive would have been the perfect cover for you. What about Brody Covington? Are you the one who had him put in the Honduran jail? Why did you jail him instead of taking him out like the others?"

"Puzzling things out to the very end? You need to have all the pieces fall into place so I can blow you away, and you will rest in peace? Believe it or not, I had nothing at all to do with that. You seem to have an array of enemies. But I was there first — and I'm here last." Frith raised his gun and aimed at me. It was a kill shot. His hand was steady. I was too close for him to miss. The look on his face was pure pleasure and greed. Options flashed through my head.

"What should you do, Annie? Or should I call you Alex? Or India? Or Lexi? I see the wheels spinning in your head… are you going to try a backflip? Are you going to fall to the right and roll? I'm a great shot, Lexi. I have an extended magazine, Lexi. How about a little kung fu? I'll tell you what, if you stand very, very still like a good girl, I promise to take you out with one bullet. You'll never know what hit you. If you try to run, I'll play with you. I'll make you scream and beg for the mercy of death. Actually, I think I'd prefer it that way.

'Small, sleek, cowering, timorous beast,
O, what a panic is in your breast!
You need not start away so hasty
With hurrying scamper!
I would be loath to run and chase you…'"

He used a stage voice as he performed for his audience of two.

"You always were a Robert Burns fan, Frith. But you know how that poem goes. That *'the best-laid schemes of mice and men, Go often awry.'*"

"Very good, little mouse! I'm impressed. And you don't seem to have panic in your heart."

"You don't scare me, Frith. You are a sad, sick little man."

A monster roiled under Frith's skin. "I'm the cat, Lexi." He licked his lips. "And you are the mouse. Run, mouse, run!"

There was a muffled blast of a bullet passing through a silencer. It hit the ground in front of me, making me startle and jump. Little pieces of macadam exploded up onto my bare legs. Then came the sound of unfettered firepower. The light of the blasts flashed in my left eye.

Laura stood facing in Frith's direction, with her eyes squinched tightly closed, firing her gun at nothing. Frith lay crumpled on the ground, motionless. I waited for her to empty her magazine, then ran over to check Frith.

"Oh my god, I killed someone. I killed Wyatt." Laura was jumping up and down, shaking her hands in the air. Gun flailing around.

I looked up from where I crouched by his side. "Believe me, Laura, if you had, the world would be a better place. Look, Laura. Open your eyes and stop hopping up and down. Frith was wearing a Kevlar vest. You knocked him out. That's all."

I picked up Frith's gun and put it in my back waistband. I pulled off his shirt and ripped open the Velcro on his vest. If Frith came to, I wanted my shots to count. I dragged the vest off and threw it to the side. I drew up his T-shirt to see how many hits he took.

The scream of sirens came from the direction of the highway moving toward us. A gray Hummer slid around the corner of the rehab center. Jack and Randy jumped out; guns aimed.

43

"CLEAR. CLEAR," I SHOUTED.

Jack looked down at the red splotches on Frith's chest that were quickly turning to nasty bruises. He looked at me. "Did you do that?"

I pointed at Laura.

Jack nodded appreciatively. "Three shots — center mass. Good job, Laura."

Laura responded with her high-pitched giggle. Manic.

"Police are heading in this direction. Deep's monitoring their response. They don't know the exact location of the gunfire. Laura," Jack had to wait until Laura's eyes focused on him, "we're going to make all of this go away. Randy is going to drive you home in your car and make sure that you're settled and comfortable. And you're going to chalk this up to a very bad day that you want to forget, so you do. Anything you say to anyone could open you up to arrest for holding Lexi hostage at gunpoint and attempted murder of Frith. You don't want to get involved with that. You want this all to go away, right now."

"I — I — I wasn't attempting murder. I was — it was self-defense."

"No, ma'am. You were never a target. Lexi was the target."

"Who?"

"Annie. Annie was Wyatt's target."

Randy took the wobbling gun out of Laura's hand and handed it to me. He bent to pick up her purse and rifled through it until he came out with a set of keys tied to a mint-green shower puff. His hand slid supportively around Laura's back, and he moved her toward her car. Laura looked back over her shoulder at me to see if I thought this was the right thing to do.

"It's going to be fine, Laura. Let Randy take you home and get you settled. Tomorrow will be better, I promise."

Laura looked up at Randy, and with the first sign of hysterics, whimpered like an injured dog. "He was a killer—a murderer. I was dating him. He could have killed me."

"You're safe, Laura. You survived. You'll never see him again," Randy soothed as he maneuvered her into her passenger seat and shut the door.

Jack was busy zip-tying Frith and snapping on his shackles. Another Iniquus car screeched into the lot. Striker's long legs were on the pavement as the car came to a stop. He jogged over.

"Lynx was missing her old life and thought she'd have some fun," Jack said.

"I can see that." Striker's muscles were taut and primed for action.

Striker looked down at Frith, who was coming around. Frith's hands in the plastic restraints reached out and grabbed Jack's pant leg. When he gave a tug, trying to down giant

Jack, Striker's boot slammed into Frith's stomach, making him puke.

"Feel better, Striker?" Jack asked.

"Considerably."

"I'm not putting him in my car covered in spew," Jack said.

"We could put a plastic bag over his head," I suggested helpfully.

Striker looked over at me with a half-smile, then turned to Jack. "Call the client and have them do the pick up here."

Jack pulled his cell from the holder at his waist. "Cops?" he asked.

"Deep called in to dispatch as an eyewitness and sent them over to an apartment complex north of here. We won't have any interference."

Striker looked over at me. "How's your back?"

"Good, thanks."

That night Striker and I lie in bed — neither of us able to sleep.

Beetle and Bella, on the other hand, were snoring loudly on the floor.

Striker stroked my hair. "I listened to the tapes again. You got an excellent confession out of him."

"Thank you." I turned over and could just make Striker out in the moonlight that glimmered through the window.

"Does it bother you what he was saying about Spyder?" he asked, tracing a finger down the side of my face.

I sat up beside him and pulled my knees in to circle them with my arms. "Frith is brilliant. He was lying, and he was manipulating me. While I knew what he was up to, it did give me pause. It was painful to hear. Somewhere inside, I must have been harboring those very thoughts. He tried to shake my foundation by making me question Spyder's relationship with me. He used enough detail so that I would say in my head, 'yes, that's true.' With enough 'yes, that's trues' running in a line, he could insert his lies, and out of habit, my brain would continue saying, "yes, that's true." Luckily, Spyder taught me that trick, and like every magic trick, no matter how good, once you know how it works, it will never fool you again."

"Spyder had no idea that you were in danger or that you were injured in any way. The only time that he heard anything about you was while he was hospitalized here in D.C. He wasn't moved to an American hospital — your case didn't make international news. I spoke with him on the way out to his assignment. He had no idea that you weren't anything but safe, whole, and happy."

"You decided not to tell him."

"And that makes you angry."

"Furious," I agreed.

"I didn't tell him because he would have dropped everything to come here to be with you. We thought you were targeted by Wilson because of Spyder. We thought that your connection to Maria was through Spyder. Bringing him in while Omega was doing a war dance would have put both of you at greater risk."

I frowned. "You were protecting me."

"I believed that I was protecting both of you."

"Riding into battle with my favor tied to your lance? You should have told me. I'm a big girl. I would have come to the same conclusion."

"You're right. I'm sorry. My instinct is to…"

"Wear a shiny suit and fight my dragons for me. I get that, Arthur."

Striker gave a half-smile. "Now that Frith is on ice and being tried for the murders, what's your plan?"

I took a long breath in, like I was drinking a glass of cold water after a long day in the sun. "You sound like you might have a few ideas of your own."

"I do," he said.

"Okay. Shoot."

"No. No shooting is involved in my plans. I think we should take a nice long vacation to somewhere beautiful, then you should go back to school, get your bachelor's in criminal science, and try to live a nice, quiet, normal life for a while."

"A wise man once told me that I wasn't wired for normal. Trying to lead a commonplace life for me was like asking a Ferrari to sit in a garage. He wondered why I would want that. Traditional doesn't mean no more loss, no more pain. He said I was an extraordinary woman. And I had to live up to that, or my soul will shrivel."

"That's not pretty — a shriveled soul."

"Exactly." I smiled.

"So, what's the plan?" Striker asked, stroking a hand down my cheek and holding my chin to plant a little kiss.

"Once Blaze is healed up, I'm going to go away with you on a long and relaxing vacation to somewhere beautiful. Then I'm going try to put a knot at the end of the rope that I've been hanging from."

"Meaning?"

"There are still some loose strands that need explanation and might leave me vulnerable. I'm going to start by finding that rat Sylanos. This time, I'll make sure that vermin is gone for good."

"Okay, Chica." He kissed me again. "But what say you to a wedding first?"

"What say you to a good night sleep first?"

Striker kissed me and pulled me into his chest, wrapping me in his strong arms. I felt safe here for the moment. But I knew I wouldn't really be safe, and no one would be safe around me until I took down Sylanos.

If Striker and I had any hopes of a happily ever after, I had to behead the Hydra.

Spyder, it's time to come home.

The End

I hope you enjoyed this next step in Lexi's story.

Find out what happens next in CUFF LYNX

Readers, I hope you enjoyed getting to know Lexi and her Iniquus team. If you had fun reading Chain Lynx, I'd appreciate it if you'd help others enjoy it too.

Recommend it: Just a few words to your friends, your book groups, and your social networks would be wonderful.

Review it: Please tell your fellow readers what you liked about my book by reviewing Chain Lynx. If you do write a review, please send me a note at hello@FionaQuinnBooks.com so I can thank you with a personal e-mail. Or stop by my website www.FionaQuinnBooks.com to keep up with my news and chat through my contact form.

THE WORLD of INIQUUS

Chronological Order

Ubicumque, Quoties. Quidquid

Weakest Lynx (Lynx Series)

Missing Lynx (Lynx Series)

Chain Lynx (Lynx Series)

Cuff Lynx (Lynx Series)

WASP (Uncommon Enemies)

In Too DEEP (Strike Force)

Relic (Uncommon Enemies)

Mine (Kate Hamilton Mystery)

Jack Be Quick (Strike Force

Deadlock (Uncommon Enemies)

Instigator (Strike Force)

Yours (Kate Hamilton Mystery)

Gulf Lynx (Lynx Series)

Open Secret (FBI Joint Task Force)

Thorn (Uncommon Enemies)
Ours (Kate Hamilton Mysteries
Cold Red (FBI Joint Task Force)
Even Odds (FBI Joint Task Force)
Survival Instinct - Cerberus Tactical K9
Protective Instinct - Cerberus Tactical K9
Defender's Instinct - Cerberus Tactical K9
Danger Signs - Delta Force Echo
Hyper Lynx - Lynx Series
Danger Zone - Delta Force Echo
Danger Close - Delta Force Echo
Cerberus Tactical K9 Team Bravo
Marriage Lynx - Lynx Series

FOR MORE INFORMATION VISIT
WWW.FIONAQUINNBOOKS.COM

ACKNOWLEDGMENTS

My great appreciation ~

To my editors, Lindsay Smith and Kathleen Payne

To my cover artist, Melody Simmons

To my publicist, Margaret Daly

To my Street Force, who support me and my writing with such enthusiasm.

To my Beta Force, who are always honest and kind at the same time.

To H. Russell for creating the Iniquus Bible—so I can keep all the details correct

To all the wonderful professionals whom I called on to get the details right.

Please note: this is a work of fiction, and while I always try my best to get all the details correct, there are times when it serves the story to go slightly to the left or right of perfection. Please understand that any mistakes or discrepancies are my authorial decision making alone and sit squarely on my shoulders.

Thank you to my family.

I send my love to my husband and my great appreciation. T, you live in my heart. You live in my characters. You are my hero.

And of course, thank YOU for reading my stories. I'm smiling joyfully as I type this. I so appreciate you!

ABOUT THE AUTHOR

Fiona Quinn is a six-time USA Today bestselling author, a Kindle Scout winner, and an Amazon All-Star.

Quinn writes action-adventure in her Iniquus World of books, including Lynx, Strike Force, Uncommon Enemies, Kate Hamilton Mysteries, FBI Joint Task Force, Cerberus Tactical K9, and Delta Force Echo series.

She writes urban fantasy as Fiona Angelica Quinn for her Elemental Witches Series.

And, just for fun, she writes the Badge Bunny Booze Mystery Collection with her dear friend, Tina Glasneck.

Quinn is rooted in the Old Dominion, where she lives with her husband. There, she pops chocolates, devours books, and taps continuously on her laptop.

Visit www.FionaQuinnBooks.com

COPYRIGHT

Chain Lynx is a work of fiction. Names, characters, places, and incidents either are the product of the author's imagination or are used fictitiously, and any resemblance to actual persons, living or dead, business establishments, events, or locales is entirely coincidental.

©2015 Fiona Quinn
All Rights Reserved
ISBN: 978-1-946661-27-2
Chesterfield, VA
Library of Congress Control Number: 2021910741

Cover Design by Melody Simmons from eBookindlecovers
Garamond and Calibri used with permission from Microsoft

Publisher's Note: Neither the publisher nor the author has any control over and does not assume any responsibility for third-party websites and their content.

No part of this book may be scanned, reproduced, or distributed in any printed or electronic form without the express written permission from the publisher or author. Doing any of these actions via the internet or in any other way without express written permission from the author is illegal and punishable by law. It is considered piracy. Please purchase only authorized editions. In accordance with the US Copyright Act of 1976, the scanning, uploading, and electronic sharing of any part of this book without the permission of the publisher constitute unlawful piracy and theft of the author's intellectual property. If you would like to use material from the book (other than for review purposes), prior written permission must be obtained by contacting the publisher at FionaQuinnBooks@Outlook.com.

Thank you for your support of the author's rights.